This book should be returned to any Lancashire
County Council Library on or before the date shown

Karen Whidd started weaving fanciful tales for her
younger brothers at the age of eleven. Amid the gorgeous
Catskill Mountains, then the majestic Rocky Mountains,
she fueled her imagination with the natural beauty
surrounding her. Karen now lives in north Texas, writes
full-time and volunteers for a boxer dog rescue. She
shares her life with her hero of a husband and four to five
dogs, depending on if she is fostering. You can email
Karen at kwhiddon1@aol.com. Fans can also check out
her website, karenwhiddon.com

LANCASHIRE COUNTY LIBRARY

3011813963146 3

Also by Nichole Severn

Rules in Blackmail
Rules in Rescue
Rules in Deceit

Also by Karen Whiddon

The CEO's Secret Baby
The Cop's Missing Child
The Millionaire Cowboy's Secret
Texas Secrets, Lovers' Lies
The Rancher's Return
The Texan's Return
Wyoming Undercover
The Texas Soldier's Son
Texas Ranch Justice
Colton's Christmas Cop

Discover more at millsandboon.co.uk

RULES IN DEFIANCE

NICHOLE SEVERN

COLTON'S RESCUE MISSION

KAREN WHIDDON

MIX
Paper from
responsible sources
FSC
www.fsc.org
FSC C007464

This book is produced from independently certified FSC™
paper to ensure responsible forest management.

For more information visit: www.harpercollins.co.uk/green

Printed and bound in Spain
by CPI, Barcelona

MILLS & BOON

All rights reserved including the right of reproduction in whole or in part in any form. This edition is published by arrangement with Harlequin Books S.A.

This is a work of fiction. Names, characters, places, locations and incidents are purely fictional and bear no relationship to any real life individuals, living or dead, or to any actual places, business establishments, locations, events or incidents. Any resemblance is entirely coincidental.

This book is sold subject to the condition that it shall not, by way of trade or otherwise, be lent, resold, hired out or otherwise circulated without the prior consent of the publisher in any form of binding or cover other than that in which it is published and without a similar condition including this condition being imposed on the subsequent purchaser.

® and ™ are trademarks owned and used by the trademark owner and/or its licensee. Trademarks marked with ® are registered with the United Kingdom Patent Office and/or the Office for Harmonisation in the Internal Market and in other countries.

First Published in Great Britain 2019
by Mills & Boon, an imprint of HarperCollins*Publishers*
1 London Bridge Street, London, SE1 9GF

Rules in Defiance © 2019 Natascha Jaffa
Colton's Rescue Mission © 2019 Harlequin Books S.A.

Special thanks and acknowledgement are given to Karen Whiddon for her contribution to *The Coltons of Roaring Springs* series.

ISBN: 978-0-263-27452-3

1219

LANCASHIRE COUNTY LIBRARY	
3011813963146 3	
Askews & Holts	12-Nov-2019
AF AFR	£5.99
NKI	

RULES IN DEFIANCE

NICHOLE SEVERN

This one's for you!
Thanks for joining the Blackhawk Security adventure.

Chapter One

An ear-piercing scream had Elliot Dunham reaching for the Glock stashed under his pillow. He threw back the sheets and pumped his legs hard, not bothering to check the time as the apartment blurred in his vision. That scream hadn't come from his apartment, but close by. Air rushed from his lungs as adrenaline burned through his veins. There was only one name that came to mind. "Waylynn."

Ripping open his front door, he made the sharp turn to his left in the darkness and faced his next-door neighbor's front door. No hesitation. He aimed the heel of his foot toward the lock and kicked with everything he had. Pain shot up his leg, but the door frame splintered, thick wood slamming back against the wall. Dust flew into his beard and face as he raised the gun and moved in. One breath. Two. Nothing but the pounding of his heartbeat behind his ears registered from the shadows. He scanned the scene, his senses adjusting slowly.

He'd gone into plenty of situations like this before, but this wasn't just another one of his clients. This was Waylynn. She mattered. He'd trained out of Blackhawk Security, offered his clients personal protection, home security and investigative services, as well as tactical training, wilderness survival and self-defense. But none of that would do Elliot a damn bit of good now. He was running off instinct. Because when it came to that woman, he couldn't think. Couldn't breathe.

Debris cut into his bare feet as he moved deeper into the dark apartment. A broken picture frame—Waylynn's doctorate degree from Texas A&M University—crunched beneath his weight. Torn couch cushions, a broken vase, a purse that'd been dumped over the floor. Signs of an obvious struggle littered the living room, but it was the trail of dark liquid leading to the back bedroom that homed his attention to the soft sobs echoing down the hallway. Blood. "Waylynn? It's Elliot. Are you dead?"

"Don't come in here!" That voice. Her voice.

"I take it that's a *no*." While his gut twisted at her hint of fear, relief spread through him. She was alive. And the scream… Something horrible had happened to make her scream like that. The front door had been locked. No breeze came through the apartment from a broken window. Elliot moved down the hallway, putting the survival skills ingrained into him since he was fourteen to good use. No sign of a break-in. No movement from an intruder. He hit the bedroom and pushed the partially open door open with his free hand. The bed had been perfectly made, brightly colored throw pillows straight. Not much damage in this room. Light from beneath the closed bathroom door stretched across the beige carpeting.

And Elliot froze.

The gun faltered in his grip as water seeped from beneath the bathroom door. Not just water. Water mixed with blood. He shot forward. "I don't care if you're naked, Doc. I'm coming in."

Elliot shouldered his way into the brightly lit bathroom and caught sight of his next-door neighbor huddled against the wall. Ice worked through him as he took in her soaked long blond hair, her stained oversize sweater and ripped black leggings, the terrified panic in her light blue eyes as she stared up at him, openmouthed.

And at the dead woman in the bathtub.

"Oh, I didn't realize this was a party." A hollow sensation carved itself into the pit of his stomach as he dropped the gun to his side. Terror etched deep lines around her mouth. Pressure built behind his sternum. Elliot set the gun on the counter and crouched in front of her, hands raised. Mildly aware he wore nothing but a pair of sweatpants, he ignored the urge to reach out for her. He'd take it slow. The woman in front of him wasn't the one he'd moved in next door to a year ago. This wasn't the woman who'd caught his attention with a single smile and a six-pack of beer in her hand when she'd made the effort to introduce herself to her new neighbor. This woman was scared, vulnerable. Dangerous.

"Who's your friend?" he asked.

Her gaze wandered to the body, far too distant, far too empty. Color drained from her face. "Alexis."

"Okay, then. First piece of the mystery solved." Elliot framed her chin between his thumb and index finger and softened his voice. He didn't have a whole lot of training when it came to trauma victims, but he couldn't keep himself from touching her. "Second question. Are you the one bleeding?"

"I'm…" She turned that ice-blue gaze back to him, her voice dropping into hollow territory. "I'm not the one bleeding."

"Now we're getting somewhere." He lowered his hand, careful of where he stepped, careful not to leave prints. He'd barged into the middle of an active crime scene. A crime scene where the most trusting woman he'd known stood in the center. There'd been a struggle, that much was clear. Things had obviously gotten out of hand, but he needed to hear the rest from her. He'd learned to trust his instincts a long time ago and something about the scene, about Waylynn's scream a few minutes ago, didn't sit right. He pointed to the bathtub. "Last question. Why is there a dead woman in your tub?"

"I don't remember. It's all a blur. I woke up facedown on the bathroom floor. Water and—" she shuddered, wrapping her arms tighter around her middle "—blood were spilling over the edge of the bathtub. I got up and then I saw her. I screamed." Tears streamed down her cheeks and she wiped at them with the back of her long, thin fingers. She worked to swallow, her knees pressed against her chest, hands shaking. She blinked against the brightness of the lighting. "It's Alexis. Alexis Jacobs. She's my assistant at the lab."

Genism Corporation's lab. The largest, most profitable biotech company in Alaska. Also one of the military's biggest prospects for genetic testing, from what he'd learned, because Dr. Waylynn Hargraves herself had put them on the map. Advancing their research by decades according to recent publicity, she'd proved the existence of some kind of highly contested gene.

Elliot scanned the scene again.

He dragged his thumb along her cheekbone, focused entirely on the size of her pupils and not the fact every hair on the back of his neck had risen at the feel of her. Only a thin line of blue remained in her irises, which meant one of two things in a room this well lit. Either Waylynn had suffered a head injury during an altercation or she'd been drugged. Or both. He scanned down the long column of her throat. And found exactly what he was looking for. A tiny pinprick on the left side of her neck. The right size for a hypodermic needle. He exhaled hard. Damn it. She'd been drugged, made to look like she'd murdered her assistant. Framed. "What's the last thing you remember?"

Anything to give them an idea of who'd done this. Because it sure as hell hadn't been Waylynn.

She blinked against the bathroom lights as though the brightness hurt. "I... I was supposed to meet Alexis here, at my apartment. She said she'd found something alarming in the recent study I oversee at work, but she didn't want to discuss it over the phone or at the lab. She insisted on somewhere private where we couldn't be overheard."

If Waylynn headed that study, anything alarming her assistant uncovered would've fallen back on her, threatened the project. But not if Alexis disappeared first. Whoever'd killed the assistant had known she and

Waylynn were meeting and planned the perfect setup. Pinning his next-door neighbor as a murderer.

"Okay. You had a meeting scheduled here," he said. "You obviously got in your car and left the lab. Then what?"

"I...don't remember." She wrapped long fingers around his arms. "Elliot, why can't I remember?"

"Sorry to be the one to tell you this, Doc, but I think you were drugged." He pointed at the faint, angry puckering of the skin at the base of her throat to distract himself from the grip she had around his arms. "Hypodermic needle mark on the left side of your neck."

"There're only a handful of sedatives that affect memory. Benzodiazepines mostly. We store them at the lab." Hand automatically gravitating to the mark, she ran her fingertips over the abrasion. Her bottom lip parted from the top, homing his attention to her mouth. That wide gaze wandered back to the tub and absolutely destroyed her expression. Waylynn worked over sixty hours a week at the lab. Stood to reason her assistant did, too. They'd probably spent a lot of time together, gotten close. Shock smoothed the lines around her eyes. Her hands shook as she covered her mouth. "But drugging me doesn't explain how Alexis... This can't be happening. Not again."

Again? Alarm bells echoed in his head and his fight instinct clawed through him. "You know, that makes me think you killed somebody in a past life I don't know about."

Movement registered from somewhere inside the apartment and Elliot reached for the gun on the counter. The metal warmed in his hand as he barricaded the door with his back.

Voices thundered through the apartment. Then footsteps outside the bathroom door. "Anchorage PD! We received a disturbance call from one of your neighbors. Is anyone here?" a distinct feminine voice asked.

"I don't know about you, but I haven't had this much excitement since getting shot at a few months ago." This night was getting better by the minute, yet Waylynn hadn't moved. "I don't mean to alarm you, Doc, but I think the police are here. And they're probably going to arrest you."

"Elliot, I think I killed her." Waylynn's fingernails dug into his arms harder. "I think I killed Alexis."

THIS COULDN'T BE HAPPENING. Not again. She couldn't go through this again.

Waylynn Hargraves pressed her elbow into the hard metal table, threading her fingers through her hair. Focus. She hadn't been charged with anything. Yet. They'd taken her blood to run a tox screen, but if Anchorage PD believed she'd killed Alexis, wouldn't they have put her in cuffs? She couldn't have killed her lab tech. She'd never hurt Alexis. They were friends. Even if… No. She'd been drugged. She'd been forced. Framed. All she had to do was remember.

Pain lightninged across her vision and she blinked against the onslaught of the fluorescent lighting above. A dull ache settled at the base of her skull. Whatever drug she'd been injected with still clung to the edges of her mind, kept her from accessing those memories. She couldn't think. Couldn't remember how she'd gotten to her own apartment, if she'd talked with Alexis, how she'd—

Waylynn swallowed around the tightness in her throat and lifted her attention to the mirror taking up most of one wall in front of her. They'd left her alone in this room, but she doubted the room on the other side of that glass was unoccupied. The weight of being watched pressed her back against the chair. "Elliot?"

The door to her right clicked open. A female uniformed officer set sights on her. Past memories overrode the present and, for a split second, Waylynn felt like the fifteen-year-old girl accused of murdering her father all over again. Scared. Alone. Pressured to confess.

Tossing a manila file folder to the table, the officer brought Waylynn back into the moment. Long, curly brown hair had been pulled back in a tight ponytail, highlighting the sternness in the officer's expression. "Dr. Hargraves, sorry to keep you waiting. I'm Officer Ramsey. I have a few questions for you about what happened tonight."

"I know how this works." Waylynn shifted in the scratchy sweatshirt and sweatpants Officer Ramsey had lent her after crime scene technicians had taken her blood-soaked clothing as evidence. This time would be different. She wasn't a scared teenager anymore. She'd left that girl behind, studied her way through school, worked multiple jobs to pay for it herself, graduated with a master of science, landed a job with the top genetics laboratories in the country as their lead research associate. The work she'd done over the last three years for Genism Corporation would save lives. But the research community wouldn't see anything other than a murder charge attached to her name. "I'm not sure how much I can tell you."

"You do know how this works, don't you?" Officer Ramsey took a seat, sliding the folder she'd placed on the table across its surface. Waylynn didn't have to look at the contents to know what they contained. Her sealed records. "You've done this before. Are you sure you don't want your attorney present?"

Done this before. That wasn't a question. That was an accusation.

Her entire career—everything she'd worked for, everything she'd left behind—crashed down around her. A wave of dizziness closed in, but Waylynn fought against the all-consuming need to sink in the chair. No. This wasn't happening. She didn't kill her lab assistant.

"I don't have an attorney. Listen, my father wasn't a very nice man. So if you're looking for some sign of sympathy when it comes to his death, you're not going to find it, but I didn't kill Alexis." She set her palms against the cold surface of the table to gain some composure. "If you read the file, then you know I was acquitted. There wasn't enough evidence to convict me of my father's murder."

She hadn't been the one who'd killed him.

"But there is now." Light green eyes pinned Waylynn in place. At her words, another uniformed officer shouldered into the room, handing Ramsey a clear plastic evidence bag and another manila file. The policeman closed the door behind him, nothing but silence settling between her and the woman across the table. Officer Ramsey held up the evidence bag for her to see. "Do you recognize this?"

A piece of paper? "No."

"Really?" Ramsey set the bag labeled "evidence" flat on the table and slid it closer. "Why don't you take a closer look?"

Picking up the bag, Waylynn studied the blank sheet of paper, not entirely sure what Officer Ramsey intended her to see. She flipped it over. A gasp lodged in her throat as a flash of memory broke through her drug-induced haze. Sharp pain as she held on to the pen. The barrel of a gun cutting into her scalp. The handwritten words fell from her mouth as she stared at the note. *Her* handwritten words. "Tell Matt Stover I'm sorry. I had to save the project."

What was this supposed to be? A confession? A suicide note?

"Crime scene technicians discovered that note on your nightstand. That's your handwriting, isn't it?" Officer Ramsey collected the evidence bag, still holding it up. "Your supervisor, Dr. Matt Stover, who you mentioned in the note, was very helpful in providing us samples."

A flood of goose bumps pimpled along her arms. That was why they'd kept her contained in this room for so long. They'd been buying their time. Dread curdled in her stomach. If someone had forced her to write that note at gunpoint, what else had they forced her to do? What else would the crime scene technicians uncover? "Handwriting analysis can't be used as evidence in court."

"Right. You've done this before. I keep forgetting." A placating smile thinned Officer Ramsey's lips, deepening the laugh lines around her mouth as she leaned back in her chair. She pointed toward Waylynn's throat. "Tell me about that mark on your neck. What'd you do? Shoot yourself up with saline to make it look like you'd been drugged?"

A pitiful laugh burst from between Waylynn's lips. "What?"

She couldn't be serious. Why would she drug—

"The tox screen we ran earlier on the sample of blood you gave us came back negative for any kind of sedatives or other drugs." Officer Ramsey folded her arms across her midsection. "I have enough to arrest you right now, Dr. Hargraves. The only thing we can't account for is the gun you used to shoot Alexis Jacobs. You worked with her, didn't you? For three years. So why don't you tell me what really happened after you lured your lab tech to your apartment to kill her and where you stashed the weapon?"

Alexis had been shot? But Anchorage PD hadn't recovered the gun. Waylynn couldn't focus. Couldn't breathe. The toxicology screen was negative, but why couldn't she remember anything after she'd left the lab? She threaded her fingers into her hair. This was insane. There was no way she would've killed Alexis. "Talk to Elliot Dunham, my next-door neighbor. He was there. He broke down my apartment door seconds after I woke up on the bathroom floor. He heard me scream. That wouldn't have been enough time for me to stash a gun."

"He's in the next room over, but I'm not stupid enough to believe anything that comes out of Elliot Dunham's or his team's mouths, Dr. Hargraves. I rely on evidence." Officer Ramsey leaned back in her chair. "All this evidence, plus the voice mail Alexis left on your phone, is telling me your assistant uncovered something in your most recent research trial for Genism Corporation. Something that would bring the entire study down. You killed her to protect yourself."

The interrogation room door swung open for the third time and Waylynn studied a single man carrying a briefcase. Early fifties if she had to guess, short, cropped blond hair, piercing blue eyes almost the same shade as hers. The tight fit of his expensive suit and white shirt accentuated lean muscle, but it was the sternness etched into his expression that raised the hairs on the back of her neck. "My client won't be answering any more questions. This interrogation is over. Dr. Hargraves, I'm Blake Henson. Your lawyer."

Waylynn straightened. "I didn't call a lawyer."

"Your employer keeps me and my firm on retainer," he said. "Dr. Stover brought me in after the police coerced him into handing over writing samples without a warrant this morning."

The less than enthusiastic tone in his voice slid through her, which she understood. Blake Henson was a corporate lawyer, not criminal. Maybe she should've called her own counsel.

"Dr. Stover gave us those samples voluntarily, but nice try." Officer Ramsey collected the evidence bag with the handwritten note and both manila file folders and stood. "But it doesn't matter. You're just in time. Your client is about to be arrested for murder one, counselor."

"Not without a murder weapon she's not. Everything you have is circumstantial at best. For all we know, Alexis Jacobs shot herself to frame my client and had someone else get rid of the gun." Leveling the briefcase parallel with the table, Blake Henson slid the leather across the surface and hit the locks. He extracted a single piece of paper and handed it to Officer Ramsey. "Regardless, Dr. Hargraves signed a nondisclosure agreement pertaining to the research she and the deceased perform for Genism Corporation. Any intellectual property Dr. Stover provided to this department wasn't his to give, and I'm afraid you don't have a judge in the state who will overturn that, Officer. Trust me, I checked."

Officer Ramsey read the document, then lowered it to her side. "You're suing the department?"

"Not yet, but if you insist on trying to charge my client of Alexis Jacobs's murder without evidence, my firm won't have any other choice than to take you and the entire department to court." Blake wrapped a strong grip around Waylynn's arm and lifted her from her seat. A rush of heavy cologne churned her stomach as he escorted her to the door. "You, of all people, can't afford that, Officer Ramsey."

Was her lawyer threatening an Anchorage PD officer? Before Waylynn had a chance to say anything, he'd directed her into the hallway, his hand still tight around her arm.

"Doc." In the blink of an eye, Elliot was there, and a flood of relief washed through her. Elliot with his handsome face, dark brown hair, strong jaw, broad shoulders and athletic build. Elliot, the only man she'd ever let give her a nickname that actually made her feel better whenever he said it. No cuffs. He hadn't been arrested, but his normally gleaming stormy-gray eyes darkened with an edge as his attention locked on her lawyer's hand. "There a problem here?"

Waylynn wrenched her arm out of Blake Henson's hold. "I'm not being charged. Yet."

"Thanks to me." Her lawyer switched his briefcase from one hand to the other, then offered his hand. "Blake Henson. Dr. Hargraves's attorney. And you are?"

"Me?" Elliot closed in on her, ignoring Blake's extended hand, his shoulder brushing along hers as though he intended to possess her. His clean, masculine scent dived into her lungs. He looked angry, which was odd considering her next-door neighbor usually went to great lengths to hide what he was thinking by layering everything out of his mouth with sarcasm or a joke. This wasn't like him. Too serious. Too...dangerous. "I'm her damn bodyguard."

Chapter Two

"You won't be able to go home. Police tend to frown on someone living in the middle of an active crime scene." Elliot pushed the SUV harder. The faster he got her to safety, the faster the knot behind his sternum might let up. He never looked for trouble, but he had no problem befriending it. And Waylynn Hargraves had been trouble since the day he'd moved in next door. The most recent example would be her dead assistant's body in the tub. And the fact he'd nearly torn a man's arm off and beat the bastard to death with it for putting his hands on her.

Not very professional. But the moment he'd seen Blake Henson's hand on her arm, it'd taken every ounce of his control not to kill the lawyer in the middle of Anchorage PD's station. Possessiveness unlike anything he'd experienced before had clawed up his throat and taken control. Nobody—not her lawyer, not the police, not him—touched Waylynn without her explicit permission.

"I remembered something." Exhaustion clung to her words. The sweatpants and sweatshirt someone at the station had lent her hung off her narrow frame, but nothing could detract from her overall beauty. The light in her ordinarily bright eyes had dimmed over the past few hours. Finding a dead woman in your bathtub could have that effect on a person. "When Officer Ramsey was questioning me, she showed me a handwritten note, and I remembered writing it. Only, in the memory, there was a gun pressed to my head." Her voice dropped as she stared out the passenger-side window. "Somebody forced me to write it."

"You're being framed for your assistant's murder, but I have a sense you already knew that." Someone had been in her home. Drugged her. Forced her to do hell knew what. And he hadn't heard a thing aside from her scream. Right next door. Elliot strengthened his grip around the steering wheel as downtown Anchorage passed in a blur. Working for Blackhawk Security certainly had its benefits. Use of the company's SUVs, health coverage, an armory of weapons, not spending the rest of his life behind bars in the middle of nowhere thanks to the founder of the firm. None of it did a damn bit of good if he lost the closest person he had to a friend. Snowy peaks along the Chugach Mountain Range glistened in the sun as they headed east, and he pushed one hand through his hair. Even in the middle of June, Anchorage gave him the proverbial middle finger. He missed the desert. He glanced toward Waylynn, then back to the road as the signal ahead turned red. "Anything else?"

"Nothing. Whoever drugged me knew what they were doing. I can't remember what happened in my apartment and the drug didn't show up on a toxicology screen. I guess I'll take that as a win-win situation. I'm not sure I want to remember what happened." Color drained from her face as she leaned her head into her hand and her elbow against the passenger-side door. Disheveled blond hair slid over her shoulder as she shook her head. The weight of her attention fell on him, hiking his awareness of her—of her flowery scent—to an all-time high. Geraniums. Her favorite. But not just from the bottle. Almost as though the scent had become a permanent part of her over the years. Now he couldn't smell the damn things without thinking of her. "Why did you tell my attorney you're my bodyguard?"

"I know you, Doc." And not because it was his job to know. He'd spent the last year as a private investigator for Blackhawk Security, uncovering the secrets his targets hid from the world, declassifying documents for his own curiosity. Hell, he kept files on every one of his teammates. His former navy SEAL boss, Sullivan Bishop, and the fact he'd killed his own serial killer father, forensics expert Vincent Kalani and the accusations filed against him back in New York, their resident computer geek, Elizabeth Bosch—Dawson, whatever she went by now—Anthony Harris's classified missions for the army, and the saddest of them all, their psychologist, Kate Monroe. But digging into Waylynn's past had never crossed his mind.

The light turned green in his peripheral vision. Car horns blared for him to get moving, but he didn't give a damn. "You're a scientist. You've spent your entire life in search of the truth and there's no way I'm going to let you get yourself killed going after this guy on your own."

"My boss was right." She hugged herself a bit tighter

and stared out the windshield. "You and I spend way too much time together."

"Or maybe Dr. Stover wants you all for himself." Couldn't blame the guy. Waylynn had a pull to her, a sort of gravity that was hard to fight. Even now, something about her urged Elliot to close the small distance between them, but he'd never cross that line. Not with Waylynn. She needed his help now and that was as far as it would go between them. Ever. He stepped on the accelerator, barely making it through the light. Her mouth parted as though she intended to deny it. "Trust me, Doc. Bosses don't usually call lawyers when their employees are being charged with murder."

Helping them escape out of an Iraqi prison was another thing.

"I think Matt is more interested in my research than what's under my lab coat." Fingers spread wide, a combination of passion and excitement controlled her hands as she spoke. She did that a lot—spoke with her hands and he couldn't do anything but pay attention. "The research we're doing is important. Have you heard of the warrior gene before?"

"Is that the movie about the boxer?" he asked.

"The warrior gene," she said. "Nearly every human being alive has a monoamine oxidase A gene, but, in several cases, individuals with low activity in that specific gene were found to have higher aggression in certain high-stress situations. It's a variant and has come to be known as the warrior gene. Identifying the subjects who possess the warrior gene has the potential to save thousands of lives a year. Active shooters could be stopped before they picked up a gun because they wouldn't be able to get one in the first place. Homicide rates would plummet. Army, navy, air force, the entire military would benefit from our research."

"What? No psychic telling you who to arrest before the vision comes true?" Elliot made a sharp right turn and floored the accelerator as they climbed Seward Highway's on-ramp. Couldn't take her to Blackhawk Security. Despite the fact its founder and CEO, Sullivan Bishop, had turned it into a fortress, Elliot wasn't willing to take the risk while the building was still under construction. It'd been five months since a bomb had ripped apart the conference room, but the best place for Waylynn right now was with him. "What you're talking about sounds like science fiction."

"It's not like that." Her hands fell into her lap as they left the city limits.

Greenery bled together in his peripheral vision, the sunlight glimmering off the Turnagain Arm waterway almost blinding. He hadn't chosen Alaska. If it were up to him, he'd have left a long time ago, but he'd keep his promise to his employer. He'd work off his debt.

"And, no, we don't have a psychic predicting violent events and the justice system would never convict a person of a crime before the actual crime was committed," she said. "But knowing who carries the gene will be a huge step forward in genetic engineering and protecting lives."

"What you're saying is everyone with the warrior gene will eventually snap when put in a high-stress situation." Elliot turned off the highway, throwing them deep into the middle of the Alaskan wilderness just before the Potter Creek trailhead that led into Chugach

State Park. The property wasn't much and he'd bought it for close to nothing, but he could keep Waylynn safe out here. And that was all that mattered. "Good thing I'm prepared for the zombie apocalypse."

"Not...everyone. But, according to the studies I've done, it's a possibility." Her voice wavered on that last part and he narrowed in on the slight twitch on the left side of her mouth. A tell. Waylynn cleared her throat as a rush of pink climbed up her neck and into her cheeks. She tipped her chin up, studying the surrounding trees as the SUV climbed up the dirt trail. Waylynn Hargraves was hiding something. "Why are you helping me?"

She could keep her secrets. For now. As long as they didn't get him killed. Because he sure as hell wasn't the sharing type. Besides, he had ways of uncovering the truth. No matter how deep it was buried. Elliot pulled off the main road, driving deeper into wilderness. No one would find them out here. And if they did, he'd come prepared. "I don't think you killed your assistant. If you had, you would've asked me for help burying the body."

A smile overwhelmed the exhaustion in her features and, for a split second, Elliot couldn't take his eyes off her. He'd never been the type to stick around long. A month here, a few weeks there. He'd made some enemies along the way, but having Waylynn next door settled the restlessness singing through his veins most days. "You have experience with that kind of thing?"

Elliot leveraged his palm against the steering wheel and stretched back in the seat. "Did I ever tell you why I came to Anchorage?"

She shook her head as the SUV bounced over fallen branches and dead foliage. He made one last turn, forcing her to reach for the handle above her seat before he brought the vehicle to a stop and hiked it into Park.

"I ran a con that ended with me on the wrong side of the Iraqi government." Reaching back behind her seat, close enough to get a lungful of her light perfume, he grabbed the duffel bag he kept stocked full of supplies and hauled it into the front. "Turns out being paid for assassination contracts you never intended to carry out constitutes fraud when the people paying you work for the government."

A weak laugh escaped from her lips as those blue eyes of hers widened. "You're not serious, are you?"

"My boss, Sullivan, was starting a security firm here in Anchorage. Needed a private investigator. I was recruited for the job." Elliot shouldered his way out of the SUV, hiking the duffel over his shoulder. He clamped his hand on top of the roof of the vehicle. "And by *recruited*, I mean he made a deal with the people who had me arrested and is forcing me to pay back the money I conned out of those nice killers until we're even. After that, who knows. Maybe my next project will be getting paid to bury bodies for people with your warrior gene."

"You don't strike me as a professional con man," she said.

"That's what makes me so good at it." He winked at her, a smile pulling at one side of his mouth, and motioned her out with a single nod. "Come on. I'll show you around."

Waylynn focused on their surroundings through his open door. He noted the exact moment she realized where he'd brought her as her mouth parted. "Please tell me you're joking."

He couldn't hold back the laugh rumbling through him and turned toward the dark green cabin. "Not this time, Doc."

A TINY CABIN.

Not an *oh-this-is-so-cute-and-perfect* cabin, but a real, featured-on-the-Travel-Channel tiny cabin in the middle of the freaking woods. Broken twigs and foliage crunched under her feet as she rounded the hood of his company SUV. Dark green paint chipping off wood planks, a single window above the shack-like door. She ran her fingers through her matted, blood-tinted hair, then cringed at the thought of what she might look like. He couldn't be serious. "Anchorage PD is going to charge me with your murder in the morning and I'm going to tell them it's because you made me stay here."

There was no way they could both fit inside this thing. No way they wouldn't run into each other in there. Waylynn swallowed hard. They'd been friends for over a year. Every night when she came home from the lab, he was there in his crappy camp chair with two beers and that damn gut-wrenching smile of his. She'd tell him about her day. He'd tell her about his most recent investigation, then they'd head inside to their apartments. Alone. But this? The idea there wouldn't be any barriers between them? It'd either destroy their friendship or push it to the next level. Either way, their relationship would never be the same if she stepped over that threshold.

"Well, now you're trying to hurt my feelings." Elliot offered her his hand, the other cinched around the duffel bag he'd extracted from the back seat. He was giving her a choice. Giving her safety if she wanted it. "It's a lot bigger than it looks."

His easygoing smile and confidence melted through her. Of course he had confidence. Wasn't that what *con man* stood for? She'd known he had a past. Everyone did. But could she trust him to keep her safe? Trust him to help her uncover who'd framed her for Alexis's murder? That was the question. Despite his revelation about the con he'd pulled in Iraq—a con that'd landed him in prison—her gut already knew the answer. Waylynn stretched out her hand, sliding her fingers up his palm. Rougher than she'd expected. Calloused, as if he'd been working with some kind of machinery or maybe out here in the woods. Desire exploded through her with a single touch, just as it had back at the police station. "It better be."

A breeze whipped through the surrounding trees, shaking them into a frenzy as Elliot reached for the door. He led her inside, a rush of heat dissipating the goose bumps pimpling along her arms. A combination of wood and spice wrapped around her as the main living space came into focus. She glanced toward him, unsure what to say.

"What'd I tell you?" Elliot released her hand, taking his body heat with him, and motioned to the unbelievably modern space with both arms wide. He set the duffel bag on the floor, then collapsed backward onto the single couch, fingers interlaced behind his head. For as small as the cabin looked from the outside, the layout worked well for the limited space. A fireplace, complete with a stock of firewood, lay dead ahead. Off to the left of that, a single countertop with bar stools on one side and a kitchen sink and stove on the other. No dining table. Not enough room. A short hallway led to what looked like a bathroom with a set of stairs leading to a space on the second level. The one and only bedroom. The decor fit the location. Wood, wood and more wood. Just as she'd expect from any other cabin stashed in the wilderness, but the granite countertop and brightly colored accents brought the entire room into the modern era. It suited Elliot. At least, what she knew of him.

"And you thought this would be awkward." He compressed his mouth against a smile.

Surprise pushed through her. "I never said that."

"You didn't have to." He swung his legs over the side of the couch and pushed to his feet. Closing in on her, he leveled that dark gaze on her and every cell in her body responded. "I read people for a living, Doc. It's what makes me good at my job."

Heat flamed up her neck and into her cheeks. She brushed a strand of blood-matted hair behind one ear and fought the urge to cross her arms. What else had he read about her? "In that case, I can't promise you I won't let you down when you look at me too closely."

"What are you talking about?" One distinct crease deepened between his eyebrows as he shifted his weight between both feet. "You haven't let me down."

"Someone is framing me for Alexis's murder." Waylynn interlaced her fingers. She used her hands to speak a lot of the time, but right now, all she wanted to do was close in on herself. To hide. From whoever'd killed her assistant. From the man standing in front of her who knew her better than any other person in her life, but she didn't want to lie to him. Ever. "This isn't the first time I've been accused of killing someone."

Seconds slipped by. Maybe a full minute. She couldn't read his expression, didn't know what he was thinking. Was controlling what others read in his body language part of being a con man, too? "Say something. Please."

Elliot ran a hand over his beard, tugging on the end. "Tell me what happened."

The same intensity she'd witnessed back at the police station consumed his expression. "I was fifteen. My father..." She pushed back the memories, but her pulse skyrocketed. "He deserved what happened to him. The cancer had already affected my mom, and police concluded she didn't have the strength to do what had been done, so I became the next logical suspect. They took me out of school, arrested me and attempted to try me as an adult, but in the end, I was acquitted. Not enough evidence. They couldn't find the gun that'd been used to kill him." The Beretta 92 pistol he'd kept stashed away in the linen closet of her childhood home. "Same as now."

That gut-wrenching smile overtook his stubborn expression, and she struggled against the gravitational pull she experienced every time he came around.

"What are the odds someone has been accused of murder twice in their life?" he asked.

"In my experience? High. Normally? Zero."

He stepped into her, setting her chin between his index finger and thumb as he had in her apartment.

Her insides turned to molten lava. Hesitation gripped her hard as he studied her. "Whoever's doing this is counting on you taking the fall for Alexis's death." He released her, the tingling sensation spreading behind her sternum fading. "I'm not going to let that happen."

All she had to do was lean forward—just a bit—to press her mouth against his. What would he taste like? Feel like?

A dull ringing reached her ears. Waylynn blinked to clear the last few seconds from her mind. She rushed to retrieve her phone from the pocket of the grungy sweats Officer Ramsey had lent her. The screen brightened with the laboratory's number. "This is probably my boss. I should answer."

Elliot swept his arms wide and bowed before retreating toward the door and, just like that, the intensity in his body language disappeared. As though it'd never happened. "By all means, use whichever part of this room you prefer. I'll grab the gear from the truck."

She stared after him as he closed the door. A small burst of disbelieving laughter escaped up her throat. No. Nothing was happening between them. That hadn't been a connection. It'd been her body's automatic reaction to a stressful situation. She and Elliot were friends and she'd keep it that way. They didn't have a future together. There *was* no future with her.

The phone vibrating in her hand brought her back into the moment. She swiped her finger across the screen and brought it to her ear. "Dr. Hargraves."

"Waylynn, I can't believe it." Dr. Matthew Stoker's frantic tenor intensified the stress lodged between her shoulder blades. "The police were here at the lab. They wanted copies of your reports to match your handwriting—"

"It's fine, Matt." Waylynn ran a hand across her forehead. Dr. Matthew Stoker had been her boss for close to ten years. He'd given her the opportunity to conduct her research and convinced Genism's board of directors to fund her projects. He was on the path to put the lab on the map for genetic research all before he hit forty. The entire company depended on him. But getting dragged into a murder investigation threatened his promising future. "You were doing what you had to for the best of the company. I don't blame you for handing the reports over. I'm sorry they came to you."

"Don't worry about me. Are you okay?" Static reached through Matt's end of the line. Or was that the sound of broken glass in the background? "I called the company lawyer for you. Blake Henson told me you'd been arrested, but they couldn't keep you in custody. Where are you?"

"I'm…" She didn't know what to say. She'd found her assistant dead in her bathtub and all the evidence Anchorage PD had recovered pointed at her. Someone had framed her for murder and the only reason she'd come out into the middle of the woods with Elliot was for her own protection. Should she trust Matt with the location?

The front door clicked open.

Elliot hauled another duffel bag inside, tossing it onto the floor, and her awareness of him rocketed to an all-time high. The zip-up hoodie he wore did nothing to hide the bulk in his arms and across his chest.

The air in her lungs stilled. She'd never noticed his physique before.

What had changed?

"Waylynn?" Matt asked over the line.

She took a deep breath to restart her system as Elliot maneuvered around her in the small space and headed for the back of the cabin. His clean, masculine scent worked deep into her lungs, became part of her, and she had the feeling that was only the beginning as she studied the rest of the tiny space. He'd brought her here to keep her safe from whoever'd killed Alexis, but what if it was him who needed protection from her? "I'm somewhere safe."

"Good. Keep it that way, because there's something you should know." The tension in Matt's voice failed to drown out the tinkling of shattered glass over the line. "Someone broke in to the lab. Somehow a fire broke out and… Everything, all of your research from the past ten years… It's gone."

Chapter Three

"Good news. I found an unopened box of peanut butter Oreos stashed under the bed." He tossed the package a few inches into the air, then caught it. Her favorite guilty pleasure. Elliot pounded down the small set of stairs and rounded the corner into the main living space from the back of the cabin.

The color had left Waylynn's cheeks, her knuckles white around the phone in her hand. The hairs on the back of his neck stood on end at the sight of her. Forget the cookies. Tossing the package onto the counter, he pulled the weapon from his shoulder holster beneath his sweatshirt and clicked off the safety, ready for war. "Tell me whose ass I need to kick."

"Somebody doesn't just want to frame me for Alexis's murder. They're destroying my life." Her voice barely reached across the small space. Confusion deepened the color in her ocean-blue gaze. "Elliot, my research... It's gone. Everything I've worked for—for the past ten years, is gone."

His gut tightened. Hell. That'd been her life's work, her career. And it was gone? Elliot didn't believe in coincidences. First, her assistant's murder in Waylynn's apartment. Now this. She was right. Whoever'd set her up to take the fall was ensuring she'd never get back up. He scanned the perimeter from the nearest window, then centered back on her, approaching slowly, and lowered the gun. Locking on the phone still clutched in her hand, he holstered his weapon. "Who was on the phone?"

"Dr. Stover. Someone broke in to the lab. There was a fire." Her voice hollowed. She somehow went even paler. Her attention snapped up as he closed the distance between them and everything inside him heated. The delicate column of her throat flexed on a swallow. "The fire department thinks it was arson. There were traces of accelerant all over my desk. Chemicals we keep in the janitorial closets."

He denied the urge to wrap her in his arms. While he hadn't taken her on as an official client—yet—the same rules applied. No getting involved with clients. "Just yours?"

She nodded but refused to let go of that damn phone. "Yes. Someone burned it all. My handwritten notes, my digital files, a decade's worth of studies and genetic testing… It was all in my desk or on my computer. What am I going to do?"

"What about a backup?" There had to be something salvageable.

"Genism doesn't allow employees to have backups other than the company server, but Matt said that's been tampered with, too." She swiped at her face, shoulders rising on a deep inhale as though her emotional reservoir had run dry. "We can't bring any foreign devices into the lab, take files out or save them to the cloud."

Of course they couldn't. That would make too much sense. And, suddenly, Elliot couldn't keep his distance from her any longer. Reaching for her, he slid his fingers up her arms. Calluses caught on her smooth skin, the rush of the scent of geraniums was intoxicating. "Waylynn, I'm sorry. I know how much your work meant— means—to you."

It was her entire life, her career. Her ticket out of a rough childhood, which he'd most recently learned included a murder accusation. She'd moved on from that life, had obviously worked hard for it. College, graduate school, becoming one of the foremost experts in the country on genetics. And in the flash of a flame, it was gone. Didn't seem fair.

"Does this place have a shower?" she asked.

"Bathroom is past the kitchen on the right." Elliot hiked a thumb over his shoulder and turned slightly to give her a line of sight. Despite the bloody tint to her blond hair, the smear of her eyeliner and mascara, and the fact she'd lost everything that mattered to her, Waylynn held her head high.

"Take your time. Clean towels are hanging behind the door," he said.

A single nod was all he got in response as she pulled out of his grasp and headed toward the bathroom.

The lock clicked into place and he didn't waste any time. Whoever'd framed her for murder had started the fire in her lab. He was sure of it. The timing. The opportunity. They both lined up. The SOB might be dangerous, but Elliot was worse. Because they'd never see him or his team coming.

Extracting his laptop from one of the black duffel

bags on the couch, he flipped it open and took a seat at the counter. Framing Waylynn to cover up a murder was one thing. Alexis's murder could've had nothing to do with Waylynn, but his next-door neighbor happened to make the perfect scapegoat with her sordid past. Coming after Waylynn's research? That was personal. Someone was hunting her.

The unsub—unknown subject—had to know about her father's murder accusation in order for the frame job to stick. Except those records had been sealed because Waylynn had been a minor at the time. Which meant the bastard was either connected to the case or had premeditated pinning the murder on Waylynn by looking for something incriminating. He couldn't discount any possibility. Not when it came to keeping her alive.

Elliot glanced toward the bathroom at the sound of water hitting tile. It'd take a few minutes for her to wash off the blood. Focusing on the screen, he pulled up the internet browser and typed in her name. His finger hovered over the enter key. Of all the people he'd investigated, of all the chances he'd had to dig into her past, he'd kept Waylynn's off-limits, respecting her privacy. He had an entire team of coworkers. Former SEALs and Rangers, an ex-National Security Agency consultant, a military investigator, Blackhawk Security's forensics expert and a psychologist. He'd worked with them for over a year, trusted them with his life, but Waylynn was different. Special. Forbidden.

And yet someone was trying to hurt her.

He hit the button. The screen brightened as headlines filled the page. Top stories included the massive progress she'd made in the bioengineering community, but one stood out among the rest. "Rhinebeck, NY, fifteen-year-old acquitted of father's murder." Elliot read through the article. Waylynn had spent over three weeks in county lockup after her arrest on school grounds. Never gave a statement, never tried to blame the crime on someone else, or offered an alibi. Police had questioned her cancer-stricken mother at the time, but ultimately concluded Nora Hargraves didn't have the strength to lift the missing handgun used to kill her husband in cold blood. Without the murder weapon, the prosecution had no other choice than to release the teen despite ample motive and opportunity. Her mother had died during the trial.

Hell. In the year they'd been neighbours, he'd known Waylynn had lost her mother when she was younger, and about the foster family who'd taken her in until she'd turned eighteen, but he hadn't realized the circumstances. Elliot leaned back in his chair to break up the tightness in his throat. He'd been on his own since he was fourteen. Voluntarily. Waylynn had everyone taken from her in a three-week span. He glanced toward the bathroom.

But none of this narrowed down a suspect pool. Nathan Hargraves had been shot nine times and died from massive blood loss. The forensic pathologist who'd signed the death certificate hadn't gone into more detail other than a final conclusion reading "homicide" and a note that reported a mere five dollars in cash had been found on the body at the time of the autopsy.

No other family. No friends who'd seemed too beat up about her father's death. No reason for someone to come after Waylynn. He'd have to do some more digging, but if Alexis's murder and the fire at the lab had anything to do with Waylynn's past, he couldn't see it. Which meant their suspect had learned about the trial, but only planned to use it to secure an arrest fifteen years later. Would've worked, too. If police had recovered the gun.

Elliot ran a hand through his hair, then rested his elbow against the counter. She hadn't told him any of this. In the year they'd been neighbors, she'd never mentioned her parents, her hometown, the fact she'd been in the foster system at the age of fifteen. Then again, how often had he talked about his parents? His hometown?

"All right, Alexis Jacobs, show me what you've got." He rolled back his right shoulder, working through the stiffness that still paralyzed the scar tissue around the bullet wound there. If the unsub wasn't connected to Waylynn's trial, then someone wanted the assistant dead for a reason. What had Waylynn said when he'd found her in the bathroom this morning? Alexis wanted to meet because she'd found something within the study they'd been conducting at the lab. But with all of Waylynn's research destroyed, he doubted the assistant's discovery hadn't been destroyed with it. He scanned through Alexis's social media pages. Three different sites. Hundreds of pictures. But this one... Elliot stopped scrolling and straightened. The redheaded beauty with freckles had taken a photo of herself a few days before her death, showing off what looked like a new tattoo of a *Q* with a heart on her wrist. The Queen of Hearts. But it was what was behind her that urged him to lean closer to the screen. A black external hard drive sticking out of the victim's purse.

"Bingo." Waylynn had said Genism didn't allow employees to back up their files on foreign devices, but what if Alexis hadn't followed company rules? He needed to get that hard drive.

The bathroom door clicked open and in his next breath, Waylynn rounded into the kitchen. Damn, he hadn't even heard her shut off the water. Hair still wet, she notched her chin level with the floor and curled her fingers into tight fists at her sides. Defiant. Strong. Sexy as hell.

"Well, don't you look nice when you're not covered in blood." Nervous energy exploded across his back as he closed the laptop, sliding it against the granite. She didn't need to see photos of the woman she'd found in her bathtub. Didn't need to know he'd looked into her trial. He drew his eyebrows together when she didn't respond. "You okay?"

"I want to know who's trying to destroy my life." Determination had cooled the day's confusion in her expression. The tears had dried, her jaw set, and she focused 100 percent on him. "You're a private investigator. I'm hiring you and your firm. Find out who did this to me."

"WE NEED TO get to my lab." There were plenty of monsters who knew how to play at being human. Which one of them had ruined her life? The possibilities were endless. Someone from her own lab. A rival geneticist. One of the volunteers from her studies. Her research into the warrior gene fulfilled her in a way nothing else had managed to for her entire life. She wasn't going to let that go. Not for anything. The person responsible wasn't going to get away with it. Waylynn settled back against the granite countertop, crossing her arms across her midsection. Then again, not all monsters did monstrous things. "Alexis said she wanted to meet with me about one of the studies. We record all of those sessions with our volunteers. So if something strange happened with one of them, it'd be on the security footage."

The weight of Elliot's gaze warmed her neck and face. Her pulse quickened. Her body surged to attention when he looked at her like that—like she was the only woman in the entire world—and her brain checked out temporarily. This place, the location, it suited him. If anything, he seemed more relaxed here than he had in the year she'd known him as her next-door neighbor. Fewer tension lines bracketed the edges of those gray eyes. If she was being honest with herself, in his tiny cabin, out in the middle of the woods trying to keep her safe, he'd never been more attractive.

"You want to be caught at yet another crime scene tied to this case? That's a terrible, horrible, incredibly foolish idea." He stood, clapping his hands together. "Let's do it and see what happens."

Reality snapped her back into the moment and she pushed thoughts of him into a dark little corner of her brain where she prayed it'd never see the light of day again. "What?"

"First things first." Elliot pointed toward her and closed the space between them faster than she thought possible. His body heat tunneled through her borrowed sweats as he slid one arm around her. Her breath caught in her lungs, surprise paralyzing her in place. In the next moment, he'd retreated, handing her a package of peanut butter Oreos. "You need to eat, then sleep. In that order."

She blinked, staring at the unopened blue plastic package in her hand. Tiny cabin. Limited space. He hadn't been stepping in for an intimate moment or to help tame the chaos eating her up from the inside. Waylynn released the breath she'd been holding. Had she wanted him to? "You know my favorite flavor of Oreos?"

"Investigating 101." He leaned back against the opposite counter. "Everything you need to know about a person is in their daily routine, and you, my friend, bring home a lot of peanut butter Oreo packages."

A burst of laughter escaped from between her lips, because if she didn't have this small release, she feared she might fall apart. "You just happened to have a supply here?"

"I may have wanted to see what all the fuss was about." He crossed his arms, emphasizing the muscles across his chest, and his boots at the ankles.

She played with the back of her earring, scraping her thumbnail along the edge of her earlobe. "And?"

"And they're addictive." A bright widening of his lips played across his mouth as he blinked at her, and every cell in her body shot to attention. How was it, after everything that'd happened this morning, he could affect her like this?

"That's what I thought." Waylynn peeled back the sticky plastic in an empty attempt to calm the uncertainty ripping through her, took a cookie, then offered him the package. Nope. Not even the combination of chocolate and peanut butter frosting could erase the last twelve hours. Alexis was still dead and her career had gone up in flames. Another flash of her writing that note skittered across her memory. She fought to steady her racing pulse and forced herself to study Elliot as he bit into an Oreo instead.

The rest of the world fell away. The charges against her, the accusing tone in Officer Ramsey's voice, the fact police would probably want to speak to her about the fire, too. In this moment, all she saw was him. Elliot. Her next-door neighbor, her closest friend who she'd spent countless hours quizzing on horrible '90s country music lyrics by text message throughout the day. Which he knew by heart. The only man who'd been able to change her breathing patterns with a single look in her direction.

Elliot laughed, pulling her back into the moment. "I promise I'm not that interesting, Doc."

Oh, no. No, no, no. She wasn't going to go down that road.

"Excuse me. I need some air." Waylynn discarded the remainder of her cookie into the sink and put one foot in front of the other until she reached the front door. She had to get out of here. Away from him. If only for a few minutes to clear her head. The wood walls blurred in her vision as she escaped out the front. The rush of a cold Alaskan breeze beat against her as she closed the door behind her. Her heartbeat pounded loud behind her ears, the pressure behind her sternum more manageable the longer she kept the door between them. She ran a hand through her damp hair easily. No longer crusted with blood.

The sudden surge of desire she'd felt for him in those

heated moments drained. She'd kept her and Elliot's friendship casual for over a year, but now... Now she'd started imagining that smile in the morning after they woke up in the same bed. How his hair would stick out in every direction as he prepared her breakfast. How they'd have the rest of their lives to test each other's knowledge of bad country music. She shook her head in an attempt to dislodge the fantasy. They were friends. Nothing more.

A ring of trees surrounded the tiny cabin, weeds cleared approximately fifteen feet in each direction. Nothing but wilderness and blue skies as far as she could see, and a sense of peace settled over her. Elliot had certainly picked the perfect spot to get away from reality. When was the last time she'd gotten out of town, away from work, took a break for herself? Waylynn took in a lungful of crisp, clean mountain air.

Short answer? Never.

After the trial, after her mother's death, she'd thrown herself into investigating what had gone wrong. Why her father's behavior had changed so drastically in such a short amount of time with no sign of disease, no evidence of cancer, tumors, mental disabilities, no added stresses at work. Why he'd suddenly turned against her and her mother. The yelling, the fights, the physical altercations. In the end, she'd tried to tell herself it didn't matter. He'd gotten what he'd deserved, but what if it hadn't been his fault? What if, like those afflicted with any other genetic disorder, he hadn't been able to control himself?

Waylynn rolled her lips between her teeth and bit down to fight back the burn in her eyes. A simple blood test had confirmed her theory. He'd been born with a variant of the monoamine oxidase A gene. The "warrior gene." By disrupting the neurotransmitters dopamine, norepinephrine and serotonin, the gene predisposed carriers to more aggressive and violent behavior. While Genism and their military contractors paid her to take advantage of those specific behaviors, she'd spent every waking minute looking for ways to neutralize them. One success. That was all it would take to change the world. To change *her* world.

Maybe then she and Elliot could become more than—

A low vibration came from the tree line, raising the hairs on the back of her neck. Movement shifted the weeds and bushes to her right and her blood pressure spiked. She unfolded her arms. The vibration grew louder, harsher, a split second before thick, brown fur and four long legs materialized at the edge of the trees. Black eyes focused on her and Waylynn couldn't move. Frizzy hackles raised along the moose's back. No antlers. A female. But with her ears flattened against her head and nostrils flared, she was just as terrifying as the male of the species.

Waylynn raised her palms in surrender, taking a step back.

Another warning reached her ears and outright fear paralyzed her in place. The creature's long, thin face dipped toward two smaller brown faces at her feet. Her babies. Newborn twins. Waylynn wouldn't hold up against a full-fledged moose charge. The damn tiny cabin wouldn't hold up against the mother defending those calves. "Elliot."

His name barely registered over the moose's low-pitched growl. With a couple of licks to the newborns, the mother refocused her efforts on keeping them safe. Waylynn lowered her hands slowly, sweat building on her upper lip. She fought to breathe around the fear clawing up her throat. Any sudden move, any attempt to escape, and the moose would charge. Licking dry lips, she tried to speak again. "Elliot."

"Don't move." Warmth flooded through her. He stepped inside her peripheral vision, so quietly she hadn't heard him come outside. As though he'd been able to feel her fear from inside the cabin and had come running. Elliot shifted in front of her, attention on the mother and her young. It was only after he'd moved between her and the moose that Waylynn understood what he was trying to do. He tossed an apple in the creature's direction. His voice leveled with reasoning. "Nobody wants your babies, Mabel. They look like a handful. So I'll make you a deal. You can have the rest of these apples, but you have to get them to go."

"I take it you two know each other?" Waylynn kept her voice low. She didn't dare look away from the cow protecting her young despite the fact all she wanted to do was run.

"We've met." Elliot notched his head back toward her slightly. "Mabel moved in around the same time I had the cabin built. Thing One and Thing Two there were born about two months ago, and she does not like the fact I vacation close by."

Mabel searched for the fruit, then brought her head back up, mouth empty. A rough exhale expanded the moose's nostrils.

"All right, Doc, she's not taking the bait, and it looks like we're in the middle of a standoff." Elliot rebalanced his weight between both feet. "When I give you the signal, I want you to run as fast as you can for the cabin. Don't look back and don't wait for me."

"What?" Waylynn took her eyes off Mabel. "I'm not going to leave you out here to take on a moose by your—"

A wall of muscle slammed her into the dirt. Her head snapped back against the ground; she couldn't see straight. He'd moved so fast she didn't have time to comprehend what'd happened until the beat of twelve hoofed feet faded into the woods. Mabel had charged, her babies had tagged along with her, and Elliot had tackled Waylynn to the ground. She struggled to breathe as he positioned his hands on either side of her, that damn gut-wrenching smile stretching his mouth thin. "That was fun."

His exhales skittered along her oversensitized skin and her heart fought to break through her rib cage in response. He'd saved her life. From a moose. "You and I have very different ideas of fun."

Chapter Four

He'd made mistakes.

Life didn't come with a set of instructions, but Elliot probably wouldn't have followed them anyway. Having her this close, in his home away from home, was a mistake. He'd been trying to save her from a life-ending stampede by Mabel and her calves but instead had gotten the up-close-and-personal Waylynn experience. Even four hours later, with her fast asleep upstairs in his bed, he could still smell her perfume on his clothing, remember the widening of her pupils as he'd looked down at her, feel the smoothness of her skin against the calluses in his palms.

He swallowed against the tightness in his throat. It wouldn't happen. Not now. Not ever. And most definitely not with her. Sure, they'd been friends for a while, but friends didn't expect or ask for commitment. Not in the same way a romantic relationship did. He'd spent the better parts of his life at the mercy of others. Never again.

The sun had leveled with the horizon hours ago, yet light still poured in through the windows. Daylight at midnight. No better time than to plan their next move.

His phone chimed with an incoming message. Swiping his thumb across the screen, he read Vincent Kalani's report. No hard drive recovered from Alexis Jacobs's apartment. The former cop and Blackhawk Security's current forensics expert had a relationship with the Anchorage police chief, which had gotten the team out of a lot of sticky situations in the past few months. Brothers in blue or something like that. But the missing hard drive triggered Elliot's gut instinct.

Someone was framing Waylynn for her assistant's murder. Either the unsub had broken into Alexis's apartment and taken the drive before police had a chance to search the place or the redhead had taken steps to make sure it would never be found if her employer came calling.

Only one way to find out.

Threading his arms through his shoulder holster, he glanced up toward the loft where Waylynn slept. No point in waking her now. If he found the hard drive, he'd bring it back here and they'd go through it together. If not, he'd have no reason to break the bad news. She'd been through enough. Elliot turned toward the door but slowed as the hairs on the back of his neck rose on end.

"You, sir, are a terrible bodyguard." That voice. Hell, that voice could move mountains. He'd recognize it anywhere, had memorized every inflection and tone.

"In my defense, you're supposed to be asleep and I was going to set the alarm." He turned toward her. Air locked in his lungs as she came down the narrow set of stairs. Long blond hair shifted over her shoulders, the muscles in her lean, bare legs flexing as she moved. Bright teal toenails reflected the flames crackling in the fireplace a few feet away. "Are you wearing my MIT shirt?"

"As nice of a gesture Officer Ramsey made by lending me her sweats so she could keep my clothes as evidence, I couldn't sleep in them. Hope you don't mind. I found it on top of a stack of shirts by the bed." She tugged on the hem but failed to make a damn bit of difference hiding all that perfect skin. "Although, not sure it matters what I'm wearing. When I close my eyes..." She folded her arms, accentuating the slight curves beneath his shirt, but not even that could distract him from the fear in those mesmerizing blue eyes. "I didn't know you'd gone to MIT."

She was avoiding the subject, the thing that kept her from falling asleep. He'd let her. For now. Everyone had their breaking point. And he had a feeling the frame job, the loss of her research—they were just the beginning.

"Mechanical engineering. Didn't last long." The dean tended to look down on students getting paid to take exams for their graduating class.

"Mechanical engineer. Con man. Private investigator." Waylynn stepped off the last step and rested her weight against the kitchen counter. "Which one of you is sneaking out of your own cabin in the middle of the night to follow a lead without me?"

Damn, she was good. "That would be the private investigator." He scratched at his beard. "You'd mentioned Genism doesn't allow employees to store their work on foreign devices, but I have a picture of your assistant with a hard drive in the background." He opened the door partway. "Want to see what kind of trouble we can get into?"

"That depends." She notched her chin parallel with the floor, the small muscles shifting in the firelight. "You're not suggesting breaking and entering, are you?"

"Give me a little more credit than that." His phone chimed with an incoming message. Elliot swiped his thumb over the screen a second time, then turned the phone toward her so she could read the message herself. "I have someone on the inside. He's already at the location. Are you in or are you out, Doc?"

Shadows fluctuated along the right side of her face from the flames, darkening the small mole beside the bridge of her nose. Waylynn rolled her lips between her teeth, unfolding her arms. "In."

"Is that what you're wearing?" As much as he hated the thought of her covering up all that smooth skin, she couldn't exactly walk around downtown Anchorage in nothing but his T-shirt and her underwear without drawing unwanted attention. "I mean, I won't argue—"

"In your dreams, con man." She turned on her heel and marched straight back up the stairs. A smile curled at the edge of his mouth as he caught sight of the delicate tattoo inked behind her right ear. A small double-helix DNA strand. He'd always attributed it to her work in genetics, but knowing now what he did about her family, about her father, maybe there was more significance in those sequences than he thought.

A few minutes later, Waylynn rounded down the stairs, dressed in Officer Ramsey's sweats once again, hair pulled back in a long ponytail, and his gut warmed. He couldn't take his eyes off her. He cleared his throat to counteract the rush of heat climbing up his neck. Didn't help. Even in a borrowed, stained pair of sweats, she was the most stunning, addictive woman he'd ever met.

"Ready to go?" She settled that ocean-blue gaze on him and the entire investigation disappeared to the back of his mind.

Wouldn't happen between them. Not now. Not ever. He'd been imprisoned long enough. First, due to his parents and his upbringing. Second, from actual prison in the middle of the hottest hell on earth and now contracted with Sullivan Bishop and Blackhawk Security. A relationship with the woman waiting for him to answer would commit him for life. Because she deserved nothing less. Elliot swung the door open completely, then withdrew his weapon as he faced the midnight sun as a precaution. "I'd say ladies first, but I'm the one with the gun."

"Such a gentleman." Waylynn took position behind him, the wild rush of geraniums still clinging to him after their close call with Mabel the Moose.

He led her toward the SUV, senses at an all-time high. He doubted whoever'd framed her for Alexis Jacobs's murder had followed them all the way out here, but he wasn't going to take the risk. Not with her.

Movement registered off to the left, past the tree line, and her long fingers latched on to his nondominant arm. Elliot slowed, trying to hear anything past the hard pounding of his heartbeat behind his ears. Not from the possibility of danger—he'd tear anyone who came close to her apart with his bare hands—but because Waylynn's touch had rocketed his awareness of her ever higher.

"Are we going to have to outrun a moose again?" Her question wisped against his earlobe.

Iridescent white eyes shifted in the bushes. Most likely a fox. A laugh vibrated through him. His nerves had run a bit too high for his taste. "Come on. I'm sure Mabel and the calves have had enough excitement for one day."

"They're not the only ones." She released her grip on his arm and moved to the passenger-side door.

They took the ride to Alexis Jacobs's apartment in silence. Tinted, bulletproof windows cast them into darkness and, despite the fact he could see her clearly in the front seat, Elliot felt her all around him. In her scent still imbedded in his clothing, to the memory of her pressed beneath him as Mabel charged. Hell, even the skin beneath his hoodie burned with memories of her touch.

He'd kept his distance, no problem, for the past year, but over the last twenty-four hours, she'd defied the single rule he'd set for himself when it came to wanting her. The only change? She needed him now more than ever and he'd been stupid enough to hide her in his own damn cabin while he hunted the bastard doing this to her. They hit the highway and headed back toward Anchorage, the combination of road and rubber pulling him back into the moment. Get control. Solve the case. Move on with their lives. That was it. They'd go back to the way things were once her apartment was cleared as a crime scene. He'd pay off his debt to Blackhawk Security and move on and she'd probably work the next decade trying to recover her research.

He squeezed his knuckles around the steering wheel for some semblance of an anchor. Who was he kidding? There was no going back. Waylynn Hargraves had worked herself beneath his skin a long time ago. Once he'd taken on her case, he'd known nothing between them would be the same.

Alexis Jacobs's apartment wasn't far from the cabin. Fifteen minutes, tops, but it sure seemed like an eternity before they hit the complex's parking lot.

"I need to make one thing clear before we go any further, Doc." Directing the SUV into a spot at the back, away from curious neighbors, Elliot pushed it into Park. He hung on to the gear shift. "I'll work this case, I'll find out who framed you for murder, who destroyed your research, no problem. I'll protect you with my life if I have to because that's what you're paying me for. We're friends, but that's it. I'm not interested in anything more."

Her arched eyebrows drew together. "Did I give you the impression I wanted more?"

"No." Which only made this easier. "Just making sure we're on the same page."

"Friends." Waylynn shouldered her way out of the SUV but turned back before she closed the passenger-side door behind her with a nod. "We'll always be friends."

"We doing this or what?" A mountainous shadow crossed in front of the SUV, arms wide. Vincent Kalani, all six foot six of him, closed in on the driver's-side door as Elliot stepped out onto the pavement. Blackhawk Security's forensics expert kept a relationship with Anchorage PD, which was the only way he and Waylynn were getting inside that apartment. And the only reason Elliot had invited the former cop along. "Generally speaking, you're not supposed to bring the client with you along for the ride."

Elliot extracted his black duffel bag all operatives were required to carry and swung his gear over his shoulder. Motioning toward Waylynn as she rounded the hood of the vehicle, he smiled. "Try telling her that. Waylynn, this is Vincent. He's the forensics expert on my team."

"Nice to meet you." She shook Vincent's enveloping hand. "Thank you for helping."

"I'm only doing this because Elliot promised he'd stop stealing my lunch out of the office fridge." The forensics expert collected a bag identical to Elliot's from the pavement a few feet away.

"Hawaiian barbecue is my favorite." Elliot winked at Waylynn, then hauled his Kevlar vest over his head and strapped it tight. He handed her an extra vest from his stash. "He still has his lunches made by his mom."

"Well, since you kept me waiting here for thirty minutes, I decided to take a look at the place myself." Clapping his hands together, the former officer widened his stance as Waylynn donned the protective gear. "Do you want the good news or the bad news first?"

Elliot crossed his arms over his vest, tugging one hand down his beard as he focused on his teammate. "Depends on how bad the bad news is."

"The seal is broken on the door," Vincent said. "Someone's already been here."

"WHO WOULD WANT to break into Alexis's apartment?" Anger was better than tears, better than grief, better than guilt. Somewhere, deep inside, Waylynn suspected everything that'd happened to that poor woman had happened because of *her*. She didn't know why, didn't know who. She'd have to live with that fact for the rest of her life unless they solved her case. She studied Elliot's and Vincent's faces in the dim streetlamps peppered throughout the parking lot. "Aside from us, I mean."

"I can think of one person." Elliot hefted his duffel bag back into the SUV, then slammed the door closed, gun in hand. "Whoever wanted you to take the fall for her murder."

A shiver raked down her spine, shaking her shoulders, and Waylynn wrapped her arms around herself. "Could they have been looking for the hard drive, too?"

"They'd had to have known about Genism's policy to become suspicious if they saw the same photo as I did." Elliot pulled back the top portion of his gun, presumably chambering a round. She didn't know anything about guns. Didn't know why he needed one now, but the confidence rolling off him in waves helped settle her nerves.

The reality of his words cleared. She unfolded her arms and stepped into him. "Wait. You think someone from Genism is doing this to me?"

"I don't know. Seems too much of a coincidence. First, Alexis is discovered dead in your bathtub, then there's a break-in at the lab, where only your research is destroyed." His expression softened, but the intensity in his eyes remained. "I made you a promise, Doc. I will protect you. Whoever is doing this might be dangerous, but I'm worse. Because they'll never see me coming."

A second shiver climbed along her back and it had

nothing to do with the investigation or the danger closing in on her. For an entire year, she'd relied on Elliot Dunham's sense of humor to get her through the rough patches. She'd catch herself smiling at work when she remembered a joke he'd told a day earlier. Every night, after she left the lab, she couldn't wait to get home and find him in his cheap folding chair outside his apartment with two beers and that gut-wrenching smile so she could hear about his day. He had a gift and he didn't even know it. The gift to help her forget the nightmares. But the man standing in front of her wasn't the Elliot she'd known. His expression was harder, his voice dropping into dangerous territory, yet she couldn't stop the explosion of traitorous desire in her lower abdominals.

"I really want you guys to have your happily-ever-after—" Vincent hiked a thumb over his shoulder "—but we have an apartment to search before someone calls the real cops."

Waylynn blinked to clear her head and dug her fingernails into the center of her palms as a distraction. The heat rushing through her dissipated. For the moment. Her mouth dried. "We're friends—"

"She's my next-door neighbor." The tendons along Elliot's neck flexed. The sharp edge etched into his expression cut through her. He nodded once.

Oh. Disappointment wrapped around her heart and squeezed the air from her lungs. Next-door neighbor now? That was quite the demotion.

"Great. Then let's get going." Rolling his eyes, Vincent shouldered his duffel and led the way up the nearest set of stairs. The sound of the forensics expert's cargo pants shifting faded. She and Elliot were alone under the streetlamp.

"You should hang back, Doc. We don't know what we're walking into up there." He tossed her the keys to the SUV. "If I'm not back in ten minutes, drive to Blackhawk Security and talk to Sullivan Bishop no matter what happens. Only him, understand?"

She closed her fingers around the keys. What was he talking about? He was coming back. If he didn't... No. She didn't want to think about that.

Elliot turned his back to her, heading after his teammate with gun in hand.

"Is that really all I'm ever going to be to you during the investigation?" Her mouth dried, but she had to get the words out. She'd never been good at handling her impulses, couldn't stop herself from closing the small space between them as he slowed at the bottom of the stairs. They'd always kept things friendly. No romantic entanglements. But his pulling away from her now, after everything that'd happened? No. She needed him. Needed that damn smile, his sarcasm. His friendship. Because without it—without *him*—the chances of her fighting back the darkness that resided deep inside grew smaller every day. "Your next-door neighbor?"

He turned his head over one shoulder without facing her. "I can't do this with you right now, Doc."

"Vincent said someone's already searched the apartment. You think going up there in two minutes rather than one is going to make a difference?" She was part of the investigation, too. She *was* the investigation. She knew the risks, understood the importance of any evidence left behind in Alexis's apartment, or what would

happen if she was caught here, but Waylynn needed
an answer now. If this friendship couldn't handle the
strain… She inhaled slowly to steady her pulse. She'd
spend the rest of her life behind bars for murder. "We've
been friends for almost a year. At least, I thought we
were. We start working together and all of a sudden,
you're pushing me away. I want to know why, Elliot."

"No, you don't." He started back up the stairs. As
though that was the end of the conversation. "It would
only make this harder."

They weren't done. Too much counted on his being
in her life. Waylynn shot her hand out, wrapping
around his arm before he could escape. "That's not
good enough."

He spun around, closing in on her until he'd sandwiched her between his body and the side of the SUV.
Despite the lingering sunset around them, his eyes
burned bright. Every muscle in his upper body strained
tight beneath his Kevlar vest as he bracketed his hands
on either side of her head.

"You've been the one constant in my life. The one
person I can count on to keep me here when all I want
to do is get the hell out of this city." The tension drained
from his shoulders, from his expression. His voice softened as he studied her, his body heat tunneling through
her clothing. "But I haven't been free in a long time,
Doc. I left the commune when I was fourteen, then
spent over a year in an Iraqi hellhole until Sullivan
Bishop pulled me out. Getting more attached to you
than I already am? That puts me in a position I don't
want to be in. So if looking at you as a friend instead of
anything more helps me keep that distance, I'm going

to do it." His hands slipped down the driver's-side door and he backed off. "I have to. For both our sakes."

She fought back the burn in her lower lash line. She wasn't a crier. She'd survived too much to break down every time something went wrong in her life, but this cut deeper than when she'd been accused of her father's murder, of Alexis's murder, of losing her entire life's work in the blink of an eye. This was Elliot. The only person she trusted. The only man who'd actually made her feel. Her friend. She swallowed to keep her voice steady despite the chaos battling inside her. "Then friends it is."

Her hands shook. One breath. Two.

"Vincent is waiting on us." Waylynn clenched her back teeth and everything inside her went cold. Circling around him, she headed for the stairs. He didn't want to be more than friends? Fine. She'd focus on the investigation, then move on with her life. With or without him. All that other stuff like relying on him to lift her mood with a joke or looking forward to that beer after she left the lab every night… Her throat got a bit tighter as she climbed the concrete steps. She'd get over it.

His boot steps echoed behind her, but she didn't dare look back to see how close he followed. Find the hard drive. Solve the case. That was all that mattered. Her life depended on it. She passed blue door after blue door on her right until the one with a broken crime scene seal came into view. Alexis's apartment. Waylynn pulled up short, not sure if she wanted to step over that threshold. Vincent had already gone inside. The sound of his search reached her ears.

Alexis Jacobs had worked directly under her for

three years. Receiving and processing DNA samples from the studies they ran, recording their findings, running the needed tests to distinguish which of their subjects carried the warrior gene. Her work had been integral to the lab, integral to Waylynn. But it'd been more than that. Alexis had been a friend. They'd spent late nights together, ordering in Chinese food while they worked. They talked about each other's lives, love interests, vacations they wished they could take. Talked about Elliot. Alexis had been five years younger, but Waylynn had gotten along with her assistant better than most researchers her age in the industry. She took another deep breath and glanced back over her shoulder, a hint of bleach on the air.

"You don't have to go in there." His clean, masculine scent worked to drown the burn of bleach from her nose. Someone must've dumped an entire bottle in the apartment.

"Yes, I do." She needed to know why. Why the killer had targeted Alexis and not Waylynn directly. Why they were trying to set her up for murder. Why they'd gone after her research. Maybe whatever was on that hard drive would give her the answers. But most of all, she owed it to Alexis.

She pushed inside, covering her nose with the crook of her arm. Blinking back against the onslaught of chemicals, she searched for the black hard drive Elliot had described. The smell had soaked into the walls. They wouldn't be able to search the apartment long before it went to their heads. "Do police normally soak the place in bleach?"

"Not unless there's a body." Elliot covered his mouth

and nose as well as he moved into her peripheral vision. Watching where he stepped, he moved toward the kitchen at the back through debris from a busted coffee table, an overturned bookcase, glass from picture frames. There'd been a struggle here. "Even then, they'd never leave the place inhospitable. Vincent, what you got?"

The former NYPD officer came around the corner, with a briefcase he must've stashed in his duffel bag. "Nothing. Place has been wiped down. No fingerprints. And I'm sure you didn't miss the fact everything's been soaked in bleach."

"We noticed." Waylynn used her sweatshirt over her hand as she pulled drawers and checked under unopened mail. No sign of the hard drive around Alexis's desktop computer. Nothing in her desk. She moved down the hall toward the single bathroom there. If Alexis had broken Genism corporate policy by loading private research onto a foreign device, she'd hide that hard drive the last place police or the company would find it. The last place a man would look. She centered her attention on Vincent. "Did you check the bathroom?"

"Checked the vents, the medicine cabinet, everything while you two were taking your sweet-ass time in the parking lot." Vincent shook his head. "No hard drive."

She didn't want to think about her conversation with Elliot right now. Finding the hard drive mattered. Clearing her name of murder mattered. Waylynn moved down the hallway and into the bathroom. Focusing on the blue-and-pink box beside the sink, she reached inside. Bingo. Pulling the solid piece of black plastic and metal from the thin cardboard, she stepped out into the hallway. She'd found the hard drive, and was holding it up for their inspection. "This is why you never send a man to do a woman's job."

Chapter Five

No identifiable fingerprints in the victim's apartment. Nothing to help them put a face to whoever was gunning for Waylynn. The entire place had been bleached down. DNA gone. Elliot exhaled hard to get the chemical burn out of his nose. Didn't help. The only lead they had now was the hard drive they'd handed off to Vincent to give to Elizabeth Dawson. In Liz's own words, Blackhawk Security's head of network security would love to have something to do other than change diapers and wash bottles all day. But even checking in with his favorite teammate out on maternity leave wasn't enough to pull Elliot out of his own head.

He caught sight of Waylynn on the balcony, staring out over the parking lot, and closed the door to Alexis's apartment behind him. Long blond hair shifted across her back, but she didn't look back at him. Hell. He'd messed up. Hurt her. Sliding his forearms across the iron railing, he took a position next to her. "You okay?"

"I am very not okay, Elliot." She intertwined her long, delicate fingers together over the railing and rounded her upper body, stretching back. Then she straightened, her bottom lip between her teeth. She unlocked her hands, then relocked them. "In the span of two days, I've lost everything. My coworker, my research. Now I'm losing you. All because someone put a body in my bathtub."

His gut clenched. Elliot turned toward her. "Doc—"

"The jokes. The sarcasm. I know it's a way to protect yourself, but you've gotten so good at protecting yourself, you're starting to push the people who care about you away." Ocean-blue eyes locked on him, full of fear, full of loss, and every cell in his body reacted. Because she was right. He didn't let people get close. She'd been the only exception, and even then he hadn't revealed a whole lot over the last year. It'd been the only way to survive. "Don't worry, Elliot. I got your message loud and clear." Waylynn turned from him, heading toward the stairs as she called over her shoulder. "I'll hire another investigator."

Like hell she would.

"No, you won't." Elliot shot his hand out, wrapping his fingers around her arm. He turned her into him and palmed the nape of her neck. Pure, unfiltered body heat worked through her clothing and down into his bones. She wasn't going anywhere. "Nobody else can protect you like I can."

"What are you doing?" Waylynn set her hands against his chest but didn't fight to escape the circle of his arm. Her pulse pounded at the base of her throat. Wild, erratic. A sharp gasp left her mouth as he held her. Her exhales brushed across his face and neck. Mere centimeters separated her mouth from his. He should let her go. Let her hire another investigator. But he couldn't. Her geranium scent filled the space between them, chasing the bleach burn from his lungs, and he was lost. In her.

"You haven't lost me, Doc." Because a life without her in it wasn't a life at all. She was the only one keeping him in Anchorage aside from Sullivan's threat of hunting him down if he skipped out on his promise. The only one who'd made it possible to think about a future that didn't include four walls and a hole in the floor. "You never will, understand?"

"I don't want you working this case if it means we can't be friends after it's over." She licked her lips, homing his attention to her perfectly soft mouth. "You're... You're the only one I have left."

He released his hold on her and enfolded her in the circle of his arms, her ear pressed to his heart. At five foot eight, she fit perfectly against him. Setting his cheek against the crown of her head, Elliot breathed her in deep. And started humming.

"Are you humming 'She Thinks My Tractor's Sexy'?" Waylynn pushed away and pressed a single hand into his chest. She tried to hide a smile but couldn't fight it for long as she stepped back. "That's cheating. You know I love that song."

"You have horrible taste in music." Elliot took her hand, intertwining his fingers with hers, and led her into a spin beneath his arm. Calluses caught on her skin, but she didn't seem to notice. Or didn't care. Damn that smile. Damn what it could do to him, how far he was willing to go to see it one more time.

He kept up the rhythm and swung her into him. One hand on her waist, the other lifting her hand out to the side. In the midnight sun, he could make out the small bit of hazel circling her pupils. A light Alaskan breeze picked her hair off her shoulders, and in that moment, he wanted nothing more than to fist it in his hands.

"You never told me you grew up in a commune." Her voice softened.

"My parents were—are—very religious." As far as he knew, they were still alive, helping take care of the communal farm and property. Elliot swung her a full ninety degrees as a distraction. This stuff… He hadn't talked about it—hadn't thought about it—in over twenty years. "Up until I turned fourteen, farming, church and chores were all I knew."

"Was it just you and your parents?" She tilted her head to block the midnight sun from his face, the laugh lines around her eyes shallower than a few minutes ago.

"I have three sisters. Two older, one younger." Wow. How old would they be now? He didn't even know if they were still part of the community they'd been raised in. "Which means I learned how to braid hair, sew a hem and do my own laundry."

"Do you keep in contact with them?" Waylynn slid her thumb up the sensitive skin on the back of his hand.

"I haven't spoken to them since I left." His throat dried. The night he'd told his parents he was leaving was the last time he'd seen them. "When I was six, we had a guy come stay with us who had a brand-new—at least, new back then—Nikon F401S camera. It was the first piece of technology I'd ever seen." He could still remember that moment clearly. "I was so enamored with this thing, kept bugging the owner to let me see it behind my parents' backs, that he actually gave it to me when he left." Her favorite song faded to the back of his mind, but Elliot only pulled her closer as the past threatened to override the moment. "I took it apart piece by piece and put it back together to see how it worked. Worked great. I'd take pictures of the farm when I was supposed to be doing my chores, hide it under my bed at night until the thing finally died. I didn't have any way to charge it. That was when I knew there was more out there than the fences we'd built around the property." He shook himself back into the present. "So when I was fourteen, I left. And I haven't looked back."

"You've been on your own since you were fourteen?" Waylynn stilled. Soft, strong, beautiful, intelligent. He was a damn fool for getting this close. No matter how often he'd tried to deny it, this woman had a pull to her, a gravitational orbit he couldn't get away from. Didn't want to get away from. "How did you survive?"

Elliot cocked his head to one side. "Well, running cons helped. Until the Iraqi government wasn't afraid to call the local police in for me ripping them off for assassination contracts I never intended to follow through on."

A lithe laugh bubbled from between her lips and, for a moment, he forgot to breathe. "Now here you are. Learned your lesson, I hope?"

"For now." A smile escaped his control. It was impossible not to smile when she looked at him like that. Like she was happy. And considering the toll the past twenty-four hours had taken on her, he'd stretch this moment out as long as he could. Elliot dropped his hold on her waist and took a step away. To prove he could. His phone vibrated with an incoming message. "Vincent handed over the hard drive to our tech. And it looks like Anchorage PD released your apartment as a crime scene a couple hours ago. Maybe we can find you something else to wear besides those sweats and my MIT shirt."

Her blue gaze narrowed in on her assistant's apartment door, but she didn't drop his hand. "We're just going to leave all of her stuff? Alexis has some family on the East Coast, but I don't know anything about them."

"Once the police are finished with whatever they're doing in there, everything will be taken care of." Elliot ran the pad of his thumb beneath her signature mole beside her nose. The dark circles under her eyes hadn't budged. When was the last time she'd really slept? Over twenty-four hours ago? "Blackhawk retains one of the best lawyers in the country. We can have her get involved to make sure it all goes where it's supposed to if that's what you want."

"Okay." Waylynn nodded but didn't move when he started down the cement corridor. "We haven't solved anything."

He didn't have to ask what she'd meant. No, they hadn't. He'd deflected the hard questions by humming her favorite song and pulling her into him. But one thing had become clear: keeping her at a distance wouldn't work. Not as long as he was investigating her case. But he didn't trust anyone else to protect her like he could.

Elliot curled his free hand into a fist. Catch-22. Because the longer he stayed with her, the weaker his resolve.

She deserved nothing less than a best friend who'd never stand her up, reassure her when she felt insecure, comfort her after a hard day at the lab. Inspire her. Help her live without and forget regrets. She deserved a man who would give in to her most intimate desires and enable her to become the most confident, sexy, seductive woman alive. Even more so than she already was.

But he wasn't that guy. He couldn't be. Elliot locked his attention on the ocean-blue depths of her fear-charged gaze and his gut twisted. "I'll take a bullet for you if it comes to that, Doc. But that's all I have to offer."

THAT'S ALL I have to offer.

The words burrowed into her bones, dug in. Painful. Crushing. But she couldn't think about that right now, refused to acknowledge the hurt building behind her sternum. She had more important things to worry about. The fact someone had tried to frame her for murder, yet again. The fact she'd have to build her research from the smallest strand of DNA up. Again.

Waylynn stayed quiet on the drive to her apartment, but the fire traveling through her veins refused to relent. The soft, white iridescent glimmer of light from Genism Corporation across town held her attention as Elliot drove them through the city. Why? Why would someone do this to her? She'd moved on with her life, left the past behind. She clenched her teeth so hard her jaw protested. It was the only way to escape when the memories found a hole in her defenses. She glanced at Elliot in the driver's seat, his knuckles stark against the black leather of the steering wheel as they pulled into the parking lot of their apartment complex.

She exited the SUV without a word, didn't bother to

check behind her to see if he'd followed. She didn't care. They were next-door neighbors as long as they were working together. He'd made that more than clear. But he was still her bodyguard. "I'll only be a few minutes."

Elliot's hand branded her upper arm as he hauled her into him, his touch burning through the material of her borrowed sweatshirt. Would she ever stop reacting to him like this? "You're not going in there alone, Doc. We don't know how deep this guy's connections run."

Doc. The word grated in her ears now. Where she'd normally taken comfort with the use of his nickname for her, she pulled out of his grasp. "Are you genuinely concerned for my safety because we're next-door neighbors or because I'm paying you?"

He interlaced his hands behind his head as a rough exhale brushed against her neck. Frustration deepened the divide between his dark eyebrows. "You are—"

"Beautiful," she said. "Intelligent, immensely talented?"

Faster than she thought possible, Elliot crushed his mouth to hers. Gripping her waist, he pulled her to her tiptoes and brought her closer. His arms caged her against him. The overload of desire rocketed her heart rate into her throat. He was all around her, the only thing keeping her upright when her legs threatened to slip right out from under her. She fisted his hoodie in her hands as the surprise wore off. He traced her bottom lip with his tongue and every nerve ending in her body fired in response as she gave him tacit permission to keep going with a slight nod of her head.

The air she breathed thickened, the investigation, Alexis's death, her torched career, were all packed into a tiny box in the back of her head as he kissed her. Kissed her as though he intended to devour her. His hands on her hips disrupted reality, helped her forget the nightmares. She never wanted it to end.

Elliot set her down, pulling away too fast. Too soon. "I was going to say *infuriating*."

Her fingers ached as she uncurled them from his hoodie. Considerable muscle and strength lay beneath the thick layer, a warm vitality that urged her to press into him. Waylynn swiped the back of her hand across her lips, then stepped out of the circle of his arms. She'd had lovers. She'd gotten serious with a boyfriend in college, but she'd ended it the day she'd found out about her genetic heritage. But that kiss... Oh, wow. A kiss like that was worth the risk. A wave of dizziness blurred her vision and she blinked to clear her head. Her lungs spasmed for oxygen. She'd forgotten to breathe. "That was..."

"Extraordinary," he said. "Phenomenal, the best you've ever had."

"I was going to say *confusing*." She took a deep breath as reality closed in. "I don't think you're supposed to kiss your next-door neighbor like that."

"You're right. I'm sorry." He shook his head, avoiding looking right at her as he backed off. He ran a hand through his hair, the butt of his gun visible as his hoodie shifted. "Small miscommunication between my brain and my mouth. It won't happen again."

"I'm going to go pack a bag." She headed for the stairs, hand on the chilled steel railing. "I'd prefer if you didn't follow me."

Waylynn exhaled his clean, masculine scent from her

system, not caring if she'd offended him. She needed space, a few minutes to clear her head. Maybe that was the problem. She couldn't think when he touched her, not when he helped her forget there was a monster out there intent on destroying everything she cared about. She swallowed back the urge to rub at her sternum as the hurt set in. Climbing the stairs to the second level of the apartment complex, she deflated. The worst part about this whole thing? She couldn't even blame her lack of resistance on lust alone. Elliot had burrowed beneath her skin, become part of her, long before tonight. She just hadn't wanted to see the truth: a relationship between them couldn't work. Not when her genetic makeup fated her to turn on him at the drop of a hat.

Stretching her hand toward the sconce bolted beside her door, she unscrewed the ornate bottom loose and caught the key hidden inside. She slipped the key into the lock, but the door swung open on its own. The rush of a combination of cleaning supplies and sweat lingered on the air. Her stomach churned. Pulling the key from the door, she remembered the crash of wood against drywall as Elliot had forced his way inside to get to her. Her apartment had been a safe haven, somewhere to wash off the pressure of the lab and pamper herself every night after she left him on the porch with a half-finished beer. But now... Waylynn closed the door behind her, back pressed against damaged wood. Too many other people had been here. Alexis. Her killer. Elliot. The police. It didn't feel like home anymore. Didn't smell like it either.

Pack a bag. Find the person responsible for ruining

her life. She wouldn't break now. She was a survivor. "You've been through worse."

Waylynn pocketed the key in her hand and headed straight through the living room to the hallway. She'd made it only a few steps when pain seared through her skull, unbalancing her, and she collapsed against the wall. Hand on her forehead, eyes closed tight, she couldn't stop the sudden rush of memory pounding at the back of her head. Her pulse sped up, lungs working overtime.

Tall male. Light brown hair, maybe blond in the dim lighting. A scar on the back of his right hand as he pressed the gun to her temple. He'd forced her to write the confession. The gunshots echoed in her ears as though there was someone shooting right beside her. Three suppressed pulls of the trigger. Alexis's eyes widened in surprise, then emptied of life right in front of her. He'd killed Alexis. He'd framed Waylynn for the murder. *You're not going to remember any of this.*

"Waylynn." Rough hands shook her back into the present.

She gasped, kicking as her fight-or-flight instinct engaged. Waylynn wedged her heels into the slightly damp carpet to escape but didn't get far before she recognized that voice. *His* voice.

"Doc, it's me. You're safe. I'm not going to hurt you." He stood, palms raised in surrender, not daring to approach. Elliot crouched in front of her and rubbed one hand into his stomach. "Damn, you've got some powerful legs."

"Elliot." She automatically studied the back of his right hand as he draped it over one knee. No scar. Blood drained from her face. Oh, no. She'd attacked him. The realization burned going down and sat like a rock at the base of her spine. The memory... She licked her dry lips, tried to swallow the tightness in her throat, and blinked to clear her head. "I'm sorry. I didn't mean—"

"You don't need to apologize to me for protecting yourself, Doc." His voice lowered an octave as he helped her to her feet. "Ever. Understand?"

She nodded but couldn't seem to let him go. "I remembered him."

Taking one hand in his, he rested her palm against his chest. The steady thump of his heart in her palm centered her, kept her from getting lost in the nightmares. The distinct line between his brows deeper, his eyes narrowing in on her. "Who?"

"The man who forced me to write that confession." She ran her free hand over her forehead, trying to release the pressure building in her head. Didn't help. She had a feeling nothing would help until whoever was doing this was caught. Her next words caught in her throat, no matter how many times she tried forcing them. "He killed her in front of me. He killed Alexis."

"You remember what he looks like?" he asked. "Recognize him?"

She shook her head, still fighting to slow her racing heart. "Not really. I think he was tall with blond hair. I feel like I should know him, though." She squeezed her eyes shut, but the pain only intensified. "He told me I'd never remember any of it, but I remember, Elliot. I saw the scar on the back of his hand. The skin looked burned."

"If his hand matches the rest of him, we'll have our

suspect by the end of the day." His voice slid through her, all that sarcasm and confidence chasing back the fear clawing its way up her throat. "If it's a recent injury, within the last five years, my lab can help narrow the suspect pool by requesting medical records noted with that kind of injury."

She'd witnessed Alexis's murder, but she couldn't remember the most important parts of it. Taking a solid breath, she reveled in the feel of strength beneath Elliot's shirt, but pulled her hand away. He'd kissed her just outside this apartment, helped her forget. But it'd been a mistake. On both their parts. He wasn't interested in taking their friendship a step further, but in reality, there was no step further. Not for her. "I need to get my stuff. I'll meet you outside."

"You sure?" Suspicion narrowed his focus as she nodded, the weight of his attention pressurizing the air in her lungs. He hiked a thumb over his shoulder toward the front door. "In that case, I'll check in to see how deep my boss wants to bury me for not filling the team in sooner."

"Just give me a couple minutes." Waylynn waited until he closed the door behind him, then headed into her bedroom with uneasy steps. Not even the bright turquoise and yellow decorations could hide the fact her apartment had been used as a crime scene. Twenty-four hours ago her room had been filled with police searching for evidence, but Anchorage PD hadn't found the wall safe. She would've heard from her lawyer by now had that been the case.

Another flash of memory threatened to cement her feet in place as she glanced toward the closed bathroom door, but she kept moving. She couldn't stop. Couldn't think about what'd happened for fear she'd bolt out the front door. Turning her back on the epicenter of the crime scene, she hauled the print of Van Gogh's *Starry Night* off its nail to reveal the safe she'd installed when she'd moved in. The small LED light turned green at the scan of her fingerprint. Passport, fifty thousand in cash, personal documents. She pushed them to the side and went for the object she'd wrapped in an old T-shirt at the back first, its physical weight nothing compared with the heaviness compressing her chest. She stuffed the rest into her bag. Just in case, but she wasn't going anywhere until she uncovered who'd turned her world upside down.

Waylynn shut the wall safe and secured it before unearthing a weekend bag from her closet. Setting the gun at the bottom, she pulled clothing from hangers and shoved them inside. She changed out of the borrowed sweats from Officer Ramsey. She was a survivor. She always had been. Slinging the bag over one shoulder, she slipped into her most comfortable flats and closed the front door behind her for the last time.

This was the start of how it all ended.

And she sure as hell wasn't going down without a fight.

Chapter Six

"Well, this crisis came sooner than expected." Elliot hit the red button on his phone's screen to end the call. Five in the morning. The sun had gotten a little bit brighter in the east and the Blackhawk Security team was all over him. Over twenty-four hours since he'd found Waylynn in her bathroom, soaked in water and blood with a dead woman beside her. Now he'd gotten the news the hard drive they'd taken from Alexis Jacobs's apartment was encrypted. It would take their network security analyst, Elizabeth Dawson, over a day, maybe longer, to untangle the information the lab assistant had stored on the device. He'd witnessed the fear carved into Waylynn's expression when he'd found her doubled over in the hallway a few minutes ago. A fear that'd burned through his whole body. They were no closer to uncovering who'd put that fear in her eyes than they were twelve hours ago.

"What crisis?" That voice. *Her* voice. Soft, sexy, alluring enough to pull him deeper into uncharted and dangerous waters with a mere word. Every nerve ending he owned shot into awareness. Always had. Waylynn moved into his peripheral vision, a brightly colored tote bag slung over one shoulder. She'd changed her clothes. The black leggings, black sweatshirt and flat shoes were perfect for her slight curves. He appreciated the pragmatism. The view wasn't bad either. "I still hope we're friends after I taser you for looking at me like that."

A laugh rumbled through him. He never could slide one past her. "Get what you need?"

"Yes. Thank you. It's nice to have my own stuff." She smoothed her hand over the bag, the hollowness at her throat and shadowing her cheeks more apparent than a couple of hours ago. "Officer Ramsey's sweats were fine. They just weren't…mine. Having something familiar makes me feel a bit better about being a suspect in yet another murder. As does a toothbrush. So what's the crisis?"

Elliot redirected his attention from the hard-edged outline at the bottom of her bag. Right. The investigation. "The drive we recovered from your assistant's apartment is encrypted."

"What does that mean for the investigation?" Waylynn folded her arms, accentuating strong, lean muscle down her biceps. She'd hit the gym at Genism every morning as long as he'd known her, and it showed. She was the most determined woman he'd ever met, stubborn, infuriating, compassionate, and… His control had cracked a little when he'd kissed her.

He'd done it to prove there'd been nothing between them, that they could work together without his emotions getting in the way, but, hell, he'd certainly been wrong about that. The second he'd set his mouth against hers, the molten lava that'd been building beneath his skin had erupted to the surface and destroyed everything in its path. Including his reasons for avoiding committed relationships. It'd taken everything in him not to sweep her into his arms and take her back to his cabin. Make her forget the investigation, the fact she'd been framed for murder. He'd have helped her forget her name given the chance.

"Means we have time for you to get some beauty sleep and put something other than peanut-butter-frosted cookies in you." He headed down the stairs toward the parked SUV.

Space. He needed space. A few feet, a couple of minutes. Anything to clear her scent from his system and break the gravitational effect she seemed to have on him.

Her flats slapped against the cement stairs as she followed on his heels. "You'd be surprised how long I can live off chocolate and peanut butter."

"I have no doubt." Wrenching open the SUV's passenger door, Elliot motioned her inside. He rounded to the driver's side and climbed behind the wheel. Less than a minute later, he pulled out of the parking lot and a low ringing reached his ears.

She pulled the phone from her bag. "It's Dr. Stover again. Probably wondering when I'm coming back to work."

"Put it on speaker." The muscles in his neck ticked at the tension straining her voice. She'd been through hell the last two days. It'd take a lot more than thirty hours to get back some semblance of normal. Elliot headed south, back to the Seward Highway on-ramp.

She tapped the speaker button on the screen. "This is Dr. Hargraves."

"Waylynn, I'm glad you picked up. Listen, I know you've been through a lot the past couple days, but I couldn't stop them." Static reached through Matt Stover's end of the line. "I wanted to be the one to call to tell you the news myself."

"Stop who? What are you talking about?" The heaviness tinting Waylynn's question pressurized the air in Elliot's lungs. Three distinct lines deepened between her eyebrows. This wasn't good.

Elliot glanced down at her phone, the screen counting the length of the call. Nothing out of the ordinary. The timer came standard with that model, but the phone in Waylynn's hand didn't have her signature cracked screen in the top right-hand corner. One night after coming home from work, she'd dropped her phone on the stairs and damaged that corner. He'd caught her before she fell, but her phone hadn't been so lucky. That'd been six months ago. She'd replaced either the screen or the phone recently. Why wait that long? "Is that a company phone?"

"Who's with you?" Dr. Stover asked.

"It's my frien—next-door neighbor. He was helping me get some of my things from my apartment." Waylynn swiped the stray hair coming out of her ponytail away from her face. "Matt, tell me what's going on."

"The board had an emergency meeting." The growl of a car engine overwhelmed Dr. Stover's voice. "In the wake of everything that's happened, you're being let go."

Elliot's attention snapped to her as they sped toward the highway. Oh, hell.

"On what grounds?" Waylynn shook her head, resting her elbow against the passenger side door. Her voice rose with each word out of her mouth. "Genism has profited off my research for ten years. They can't fire me."

It was five o'clock in the morning. Why would her boss—former boss—call Waylynn that early unless he knew she wasn't asleep? His instincts screamed warning as he wrenched the wheel to the left, turning them around. "Hang up the phone."

"What?" Those ocean-blue eyes widened with confusion. She planted her free hand against the dashboard to keep her balance as they turned back the way they'd come. "What's wrong?"

"Waylynn?" Matt Stover asked. "What's going on?"

Elliot grabbed for the phone and tossed it out the window.

Waylynn spun in her seat to track the phone's landing out the back window. "What are you doing?"

"Your assistant broke corporate policy to store company information on that drive we recovered. Which means whoever killed her had to have known she'd taken it in the first place." Elliot pressed the accelerator to the floor, glancing into the rearview mirror for a tail. Damn it, he should've noticed the phone before now.

"Okay, so it had to be someone in Genism. That doesn't explain why you threw my phone out the window." Her voice hollowed as she straightened in her seat. "I got a new phone a few weeks ago after Matt noticed I'd broken the screen on the last one."

"I knew I never liked that guy." Elliot shook his head, knuckles white on the steering wheel. "The bastard has been tracking you through your company phone. Probably listening to all of your conversations."

"Matt wouldn't do that. We've worked together for years. We're friends," she said. "Where're we going? Your cabin is in the other direction."

"Blackhawk Security." The light turned green up ahead and he pushed the SUV harder. Downtown Anchorage passed in a rush out the side windows. Theories as to why Genism would be tracking Waylynn crossed his mind, but he couldn't think about that right now. He forced himself to focus. Get her to safety. Then track down the SOB who'd dared come after her. "You're officially in protective custody." He used the controls on the steering wheel to call the team.

"I just got off the phone with you." Blackhawk's founder and CEO's voice filled the interior of the car. Sullivan Bishop didn't wait for an answer. "Please tell me you haven't already dug yourself a deeper—"

"Mango." His boss would know what the code word meant. Elliot checked the rearview mirror again. No movement.

"ETA?" The former SEAL's tone dipped into dangerous territory. Sullivan had formed the team to protect those whom the police and other law enforcement agencies couldn't or wouldn't bother with. Waylynn Hargraves qualified. His boss—and the entire Blackhawk Security team—would do what was necessary to keep her safe.

"Two minutes." He studied Waylynn. The tension tightening her grip on the edge of the seat was enough to lock his jaw. He should've noticed her phone earlier. They could've gotten ahead of this thing for once. "One civilian."

"We're ready." Sullivan ended the call, but Elliot couldn't relax yet.

The front of the SUV crossed into the intersection. Two more minutes and she'd be safe. She'd—

Headlights brightened through his window a split second before the crash. Rubber on asphalt screeched in his ears as Waylynn's side of the vehicle slammed into the light post. Glass shattered around them, metal screaming against metal.

Momentum rocked Elliot sideways in his seat, smashing his head against the window as air bags deployed. The smell of burned rubber and gasoline filled his system. Son of a bitch. He hadn't seen that coming. A wave of dizziness and pain darkened the edges of his vision and he rubbed the base of his palm into his eye. One breath. Two. Headlights from the vehicle that'd T-boned them flickered. Copper and salt filled his mouth. Blood. He squinted away from the blinding light, searching for her in the passenger seat among the air bags in his way. She'd been wearing a seat belt, right? He couldn't remember, the pounding at the crown of his head overwhelming. Reaching out, he brushed his hand against her arm as glass crunched outside the vehicle. Footsteps. Elliot disengaged his seat belt, his vision clearing in slow increments. "Waylynn."

She didn't answer. Didn't move.

"Waylynn." He pushed every ounce of energy he had into her name. Dread curdled in his gut. He slid his hand along the side of her face and turned her toward him. Planting his fingers at her throat, he exhaled hard in relief. Strong pulse. She was alive. There was no way they'd be able to get out of the SUV through either of the doors with what looked like another SUV on his side and the streetlamp on hers. Elliot compressed the button to her seat belt. They'd have to go out the back. He shook his head to clear the high-pitched keen ringing in his ears. The mission hadn't changed, only the circumstances: get her to safety. "Come on, Doc. We gotta get out of here."

He climbed over the seat into the back row, his boots sliding against broken glass on the floor, and pulled a lockbox from under the hidden compartment beneath the floor mat. Thumbing in the combination, Elliot pocketed the gun's extra magazine and ammunition and tucked the small handgun down the waistband of his jeans at the small of his back. No sirens. Blackhawk Security SUVs came loaded with trackers. The team would find the vehicle in the next few minutes, but his instincts said they didn't have that long. Genism had been tracking Waylynn for weeks. No telling whom they'd sent after her, but a company with that many resources and that much power wouldn't hire an amateur. He leveraged his weight into the back of the seats and kicked the rear window as hard as he could. The bulletproof glass dislodged in one piece, crashing to the ground.

Movement registered off to his right, beyond the vehicle that'd smashed into them. The driver? Had they made it out okay? Rough breathing reached his ears over the shuffling of broken glass. "Help." The man's voice rocketed Elliot's blood pressure higher. "I need help!"

"Hang on, buddy. I'm coming." Elliot didn't hesitate. He climbed from the back of the SUV, but an earth-shattering wave of pain from the crash shot down his spine and unbalanced him. He landed on top of the bulletproof glass, a groan working up his throat. He was going to feel that in a couple of hours. His head pounded loud behind his ears, but the ringing had stopped. "I'm okay."

The streetlamp reflected off a classic pair of dark oxford shoes as he rolled to his side. Two Taser nodes latched on to his shirt, but before he could reach for them twelve hundred volts of electricity shot through him at the push of a button. Fire burned his nerves and muscles. Elliot rolled onto his back, unable to control his movements. His jaw clenched hard, his entire body rigid from the current. The headache at the back of his skull exploded in a haze of white light. A growl ripped from his throat. Waylynn. He had to get to Waylynn.

The current faded, but his peripheral nervous system had yet to get the message. Elliot struggled to keep his eyes open, to reach for his gun. To do anything but lie there, leaving Waylynn vulnerable. "Don't…touch her."

The masked assailant who'd tasered him crouched low, retrieving the Taser's electrodes one by one. "Try to stop me."

SHE GASPED INTO consciousness as a high-voltage shock wave of fear slid down her spine. Pain exploded from the right side of her head. They'd… They'd been in an accident. They'd been hit. Waylynn fought to raise her head, but the darkness, the fatigue, tempted her to close her eyes again. Go to sleep. No. She had to stay awake. Dim lighting glinted off the broken glass in her lap. She set her head back against the headrest and scanned the rest of the vehicle. "Elliot?"

His name clawed from her dry throat as she searched the empty interior. She swallowed against the bile rising up her throat. Oh, no. The driver's side window had been shattered. Had he been thrown from the SUV? Panic overwhelmed her as she reached to unlatch her seat belt, but found the buckle already unlocked. She was sure she'd buckled herself when she'd gotten in the car. Had to be Elliot. Where was he? Her muscles protested as she climbed across the center console. Ignoring the slice of glass in her palms, she rested her weight against his still-warm seat. Distant sirens reached her ears. The police were on their way. "Answer me, Elliot."

"Sorry, Dr. Hargraves, your bodyguard won't be answering anything for a while." Gloved hands shot through the driver's side window and pulled her from the SUV.

"Wait, I have to find my friend. He was in the vehicle with me. He could be hurt." Waylynn struggled against his vise-like grip, unwilling to leave the scene until she recovered Elliot. No. She wasn't going to the hospital. Not without him, but the man pulling her from the crash was too strong. So much bigger than her and her injuries had taken a lot of her strength. The scene of the crash blurred as he set her on her feet and spun her to face him. Her head throbbed in rhythm to her racing pulse as the dizziness cleared. The black ski mask hiding his features plunged dread straight through her. What kind of emergency personnel wore a mask? The hardness in his impossibly black eyes and his hold still wrapped around her wrists told her the answer. They didn't.

His six-foot-plus frame towered over her. Black ski mask, dark jacket, black pants, black shoes. Gloves. "He'll be fine once he wakes up."

He'd called her Dr. Hargraves. She'd never told him her name.

"Let me go." She pulled at her wrists locked between his hands, the scent of cigarettes burning her nose. This wasn't the man from her quick flash of memory back at her apartment. He'd had blue eyes, but fear skittered through her all the same. She glanced at the smoking vehicle that'd T-boned them in the intersection, the driver's-side door propped open. No driver to be seen. Because he was standing in front of her. Waylynn swept her tongue through the saltiness in her mouth. "You caused the crash?"

"You should've taken the fall for Alexis's murder, Waylynn." Her masked assailant pulled her into him, repositioning one hand around her throat. "Would've made this so much easier. Shame, too. I think your work could've changed the world."

Could've?

His hand shot to her throat, cutting off her oxygen. Waylynn tried to pry his grip from her, but he pulled a gun from the waistband of his pants and lodged it into her rib cage. Black cobwebs snaked into the edges of her vision. "P-please—"

"Why don't you point that thing at someone your own size?" That voice.

A combination of recognition and hesitation slid through her. She'd know that voice anywhere, but right now, it sounded…different. Waylynn searched the wreckage through the holes that hadn't darkened in her vision, jerking in her captor's hold. Movement registered from the back of the totaled SUV, urging her to step back, but her abductor kept a tight grip. Shadows retreated from his face as Elliot moved beneath the pool of light from the streetlamp. A gasp caught in her throat. Blood chilled in her veins, yet beads of sweat slid from her temples. He was alive. Goose bumps prickled across the small of her back. He was…not the Elliot she knew.

No. The shadow standing ten feet from her had turned into something far more threatening. Waylynn pulled at her attacker's wrist, her body screaming for air. Pressure built in her lungs. A single second stretched into hours, the darkness closing in faster.

"I'll have to use a higher voltage on you next time." Her abductor's hand loosened enough for her to gulp down a lungful of oxygen as he took aim at her best friend.

Warning trickled down her spine.

"There won't be a next time." A predatory growl escaped from Elliot's mouth, raising the hairs on the back of her neck. Violence stared out through the gray eyes she'd dreamed about for months. A shadow of that same violence darkened his expression. "Now get your damn hands off her."

Elliot didn't wait for an answer and rushed forward.

She wanted to scream. Couldn't with the hand around her neck. The explosion of gunfire rocked through her. Her ears rang as his shoulder ripped back from catching the bullet. His guttural groan ignited the burn of desperation. Waylynn tried to lunge forward to catch him before he hit the ground but was pulled back into her attacker. She launched her elbow into a wall of muscle, only her captor's exhale an indication she'd done any damage. That small amount of vulnerability pushed her harder.

Elliot had collapsed to one knee, his knuckles against asphalt, eyes shut tight.

Slamming her heel into the top of her assailant's foot, she got him to release her. She twisted out of his reach, gulped as much air as she could, and rocketed the base of her palm into where she thought his nose might be under the mask. "Get off of me!"

The satisfying crunch of bone reached her ears. She raced to take control of the gun in his hand, but she wasn't fast enough. A strong backhand across her face knocked her to the ground. Stinging pain lanced through her head as she fell, the city street nothing but a blur.

"You shouldn't have done that." Elliot's swing unbalanced the gunman, but another squeeze of the trigger arced a bullet wide over Waylynn's head. They had to get out of here. "Waylynn, run!"

She covered her head in a vain attempt to stop the bullet with her hands. The sirens she'd heard earlier seemed to fade. Where were the police? Why wasn't anybody helping? Blood dripped from Elliot's shoulder. His movements were slowing. He wouldn't last much longer without help. Shoving to her feet, she searched the scene for something—anything—he could use as a weapon.

The crunch of glass against asphalt followed by a rough groan from over her shoulder forced her to turn back to the fight. Her attacker had pinned Elliot against the colliding vehicle and raised the gun once more. Another hit to the face twisted his head in one direction. The second hit wrenched his head again. "Stop! You're going to kill him!"

Her attacker punched Elliot over and over, those dark gray eyes locked on her.

"No!" Waylynn pumped her legs hard, then latched on to the masked man's arm to give Elliot a fighting chance. But a solid kick to the midsection sent her flying back. She couldn't breathe. Couldn't think. Only adrenaline kept her moving. There. Waylynn crawled toward a piece of the damaged streetlamp, loose gravel digging into her knees. Sliding her fingers around the metal, she pushed to her feet and hiked the steel above her shoulder on unsteady legs. "Get the hell away from him. Now."

"Waylynn…run." Blood trickled down Elliot's bottom lip as he swayed on his feet, the skin swollen and cracked.

Waylynn fought off the paralysis threatening to overwhelm her. She'd never attacked another human being before. Never wanted to hurt someone as much as she wanted to hurt the man with the gun right now. "I said back away."

She adjusted her grip around the pipe and swiped her tongue across her increasingly dry lips. Her gut clenched as Elliot slid down the side of the vehicle, his normally bright gaze clouded. He was losing blood too fast. She had to get him to the hospital.

"You should've listened to your bodyguard, Dr. Hargraves. You should've run while you had the chance."

A low rumble of a laugh filled her ears, dread pooling at the base of her spine. No matter what happened in the next few minutes, she'd remember that laugh for the rest of her life. Something pure and evil crawled over her skin. That black gaze forced ice through her veins. "Those sirens you heard? A distraction of mine. Anchorage PD won't have enough patrols to answer this call. Nobody is coming to save you."

She glanced at Elliot losing consciousness at her feet. The bullet could still be inside him, could be causing permanent damage. Not to mention the other dozen injuries he'd incurred since the crash. They were running out of time. Elliot would die right here in the middle of the street if she didn't do something. He'd protected her this far. Now it was her turn to return the favor. "I don't need anyone to save me."

Waylynn swung the pipe as hard as she could.

Her attacker caught it midswing and wrenched the steel from her hand. She didn't hesitate, lashing out at him with her opposite hand, but the strike did nothing. She didn't work for Blackhawk Security. She hadn't been trained in hand-to-hand combat or joined the military. She was a scientist, a researcher. She spent most of her days glued to the computer screen analyzing genetic samples under her microscope.

But she wouldn't let him take her and she wasn't going to let Elliot die.

The clang of metal on asphalt rang loud in her ears as he tossed her makeshift weapon and advanced. She stumbled back, the heel of her flats catching on chunks of loose debris from the crash. No. Waylynn fisted her hands, taking a stand. "His team is already on the way."

"They can't help you now, Dr. Hargraves. You brought your bodyguard into this mess, and he'll die because of you." Her attacker raised the gun, taking aim at her head. "Then it'll be your turn."

Chapter Seven

"Over here!" an unfamiliar voice called.

A bright light passed over him, footsteps and shouts close enough to pull Elliot from unconsciousness. Pain shot across his shoulder and down his arm. His head throbbed at the base of his skull.

"Tell me he's not dead." Now, that voice he recognized. Sullivan.

Cold fingers slid across his neck and he hissed in reaction. "Pulse is weak, but he's alive. He's lost a lot of blood."

Different voice.

"You say the nicest things, Kate." He struggled to see the psychologist's face. Squinting against the circle of flashlights around him, Elliot moved to lift his arm to block the light but couldn't. Right. A bullet tended to have that effect. He ran his tongue along the split inside his cheek, then leaned over and spit blood. Digging his heels into the ground, he pressed his back against the vehicle behind him and pushed to his feet slowly to face the team. Oh, hell. He felt like he'd been hit by a train. Or at least a Mack truck. Pieces of memory bled into place. They'd been attacked. The son of a bitch had gone after Waylynn right before he'd lost consciousness. "Where is she? Where's Waylynn?"

"You tell us." Sullivan Bishop centered himself in his vision as Kate Monroe, Blackhawk Security's profiler, moved out of the way. Vincent, Glennon, Anthony, Elizabeth. Even Elizabeth's baby daddy, Braxton, stood around him. The gang was all there. "What happened?"

"Bastard plowed into us. Tasered me to get to her. I fought him off, but he put a bullet in my shoulder. Lost too much blood." The haze cleared with every inhale. He was still losing blood. Then he spotted the piece of pipe she'd threatened to bash her attacker with in the middle of the street. Rage diluted the pain and spread like wildfire. Her abductor wanted a battle? If the son of a bitch damaged a single hair on her head, Elliot would bring a war. He shoved through the semicircle his team had built around him. "Get out of my way."

They couldn't have gotten far. Everything about this investigation—the death of Waylynn's assistant, the destruction of her research, the recovered hard drive, the tracking device in her phone—it all tied back to Genism Corporation. He'd never met Dr. Matthew Stover, but it stood to reason he was the one who'd been tracking her since giving her the phone a few weeks ago.

Anthony Harris, the team's weapons expert, barricaded himself, arms folded, in front of Elliot's escape route. "I've seen that look, man. Hell, I've given that look to everyone who came between me and Glennon. You've lost a lot of blood. Tell me what you need, and I'll recover her while you get patched up."

His reflection stared back at him from Anthony's damn aviator sunglasses. Blood dripped down his face, his lip busted. Not to mention the injuries he couldn't see. The bullet in his shoulder, the possible cracked rib he'd taken to give Waylynn a chance to run. He'd failed her once. It took every ounce of energy he had to keep standing, but he wouldn't fail her again. He'd take a hundred more bullets if it meant keeping her safe. Rolling his shoulder forward, he clenched his teeth against the pain screaming through his arm. The bullet was still inside, tearing through muscle and tendon, but every second that bastard had Waylynn led to a higher chance he wouldn't be able to find her. And that wasn't an option. He wouldn't lose her. Not now. Not ever. Elliot stretched out his hand. "Keys."

"Take mine. None of you have wrecked it yet. Want backup?" Kate didn't hesitate, a half smile curling at one edge of her pale mouth as she tossed the keys. He shook his head. This was something he had to do on his own. The psychologist-turned-profiler folded her arms. Medium-length, platinum blonde hair framed a thin face and wide green eyes. At five foot ten, Kate Monroe demanded attention with a single look, but the shroud of grief from losing her husband to a former patient last year kept most people at a distance. But Elliot knew the truth. Of all of the men and women on this team, Kate was the biggest softy of them all. She nodded. "You've been shot, beaten and we found you unconscious."

"I'm fine." Nothing would stop him from getting to Waylynn.

"Try not to get yourself shot again," Vincent said. "Or killed."

Elliot curled his hand around the keys, then circled

around Anthony without looking back at the rest of his team. He wouldn't need backup. Didn't need a weapon. He'd tear the son of bitch who dared take Waylynn from him with his bare hands.

A thin veil of snow dusted the ground as he rounded to the driver's side of Kate's SUV and climbed in. What kind of hell city snowed in the middle of June? The engine growled to life at the turn of a key, the entire team staring at him through the windshield as he spun away from the scene.

Red and blue police cruiser lights flashed across his vision as he programmed Genism's address into the vehicle's navigation system. Sullivan and Anthony would stall Anchorage PD as long as they could. Elliot had more important things to worry about. There was only one place this could end, one place he bet the man who'd framed Waylynn for murder would take her.

"I'm coming for you, Doc." Headlights reflected off wet road, but Elliot only pressed the accelerator harder. He squeezed his knuckles around the steering wheel, the scrapes and cuts along the back of his hands still bleeding. Whoever had come after her wasn't some geneticist. He'd never known a lab researcher to fight like that. He swiped at the blood running down his mouth. No, the son of a bitch who'd taken Waylynn was something more. Former military, maybe a trained federal operative. But that didn't explain the connection to his next-door neighbor or her employer. Unless Genism Corporation had hired someone to come after her on their behalf.

Didn't matter right now. Getting Waylynn back, having her in his arms again, that was all that mattered.

They'd deal with the rest once he recovered her. Together. The slight sigh that'd escaped from her as he'd kissed her replayed in his head. Blistering-hot blood rushed through his system. He'd get her back. He had to. "You better be alive."

Tires screeched on pavement as he fishtailed the SUV into Genism Corporation's main parking lot. Streetlamps flickered, then died, the sun peeking out from behind the Chugach Mountain Range. No sign of another vehicle. Nothing to indicate her abductor had brought her here. His gut said he was in the right place. Stretching his arm into the back seat, Elliot suppressed a scream working up his throat as he reached for the lockbox under the bench seat. A faint pop registered beneath muscle and he exhaled hard through the pain. Damn bullet wouldn't stop him from finding her.

Nothing would.

Slamming a fresh magazine into his spare Glock, he loaded a round and checked the safety. His boots hit the ground, the hairs on the back of his neck standing on end. As though he'd been centered in someone else's crosshairs. He scanned the lab's rooftop—still nothing—then headed for the main doors. Warning exploded through him, but what was life without a little risk? Elliot tightened his grip around the gun. He wrenched the glass door handle and raised the gun, pushing his way inside the stark white lobby.

Silence. No cars in the parking lot, no security on location. Yet the lab's front door had been left unlocked. "That doesn't seem very responsible."

A pair of black shoes sticking out from behind the large receptionist desk pulled him forward. Checking over this shoulder, Elliot crouched beside a female guard who'd been relieved of the weapon that was supposed to be in her holster. A line of blood trickled onto her cheekbone, but the rise and fall of her chest indicated she'd only been knocked unconscious. He pulled his phone from his pocket and requested an ambulance to the lab. Scuff marks veered off to the left, stark black against the white tile leading deeper into the lab. Caused by Waylynn's shoes as her abductor dragged her down the hall? Shoving to his feet, he hefted the gun to shoulder level. Pain exploded down his arm, but it wouldn't slow him down. Anchorage PD was about to have their hands full with another body on this case.

A high-pitched scream echoed down the hallway, an all-too-familiar sound that jacked his blood pressure higher.

"Waylynn." Every cell in his body caught fire as he followed the sound. White walls and tile blurred in his vision, his gut tight. Clear glass windows and expensive equipment was all he could see as he passed lab after lab. He'd heard her—she'd been close—but there were too many rooms in this damn facility to know where the SOB had taken her. Elliot slowed. Focused. His lungs worked overtime, but he forced himself to listen harder. She was here. She was alive. He was close.

"You don't have to do this." Her voice shook and Elliot slowed. The scent of geraniums filled his lungs and he breathed her in deeper as he pressed himself back against the nearest wall for cover. Waylynn. "Nobody else has to get hurt. Please."

The static sound of tape coming off the roll filled the silence. Elliot chanced a glance around the corner. There, in the center of the room, Waylynn had been duct taped at the wrists and ankles to a black office chair. Right in front of her stood the bastard who'd taken her with another piece of tape stretched between his hands. Her abductor leaned forward to secure the strip over her mouth. She struggled to free herself from the grip at the back of her neck and Elliot tightened his hand around the Glock. The SOB had hit her once. He wouldn't touch her again. Elliot swung gun-first into the lab, the scent of chemicals strong in the air. "Looks like I'm late to the party."

Only the man's dark eyes were visible through the black ski mask, the shooter's hands raised in surrender. One wrong move. That was all it would take to give Elliot a reason to pull the trigger.

"That was easy." The gun wavered in his hand as he closed in on the suspect. "What? You're not going to shoot me again? How about another round of electricity?"

Waylynn struggled to speak through the tape, but only mumbled sounds reached his ears. Warning flared in her gaze.

Fluorescent lighting reflected back off some kind of liquid on the floor. The chemical smell. Elliot caught sight of the empty bottle on the desk beside Waylynn— isopropyl alcohol—and the lighter in the shooter's hand. "Oh, hell."

THEY WERE DEAD.

Relief at seeing Elliot alive warred with the suffocating panic clawing up her throat. If her kidnapper let go of that lighter, everyone in this room would burn.

And there wouldn't be a thing she could do about it. Waylynn pulled at the tape securing her to the chair. One edge slipped off the hem of her sweatshirt and her pulse jerked a bit higher. Could she get to the kidnapper before he killed them all?

She twisted her wrists again, attention on her attacker. She'd almost lost her best friend once. She couldn't do it again, couldn't watch him die in front of her. Although the entire bottle of alcohol her abductor had emptied onto the floor around her might solve that problem faster than she wanted.

"Drop that lighter and I'll make you wish you'd killed me when you had the chance." Blood stained Elliot's jacket and jeans. Awareness flooded through her as he flinched against the pain he must've felt from the bullet.

"You couldn't stop me after the crash. You can't stop me now, Dunham." He knew Elliot's name? Of course he did. He knew everything about them it seemed. Her name, where she worked, knew Elliot. A sharp hiss escaped the lighter as the attacker who'd run them off the road ignited the flame. No. No, no, no, no. This wasn't happening. "Dr. Hargraves isn't walking out of this building alive. Nothing personal."

It sure seemed personal to her.

Her kidnapper dropped the lighter.

"No!" Elliot launched forward.

She screamed through the tape as her captor bolted for the lab's side door. Flames ignited all around her, the heat instantly too much to take. Fists clenched, she pulled at the tape around her wrists, but where there'd been leeway before, she couldn't break the binding. Elliot pulled up short outside the ring of flames. Her heart threatened to beat out of her chest. He couldn't get through. Couldn't get to her without getting burned. Black smoke climbed toward the ceiling as one of the nearby desks caught fire. The sprinklers would put out the flames before they reached her. Everything would be okay.

"Waylynn!" Elliot holstered his weapon, then covered his face as the fire lashed out at him.

She wedged her toes against the floor and tried to push away from the flames. In vain. Her abductor had sandwiched her between a lab desk and the ring of fire. There was no way out. Why hadn't the emergency system responded? No alarms. No sprinklers. A sob broke through the panic and she closed her eyes. No. She couldn't die like this. Blue-based flames inched their way toward her as the linoleum beneath the alcohol melted from the heat.

"Hang on, Doc." Elliot covered his mouth and backed up a few feet. "I'll get you out of here."

He was going to jump through the fire to try to save her. He'd burn right in front of her and there was nothing she could do to help him. No. He needed to get out of here. Needed to go after the shooter who'd put a bullet in his shoulder. Waylynn shook her head, pressing herself back into the chair. She flexed her jaw, worked at the tape around her mouth. Heated air burned down her esophagus and she couldn't yell for him to stop. An acrid smell dived deep into her lungs as the edge of the office chair singed. Sweat beaded along her hairline and at the nape of her neck. Her feet had been taped too high off the ground. She couldn't move. She shook her head again.

Elliot jumped.

The tape kept her scream at bay. Blood rushed to her head, too fast, too hard. The small amount of air she'd been holding pressurized in her lungs, but faster than she thought possible, rough hands were tugging at her wrists. She pulled at the duct tape again, trying to get it off as fast as possible.

"I always thought you were smoking hot, but this is a bit much, don't you think?" Elliot cut the tape from her wrists with a small blade in his hand, then crouched in front of her to get to her ankles.

She doubled over to work at the other side, then pulled the tape from her mouth. Standing, she shoved him. "What were you thinking? You could've died, and I wouldn't have been able to do anything."

He slid an arm around her waist and pulled her into him. The flames threatening to consume the entire lab—chemicals and everything—were nothing compared with the heat in his eyes at that moment. "I protect what's mine."

Waylynn sucked down a lungful of tainted oxygen. His? The growing heat around them battled with the tingling at the base of her spine. There was nowhere to go. The fire had spread too fast, but he'd protect her. She fisted his jacket, holding on to him with everything she had. "We're trapped."

"Climb up on the desk." Calluses scraped against her oversensitized skin as Elliot helped her onto the office chair she'd been bound to, then onto the desk. He followed after her, shedding his jacket in the process. Blood had spread across his white T-shirt, but he didn't seem to notice. "The smoke is getting thicker. Cover your mouth with this and follow my lead."

Dried blood flaked against her fingers as she held the jacket up to her face. Her eyes stung, smoke filling every square inch of the room. Where were they supposed to go? The exits had been blocked by the flames. More sections of the floor were melting. Fire ate oxygen. They'd suffocate from smoke inhalation if they didn't get out of here soon. Waylynn clung to the wall of muscle somehow keeping her calm in the middle of a burning building.

Elliot spun her into him, the whites of his eyes reddening. Sweat dripped down into his beard. "Do you trust me?"

Trust him? He'd saved her life twice in the span of twenty-four hours. He was the only person in this world she could count on, the only man she'd let close. The only man she'd considered a friend. She nodded. "Yes."

"Then I need you to get up into the vent above us." Elliot crouched on top of the desk, then gazed up at her. "I'll give you a boost. Get as far from the fire as you can, get in the SUV and call my team."

Waylynn craned her neck to spot the vent through the thickening smoke. Okay. She could make it to the opening with a boost. Locking her gaze on him, she dropped the jacket beside her. She placed one foot in his cupped palms and latched on to him. Tiles fell from the ceiling a few feet away and she turned away from the embers flying through the air, nearly losing her balance. Strong arms pulled her back into him. Heat blistered along her back, the fire getting closer every second they wasted talking, but his words finally registered. *She* would get as far from the fire as she could. *She* would get to the SUV. *She* would call his team. "What about you? How will you get up?"

"I'll be right behind you." He glanced up at the vent again. "Come on. This desk isn't going to hold both of us for much longer."

But Waylynn didn't move. "For a recovering con man, you're not very good at lying."

"Maybe you're just the one person who can see through me." His hands feathered over her arms, only a hint of his clean, masculine scent surviving the hotter-than-hell temperatures. Putting his life in danger with the moose, taking a bullet for her back at the crash scene, now this. Elliot intertwined his fingers through hers and brought her palm to his mouth. His beard bristled along the skin there and a different kind of warmth trickled down her spine despite the encroaching flames. He closed his eyes for a split second and an understanding passed between them. He'd told her before: he'd do anything to keep her safe. Without warning, he crouched, wrapped his arms around her legs and hefted her above him.

"Elliot, no!" She pushed off the ceiling with one hand, clinging to him for balance with the other. "I'm not leaving you. I can't do this without you."

"Yes, you can, Waylynn." A groan escaped up his throat as he pushed her higher with his injured shoulder. He never called her Waylynn. Which meant… "Get in and don't look back. Do not come back for me."

No. She pulled at the metal seam of the vent, flinching as the crash of steel on wood reverberated through her ears. Scrambling straight up into the duct, she exhaled hard at the burn of metal against her skin. Pitch-black darkness greeted her on either side. With some maneuvering, she leveraged one hand on the edge of the opening and reached back through to him. "Grab my hand. I can pull you up."

"Get out of here, Doc. That vent can't support us both." Elliot protected his face as one corner of the desk they'd stood on together caught fire. They were running out of time. Any minute now, their island of safety would burn right out from underneath him. He gathered the jacket from the table and covered his mouth and nose. "I'll find another way out."

"There is no other way out. Elliot, grab my hand!" She'd thought she'd lost him once. She couldn't do it again. Screw the investigation. Screw being framed for murder. Screw her research. Elliot Dunham was the only person in this world who mattered, the only person who was more important than breathing. More important than food or water or her apartment. He'd risk all that? Smoke dived deep into her lungs, burned her eyes, and she moved to cover her mouth with her arm. She couldn't last up here much longer. The smoke was pooling inside the vent system, but she wouldn't leave him behind. Never. "How are you supposed to protect me if you're dead?"

"I've survived this long, haven't I? Get out of the building, Waylynn. I'll find you." He shifted closer to one edge of the desk without looking up at her.

And jumped.

Aluminum cut into her palms as she gripped the vent opening. "Elliot!"

Chapter Eight

Son of a bitch. When would people stop trying to set him on fire?

Waylynn's scream died as the fire roared loud in his ears and he hoped like hell she was getting as far from this building as possible. He would've climbed into that vent right after her if he'd believed the airshaft would take both of their weight. Alas, that was not the case.

A rafter splintered above him, cracks in the exposed wood a bright, glowing orange. He'd run out of time. The isopropyl alcohol Waylynn's abductor had emptied onto the floor wasn't the only chemical the lab kept on hand. This entire building was a Molotov cocktail waiting to explode. "Right. Exit plan."

Going out the window wasn't an option. The bookcases, desks and chairs had already been consumed by the flames. Another foot toward the flames was too much for his exposed skin to take. Elliot squinted into the brightening fury closing in on him. Smoke clouded his airway and he jumped to the floor. Memories of a downtown apartment, a stalker, a crowbar to the head and Sullivan Bishop throwing him over his shoulder rushed to the front of his mind. He and his boss had been working Jane Reise's case a few months ago and the suspect they'd been tracking hadn't been too happy about their coming into his personal space. Well, at least no one had knocked him unconscious this time. If he played his cards right, he could make it through the small line of tile that hadn't been affected by the fire yet. "I'm going to regret this."

He protected his face and ran straight to the nearest door through the narrow untouched space. Testing the handle with his jacket around his hand, he slammed his uninjured shoulder into the thick steel. The damn thing wouldn't budge. The lab's biohazard procedures must've locked down the entire room. But then why hadn't the sprinklers come on? He rammed his shoulder into the door one more time, a heavy thud barely registering over the crackling of fire. The bastard who'd started the fire must've turned them off. The room would've gone into quarantine at the sign of a fire or biohazard leak, but the sprinklers and other precautionary measures were useless now. Elliot spun to go back the way he'd come, but the clear path that'd been there a minute ago was gone. "Huh. Mom was right. I really am going to burn in hell."

Well, then at least he'd have the chance to see her again. A burst of nervous laughter escaped but died as the seriousness of the situation took hold. He was going to die in this room. His family could take care of themselves. They always had. His team might mourn him, but they'd move on. But Waylynn? She didn't have anyone else. No family. No friends other than her colleagues and her work to keep her company. Even that had been destroyed. Elliot curled his fingers into his palms. He'd spent the last year telling himself nothing could happen between them after everything he'd been through, that his freedom, his happiness, took priority.

But, hell, Waylynn made him happy.

That smile when she spotted him with a beer when she came home after a long day of work, the fact humming "Gangsta's Paradise" brought out her infectious laugh every time, her determination to move on with her life despite her past. Everything about her made him want to be the man she deserved, made him want to be more than a con man. More than a private investigator. More than a friend.

Sweat slid down his face beneath his T-shirt. No. This wasn't how he was going out. Elliot reached for the gun in his shoulder. He'd shoot his way out if he had to. But came up empty. He searched the floor, spotting his gun a few feet from the desk he and Waylynn had used for a brief moment of safety. No way he could get to it now. New plan. Wrapping his jacket around his arm, he hiked his elbow into the pane of glass in the door. Two times. Three. He pushed the last remnants of his draining energy into the next three strikes, but the glass didn't so much as crack. The glass was meant to withstand an explosion in the lab, sealed to keep toxins in, in case of a biohazard lockdown. He wasn't getting through it without something heavier. He stepped back. He needed a microscope, a chair—anything—to punch through.

Without warning, the butt of a fire extinguisher crashed through the glass. Shards fell from the frame onto the floor. Those ocean-blue eyes settled on him. Ash streaked Waylynn's face, darkened the bruise across her cheek. Pieces of her long blond hair had singed ends. "You are not getting away from me that easily."

"What are you doing here?" A blend of fury and admiration flooded through him. He didn't know whether he wanted to kiss her or hike her over his shoulder and run for putting herself back in harm's way. Black smoke broke free through the broken glass. Escape first. Decide later. "I told you to get as far from this building as possible."

"I'm saving your life." She set the fire extinguisher on the floor and reached through the opening for him, fisting his T-shirt with skinned and bloody fingers. "But, sure, let's take the time we don't have to argue about it some more."

"Fine." Elliot hiked one leg through the broken windowpane, then fell onto the tile on the other side of the door. He couldn't suppress the groan working up his throat as pain spread through his shoulder and down his spine. His lungs spasmed with the rush of clean oxygen. He closed his eyes to relieve the sting, but they weren't out of the woods yet. The fire would spread to this room—and every room—now that Waylynn had shattered the window. They had to get out of there. And find the bastard who'd tried to kill them. "Tasered. Shot. Nearly burned alive. What else could go wrong today?"

"Elliot." His name on her lips—almost breath-like—raised his awareness of her to all all-time high. Something was wrong.

Elliot cracked his eyes. His shoulder protested as he hiked himself to his feet, but pain was nothing compared with the fire burning through his veins at the sight of that masked SOB pointing a gun to Waylynn's head. "Speak of the devil and he shall appear."

"Move and she's dead, Mr. Dunham," the arsonist said.

Waylynn flinched as her captor's grip on the tendon between her neck and shoulder visibly tightened.

"I don't think you want her dead. Otherwise you would've killed her already. You had opportunity. Motive is still a mystery, though." He might not be able to read the bastard's expression through that damn mask, but Elliot had already started putting the pieces together. Reading people was what he did. Everything he needed to know about a person was in their routine, in their actions. In the choices they made. All he had to do was solve the puzzle. It was how he'd conned so many people out of their money until a few years ago. And how he'd ended up in an Iraqi prison. "You started by framing her for murder, but when she hired a private investigator to clear her name, you destroyed her research, hoping that would bruise her enough to stop looking deeper. It didn't work so you had to try kidnapping, and the arson gave her enough time to get free. Even now, I can tell the safety on your gun is on. Either you don't want Waylynn dead or you're the worst killer I've ever seen."

The arsonist's gloved hand twitched alongside the gun as he shifted his weight between his feet. One second. Two. He turned the gun on Elliot and clicked off the safety. "You think you have me figured out, but I've done my research, too, Mr. Dunham. I know everything there is to know about you. How many people you've hurt, how much money you've stolen, where your family lives."

"You don't know anything about me if you think a threat like that is going to make me react." If anything, it was the shooter's hold on Waylynn that heated his blood now. That, and the fire threatening to kill them all. He glanced at her, at the slight movement she made with her eyes to the right. Without making it obvious, Elliot spotted the fire extinguisher beside him. Wouldn't survive against another bullet, but it was better than nothing. He nodded enough for her to notice.

"Put down the gun and let Waylynn go or I'm going to make you bleed. You don't want her dead, which means you need her for something." Sweat built down his spine as flames licked up the sides of the opening at his back. Shock slammed into him with the force of a knife to the gut. "Or you know her."

Waylynn stiffened.

"Funny how you think you know someone. How you think you can trust them." The bastard pointed the gun at her again and a rush of fury exploded behind Elliot's sternum. Her attacker wrenched her hair back, exposing her neck, and traced the column of her throat with the barrel. A thin scratch appeared in the path. "Then you discover what kind of monster they are. You know her secret, don't you, Dunham? You know what she's capable of."

Elliot lunged. Catching the shooter by surprise, he wrapped his hand around the gun's barrel with one hand and pushed Waylynn to the floor with the other, out of the way. A hard right hook ignited white streaks behind his eyelids. He went down on one knee. Slamming his elbow into her abductor's knee, he brought the arsonist down, too. But not for long. Another hit landed Elliot on his back and before he had a chance to dodge, the masked assailant was on top of him. One strike wrenched his head back into the white tile. A second darkened the edges of his vision.

His attacker dug his thumb into Elliot's bullet wound and a scream ripped from him like nothing before. A black haze descended over his vision, but he fought to stay conscious. He'd promised to protect her. He wouldn't fail her again. Pulling back his elbow, he gripped the masked assailant's shirt and launched his fist into the bastard's face.

Three gunshots exploded from over his head.

The man above him straightened, those dark brown eyes wide a split second before he collapsed to the tile beside Elliot. "He wasn't supposed to…kill Alexis."

Waylynn stared down at him, gun shaking between her hands, lips parted as though she couldn't believe what'd just happened. Stray stands of long, blond hair puffed with her strained exhales. She let go of the gun, metal meeting tile loud in his ears, as he pushed to his feet, then stumbled away from him. She shook her head. "I'm not a monster. I'm not a monster."

SHE'D KILLED HIM. The man who'd kidnapped her, strapped her to a chair and tried to burn her alive. And it'd been easy. It'd felt right. Because there was no way she was going to watch Elliot die right in front of her. She'd already lost too many people she cared about. Waylynn's hands still shook as she pushed hair out of her face. Red and blue patrol lights claimed her attention as the EMT beside her finished checking her blood pressure and other stats in the back of the ambulance. She didn't even know her attacker's name, didn't know why he'd targeted her. He'd known Alexis. That much was clear.

But it wasn't over. Not yet. The man who'd done those things tonight wasn't the same one who'd drugged her and killed Alexis. At least, not from the small bits and pieces she'd been able to recover of that night.

And Elliot...

She'd shot and killed someone with his own gun in Elliot's defense. What would he see when he looked at her after giving his statement to the Anchorage PD and the fire department? A monster as her attacker had claimed? Waylynn pulled the blanket around her tighter, ice freezing deep in her muscles. Odd, considering parts of Genism Corporation were still on fire.

"Dr. Hargraves." Officer Shea Ramsey, dressed in plain clothes, closed in on her from across the parking lot. Jeans, T-shirt, long curly hair burying her shoulders. Not on duty. "I heard everything on the radio. I'm glad you're okay."

Surprise rocketed Waylynn's pulse higher and she hopped down from the lip of the ambulance. "Officer Ramsey—"

"Shea, please." The officer motioned for her to sit, then took a seat beside her. A combination of pine and honey filled Waylynn's lungs. Officer Ramsey's caramel-colored eyes assessed the scene but watched the gurney being wheeled out the lab's front doors by two men from the coroner's office. "Have you talked to anybody about it yet? I mean, besides giving your statement to police about what happened? I can't imagine what you're feeling."

"No." Waylynn stared down at her hands. She'd never shot anyone before. Never taken a life despite popular belief. But it was inevitable, right? That was what she'd been trying to prove all these years with her research. The warrior gene turned normal, healthy, happy individuals into monsters in the blink of an eye. It was genetics. Fate. She just hadn't expected this day to come so soon. "What's there to talk about? I shot a man—" she swallowed around the bile working up her throat, the sight of so much blood still fresh in her mind "—to save my best friend. Elliot wouldn't be standing over there if I hadn't."

And she'd do it again.

"But he was your boss." Officer Ramsey's expression smoothed over. She narrowed in on Waylynn. "You worked beside him every day and you had no idea he wanted you dead?"

Air rushed from her lungs. No. That wasn't right. "What did you say?"

"They didn't tell you." Shea Ramsey ran a hand through that mass of hair and pushed off the back of the ambulance. She shifted her weight between both feet in agitated movements. "I'm sorry. I didn't mean... I thought you knew Dr. Matthew Stover was the attacker you shot. Uniformed officers are at his house now. He had surveillance footage of you, recordings of calls from your cell phone, original newspapers from your trial fifteen years ago."

The blanket fell from her shoulders as Waylynn stood, attention on the gloved hand peeking out from beneath the white sheet on the gurney. That hand had started the fire meant to kill her, had pointed a gun at her head. Couldn't be Matt's. He was her friend, her supervisor, the one who'd given her a job when she'd needed it the most. He'd run the warrior gene trials based off her research, supported her, stood up for her against the board members' threats to shut down the study because of funding.

What had Elliot said before she'd put three bullets in her attacker? *You don't want her dead, which means you need her for something. Or you know her.*

"Dr. Hargraves?" Officer Ramsey's voice sounded far-off, distant, and it wasn't until Elliot barricaded himself in front of her path that she realized she'd bolted for the body on the gurney.

"Waylynn." His voice washed through her, threatened to distract her.

"I need to see his face." She angled herself to see around his bandaged shoulder, to see the body as the coroner loaded it into the back of his dark van. Her breath sawed in and out of her lungs, a combination of smoke and man spreading through her system. No. Wasn't possible. Matt wouldn't have turned on her like this. Her gaze snapped to Elliot's, those mesmerizing gray eyes pulling her out of the haze of confusion, and a tremor cartwheeled down her spine. Would it always be like that? Would her body always want to give in to this unfiltered need to burrow into his arms whenever she laid eyes on him? Her heart beat too hard in her chest, but she met his stare straight on, hoping to appear stubborn and determined rather than out of her mind. "You said he didn't want to kill me. He knew me. You said that."

"Yes." He refused to budge. Sliding the hand of his uninjured arm up her neck, he framed her face. A muscle twitched in his jaw. "But seeing his face will only haunt you for the rest of your life. You have enough nightmares keeping you up at night. Trust me."

She did trust him. He'd saved her life. Three times now. Once by being willing to sacrifice himself for her safety. Nobody had ever done that before. Put her needs above theirs. Chancing one more glance at the gurney as the medical examiners shut the heavy van doors, Waylynn nodded. She closed the small space between them, the need for his touch so overwhelming. She buried her head in the hollow of his neck, exactly where she needed to be. A shiver rushed through her, warm tingles replacing the dread heating her blood. "Was it him? Was it Matt?"

"He was carrying his Genism Corporation ID. Must've used it to get access to the building after taking you from the crash site." Elliot wrapped his uninjured arm around her, pressed her tight against him. The steady rhythm of his heart helped control hers the more she focused on the sound, but the aftereffects of having taken a life still clung to her nervous system. "Explains how he knew how to disable the emergency system so the fire wouldn't be detected until it was too late."

A tremor shook through her from the top of her head and worked its way all the way down to her toes. A sob gushed from her lips and she held on to him tighter. "I was afraid he'd killed you."

"Not going to lie." Elliot planted a kiss at the crown of her head. "Being tasered and then shot sucks."

That earned him a laugh and suddenly, the fire, the betrayal, the explosion of bullets in her memory, it all slipped away. In such a short amount of time, Elliot had become the center of her universe. Her skin pimpled with awareness. Of him. Exhaust filled her lungs as the coroner's van pulled out of the lab's parking lot, but even with Matt Stover's body in the back, the nightmare wasn't over. Waylynn closed her eyes against the quick flash of memory from the scene at her apartment, but she couldn't shake the knowledge her boss hadn't killed Alexis. No. The man who'd forced her to write that confession at gunpoint was still out there. Maybe still targeting her.

"Your lawyer is here." Elliot's voice dropped into dangerous territory. Sure enough, Blake Henson climbed out of his town car and headed toward them. On the other side of the parking lot, two black SUVs pulled up alongside one of the ambulances. The Blackhawk Security team had arrived. With one last kiss planted on the top of her head, he released her. "Don't go anywhere. I'll be right back."

"Considering I'm wanted for murder, there aren't many places I can go." A smile tugged at one corner of her mouth as he met with the other members of his team. From what he'd told her about them during their long talks and beers after work, she assigned names to the operatives she spotted.

The one with the immovable expression had to be Sullivan Bishop, former Navy SEAL and the CEO and founder of the security firm. The tall, striking blonde…

Waylynn guessed she had to be Kate Monroe, and her stomach sank a bit. Elliot had told her about one of Kate's patients who'd killed the psychologist's husband last year, but being back at work looked good on her. The others were easily identifiable. Elizabeth with her black leather jacket and fingernail polish and dark circles under her eyes. New mom. She'd met Vincent. Anthony Harris was most recognizable with a pair of aviator sunglasses and an armory strapped to his Kevlar. The woman at his side had to be his wife, the army investigator and newest recruit to the team, Glennon.

Elliot greeted each of them with a smile and a laugh, as though they were family. Considering he'd spent the last year with them day in and day out, she imagined they were the only family he had left. They protected each other, fought for each other, supported each other. A strange sensation spread from behind her sternum. What she wouldn't give to be part of a family like that again. To be loved.

"Dr. Hargraves, I came as soon as I'd heard the situation over the police scanner." With his perfectly pressed Italian suit, Blake Henson ripped her back into the present moment. Cruiser lights deepened the fine lines around his mouth as the sun rose above the peaks of the mountains, but it was the light color of his eyes that paralyzed her from head to toe. Light blue. Just as she remembered from the flashes of that night in her apartment. "From what I understand, you're lucky to be alive. No permanent damage, I hope."

"Lucky. Right." Had nothing to do with the fact her next-door neighbor had put himself in the line of fire to protect her. Waylynn took a step back. "I'm sorry you had to come all the way down here, but as of two hours ago, I'm no longer an employee of Genism. The board decided to…" She paused around the building lump in her throat as her conversation with Matt before the crash replayed in her head. "They decided to let me go. So I guess I need to find another lawyer."

"Considering the circumstances and the fact your direct superior tried to murder you, I think I'll be able to negotiate with the board after all this damage is repaired." Blake Henson stretched out his hand, a business card between his index and middle finger. "Call me tomorrow and we'll work out the details to bring you back on board."

"Back?" She couldn't believe it. She took the card from the attorney, her attention automatically lowering to the back of his hand. Searching for a scar that wasn't there. Air rushed from her lungs and she relaxed a bit more. He might have the same-colored eyes as the man from her drugged memory, but she couldn't imagine a reason for Blake Henson to drug her, kill Alexis and frame Waylynn for murder. He was one of the company lawyers. While his job might involve keeping company activities and indiscretions from the press, he'd never looked at her twice in the ten years she'd worked for Genism. The past couple of days had messed with her head. She'd become suspicious of everyone. "Thank you."

"Everything okay?" Elliot's warmth tunneled through her clothing and straight to her bones as he wrapped his uninjured arm around her again. Relief spread like wildfire, but she drowned the urge to lean into him. Until they were alone.

"Get your rest, Dr. Hargraves. We'll talk tomorrow." Blake Henson turned back the way he'd come and climbed behind the wheel of his town car. Within a minute, he'd swerved out of the parking lot and disappeared.

"Everything's fine." At least, it would be. But right now, she wanted nothing more than to wash the smell of smoke from her clothes and gorge herself on real food. She studied the aftermath of the fire, the scorch marks and broken windows. An hour ago, she'd almost died in that building. Notching her chin higher, she tamped down another tremor shaking through her. "I'm ready for you to take me back to the cabin."

Chapter Nine

A broken woman made the most dangerous kind of warrior.

As Elliot led her back into the cabin, dried tear streaks cutting into the ash smudges on her face, he believed that 100 percent. She was a survivor. Always had been. And, damn, it looked good on her. Handing her the bag she'd packed at her apartment, he nodded toward the bathroom down the hall. Lucky the Blackhawk Security team had thought to grab it from the wreck. Otherwise, she might've been stuck wearing his MIT shirt again. He swallowed against the image of her dressed in nothing but that shirt earlier. "Why don't you go clean up? I'll round up something other than peanut-butter Oreos for—" he checked his watch "—breakfast, apparently."

Waylynn ran a hand over her arm, dead on her feet. She moved toward the kitchen. "You don't... You don't have to do that."

"You're dead on your feet, Doc." He gave in to her gravitational pull, closed the distance between them. Her perfume mixed with the smell of smoke became part of him. "You hired me to protect you. So I'm only going to say this once because I know you'll push yourself over the edge if I let you. I need you fed, cleaned up and in my bed within the hour. No argument."

Her mouth thinned as she crossed her arms and shifted her weight onto one foot. Defiance sparkled in those ocean-blue eyes as she hitched one knee to the side, every bit the brazen, smart-mouthed woman he couldn't get out of his head for a minute straight. Hell, her middle name was *defiance*. She'd pushed at his boundaries at every turn, buried herself beneath his skin to the point he didn't know how to get her out. Wasn't sure he wanted to, to be honest. "You realize I killed the last man who tried to boss me around, right? You sure you want to go down this road?" Sadness colored her voice.

She wasn't in the mood for joking. Elliot had embraced a special kind of darkness that allowed him to become whomever he needed to be in order to get the job done. He'd tricked dozens of targets into handing over their money, convinced them they were getting the better end of the deal, made them trust him. And she blew that all straight to hell when she looked at him like that. Like she was up for the challenge. And, damn, if that wasn't the sexiest thing he'd ever seen. "I think I can handle it."

"Be careful what you wish for." Leaning into him, she planted her palms on his chest and rose on tiptoe. Her mouth leveled with his ear. His blood pressure shot into overdrive as she dropped her voice. "The devil comes disguised as everything you think you want."

Her fingertips brushed across the oversensitized skin down his arms as she headed for the bathroom, not a single glance back. His heart restarted as the bathroom door lock clicked into place. Seconds ticked by. A minute. He didn't know how long he stood there debating whether he should give in to the temptation to knock on that door. Elliot curled his fingers into fists. The moment he gave in, there would be no turning back. All too easily, he imagined her under the shower spray, nothing between them but rivulets of water, and every muscle he owned urged him to follow through.

No. He wouldn't barge in on her. She'd been through more than most the past two days. They both had, and he wasn't about to take advantage. He'd keep as much distance between them as he could in a tiny cabin. Which wasn't much. He forced his feet toward the kitchen instead of down the small hallway. Wrenching open the fridge door with his injured arm, he slammed a hand over the bullet wound in his shoulder. The pain kept him in the moment. Kept his mind on getting a meal together and nothing more.

The sizzle of olive oil and chicken in the pan drowned her approach, but the slight humidity crawling through the kitchen announced she'd finished in the shower before she appeared in his peripheral vision. "What's for breakfast?"

He didn't dare meet her gaze as he chopped asparagus, but everything about her—the way she spoke, how she brushed her hair behind her ears, even how perfectly she fit against him—drew him in. Always had. Tossing a pinch of salt and pepper into the skillet, Elliot faced her. And the air rushed from his lungs. The world's most exotic, alluring women had nothing on the blonde beauty in front of him. Baggy sweats and an oversize

T-shirt hung off her lean frame but didn't detract from her overall attractiveness. If anything, his mind wandered to all the possibilities hiding under the thin fabric of her shirt. "Asparagus sweet potato chicken skillet."

He cleared his throat. Her hair hung in wet strands, accentuating the sharpness of her cheekbones and vividness in her stare. He tightened the grip on the knife in his hand.

And sliced his finger clean open.

Dropping the knife, Elliot reached for the hand towel hanging from the oven and wrapped his finger as fast as he could. "Damn it."

"Are you okay? Here, let me see." Waylynn hurried around the counter and took his hand in hers, mere inches between them. Smooth skin brushed against his as she studied the wound, but he barely noticed the pain. Every sense he owned had heightened in awareness. Because of her. Because of the concern etched into her expression, the sympathy in her voice. His heart thudded hard behind his ribs, almost as if the damn thing were trying to reach her. He'd kissed her once to prove there was nothing between them. No heat. No passion. It'd been rushed and rough. And he'd been dead wrong. There'd been nothing but heat. Nothing but passion and, hell, he couldn't stop thinking about that kiss now. Couldn't stop thinking about the next one either. "Doesn't look like you'll need stitches." She raised her head. "Something's burning."

He blinked to clear his head of her, her words registering through the Waylynn-induced haze. Damn it. Elliot ripped his hand out of hers and spun toward the skillet. Sure enough, black smoke and the scent of burned oil and chicken filled the kitchen. He twisted the knob to shut off the gas and exhaled hard. "I think we've had enough fires for one day. How about I go get us something?"

"There aren't any places open this early. How about you get your finger taken care of and I'll take care of this?" Waylynn brushed past him, that bright smile destroying the deepest part of him, the part that'd sworn off commitment in order to keep his freedom. She moved the skillet to another burner with a hot pad. Picking up the spatula he'd set beside the oven, she turned back to him and pointed with it. "Go. I promise not to burn your cabin down. Although, it wouldn't be hard because it's so small."

"I'm sensing some hostility toward my top-secret safe house." He pulled a first-aid kit out of the top drawer of the kitchen and wrapped a bandage around the wound. "It's not that bad. Come on. Where else can you say you almost got trampled by a moose and her young?"

No reaction. She pushed the burned mess around the skillet with the spatula. Her hands shook and she set the utensil onto the granite. "I'm sorry. I didn't mean... I appreciate everything you've done for me. I do. I've been through all of this before when I was accused of killing my father, but I—"

"Wasn't expecting you'd have to shoot your boss? I can't imagine what you're feeling, Doc." Elliot tossed the first-aid kit back into the drawer and bumped it closed with his hip. "I never said thank you, did I? Without you, I probably wouldn't be standing here. Also, how in the hell did a geneticist beat the crap out of me?"

Waylynn stepped into him. Reaching for his wounded shoulder, she brushed her fingers over the fresh gauze and tape. "Matt's been involved with MMA fighting for years. Said it kept him in shape. I never considered he'd… I never thought he'd be the one to turn on me." She raised her gaze to his, her hand framing his jaw and one of the bruises on the side of his face. The small muscles there twitched in response to her touch. "I'm sorry, Elliot. For everything. You wouldn't have been beaten, shot or almost burned alive if it weren't for me."

"Don't forget tasered." He sure wouldn't. He snaked his uninjured arm around the small of her back, pressing her against him. Right where she belonged. His smile died. She blamed herself. For all of it. That was the kind of person she was. Forced to grow up too fast after losing her parents, taking on more responsibility than a fifteen-year-old should've had to have dealt with. She'd lost an entire childhood—like he had—but she felt responsible because he bet that was the only way for her to keep it together. "Waylynn, you're not responsible for any of this. Not for the crash, not what happened to me. You *are* responsible for Matt Stover's death but nobody's going to hold that against you. Whoever killed Alexis Jacobs and got your boss to do their dirty work did this. And I'm going to find them."

"Right. A psychopath is targeting me because I like puppies and rainbows." A humorless laugh escaped her mouth. She traced a seam in his shirt with her thumb but backed out of his reach. After threading one hand through her hair, she crossed her arms beneath the baggy shirt, accentuating her small frame. Her attention traveled to the front door as she bit her thumbnail.

Color drained from her face as she steadily walked toward it and secured the dead bolt. "I feel as though I'm losing my mind. Two days ago, I got a message from Alexis to meet me at my apartment, and now she and my boss are dead."

Her tightly held control had started to crack.

"You're safe here." Spinning her into him, he forced Waylynn to look him in the eye. The outright terror in her expression raised his protective instinct. "I will protect you. No matter the cost. Physically, mentally, I will do anything to keep you safe."

"I know you will, but for how long? Another day? A week? It could take months to identify whoever framed me, Elliot." She rolled her lips between her teeth, her gaze drifting to the front door again. To double-check the lock?

"However long it takes, Doc." He pulled her into him, those blue eyes locking on his mouth for the briefest of moments. "I'm not going anywhere."

BEING IN HER life was a death sentence. That was clear now. First her father, then her mother. Now Alexis and Matt. Waylynn forced herself to take a step back, forced herself to take her eyes off his mouth, and suppressed the chaotic need burning inside her to stay in his arms. She couldn't let Elliot be next. Couldn't let him become a victim of her genetic code down the line. He was too important. He was…everything.

Her blood heated at the realization. Holy mother of peanut-butter Oreos. Her throat dried. She'd always found him attractive, charming, funny. But now? Now, she couldn't stop thinking about how much time she'd wasted over the last year. How she'd hidden her crush, how much she looked forward to seeing him every day after work for that beer. The way they recited bad country songs to make each other laugh. They'd almost died in that fire. He'd been shot trying to save her life. In the blink of an eye, she could've lost him forever. And she wasn't going to waste another minute. "Kiss me."

Waylynn didn't wait for an answer. Interlocking her fingers around the back of his neck, she crushed her body against his. Hard muscle pressed into her as he wrapped her with his uninjured arm. She notched her mouth higher to meet his lips as she came up on her toes. The difference between their sizes was laughable, but somehow, it worked. Everything about Elliot Dunham defied the fantasy she'd built in her head of the perfect man over the years, when she'd allowed herself to imagine a long-term relationship with a partner. His occupation, his height, even the color of his eyes. But right now, if only for tonight—no, forever—she wanted him. "Am I hurting you?"

"If you stop, I'll be in a lot more pain than I am right now," he said.

A smile stretched her mouth thin. She'd tried to stay in control for the last two days, tried not to let herself splinter, tried not to let him see how much she needed him. But it'd all been in vain as he slipped his tongue into her mouth. She had no control. Not when it came to him. Sliding her palm down his stomach, she reveled in the strong, muscled ridges and valleys beneath her fingers. His heartbeat changed. Sped up. She'd done that. Despite his insistence of keeping things between them professional, she'd elicited a reaction from him.

Because he'd been made for her. No other man had ignited this craving to be touched, to be loved, and she couldn't get enough.

Pressing her back against the counter, Elliot caged her between him and cold granite, the difference in battling temperatures fighting for dominance. He kissed her deeper, faster, and the ridiculous-sized cabin, the investigation, the fact she'd killed her boss to save his life less than two hours ago vanished. There was only him.

And with a deep trail of kisses down her throat, he had the power to break her. Elliot intertwined his fingers with hers, then raised her raw knuckles to his mouth. One by one, he kissed the wounds, sending small electric pulses through her nervous system. "I don't care what that bastard said. You're not a monster, Doc. You're a survivor. Always have been. Only now it's written all over your body."

I'm not a monster. Her words as she'd pulled that trigger drained the burning heat smoldering beneath her skin. She didn't want to think about that. Not now, not after he'd just started to make her feel. Monsters killed. Deep inside, everyone had the potential to kill, but according to her own research, the odds had increased for her the moment she'd been born. One day she could be Dr. Jekyll, the next Ms. Hyde. "How can you be sure?"

"I've met real monsters, Waylynn. You might've shot a man a few hours ago, but I'll tell you right now, you're not one of them. You're kind, you're generous, you put others first and strive to do what's right. You came back for me in the middle of the fire at the cost of putting your own life in danger." He smoothed his thumb across her knuckles. "And you can either fight that fact or accept it. You can let that fear control you or take the control and move on with your life. Those are your choices."

What she wouldn't give to believe every word out of his kiss-swollen mouth, but the truth remained. She couldn't outrun genetics. Nobody could. Tears burned in her lower lash line, thick salt coating the back of her throat and behind her teeth. Twisting away, she put as much distance as she could between them in the limited amount of space. The fantasy she'd built up inside her head was just that. A fantasy. How could she have been so stupid to let it tint the real world? "There is no choice, Elliot. Not for me."

"Why not?" A strong hand wrapped around her arm and spun her back into him. "Why don't you get to be happy?"

"I have the warrior gene!" Waylynn clamped her hand over her mouth, the tears finally falling. She couldn't hide the truth anymore. Couldn't live with the weight by herself. Swiping the back of her hand across her face, she sniffled. Control. She forced a weak smile. "So you see? Even if we find the person responsible for framing me, I don't get a happily-ever-after, Elliot. I don't get to spend the rest of my life with the man I've fallen in love with. I don't get to have the family I've always dreamed of having. Because one day, my DNA will force me to turn on them. Just like my father's did."

Elliot suddenly seemed so much…bigger as a sharp edge cooled the gray of his eyes. Dropping his hand, she lost the little bit of body heat she'd been able to hold on to since shooting Matt Stover. Panic flared the longer he stared down at her, unreadable, unmovable.

What did he think of her now? What did he see? His throat worked to swallow. "The man you've fallen in love with?"

There were two kinds of secrets. The one she'd kept from others and the one she'd kept from herself. But she couldn't shoulder either. Not anymore. She wasn't sure when it'd happened. Maybe that first time he'd waited for her after work with a beer and a smile. Could've been the moment he'd come running to help her after she'd discovered Alexis in the tub and screamed. Or was it when he'd taken that bullet back at the crash scene to distract her boss from kidnapping her? Did it matter? Wiping her face, a strained laugh escaped past her lips. "Come on now. You're a private investigator, remember? You're trained to read people. Isn't that what you said? You had to have seen it. I'm not that good of a liar."

Elliot blinked, running his palms down his face. Turning away from her, he kept his body language neutral, but none of that screamed *reciprocating feelings* and her stomach sank.

What did she expect? He'd made himself perfectly clear. Nothing would happen between them. Living in the commune, spending over a year in an Iraqi prison, being in a committed relationship. They were all the same to him. Prisons. Barriers to his own happiness. She'd cut herself off from any kind of human interaction past a professional level in a sick attempt to protect others. Her throat tightened as rejection took hold. Maybe she should've been more concerned about herself. "Elliot—"

"I don't care," he said.

Everything inside her shattered.

Smudges of ash darkened the angles of his jaw, hardening his expression. Elliot shook his head. "Wait. That came out wrong. I don't care about your genetics, Doc. I don't care if some gene changes you into someone else down the road. I know who you are." He closed in on her, the scent of smoke and man filling her lungs as he took her beat-up hands in his. "Every second I get to spend with you is better than losing you altogether."

She swallowed back the salty taste in her mouth. "What?"

"You're going to make me say it all over again, aren't you?" That gut-wrenching smile of his rocketed her blood pressure higher. In an instant, it vanished. Smoothing his thumbs across her knuckles again, he softened his stance. "You've got blood on your hands, but I don't see a monster when I look at you. I see my best friend. The woman who means more to me than anyone else in my life. The woman I'll do anything to keep for myself."

"You're not scared of what I might turn into." Not a question. He had to have read her father's file, read hers and her mother's statements after his body had been recovered. Nathan Hargraves had terrorized his family until the day he'd died. Elliot understood the risks, yet he still wanted her. The slight tenderness of her lips from his kiss was proof, wasn't it? He was willing to break the rule he'd set between them: no emotional attachments. For her. "You don't have to do this. We can stay friends like you wanted. We'll figure it out—"

"What's life without a bit of risk?" Elliot shrugged with his uninjured shoulder.

She couldn't contain the smile spreading her lips thin, fisting her fingers in his shirt to drag his mouth down to hers. Grazing her bottom lip along his, she nipped at him before pulling away. "Don't say I didn't warn you."

Her gut clenched at another sight of that tingling-inducing smile as he pressed his mouth to hers. Her laugh broke free at the sound of her stomach growling. Right. They hadn't eaten anything in... She didn't know how long. Waylynn released him. "Well, that certainly ruins the mood."

"Nah." Elliot interlaced his fingers through hers and flipped her palm toward the not-so-high ceiling. With his gaze locked on hers, he kissed the overly sensitive skin along the inside of her wrist. "Just postpones it a bit."

Her nerve endings burned with awareness. Nearly a lifetime of fear for the future drained from her system. Because of him. He'd given her reason not to escape the darkness. Instead, maybe she could learn to love herself there with his help. "All right. Food. Sleep. Then making out."

Elliot winked at her as he started working on saving the chicken and oil in the pan one-handed. "It's good to have priorities."

Chapter Ten

She'd fallen asleep in his arms, both of them too exhausted to do much else after gorging themselves on the bits of chicken and vegetables he'd managed to save. It hadn't taken more than a few minutes for him to fall asleep with her safe in his arms, her clean, flowery scent clinging to his shirt and boxers. Hints of her perfume filled his lungs now, but, when Elliot reached across the sheets, he discovered it to be a figment of his imagination. The bed was empty. Sunlight streamed through the pane of the massive triangle-shaped window out the back of the cabin. He checked his watch. Noon. He'd been asleep for close to eight hours. And, hell, it'd been the best sleep of his life as far as he was concerned.

Some guys just couldn't handle a bullet to the shoulder.

Him being one of them.

Running a hand through his hair, he threw his legs over the side of the bed and pushed to his feet. Strapping his arm into the sling the paramedics had given him at the scene after treating him, Elliot rolled back his shoulder to stretch the injury. With pain came clarity. His muscles protested as he moved toward the stairs, but the deafening silence pulled him deeper into the small space. "Doc?"

No answer.

Cold hardwood creaked under his weight as he hit the bottom step. The smell of coffee fought to distract him, but his heart jumped into his throat as he caught sight of her. Lean muscle and strength stretched and contorted into shapes he'd never seen a human body execute. Shadows deepened the ridges and valleys across her exposed midsection and back around her sports bra. Neon leggings left little to the imagination as she balanced precariously on both hands—no support—and lifted the crown of her head toward her toes in an impossible backbend. He'd never seen anything like it. Never seen anything quite like her.

How could someone so beautiful, so strong, believe she'd turn into a monster? Elliot rested his uninjured shoulder against the wall, watching the sweep of her arms and legs in a hypnotic dance.

Floating her legs back to the floor, Waylynn exhaled hard as she turned. She jumped with a small scream, a hand on her collarbones, as she spotted him across the room. She pulled wireless headphones from her ears. "How long have you been standing there like a creepy stalker?"

"Long enough to think you've been possessed by a poltergeist. I considered calling a priest to exorcize it from your body." It was only when she reached for a towel off the back of the bar stool that he noticed the sprawl of papers and his laptop open on the counter.

"If there's one thing I learned cramming through the night during my doctoral program, it was exercise helps me focus." Waylynn set her headphones on the counter. Small beads of sweat built in her hairline, the bruise along her jawline from where that bastard Dr. Stover had backhanded her more purple than black now.

It'd been a damn good thing Waylynn had gotten to him first. Elliot had wanted nothing more than to finish the job himself after what her boss had put her through. Rage flooded through him at the vile memory, but he forced himself in check. Hell, maybe he needed to exercise, too. The Genism Corporation logo caught his attention on the stack of papers she'd left on the counter. He spidered his fingers over the top one and turned it toward him. Handwritten notes detailed possible suspects within the company, starting at the very top, then navigating to the bottom on what looked like official letterhead. "Look at you taking up the private investigator mantle. Any leads?"

"If I go with the theory someone within Genism wanted to hide the results of our warrior gene trials, no. There are too many suspects to count, and it would take months to sift through it all. Every executive had reason to protect the lab. Money, reputation, the fact Genism is in direct competition with a few other labs for pharmaceutical company contracts. Not to mention military contracts. The list goes on." She wiped the towel across her collarbones with one hand and moved another sheet of paper out from under the stack with the other. "The only thing I'm certain about is whoever killed Alexis gave Dr. Stover my DNA results so I would be labeled a monster capable of murder. With my past, it wasn't hard, but framing me didn't do the job, so they escalated to direct attack. I just don't know how they got that DNA information. I assigned numbers to each volunteer in the study, including myself when I submitted my blood work. There weren't any names on the dozens of reports I filed. No way they could've read a result and assigned it to a specific subject. Matt didn't have access to that information."

"You had to have recorded them somewhere," he said. "Companies like Genism cover their asses. Did the subjects sign releases, legal documents?"

"Yeah. Of course they did. If the suspect works in Genism's legal department, they'd have access to all of the waivers with subjects' personal information and the numbers I'd assigned. All they'd have to do is look at the results for a match. Which narrows it down to about... one hundred people with access to that information." Her shoulders deflated. Draping the towel onto the back of the chair, she shuffled through the paperwork searching for another hand-drawn diagram and picked it up. An employee flow chart. In her next breath, she tossed it back to the counter. "I take that back. That does not narrow the suspect pool."

Only one name came to mind.

"What about your lawyer? What's his name again?" The SOB who'd dared put his hand on her at the police station after her interrogation.

"Blake Henson? He didn't have a scar when he handed me his business card at the crime scene. Believe me, I checked. Has to be someone else." Waylynn bit her bottom lip before running one hand through her hair. The weight of her gaze pressurized the air in his lungs as he studied the almost-completed list of personnel she'd constructed from memory. "Are we going to talk about what's on your computer?"

"It's not mine. I'm holding it for a friend." A laugh rumbled through him at her smile, but he knew exactly what she was referring to. The file folder. The only file folder on his desktop. Smoothing his uninjured hand against the counter, he straightened. "How'd you get into it?"

"I made it through twenty years of school. It wasn't hard to guess your password." Maneuvering the laptop toward him, she presented the individual files he'd been collecting the day he joined the Blackhawk Security team. Coworkers. Clients. People he'd investigated for his clients. Every shred of their lives was in that file. Bank records, mortgage paperwork, daily schedules, family, affairs, where their children went to school. Everything he needed to know to do his job sat in a password-protected folder only he'd had access to. Until now. Okay, he hadn't needed it all, but knowing the people he came into contact with—sometimes on a daily basis—fed his inner survivalist. Never knew when a bit of blackmail could help the situation. "I didn't read them, if that's what you're worried about. My only question is where's my file?"

"You really want to know?" Hesitation showed in her gaze and he couldn't help but smile. He could draw this out, have some much-needed fun after what'd happened over the last few days, but he tapped his index finger against his temple. "In my head."

"You don't have a physical or digital file?" she asked.

"Nope." Rounding the counter, he tugged a cabinet door open and took down two mugs. Seconds ticked by.

Maybe a full minute as he poured coffee into the mugs and offered her one. Black. The way she liked it. He handed her a cupful. "Why? Are you feeling left out?"

"No, it's just… You've run background checks on the people you work with, even your boss, and, from the looks of it, anyone who might've even road raged at you on the freeway." Sipping on her coffee, she steered her focus back to the computer screen. "Why not me?"

Elliot took a gulp of dark liquid, reveling in the burn down his throat. Settling his lower back against the opposite counter, he increased the space between them. A lie would be easy. He hadn't gotten around to it. He knew everything he needed to know about her. She wasn't interesting enough to investigate. Lie. Lie. Lie. If he was being honest with himself, there was only one reason he hadn't dug into her personal life as he'd done with everyone else he came into contact with. He couldn't stand the thought of losing *her*.

"Because you're the last person I think of at night when I go to sleep and the first person I think of when I wake up." Setting his coffee on the granite, he rubbed the muscle by the hole in his shoulder. He stepped around the counter. "You're the only woman I know who can recite every bad '90s country song from memory and make a crappy day better with a single smile." His body craved hers as he slowly closed the distance between them. "You're the most intelligent, beautiful, sexy and puzzling scientist I know and I guess, when it came right down to it—" Elliot lowered his mouth over hers "—I didn't want to spoil the surprise."

"How thoughtful of you." She notched her chin higher to meet his mouth. "So what now?"

Sliding his uninjured arm across her lower back, he hiked her into his chest. Ferocious need raged through him. Dangerous. Intoxicating. Lethal to the single rule he'd laid out for himself when he'd gotten out of Iraq: no emotional attachments. But, right now, the thought of losing freedom to this woman only strengthened that need more. "Well, we've eaten and caught up on some sleep. I think we need to stick to our plan and make out."

"I do love a man with a plan." Waylynn intertwined her fingers with his and tugged him up the stairs after her.

He'd broken his rules. For her.

The thought coaxed a smile as she set her ear against his bare chest. Ridges and valleys of muscle flexed beneath her as she planted a kiss on his sternum. What she wouldn't give to stay here forever. Forget Alexis's murder. Forget that'd she'd been framed for killing her own assistant. Forget finding the person responsible or the fact she'd been let go from the only job she'd ever cared about. How much more did they have to go through before giving up was okay? How much more before she got her life back?

Resting her chin on his sternum, she studied the details of his face and filled with heat all over again. Her pulse hammered behind her ears. She loved him. She'd known it before, but she was sure of it now more than ever. What other reason was there for having such a strong reaction to him? The last few hours in this bed had been everything and more. Not only physically but mentally, emotionally. For a little while, she'd forgotten the need to survive and…lived. And the idea she'd have to go the rest of her life as just friends from here on out threatened to shred her apart on the inside. Wasn't going to happen. They'd forged something new, something better, stronger than before. Not even he could deny that.

"I know what you're thinking." Slowly, he traced a fingertip over her spine and a shudder of pleasure washed through her. She squirmed against him, the wrinkled sheets pulling away from them as she narrowly avoided his injured shoulder. "How in the world did we go this long without jumping each other?"

She set her forehead against his chest and planted a soft kiss over his heart. "More like how did we do it all those times without tearing your stitches."

Following the bruise pattern along her jaw, he kept his touch light. Darkness chased the desire from his eyes in an instant—most likely brought on by the memory of how she'd gotten the bruise in the first place—and she ran her hand through his beard in an attempt to keep him in the here and now. "Even if I did, it would have been worth it."

"I'm glad you think so, but sooner or later, we've got to leave this cabin." Waylynn slipped her hand over the back of his, then brought it to her mouth as he'd done downstairs before she rolled away from the comfort of his warmth. Wrapping one of the sheets around her body, she threw her legs over the bed to stand, but was pulled back to the mattress. A shout escaped from between her lips as she fell straight into his arms. He hovered above her, that gut-wrenching smile raising her desire all over again.

"I've got food storage under this bed like you

wouldn't believe. We don't have to go anywhere." He placed a kiss on the tip of her nose, her senses going wild. Would it always be like this between them? This undeniable excitement whenever he touched her? "But if you insist, we can always hook up the cabin to the SUV and travel, get out of Anchorage."

"You're joking, right?" He couldn't be serious. "What about your deal with Blackhawk Security? Won't the men you conned out of their money come after you if Sullivan stops paying?"

"Can't come after me if they can't find me," he said. "I've still got contacts and cash. We could change our names, hit the road. Never look back."

Waylynn sat up, twisted around to face him. She clutched the sheets around her, the heat between them draining from her veins every second he actually considered picking up and leaving. Had that been his plan all along? Pay his debt, then disappear? Would she have come home from work one day to find his cheap camping chair on the front porch empty and his belongings gone? "You've thought this through."

"I've never been good staying in one place," he said.

Her brain automatically searched for the sarcastic remark that would sweep all this talk of him leaving under the rug, but nothing came to mind. "I don't know what to say."

"Say you'll come with me." He slipped his hand into hers. "You've got nothing left here, Doc. Your family is gone, the lab's board of directors let you go. And don't forget the killer who put a target on your back. Say yes."

He was right. She had nothing left here. The realization tightened the grip she had on the sheets. She opened her mouth to answer, but a high-pitched ringing shot her blood pressure higher. Waylynn exhaled hard as he reached for his phone beside the bed. Saved by the bell.

"It's Kate. I asked her to construct a profile on this guy. Hopefully she has something useful." He shoved off the bed and answered the phone. "Go for Dunham."

Leveraging the phone between his uninjured shoulder and jaw, he pushed his legs into his jeans, then disappeared down the stairs, only tendrils of his conversation audible from this spot where she'd gotten a glimpse of the future. "When?"

Leave Anchorage? Reaching into her overnight bag, she pulled fresh clothing from the bottom, ignoring the heavy weight inside, and dressed as fast as she could. What were they supposed to do? Ignore the fact she'd been framed for murder by running? She was still the main suspect in Alexis Jacobs's investigation. Dr. Stover's attempt on her life had only derailed the case, not solved it. Anchorage PD wouldn't let her leave the city, let alone leave the state. They'd issue a warrant for her arrest and, given the theory somebody from the lab had started this nightmare, she wouldn't get far. Genism Corporation was one of the largest genetics laboratories in the country. Their reach—their resources—extended further than Waylynn could ever imagine.

She didn't want to spend the rest of her life looking over her shoulder.

Beeping from Elliot's security panel rang loud in her ears as he stepped outside onto the cabin's small front porch. The door clicked closed, leaving her alone for the first time in days.

She'd grown up here, built her life, built a career.

She'd stared down an entire city of citizens convinced she'd murdered her father and held her head high and her middle finger higher. She deserved to be happy here, had given everything to this town. Could she really give that up?

No.

Not because some psychopath had destroyed her life's work, and not because the man she'd fallen for had his own ideals of freedom. If Elliot wanted to leave Anchorage behind, leave *her* behind… Her throat threatened to close in on itself. She'd survive. Just as she'd survived everything else in her life. Making her way downstairs, she dived back into the work she'd started before she'd given Elliot everything she had left. She could rebuild her research. It might take another decade, she might never find another lab to take her on and finance the trials she needed, but she could do this. She'd done it once. She could do it again. If she could get to Genism's server, she might be able to salvage what was left of her career.

Typing in her login and password to the lab's remote access, she nearly cried from relief. The board hadn't shut down her access yet. Her trial notes, her research, patient results, everything was there. But hadn't Matt said the files were damaged during the break-in? Scrambling to save ten years' worth of research as fast as she could, Waylynn swept a hand through her hair to fight the anxiety climbing up her throat. The lab's IT department might've been waiting to see if she'd try her access. Even though she'd poured her soul into this work, the research technically belonged to Genism. She couldn't copy and paste it into her next job, but she could use it to rebuild. She didn't have to start from scratch as she'd feared. Shoving Elliot's thumb drive into the port on the laptop, she waited for the device's window to load.

Then froze.

There was only one other file on the drive. Labeled with Nathan Hargraves's name. The thumbnail detailed the contents. Her father's police report. Her stomach dropped, the edges of her vision darkening as she held her breath. Elliot had lied to her. He'd claimed he hadn't investigated her past. Waylynn swallowed through the gravitational urge to run. He'd obviously read the report. Had he discovered who'd really killed her father?

The security system announced his opening the front door, and a rush of cool morning air raised the hairs on the back of her neck. Or was that the weight of his attention drilling into her spine? "We've got a problem."

Waylynn clicked off the thumb drive's window, leaving only Genism's server screen visible on the laptop. After everything they'd been through, after what they'd shared upstairs in that bed, why would he lie to her about his own private investigation? Her heartbeat thundered behind her ears. The police hadn't been able to solve her father's murder, but Elliot wasn't police. He wasn't held back by the same laws, wasn't scared to cross the line when it came to solving a case. And it wasn't in his nature to let things lie when the evidence ran out. She trusted him with her life, thought she loved him. He was good and intelligent and her best friend. But if he'd read that file, then he knew the truth Anchorage PD hadn't been able to prove without the murder weapon and there was nothing she could do about it.

Bile worked up her throat. Her body felt heavy, weighed down, but she stood strong.

Crossing her arms across her midsection, she sat on the edge of the bar stool and fought the nervousness blazing through her. "Just one problem? Last time I counted, we had more than that."

Tossing his phone onto the counter beside the laptop and her headphones, Elliot ran a hand down his thick beard. Those hands had touched her oversensitized skin less than an hour ago, had awakened things inside her she'd fully believed she couldn't have. He'd saved her life—twice—but, more important, had saved her future. A future with a man who wasn't afraid of what she might become.

She studied him. No smile. No sarcastic remark. Pushing away from the bar stool, she closed in on him as his fisted hands shook at his sides. The tendons between his shoulders and neck strained to the point she again thought he might tear open his stitches. Panic flared hot and bright behind her sternum. "Elliot? What happened?"

He locked violent gray eyes on her. "Someone broke into Liz's home and stole the hard drive."

Chapter Eleven

The bastard had gone after his team, threatened Elizabeth Dawson, her family. Blackhawk's network security analyst and her baby had been able to get out of the house while Liz's significant other, Braxton, had taken shots at the SOB. Police were at the house now, taking statements, but this could've gone a whole other direction. Elliot pushed a hand through his hair. Damn it. He hadn't meant for this. Hadn't meant for any of this when he'd handed over that drive.

"Is she okay?" Concern deepened the lines around Waylynn's mouth as she sank against the bar stool again. "She has a baby—"

"Everyone is fine. Just a bit shook up." He said the words more for himself than to comfort her. Anything to keep himself from charging down there, leaving Waylynn unprotected and tracking the suspect down himself. "Kate's with them at the house. Wanted me to know they didn't mention the hard drive to the police."

Waylynn nodded. "Genism would've claimed intellectual property and taken the drive before we could read what was on it. Probably destroyed the device to hide whatever was on it to prevent a leak."

"Yeah, well, Liz hasn't been able to get much other than the lab's logo off any of the files yet, so I'm not sure how much use the drive is going to be." How the man who'd broken in knew about it in the first place was a mystery. Alexis Jacobs's apartment had been searched and cleaned before they'd gotten there. Could've been the same perp who'd broken into the assistant's apartment and Liz's home. "But it proves Alexis broke company policy. Something in your work together was important enough for her to risk her job and a possible lawsuit. The killer has to know exactly what's on that hard drive and wants it enough to kill for. Otherwise, why go after it at all?"

"Your stitches are bleeding." Waylynn crossed the small space between them, her geranium scent tempting him to pull her back up the stairs. She smoothed her fingers over the bandage and peeled back a corner, but the mutual pleasure they'd shared less than an hour ago had cooled. Significantly. Maneuvering him to the bar stool, she turned her back to him. "Sit down. I'll grab the first aid kit."

He hadn't noticed the blood, his head too wrapped up in the investigation, in her. Elliot slid his hand around hers, turning her into him. "We're going to catch this guy, Doc. He'll never touch you again."

"I know." Her voice hollowed as she ran a hand through her hair, a nervous habit she'd formed over the last few days. "But how many more people are going to get hurt in the process? First Alexis. Then Matt. Now the people on your team are in danger. Their families. I…" Waylynn pulled her hand out of his. "I've lost everyone close to me. I can't lose you, too."

"First off, I've been doing this job long enough to know the risks, and so has my team. They're prepared for the worst. Trust me when I say they can take care of themselves. The son of a bitch was lucky Braxton didn't put a hole in him for coming near his girls." Elliot stood, bringing her in to him. "And, second, you're not going to lose me. I made you a promise and I intend to keep it. No matter the cost."

"Okay," she said. "Then I can tell you our next move. If the killer knows what's on that drive, it makes sense that he knew Alexis. Maybe had a relationship with her."

"I'm impressed." He focused on the laptop as she pulled away from him and sat on the bar stool. "Did she ever mention a boyfriend? An ex? Someone she spent a lot of time with at the lab?"

"Not that I remember, but the company looks down on interoffice relationships." Waylynn's fingers hit the keyboard in rapid succession and the screen flickered to life. "She wouldn't have told me she was seeing someone in the lab, but I was able to log into Genism's servers to recover all my research that'd been destroyed. If your teammate wasn't able to decrypt the hard drive before it was stolen, we might be able to find out what Alexis stored on it by reviewing her server history. So far the medical records I was able to access through the server haven't turned anything up on recent hand injuries, but I'm searching for Alexis's trail now."

Anticipation burned through him. They'd been waiting for a break in the investigation, waiting to see what Waylynn's assistant had died for. Elliot forced himself to breathe evenly. He'd been waiting to find the bastard who'd dared come after his woman. Because she was his to protect, his responsibility. But he didn't believe in luck. Didn't believe in coincidence either. Her boss had gone as far as to put a tracking device in Waylynn's phone in order to take her out himself. There was no telling how far the lab executives she'd dedicated ten years of her life to would go to protect themselves and the company. "When did you find out you still have access to the servers?"

"After you went outside." Her fingers stilled on the keyboard, but she didn't look up at him. "This isn't going to define the rest of my life. The pain, death and violence have been threatening to pull me under, but I'm going to keep my head above water. I'm going to rebuild my life and I'm going to rebuild my research." She nodded once. "I've done it once. I can do it again. You showed me that."

Damn straight she could. And he'd be right there at her side. Her biggest supporter. No matter how long it took, he'd help her rebuild everything she'd lost and more. "Did you practice that in front of the mirror?"

"Maybe a little." Her laugh cut through him and in the span of three seconds, it was the most exhilarating and life-altering experience of his life.

He loved this woman. Down to his bones, couldn't live the rest of his life without her, without loving her. Waylynn Hargraves was the strongest, most fearless woman he'd ever known. She'd stared death in the face and laughed. She'd decided fear wouldn't control her as it would so many others in the same situation and he couldn't take his eyes off her. Possessiveness exploded through him. He reached out, curling a strand of hair around his finger. Whatever that meant for their future—if they had a future together—he didn't know. But he was willing to give it a try. Screw the past. His parents, the prison guards. They were nothing like the woman in front of him. She wouldn't try to imprison him, wouldn't betray him. She didn't have the heart. "If I haven't made it clear before, if you do ever end up killing someone, I'll help you bury the evidence."

"Just what every woman wants to hear." Another flash of that brilliant smile. The laptop beeped, bringing her focus back to the screen. "I've got it. Looks like Alexis was singling out certain subjects and separating them into a new file."

"What made those subjects special?" Elliot rested his uninjured arm against the back of the chair and leaned in over her shoulder. Her breathing patterns changed and he couldn't help but revel in the knowledge that his closeness was the reason. He'd done that to her, made her breath hitch, affected the pulse at the base of her neck.

"I don't know. They're labeled by their trial numbers I assigned to each volunteer. No names, but every one of them were positive for the warrior gene." Waylynn leaned back in the chair. "I won't be able to match them without the waivers I handed over to the legal department when the subjects applied to be part of the trial."

"Can you access those files from the servers, too?" he asked.

"It's worth a try." Waylynn clicked off the current screen and slid her fingers across the track pad. A minute—maybe two—later, she shook her head. "I don't have access to those files. We'd need someone from

Legal to get them for us, but I know someone who might be able to help." She rolled her lips between her teeth, then headed for the stairs without another word. Within thirty seconds, she hit the bottom step, holding a small white rectangle between her fingers. "Blake Henson gave me his card back at the scene. He wanted me to call him today to work out reinstating me with the lab, but he might be willing to help us if we explain someone in his department is a murderer."

"Let me get this straight." Elliot ran a hand down his beard. "We're going to ask an employee paid to protect the company he works for to hand over confidential corporate documents to help our illegal investigation."

"You think it's a bad idea?" Uncertainty deepened the lines between her eyebrows as she studied the business card, and damn, he had to fight the urge to smooth them away.

"No, I just wanted to make sure I heard you right." He closed the distance between them. "We'll find him. No matter how long it takes or how many different plans we need to come up with. We're in this together."

"So you're not going to try to sneak out of the cabin in the middle of the night to follow evidence again, then?" she asked.

"I knew you were going to hold that against me." He framed her jaw with one hand and moved his mouth over hers lightly. An explosion of that unchecked need pressed his body against hers. "But, no. For better or worse, you're stuck with me."

Her face lit up and every muscle he owned coiled tight. She rose up on her toes, leveling that intoxicating blue gaze with his. Cocking her head to the side, she wrapped her arms around the back of his neck, careful to avoid the hole in his shoulder. "It'll probably be for worse."

A laugh rumbled through him. Then he kissed her. Hard. Fast. It was too late to turn back now. She'd claimed him from the inside out and he would have handed his soul over willingly. He came up for air but couldn't suppress the wild addiction he had for her flooding through him. "I knew that the moment I met you."

WELL, THEY WEREN'T best friends anymore.

The haze surrounding her brain had taken a stronger hold than before, to the point she'd lost track of time. Nothing remained but him and his clean, masculine scent in her lungs. Three days. That was all it'd taken to change her life, to discover a connection stronger than the one her genetics had forged on her future. She wasn't sure how long they'd stood there, his mouth on hers, her pressed against him. Stepping back for air, Waylynn flitted her fingers over the edge of the gauze taped to his shoulder. They'd gotten distracted. She set her palms against his chest, his heartbeat strong beneath her touch, and backed off. "As much as I'd love to make out with you all day, we need to change your bandage, then call my lawyer."

"Forget it. Let it get infected." He moved to close the space she'd put between them.

She countered his approach, a rush of gut-clenching delirium threatening to help her get lost in him all over again, but she wouldn't wait for whoever'd framed her to find her first. "That was a nice way of me saying we need to brush our teeth and you most definitely need to shower. You still smell like smoke."

"Yeah, all right." Elliot moved to the single kitchen drawer and pulled the first aid kit free. "But as soon as I'm done, I can't promise I'll keep my hands off you."

"I've been warned."

A few moments later, the door clicked softly, followed by the sound of water hitting tile as he disappeared into the bathroom. She picked up her lawyer's business card and Elliot's phone from the granite countertop. The zing of cold stone against her skin cleared her head of him. For now. What she wouldn't give to forget everything that'd happened the last few days, but without that chaos, she and Elliot would've kept up with their evasive dance. She would've come home from the lab every night, compete in the lyric trivia battle they'd created, drink his beer and go inside her apartment. Alone. Never knowing what it'd be like to kiss him, never knowing his touch, or what it'd feel like to have the kind of protection he offered. Never knowing love.

Inhaling deep, she fought to keep her head in the game. It wouldn't last long. Elliot Dunham had worked his way beneath her skin, down into her bones, and had become part of her. But she'd take advantage of the clarity to find the Genism employee who obviously wanted her dead. Dialing Blake Henson's number from his business card, she brought the phone to her ears.

Two rings. Three.

"Come on, pick up." Nervousness lodged in her throat. According to Alexis's corporate server history, someone in the legal department had orchestrated this entire puzzle. Blake Henson was the only resource they had to find their suspect. Without his willingness to hand over confidential documents identifying the subjects of her trials—the same subjects Alexis had compiled in her list—she and Elliot had nothing. She'd spend the rest of her life looking over her shoulder, paranoid about the next attack. She bounced on her toes as anxiety clawed up her throat. "Pick up the phone."

The line clicked. "Blake Henson."

Relief crashed through her. "Mr. Henson, it's Waylynn. Sorry, Dr. Hargraves. You know, the former employee currently under investigation for murdering my lab assistant."

"Doesn't ring a bell. I'm kidding, Dr. Hargraves. Of course I recognize your voice." A deep laugh reached through the line. "I was getting worried you wouldn't call, but I'm about to meet with the board of directors about your reinstatement. Can I call you back?"

"Actually, I wasn't calling about that. I need your help with something else." She dug the corner of his business card into her index finger. This had to work. There weren't any other options. "According to the Genism server history, my assistant was in the middle of compiling a list of subjects who volunteered for trials testing for the warrior gene. Each volunteer filled out a waiver before the trials began and was assigned a subject number to guard their privacy—"

"But you need the waivers to identify them to help clear your name of Ms. Jacobs's murder," Blake Henson said.

"Yes." Her throat threatened to close, and she gripped the business card harder. Would he help them, or would he report her request back to the board and terminate any chance she had of getting her job back? She didn't know him well enough to make a guess. He'd defended her during Anchorage PD's interrogation because it'd been his job—to protect Genism Corporation employees. But now that she wasn't an employee any longer… "I know what I'm asking you to do, but you're the only chance I have of finding who killed my assistant."

Seconds ticked by in silence, a full minute.

She checked the screen to ensure the call was still connected, but he hadn't hung up. Was he having the receptionist call the police as they spoke? Waylynn breathed through the pressure building behind her sternum. "Mr. Henson?"

"You said Ms. Jacobs was compiling a list of subjects who tested positive for the warrior gene. The only way she would've identified them was if someone from the legal department gave her the very same documents you're asking me to hand over." The lawyer's voice lowered to a whisper, and she had to remember he was about to meet with the board concerning her reinstatement. "Does that mean you think one of my colleagues is a murderer?"

The click of the bathroom door put her face-to-face with a wall of muscle that threw her saliva glands into overdrive. The breath rushed out of her as the raw edges of his wound glimmered under the single lightbulb above the counter. Elliot carried fresh gauze and tape at his side but didn't move to repatch the bullet wound. She hit the button for speakerphone to bring him into the conversation. "I'm not sure, but anything you can provide may help the investigation."

"If I get you the documents you're asking for, I could

lose my job. I could get sued by the lab, and believe me when I say they have a horde of bulldog attorneys I've worked with for years who will make sure I never practice law again." His hesitation slithered through her. One second. Two. "You'll have to meet me out of the city, away from Genism. Can you meet at Cliffside Marina in Whittier in two hours? Alone?"

Elliot shook his head slowly, a hint of that raging violence consuming his gaze. Gripping the towel around his hips, he accentuated the bruises and cuts along his white knuckles.

This was the only chance they had of uncovering what got Alexis Jacobs killed and why someone had framed her for it. Waylynn kept her focus on the man in front of her. "I'll be there."

"See you then." Blake Henson ended the call.

"What were you thinking agreeing to meet him alone?" Elliot asked.

"I was thinking it'd be nice if I didn't have to look over my shoulder for the rest of my life, that I could end this nightmare, and move on." She set his phone back onto the counter, taking a deep breath. "I told you. Blake Henson isn't the man who drugged and framed me for Alexis's murder. He's taking a risk to help us."

"Someone is out to destroy you, and we've already proved your boss was involved, Doc. What makes you think whoever started this doesn't have someone else working for him?" Elliot ran a hand through his still-wet hair, shaking his head. The violence had cooled in his eyes, but tension tightened the muscles down his back as he turned away from her. "There's no way I'm letting you meet this guy by yourself."

"Here, let me help." She reached out for him, sliding her hand over his arm. Taking the gauze and tape from him, she crowded him until he sat on the bar stool. Someone had gone out of their way to destroy her and she wasn't stupid enough to meet her lawyer on her own. Didn't matter Elliot had lied about investigating her past or the fact he might pick up and leave Anchorage at the drop of a hat. She wanted him by her side. Forever. Because that was what love was. Compromising. Strong. Honest. The con man, the MIT drop out, the investigator, she loved them all. Waylynn cut a piece of gauze to size, then placed his hand over it while she ripped the last two pieces of tape from the roll to secure it in place.

He clamped a hand over hers as she pressed down the tape, running the pad of his thumb over the back of her hand. Her breath caught as he dragged her closer, the towel around his hips riding up his powerful thighs. Clean man and a hint of their burned breakfast from that morning filled her lungs, but every cell in her body stood at attention. For him. "Your safety is the only thing that matters to me, Doc. You're mine to protect. I failed once. It won't happen again."

"I know." But if her lawyer suspected she'd brought backup or that she'd been followed, he'd disappear with the files they needed to clear her name. Elliot's body heat beat against her and she finally looked up into those mesmerizing gray eyes. "What if I'm the only one Blake Henson sees? You'll be there, but in the background. Close enough to get to me if something goes wrong and we'll get what we need to identify the subjects Alexis was focused on."

"I'm calling in backup." He pushed to his feet, a corner of the gauze still free. "If the bastard comes at you again, we'll be ready."

"If that will make you feel better, then let's do it." Hell, having an entire team of trained professionals made *her* feel better. She slid her thumbnail around the empty roll of medical tape. "You ran out of tape, but I think I might have some in the first-aid kit I brought from my apartment."

He pulled her back into him by the hand, planting a hard rush-inducing kiss on her lips. "I'm going up to get dressed anyway and you still need to brush your teeth. I'll get it."

"All right. It should be in the bottom of my bag." Her fingers slipped from his as he headed upstairs. A smile played on her lips as he threw the towel over the balcony and she bit down on her thumbnail to keep herself in place. Together forever? That was a lot of horrible '90s country battles. Turning her attention back to the laptop and not to her imagination of him upstairs, she pulled more of her research off the servers as fast as she could before the IT department cut off her access. It was a miracle her login had worked this long. "Did you find the tape?"

Hardwood protested under his weight as Elliot came back down the stairs. "What the hell is this?"

Waylynn lifted her gaze, the smile disappearing. Her hand automatically clenched the edge of the granite countertop as she locked on her overnight bag in his hands and the gun she'd hidden in the bottom. No. No, no, no, no. She straightened, trying to control the panic exploding behind her sternum. "Elliot, listen to me, it's not what you think."

"Really?" He moved in on her, all predator and her the prey. "Because this looks a lot like the gun that was used to shoot your father fifteen years ago."

Chapter Twelve

Betrayal didn't start with big lies, but with small secrets.

And Waylynn holding on to the evidence in her father's murder investigation all these years was possibly one of the biggest betrayals he'd ever experienced. "Forget about the stash of cash and your passport. Why do you have the gun, Waylynn?"

Her mouth fell open. Ocean-blue eyes snapped to the weapon. "You have to understand, I was fifteen. I was scared. I hid the gun thinking it would all go away. I knew it was wrong, but I thought if the police never found the murder weapon, they'd forget the whole thing."

The world fell out from under him. All this time, she'd kept evidence out of police custody, and a flood of fury burned through him. She'd spent the last four days trying to convince him she'd become the monster she'd feared, but he hadn't listened to any of it. Not her. Not the woman whose smile turned his entire day around. Not the woman who'd held her own in their private country competition. Not the woman he'd fallen in love with over the past ninety-six hours. He'd been wrong. Elliot pointed one finger at her, the weapon tight in his hand. "You lied to me."

"No. I never lied to you." She moved forward, but he countered her advance. Her expression fell as she slowed a few feet from him. "I just didn't tell you the whole truth."

"Then tell me the truth now." Whom the hell had he been protecting? Whom had he taken a bullet for back at the crash site? All this time she'd played the victim, manipulating him to believe her innocence. Had he been staring at—making love to—a murderer instead? Bile pushed into his throat. He'd done a lot of bad stuff in his life, but he'd drawn the line at murder. And Waylynn... "Did you kill your father?"

She picked at her chipped nails, her throat working to swallow. Her shoulder rose on a deep inhale and she dropped her hands to her sides, her mind made up by the sternness in her expression. "I can't tell you that. Because if I do, you won't see me as a friend anymore... as a partner. I need you to trust me."

"Can't? Or won't?" He turned his back to her, the gun still in his hand. How had he not seen it before? He'd read the police report of that night. Police hadn't been able to recover the murder weapon and he'd chalked it up to human error. Evidence went missing all the time in high-profile cases like Nathan Hargraves's. In reality, the truth crushed the air from his lungs. "I just found a gun from a fifteen-year-old murder in your bag. Any trust you earned with me is gone."

"Please." She reached out for him, but suddenly thought better of it. "Elliot, I wish I could—"

"Could what?" Twisting around, he struggled to contain the rage exploding through him. "Take it all back? Tell me the truth from the beginning? I put my life on the line, took a bullet and nearly died in a fire for you. Because I believed you were innocent." Pain set up residence behind his sternum. She'd played him, manipulated him. Used him. Just as his parents and the Iraqi guards had with their head games and steel bars. "You're just as guilty as the bastard targeting you, aren't you? You killed your father and hid the evidence to avoid prosecution. I guess you were right before, Waylynn. You are a monster."

He regretted the words the moment they left his mouth, but the damage had already been done. No matter how much his instincts protested that statement, she'd killed a man in cold blood and kept the evidence hidden.

And he couldn't love her.

Waylynn blinked as though shock had punched her straight in the stomach and shot her hand out toward the counter for balance. Swiping her tongue across her bottom lip, she nodded, but refused to look at him. Shame. Guilt. Reality closed in on her features, and his gut clenched. In an instant, the grief had passed, control crossing her expression as she nailed him with her cold gaze. "What about the lies you've told, Elliot? What about the people you've hurt or the money you've stolen?" She pulled the storage device from his laptop and held it up. "What about the fact you swore to me you've never investigated my background, but have my father's police report on this thumb drive?"

"You're comparing my job protecting you to homicide?" He shouldn't have lied about the investigation

into her past, but he'd told her the truth. There was no
file on her. He hadn't started gathering information to
use against her like he had the others. He hadn't had any
intention of ever blackmailing her down the line. He'd
requested the report from Vincent to make sure what
was happening now wasn't tied to her past. That was his
job. The second they'd tied Genism to Alexis's murder,
he'd pulled the file into the trash. Only he hadn't realized there was a copy left on the thumb drive. Elliot set
the gun on the counter, leaving it wrapped in the old
T-shirt—the one spotted with blood—to preserve any
fingerprints it might've held on to over the last fifteen
years. It took every ounce of energy not to sink to the
floor as his heart tore itself to pieces. "I'm only going
to ask you one more time and I want an answer. Did
you kill Nathan Hargraves?"

"I think you already have the answer you want. I'm
a monster, remember?" Anger hollowed her voice, but
she'd had to have known this day would come. Ripping her overnight bag from his grasp, she tucked it
under her arm and headed for the front door. Hand on
the dead bolt, she slowed. "Are you going to turn the
gun in to the police?"

The bullet wound in his shoulder burned with renewed vigor. The last four days—aside from getting
tasered, shot and nearly roasted to death—had been the
best in his life. She'd given him a glimpse of real happiness. Given him a glimpse of the future. One where
he didn't have to worry about the debt hanging over his
head, putting his life on the line every day for people
he didn't know, or looking over his shoulder the rest
of his life for victims of his past. There was only her.

And she was going to throw that all away. Blackhawk Security operatives protected those who couldn't protect themselves, by any means necessary. They broke laws, avoided authorities, kept their clients alive at the cost of their own lives. They hunted murderers. They didn't become them and they sure as hell didn't protect them. "Yes."

She nodded but refused to look back at him. She wrenched the door open. "I trusted you, too, Elliot. Remember that when you realize the mistake you've made, but don't you dare come looking for me. I don't *ever* want to see you again."

The cabin windows shook as she slammed the door behind her.

He should go after her. They were in the middle of the woods, for crying out loud. Chances of her getting lost, running into Mabel and her calves or something far worse happening increased with every step she took outside the perimeter of the cabin. But he couldn't force himself to move. He stretched the fingers of his uninjured hand, only now realizing he'd drawn blood with his nails. Pressure built in his head the longer he stared after her. He didn't protect killers and that was exactly what she was. A cold-blooded killer.

"Son of a bitch." She shouldn't be out there on her own. She'd betrayed him, manipulated him, but he didn't want to find the woman dead in the morning. The sun had met the horizon, darkness was closing in. Elliot scooped his phone, the gun and keys from the countertop and hit the speed dial for Blackhawk's forensics expert on his way to the front door. Two rings. Three. He exhaled hard as Vincent Kalani's voice mail filled the line. "I promise to stop stealing your lunch from the office fridge if you call me back in the next two minutes. No promises after that."

He hung up. Falling snow melted against his exposed skin as he wrenched open the SUV's driver's side door and climbed behind the wheel. Tossing his phone into the passenger seat, he engaged the headlights. Hell, he hated the snow. Pulling a flashlight from the supplies stashed under the back seat, he scanned the clearing around the cabin. Nothing but thick trees stared back at him as his boots hit the ground and he headed deeper into the forest. The headlights helped, but not much. "Waylynn!"

No answer.

Footprints imprinted in the dirt at the bottom of the cabin steps. Hell if he knew the plan when he found her. Turn her over to his team at Blackhawk Security? Drive her directly into Anchorage PD custody? He had to find her first. He'd worry about the plan later. Elliot brushed aside low-hanging branches, dry foliage and twigs crunching beneath his weight. He followed her shallow footprints. "Come on, Doc. Where are you?"

She couldn't have gotten that far on foot. Not in the dark. The road they'd driven up was the only clear path to the main highway, but sooner than he expected, her footprints disappeared. The ground was too dry here. Slowing, he held his breath to listen for any sign of movement, any sign she was close by. An owl hooted above him, kicking his nerves into high alert. "Waylynn!"

Running a hand through his hair, he dislodged snowflakes and wiped his hand down his jeans. Tendrils of their conversation—of him finding the gun—played through his head on repeat. No. The only reason he'd come out here was to make sure she paid for what she'd done. Nothing more. Elliot swung the flashlight into the tree line on either side of the road. No sign of her. He exhaled hard, dropping the flashlight to his side. His senses adjusted slowly to the dark, but it didn't make a damn bit of difference.

He was too late.

She'd disappeared.

YOU ARE A MONSTER.

Waylynn swiped at her face for the millionth time as she pushed through thick wilderness and dead leaves. Branches scraped at her skin, drawing blood, but she couldn't stop. Couldn't go back. Hadn't she gone far enough to reach the main road?

Exhaustion claimed her muscles as she'd practically run from the cabin—from him—but she hadn't had any other choice. He was going to turn over the gun used to kill her father to the police. She locked her teeth against the truth. He was going to turn *her* over. Her side of the story wouldn't matter. Not when it came to homicide. Even fifteen years later. The statute of limitations would never run out.

She had money. Her passport was still valid. She could run. She'd stored the thumb drive with her research into her bag. There were plenty of labs around the country who'd be willing to take her on. She'd be cleared of Alexis's murder. Officer Ramsey had all but indicated she was before Waylynn had left the scene of the fire at Genism.

Instead, she slowed her pace as dead silence and

blackness surrounded her. A short burst of laughter escaped up her throat. Whom was she kidding? Unless she changed her name—started a whole new life—Elliot would find her. That was his job. Hugging her bag closer, she leaned against a large tree for support. She struggled to catch her breath and checked over her shoulder. Only hints of sunlight reached this far into the forest. She'd stuck to the road leading to his cabin for a few hundred feet but trailed off as she'd heard him call her name. No. He didn't get to come after her, didn't get to apologize.

He didn't get to play the hero this time.

"Come on, Hargraves. You've got to move." Blinking back the haze of anger, she forced one foot in front of the other. She couldn't stay out here all night. Snow had started falling again, temperatures dropping even in the middle of summer. Elliot had unloaded the tiny cabin close to the mountain range and if she got stuck out here for another hour, she'd freeze to death. And she just couldn't give him the satisfaction.

Frigid wind slammed into her, cutting through the light sweatshirt she'd brought with her. Straight down into bone, but she pushed on. Where was the damn highway? Her teeth chattered as a thousand different emotions bubbled inside her. Fury, confusion, hurt. A sharp ache expanded from behind her sternum. Or was it from the invisible knife he'd stabbed into her back? She'd protected herself—kept herself from opening up to anyone—for the past fifteen years, but Elliot Dunham had shoved her from one end of the emotional gauntlet to the other in seconds. Mere hours ago, she'd been wrapped in his arms, whispering promises, making plans. He'd made her believe they could be happy, that he didn't care about the darkness ingrained in her genetic code.

Then he'd destroyed it all. He'd confirmed the fear she'd carried with her since taking her very first blood test in Genism's warrior gene trial, the trial based off her research.

She'd let him in. And he'd betrayed her.

How could she have been so stupid? A growl escaped from between her lips, embarrassment heating her from the inside, but it wasn't enough to make a difference in her frozen fingers or numb toes. She shook her head and tried to bundle deeper into her sweatshirt. Maybe if she kept thinking of all the stupid decisions she'd made over the last four days—how she'd actually believed he could love her—she'd generate enough body heat to keep her alive out here.

"Where is the damn road?" Waylynn slowed again, listening for any sign she was headed in the right direction. Elliot hadn't driven more than twenty minutes off the main highway. She'd covered at least a mile on foot, what she could feel of her feet aching in the thin shoes offering no support. What exactly was her plan once she reached the road? Flag down a vehicle? Hitchhike to the meeting with her former lawyer at the marina? Chances of finding someone going straight there were slim. She deflated on the spot, knees weak, exhausted. And her heart… She rubbed at her chest as a fresh wave of tears burned in her eyes. Her heart was tired, damn it.

White light moved over her, and she raised her hands to block the beams. The air rushed from her lungs. Headlights. The sound of tires on road grew louder, then softer within a beat of her pulse. Shoving to her feet, Waylynn ignored the pain and followed the retreating vehicle until her shoes hit solid ground. A burst of relieved laughter escaped her throat. She'd made it and another car was approaching.

"Hey!" She stepped out a few feet into the road, swinging her arm overhead. The car arched away from her, didn't stop. Two more cars passed, neither pulling over. She couldn't miss the meeting with Blake Henson. Everything—finding Alexis's murderer, avoiding a murder in the first-degree charge, getting her job back—depended on it. She should've stolen Elliot's keys and taken the SUV, but she'd had to put as much distance between them as possible. Walking backward, Waylynn stuck out her thumb as another vehicle approached. "Please pull over. Please."

The car drove straight past her.

"You've got to be kidding me. Really? Is there no such thing as human decency left in this city!" Dropping her hand, she kicked hard at a loose rock on the shoulder. Clouds turned violet, blue and orange as the sun continued its slow crawl across the horizon, barely making the road in front of her visible. Screeching tires filled her ears and she snapped her head up. The sleek black car had stopped in the middle of the road. Waited. For her? Exhaust and a hint of gasoline filled her lungs as she took a single step toward the vehicle. The hairs raised on the back of her neck, her scalp pulling tight in warning. That car was the only one that'd stopped, was her only shot of getting out of here and to her meeting, but no matter how hard she pushed for her feet to move, they wouldn't obey.

No. Something wasn't right about this.

Red taillights highlighted asphalt as the driver put the car in Reverse and her instincts kicked into a nervous overdrive. She twisted around, headed in the opposite direction. Shoving her hands into her pockets, she held her bag close to her ribs. She should've grabbed the gun before running into the woods. She scanned the road in front of her. Twigs. Small rocks. Nothing that could really be used to protect herself. Air froze in her lungs as the car reentered her peripheral vision driving backward down a seventy-mile-an-hour highway.

The passenger side window slid down, the outline of the driver clear, but she refused to look up. Another car sped past, but she caught the driver's question above the noise of tires and road. "Need a ride?"

"No, thank you." Waylynn pushed the pain in her feet to the back of her mind. She had to keep walking. Sweat beaded at her temple despite the dropping temperatures. "I'm fine."

Shoving the vehicle into Park, the driver hit the pavement, one arm draped over the roof. "Come on now, Dr. Hargraves. Get in. At least let me get you to the meeting with your lawyer."

She stopped cold. Puffs of crystallized air formed in front of her lips, every muscle in her body strung tight. She raised her gaze, only the shadowy outline of the driver visible. Male. Tall. At least six feet. Wearing a baseball cap. No facial features she could make out. Nothing to suggest she'd met this man before. "How do you know my name?"

How did he know about the meeting with her lawyer?

"I know everything about you, Waylynn." He slammed

the door closed and rounded in front of the headlights. The falling snow, coupled with the fact he was too tall for the headlights to identify him, pooled dread at the base of her spine. But it was the gun in his hand that claimed most of her attention. "And the best thing you can do for yourself is get in the car."

Waylynn ditched her bag and ran like the devil. Broken branches and vines threatened to trip her as she headed for the trees. She wouldn't look back. Wouldn't see if the driver had followed her. Wouldn't give up that easily. She was a survivor and she'd fight like hell to stay that way. Her lungs burned with shallow breaths, but she didn't slow. Because the crunching sound of dead foliage and twigs behind her meant he'd come after her. Pain pulled at her, slowed her down. No. This wasn't how she was going to die.

Two gunshots exploded in her ears and she wrapped her hands around the back of her head in an attempt to protect herself from a bullet. Pain erupted through her left arm instead and she screamed as her nerve endings caught fire. She plowed into a tree shoulder-first as the initial shock took hold, momentum spinning her toward the shooter. Her flimsy shoe caught on a root climbing from the earth and she fell back. Dead leaves and dirt worked into her eyes and mouth as she rolled down the small incline. Waylynn shot her hand out to grab something—anything—to keep her from falling and latched on to a loose root.

The world fought to right itself as the dizziness fled. She pulled at the root with her uninjured arm, but adrenaline could push her only so far. She was exhausted, bleeding. Her ears rang, but through the high-pitched

keen, she picked up the sound of rushing water. A river.
Looking down at her feet, she suppressed the scream
working up her throat at the sight of how close she'd
come to death. She struggled for purchase no more than
twelve inches from the edge of a small cliff that ended
in a raging river below. She couldn't breathe, couldn't
think, her hand gripped tight around the root. If the
madman who'd shot her in the middle of the damn wilderness didn't kill her, the river would. Waylynn tugged
at the root again, but it gave way. Another scream escaped as reality set in. No one could help her now.

A rough hand clamped onto her arm a split second
before she plunged into the violent waters below, a hand
with a raised scar across the back. "Oh, no, Dr. Hargraves. I'm not finished with you yet."

Chapter Thirteen

You are a monster. Had he really thrown that in her face? The constant replay of their conversation echoed in his head as he hiked through another trail leading toward the main road. It was stupid to give in to the guilt eating him alive from the inside when he finally understood what she was, but the emotion proved too strong to fight. He'd used her one fear against her and now she was missing. Damn it. As far as he could tell, she'd headed straight into the woods to lose him.

Three sets of headlights illuminated the trees and brush around him. He tapped the earpiece he kept on hand to connect to the rest of the team when they came into range and stepped out into the small dirt road leading up to the cabin. Vincent, Elizabeth, Sullivan and Anthony all hit the dirt at the same time and surveyed their surroundings. Just as they'd been trained. "Hey, look. It's the strippers I ordered."

"You can't afford me." Sullivan Bishop took the phone Vincent offered him, swiping his thumb over the screen, and held it up. He turned in a wide circle. The former Navy SEAL had come strapped and ready for war. They all had. "How long has she been on foot?"

Elliot strangled the guilt and rage. He never should've let her walk out that door, but neither did him a damn bit of good right now. Now all he could do was find her. "An hour. She headed down the road for about two hundred feet, then veered north, straight into the woods. I've searched four grids, all around the spot she took cover in the trees. No sign of her."

"We're out of range." Elizabeth stuffed her own phone into her pocket. "There's no way she would've been able to call someone for a ride. She has to still be out there."

Not only were they out of range, but he'd also ditched her phone when he'd determined it was tapped, right before the car accident. No. She couldn't call anyone. Couldn't ask for help.

"By 'took cover' you mean went into hiding?" Sullivan asked. "What the hell happened, Dunham? Last time I checked, that woman wouldn't leave your side."

Elliot ran his uninjured hand through his hair. What'd happened? He'd screwed up. That was what had happened. There were at least a dozen other ways he could've approached the subject of the gun, but instead, he'd taken her betrayal personally. Searching for her a quarter mile in every direction, clearing his head, worried he'd find her body out here, he'd realized she hadn't kept her father's murder weapon to hurt him. She'd kept it to protect herself. Physically or from a murder charge, he had no idea. Didn't change the fact he'd trusted her, believed her innocence, had slept with her, but he never should've judged her for how she'd chosen to survive. As she'd rightly pointed out, he'd done things—hurt people—to do the same. Waylynn was gone, but he sure as hell wouldn't give up on finding her. "All that matters is that we find her."

Wrenching his SUV driver's side door open, he gripped the gun Waylynn had left behind and handed it to Vincent with the old T-shirt still wrapped around the handle. No more lies. No more secrets. The forensics expert would tell him who killed Nathan Hargraves and then he would get back out there and search this entire state if he had to, to find her. "I need you to run prints on this as soon as possible."

And if they came back as Waylynn's... He'd figure it out after he found her.

"All right. I'll do it." Vincent Kalani towered over him, a Hawaiian giant with tattoos up and down his neck and curly, black hair that extended to the middle of his back. Unfolding his arms, the former cop pointed a single finger at him with one hand and took the gun with the other. "But only if you swear to stop stealing my food."

He'd do whatever he had to, to get to the truth. His future depended on it. "Deal."

"I've got my equipment in the SUV. Give me a few minutes." Vincent headed toward his vehicle with the gun in hand.

"I'm going back out there." Someone had targeted Waylynn. Set her up for murder. Even if she got to the main road, she wouldn't last long on her own. No matter what Vincent's final report indicated or what Elliot had said to her before she'd run out the door, this wasn't over. He checked the batteries in his flashlight, then the magazine in his Glock, and reholstered the weapon. "Even if it takes all night."

Anthony handed Kevlar and weaponry to Elizabeth, Sullivan and Elliot.

"Tell us where you want us." Sullivan waited for an answer, the rest of the team's weighted attention on him. Every one of them had dropped what they'd been doing to aid in the search for Waylynn. Anthony and Elizabeth both had kids now, were risking their lives and their family by getting involved. Blackhawk Security's team leader and founder had proposed to his army prosecutor. Vincent didn't have anybody as far as Elliot knew, but that didn't stop him from showing up and doing what he could to help. They'd all come out here because he needed them.

Because they were his team. Because they were the only family he had left.

Warmth spread through him at the thought. His parents hadn't given a damn about him. He'd been another set of hands to work the land. The Iraqi guards hadn't given a damn about him. He'd been their prisoner, someone to punish. But these people did. Waylynn did. Elliot curled his fingers into his palms. And he didn't deserve any of it. The moment she'd gotten close, gave him a glimpse of what could be, he'd searched for an excuse to wedge between them. All because he thought he knew what real happiness was. In reality, he'd had no idea. Not until he'd met her. Then again, murder was a pretty good excuse not to commit to someone. "Elizabeth and I will search the remaining grids to the north. Sullivan and Anthony, work your way down the road in case she doubled back. Meet back here in thirty minutes."

"You heard the man. Let's move out." Sullivan and

Anthony moved as one toward the road as headlights filtered through the thick trees. Another SUV climbed up the small incline toward the cabin and the team visibly tensed. "Stand down. It's Kate with the profile you asked for. She tried relaying the intel earlier, but we got disconnected on the way out here. Your cell service really sucks."

Yet Waylynn had been able to get through to her lawyer without any problems.

"I'll keep that in mind." As much as Kate's profile might help them narrow the suspect pool, it wouldn't do them any good until they recovered Waylynn. Even now, his nerves were fraying at the ends for not having her close. And if something had happened to her out here... Nausea churned in his gut. He'd spend the rest of his life with that weight. Whatever her crimes, she didn't deserve to be hunted like an animal for the rest of her life. He closed in on Kate's SUV as the former psychologist climbed out of the driver's seat.

And slowed.

Where grief normally shadowed the blonde's expression, the hopelessness in her gaze pierced him straight to the core. "Something's happened."

"I'm sorry, Elliot. I pulled over on the side of the highway at the road entrance to see if she'd made it that far." The team converged on their profiler as Kate reached into the SUV, her focus entirely on him. She slammed her door closed, holding a medium-sized brightly colored bag at her side. "And I found this."

Waylynn's bag.

A high-pitched ringing filled his ears, a cold sweat shooting down his back. He forced himself to reach for the bag and curled his fingers in the faux tanned leather. The weight pulled at him and he didn't have to look inside to know it was still full of her clothing and toiletries. "Where?"

Kate crossed her arms and leaned her weight against the SUV, her voice hollow. Platinum blonde hair escaped the tight bun at the back of her neck as she pulled her phone from her signature green cargo jacket, her husband's. She offered him the device. "About thirty yards from the road. I took a picture before moving it. Looked like she'd ditched it in a hurry. I had to recollect some of the items that'd fallen out. Including this."

Blackhawk's profiler handed him an all-too-familiar storage drive.

The one Waylynn had used to save her research.

Elliot tightened his grip on the phone. Kate was right. From the looks of it, Waylynn had obviously ditched the bag in a hurry, but she never would've left her research behind. Which meant… "He has her."

"What's the profile say, Kate? We've got to find this bastard before someone else gets hurt." Sullivan took the phone before Elliot could crush it in his hand and studied the photo.

Elliot didn't hear a damn word. Forget the investigation. Forget the profile. Forget Vincent's report. The SOB who'd framed Waylynn for murder had reached the end of his rope. He was going to kill her. Racing for the SUV, he ignored the pain shooting through his shoulder and ripped open the driver's-side door. He tossed her bag in the back seat and shoved the keys into the ignition.

"Elliot, you're not going to find him on your own."

Elizabeth Dawson planted her palms on the hood of the vehicle, short dark hair swinging forward from behind her ears. "We're a team. You need us."

"You're not going to want me on your team after you see what I do to him." The words growled from his throat. He revved the engine. He'd never hurt Liz, but he had no problem making her think he would to get to Waylynn. She was the only one who mattered. She was...everything. And he loved her. Didn't matter if she'd killed her father. Didn't matter she'd hidden the evidence for the last fifteen years. Or if she'd turn into someone he didn't recognize years down the road from some genetic marker. She was his. And he had to get to her. Now.

"Probably." Elizabeth held up her phone, the Genism logo clear in the upper left-hand corner of the screen. "But I'm the one who knows how to find her."

He put the SUV in Park and got out. "What is that?"

"I was able to save a chunk of data to my computer from the hard drive before it was stolen. Braxton's been working on it since the break-in. Says he's going to kill the guy himself if he finds him." Elizabeth offered him the phone. "He recovered a readable copy of the list Alexis Jacobs was building from the genetics trials and just sent it to me. Names and everything."

Elliot ran his finger down the side of the screen. Adrenaline sharpened his senses, hiked his blood pressure rate higher. They had a lead. If one of the people on this list put their hands on Waylynn... He focused on one name in particular, reading it three times before the puzzle pieces fell into place, and let the violence boiling inside him take control. "I know where he took her, and I know who he is."

A HIGH-PITCHED WHIRLING sound pulled her from unconsciousness.

Waylynn swallowed around the horrible taste in her mouth. Dirt and…salt? Straightening her neck, she oriented herself and blinked to clear the haze. Her shirt had plastered to her skin, soaked. With blood. Where was she? Movement registered a few feet away from her and she tensed. But couldn't move. Panic exploded through her and she pulled at her wrists as the flood of her last moments before her attacker injected her with a syringe rushed forward. She shut her eyes tight to work through the burst of pain in her arm. How could she have forgotten she'd been shot? "You shot me."

A wave of dizziness pitched her stomach into nauseous territory. Or had the white stuccoed surface beneath her actually moved?

"I've seen what you're capable of, Dr. Hargraves, remember?" Her lawyer, Blake Henson, crouched in front of her, a drill in his scarred left hand. The opposite hand he'd used to give her his business card back at the lab. Fear climbed up her spine, tightening the muscles down her spine. It was him. Blake Henson killed her assistant. Drugged her. Framed her for murder. Impossibly blue eyes steadied on her as she fought the churn of nausea working up her throat. "I couldn't take any chances."

"In that case, I have a problem with the customer service here. Can I speak to the manager?" She forced herself to look past him, to the steering wheel and small windshield, the padded seats, the clean, tan-and-navy

color scheme. Salt and humidity dived into her lungs.
They were on a boat. Maybe at the marina where she
was supposed to meet him. Only now she understood.
He'd never intended to hand over those documents and
help clear her name. He'd set all of this up from the beginning. But none of that explained the drill in his hand.
Didn't matter. She wasn't going to hang around long
enough for him to use it. Stretching her fingers behind
her, she brushed against the seat at her back but didn't
feel anything that could be used to free herself. "You
killed Alexis. Destroyed my research. Framed me. What
did I ever do to you?"

"Yes, well, I had to make it look like you'd do anything to protect your precious warrior gene trials after
I killed Alexis." Henson slipped his index finger over
the trigger of the drill. "Shame, too. I was actually starting to think she and I had a future together. I was going
to propose." His expression hardened in the dim light
coming off the horizon. "Then she started compiling a
list of Genism employees and consultants who tested
positive for the warrior gene, my name included. When
my firm had first been put on retainer, we were asked
to provide a blood sample by the board of directors.
Genism policy. Once she confirmed I carried the variant, too, she'd started pulling away. Wouldn't return my
calls." Her lawyer gripped the drill so hard in his apparent anger, he didn't notice the extra drill bit magnetized
to the base of the tool had slipped to the boat's deck.
"She was going to go to the board, cost me everything
I'd worked for the last fifteen years. She was going to
leave me. And I couldn't have that."

Waylynn positioned her foot over the slim piece of

steel. It wasn't much as a weapon, but it was something. Maybe enough to cut the plastic around her wrists. She just had to keep him talking. "And somehow you learned about my past."

"Your previous murder accusation did come in handy." Anger consumed his expression, a glint that was dark and violent and utterly menacing, but she'd seen scary. And this man? He didn't have Elliot's smile. "Who better to pin your assistant's death on than a woman who's already shown she's capable of murder?"

Her heart panged at the simple thought of Elliot's name, but she bit back the urge to react. She had to stay in control. She had to get out of this. Because he wasn't coming to save her this time. Pulling her foot inward, she maneuvered the drill bit that much closer toward her hand. She didn't bother denying her lawyer's allegation. The courts had brought the charges against her fifteen years ago despite the truth and he wouldn't give a damn about what'd really happened. A few more inches. That was all she needed. "And Matt? What did he have to do with any of this?"

"A tool. Nothing more." Blake Henson stood, his knees popping as he straightened. Two steps. Three. He placed the drill above a large, clear, plastic box she hadn't noticed until now and compressed the trigger. The high-pitched whirling started again as pressure built in her chest.

Waylynn dug her heels into the deck. Oh, no. No, no, no, no. This wasn't happening. Darkness closed in around the edges of her vision, her breath coming in short bursts. Pulling at the zip ties again, she locked her jaw against the scream working up her throat. She wasn't going in that box. Stretching to reach the drill bit sticking out from beneath the heel of her shoe, she cut the edge of her finger.

The sound of the drill died as Blake Henson pulled the steel bit from the box. "Alexis showed me the list she built identifying subjects who carried your little warrior gene. Of course, I was surprised to find you on the list, Doctor. Didn't think you had it in you. No pun intended." His short burst of laughter only solidified the dread pooling at the base of her spine. "From there it wasn't hard to aim Matt Stover in your direction. He felt lied to, manipulated, believed you'd destroy everything you and he had built for Genism for your own gain. Of course, some of those ideas might not have been his own. I gave him the idea to start tracking your phone, to wait for the perfect opportunity to strike when you were released from police custody."

"Why defend me at all?" she asked. "Why not let the police charge me with murder? You said you were my lawyer!"

"I wouldn't be playing my part if I hadn't shown up in my legal capacity. It would have been conspicuous by my absence." A furrow appeared between his eyebrows, as though his answer hadn't been obvious. "I needed you close. I needed you to not suspect I was the one who'd killed Alexis in case your memory returned. The cocktail I dosed you with that night is powerful, but not always reliable."

"So many bodies." But she wouldn't be one of them. Waylynn palmed the drill bit and worked at the zip tie behind her back. No. She'd fight because she'd had to her entire life. She didn't know how to die quietly. Was the drill bit cutting through the plastic? She had no idea, but she wasn't going to sit here and let Blake Henson decide what to do with her. And she was done being his puppet. "You're a psychopath."

"I prefer *creative*." He set the drill down on the driver's seat and hefted the lid off the box. "Like it? I'd like to say I came up with the idea all by myself, but your colleagues were really the ones who gave me the idea. You see, this plastic is near unbreakable. It can keep a number of contaminants from escaping the lab, only I've made a few adjustments to suit my needs."

She was running out of time. The drill bit hadn't cut through the zip ties as fast as she thought it would and Blake Henson's tone suggested he'd started winding down. "What did you drug me with that night? Why couldn't the toxicology report find anything after the police took my blood?"

"You're stalling, Dr. Hargraves." Her lawyer laid the lid to the box—her intended coffin—against the side of the boat. In her next breath, he stood over her. "Whatever you're planning, it won't work. I made the mistake of trying to come at you indirectly twice now, but I've learned my lesson."

Desperation clawed through her. Time had run out. Waylynn tugged at the zip ties. "You don't have to do this. Just because you're a carrier for the warrior gene doesn't mean the board will let you go. I can help you. I can—"

"I'm not interested in your help, Doctor. You've already cost me everything I cared about." Gripping her arms, Blake Henson ripped her from the deck. The boat swayed, forcing her into him. He tugged her toward the clear box, the one he'd drilled holes into. "And now it's your turn."

"All this talking is giving me a headache." Trying to wrench out of his hold, she aggravated the bullet wound in her arm and nearly lost consciousness from the agony tearing through her. How could Elliot still stand after taking a bullet in the shoulder? Her flimsy shoes slipped on the boat's deck, but he only held her tighter. He was so much stronger, so much bigger, but she kept fighting. She'd die in that box if she gave up now. "No!"

The zip ties snapped. Swinging the drill bit as hard as she could, she planted it straight into his arm, in almost exactly the same location he'd shot her. His roar threatened to burst her eardrums a split second before the back of his hand met her face. Waylynn hit the deck. Hard. Temporary blackness clouded her vision, but she pushed to her feet. Couldn't stop. Pain lightninged through her arm, threatening to undo her, as she lunged for the back of the boat. "Help!"

A bloodied hand wrapped around her mouth and pulled her into her attacker's chest. Blake Henson's mouth pressed against her ear. "You're going to pay for that."

She wrenched her elbow back as hard as she could but lost momentum as he hefted her off her feet. The boat, the marina, everything blurred as her lawyer tossed her over his shoulder in a fireman's carry. Kicking, punching, she battled to get free with every last ounce of strength.

It wasn't enough.

Dumping her into the plastic box he'd prepared, Henson knocked the air from her lungs, momentarily paralyzing her long enough to get the lid in place.

"No! No!" She pounded on the plastic, each hit reverberating through the box. Kicking at the bottom of the container, Waylynn struggled to lift her knees up enough to gain leverage. There wasn't any room. Small holes provided enough oxygen, but she'd never felt so claustrophobic in her life. He'd sealed her inside her own coffin. She set her palms against the lid as tears streaked down her face into her hairline. "Please. Don't do this."

"The holes I've drilled into the bottom of the box are small enough to ensure you don't die too quickly. Wouldn't want you not to suffer, now would we?" Blake Henson watched her struggle from above. Anchoring his hands on either side of the plastic container, he bent over her. Face-to-face with two inches of biocontainment plastic between them. "Don't worry, Dr. Hargraves. Genism will be fine without you."

Without another word, her lawyer straightened, then hauled her and the box toward the back of the boat. Her throat stung from screaming, her knuckles bled from hitting the lid with everything she had left. No. This wasn't how she wanted to die. Her attacker slid the bottom of the box out the back of the boat, nothing but a sea of black below.

A flashlight beam caught her attention through the plastic.

"Waylynn!" Elliot pumped his legs hard across the dock and she pressed her hands against the lid in an effort to reach out for him.

Right as Blake Henson dropped her into the ocean.

Chapter Fourteen

She was in the water.

Bullets ripped past his head as Blake Henson balanced on the back of his boat, but Elliot had only one focus.

"Waylynn!" His lungs struggled to keep up with the rest of his body as he hurdled over a coil of rope toward the spot he'd seen her go in. If anything happened to her, the bastard would pay, but he couldn't go after the lawyer now. Gunfire erupted from the docks and forced Henson to take cover. Elliot's team had his back and it would have to be enough for now. He tossed the flashlight. One step. Two. He launched himself off the end of the dock.

Freezing water shocked every nerve ending he owned as he hit the water, but it wasn't enough to stop him from diving deeper. Bubbles and darkness made it nearly impossible to see through the water. His ears popped as he sank lower, pressure building in his lungs. He couldn't see her. Stretching out his hands, he grazed something hard and latched on to the smooth edges of what felt like a large aquatic box for swimming with sharks. His senses adjusted slowly, murky water and seaweed clearing just enough—enough to see her terrified expression through the container Henson had sealed her in.

She beat against the lid wildly. Bubbles escaped the small holes down by her feet, the water level slowly rising inside the clear coffin. She was going to drown. Elliot slid his fingers around the edge of the box, ignoring the rush of pain in his shoulder. How the hell had her kidnapper sealed this thing? His heartbeat pounded loud behind his ears as the frigid temperature slowed his movements. Low thumps reverberated through him, bullets from the battle above slicing through the water around them. The water level had reached her knees as the weight of the box pulled her deeper into the ocean.

They were running out of time.

Gripping the edges of the box, he tried hauling it toward the surface. In vain. The damn thing was too heavy, and his muscles had lost strength due to his wound. Elliot tapped on the glass to get her attention and pointed to the ocean floor. He'd swim down to find something—a rock, a stray piece of metal, anything—to pry the container open. Her palms flattened against the clear plastic as he swam deeper into the gloom below them. Tons of water threatened to crush him as he reached the sandy bottom of the marina. Skimming his hand along the surface, he gripped a sharp rock and headed straight back up to where he thought her last position to be.

She wasn't there. Waylynn and the box had shifted with the undertow.

His lungs ached. His body had burned through his oxygen supply faster than he'd estimated. Catching sight of her outline as she sank farther into the depths, El-liot had to make a choice. Surface for air and risk get-ting shot in the process. Or lose consciousness trying to get her out now. Every instinct protested leaving her down here alone, but he had to surface. Rock in hand, he struggled topside. His clothing pulled at him, his boots heavy.

A bright wave of fire consumed the surface as a blast knocked him off course.

Elliot curled in on himself and pushed away from the surface as debris hit the water from an explosion above. An entire leather seat crashed directly above him, but he couldn't kick fast enough to avoid the colli-sion. Metal tore into his thigh, ripping through his jeans, skin and into the muscle. A garbled scream pulled re-served air from his lungs as he clamped a hand down on the wound. The debris had missed major arteries, but he wasn't sure how much time he had left before he passed out from blood loss. He couldn't hold his breath any longer. Every second he wasted cost Way-lynn valuable time and the more he bled, the more pred-ators would start hunting. He pushed to the surface and gasped for oxygen. Pain burned through him with each kick. "Holy hell, that hurts."

"Over here!" Kate screamed over her shoulder from the dock and reached for him. "Give me your hand. I'll pull you out."

"She's stuck down there, Kate, and I can't get her out. I'm not going anywhere." He sucked down air as fast as he could, trying to expand his lungs for another chance. She was alone. She was scared. Heat seared along his face and neck. Pieces of burning wood floated around him. "Find me a tool. A crowbar. Anything that can break through thick plastic."

"Kate! Gear up!" Footsteps sounded on the dock behind her. Vincent appeared at her side, hauling an oxygen tank from his shoulder and dropping scuba gear to the dock. Blackhawk's forensics expert pounded the end of a flare against the pier, bright white magnesium lighting a marina already on fire, then tossed it into the ocean. The red glow flickered as the flare sank. He sparked another and threw it down. "These should help."

"Where's Henson?" he asked.

"Elliot, get down there." Kate ripped her husband's jacket off and stripped out of her shirt. Medium-length, flowing blond hair skimmed her sports bra as she pushed her jeans down her legs. "I'll be ready in fifteen seconds. Go!"

He'd have to ask about the explosion later. After he got Waylynn out of that damn box. Elliot dived. Swimming with every last ounce of strength he had left, he followed the trail of small bubbles coming from the blackness below, lit by Vincent's flares. She still had oxygen. How much, he had no idea, but it wouldn't last forever. Tendrils of blood seeped from both wounds and wove in front of his face, but he only pushed harder. She might've given up on him, but he wouldn't leave her to die.

The light from the flares reflected off a solid surface below. Waylynn. The panic in her ocean-blue gaze cut through him as he gripped onto the edges of the box again. The undertow pulled to rip him away, but he only held tighter. He wouldn't fail her again. Not this intelligent, mind-blowing, sexy creature who'd crashed into his existence and defied everything he'd known about what real happiness was. The box had leveled out along the sandy floor, submerging her in water from head to toe. Water lapped at the edges of her temples as she screamed, dark mascara running down her face.

A gloved hand slipped over his shoulder and he spun to find Kate in full scuba gear beside him. She pulled her mouthpiece free and handed it to him. Exhaling the air he'd been coveting, he maneuvered the rubber into his mouth and inhaled deep. A burst of cold oxygen filled his lungs and he handed the mouthpiece back. The tank had enough oxygen to last the two of them for at least another thirty minutes, but Waylynn...

She wouldn't last much longer.

A sharp pain lanced through him. That wasn't an option. He needed her. He wasn't sure how much until this very moment, but there was no denying it now.

He wedged his hands on either side of the box and kicked with everything he had. The lid didn't budge. The bubbles escaping through the two small holes in the bottom of the container tickled along his skin and face. They had to stop the intake of water. Tapping on Kate's shoulder, he pointed to them. She nodded, swimming behind him and plugging them with her gloves as much as she could. It wasn't a permanent fix, but it'd give Waylynn more time. The water lapped at her mouth and nose as she pressed against the lid of the box. He searched the marina floor, this time in the light of two flares still burning bright a few yards away. Magnesium burned hot enough to melt through the thickest metal. Plastic shouldn't hold one of those flares back. But he could hit Waylynn's skin in the process.

His movements slowed as the frigid temperature cut through his clothing, past skin, past muscle and straight into his bones. He was losing blood with every pump of his legs as he closed in on the nearest flare. Careful not to stare at the magnesium fire directly, he grabbed what was left of the casing and swam as fast as he could to Waylynn.

They were going to get her out. Because if they didn't… He'd go back to prison. Nobody would be able to stop him from tearing Blake Henson apart with his bare hands.

He moved the flare over the lid, shocked to find a wide, dark stain blooming across her white shirt he hadn't noticed before. Blood. Rage threatened to consume him. What the hell had that bastard done to her? Elliot forced himself to focus, forced himself to ignore the haze of red spreading across his vision. One second. Two. Putting the flare to the plastic would get the job done, but there was no way he could protect Waylynn from the heat. He didn't have any other choice. The water lapped at her mouth and nose. She gasped for air, pressing her palms against the container wall.

They were out of time.

Elliot set the flare against the lid. Plastic instantly melted then cooled in the freezing water, but within seconds left a hole wide enough for him to reach his hand through. The clear coffin immediately filled with water, submerging Waylynn completely. He shoved his hand inside the crude hole and ripped the lid from the box.

She was free.

Hauling her into him, he ignored the protest of his body and pumped his arms and legs hard for the surface.

But he'd already lost too much blood. His lungs burned with the need for air. No. He'd just gotten her free from Henson's crude coffin. He wasn't going to let his body be the thing keeping her from staying alive now. His grip lightened on Waylynn and she slipped out of his hand. He grew heavier as he struggled the last five feet toward the surface.

Someone—Kate?—gripped under his arm and pushed him above water. Another gasp reached his ears. Waylynn. Relief flooded through him as Kate helped them maneuver around burning debris toward the dock. Sullivan, Elizabeth and Vincent each bent down to pull them from the water. His back hit the old wood and his breath wheezed from his lungs, momentarily cutting off his air supply and leaving him dizzy. "Let's never do that again."

Waylynn set her cheek against the dock, blue eyes heavy, skin pale. She wouldn't look at him, but it didn't matter. She was alive.

Movement registered out of the corner of his eye near the remnants of Blake Henson's boat. A hand slapped onto the dock, soaking wet, followed by the rest of the SOB who'd taken Waylynn from him.

"There's blood on her clothing." Elliot pushed to his feet, his steps unbalanced. He forced his feet to move, then again, his strength returning in small increments as oxygen filled his bloodstream. "Have her checked out. And if anything else happens to her, I'll put my files on every single one of you to good use."

Vincent hauled Kate's oxygen tank off her shoulders. "What files?"

Waylynn huddled beneath the blanket Sullivan wrapped around her. "Wh-w-where're you going?"

"There's something I need to finish." He tracked Henson onto what remained of the boat. The bastard better have a weapon stashed down below. He was going to need it. Elliot stepped onto the burning deck, his target straight ahead. "Permission to come aboard, Counselor."

GUNSHOT WOUND TO her arm. Mild hypothermia from nearly drowning in the ocean. Days of emotional havoc. Waylynn fisted the blanket one of the men on Elliot's team had provided for her as she waited to be cleared to leave in the back of the ambulance. Paramedics had pulled the bullet from her arm, stitched her up and stabilized her stats. She'd live, but her attacker? He had no idea what kind of violence she'd caged for the last fifteen years. But she'd show him.

A single officer escorted Blake Henson down the dock in cuffs.

Now was her chance.

She dumped the blanket onto the floor and slid from the back of the ambulance. The fishing knife she'd picked up after the Blackhawk Security team pulled her from the water warmed in her hand. No. Henson didn't get to waste away behind bars for the rest of his life. He was going to know exactly what kind of terror he'd put her through the last five days. Even if police apprehended her afterward, her lawyer had already taken everything from her. She had nothing left to lose. She was the only one who could make him pay.

A monster to destroy a monster.

A calloused hand wrapped around hers and the knife, his mouth pressed against her ear. Salt and humidity filled her lungs, his clothing still damp against her arm. "Never considered you the stabby type, Doc."

"Let go of me." Waylynn tried to pull her hand free. Heat burned through her veins as the officer forced Blake Henson into the back of a black-and-white cruiser. The man who'd destroyed her life stared right at her, a small curve to his mouth as the door slammed behind him. Hollowness settled in the pit of her stomach. She snapped her gaze to Elliot's, felt a pull at the sight of those mesmerizing gray eyes. She struggled to wrench out of his reach, the base of the blade cutting into her hand, he held it so tight. The cruiser pulled away and everything inside her went cold. Colder than the ocean the lawyer had left her to drown in. She turned on Elliot, shoving her uninjured hand against his chest. "Why did you stop me? I could've ended this for good."

Blake Henson was on retainer for one of the top genetics labs in the country, which meant he was a damn good lawyer. Genism Corporation hired only the best. Even if he defended himself during the trial, there was a chance he'd be free within months. The attorney blamed her for ruining his life.

She might not survive the next time he came after her.

Elliot held strong despite the leg injury he'd endured trying to save her life. Blood still soaked through his jeans and her shirt, a violent reminder of the night's events. His expression hardened, but his grip on her wrist lightened. "You're not a killer, Waylynn."

She froze. He wasn't serious, was he? Her skin felt

too tight for her body under the weight of his attention. Red and blue patrol lights softened the edge to his expression but weren't enough to change her mind about him. "That's funny coming from you, because the last time we spoke, you called me a monster, you practically accused me of murdering my father and said you'd never trust me again."

"I was wrong." His fingertips traced the vein leading from the oversensitized skin of her wrist upward and a shiver, one that had nothing to do with the dropping temperature, chased down her spine. "About all of it. I'm sorry."

"You're sorry." Waylynn pried her wrist out of his hand, severing contact between them. "You took my biggest fear I believed about myself and you used it against me, Elliot. You hurt me deeper than anyone ever has before, deeper than when my father turned on me and my mother. I trusted you. You were my best friend, the only person I counted on to keep me safe. I... I loved you. But that wasn't enough, was it?" The cold that'd taken residence in her muscles reached her heart.

It took everything in her to turn around and head for Officer Ramsey waiting by her police cruiser. Her apartment wouldn't be the same, wouldn't give her solace like it did before she'd found Alexis Jacobs in her bathtub, but she couldn't stay here. Couldn't face him again—

"I'm not done with you, Doc." His fingers slipped around her arm, twisting her into him. Flecks of ice speckled his hair and beard from his dive into the ocean after her. Tension strained the cords between his shoulders and neck, and the memories of their twenty-four hours spent in passion flashed before her eyes.

She'd hired Blackhawk Security—hired him—to protect her. She owed him her life. She would've died in that coffin if he and his team hadn't intervened, but that had been their job. And none of that changed the fact he'd accused her of murder. Her. The woman he'd contemplated a future with, the woman he'd said he'd take a bullet for. Waylynn set her hand against his chest and closed her eyes to count off his heart rate.

One year. That was all it'd taken to fall in love with him. The beers after work, the '90s country battles, the slow sway of his body against hers outside her assistant's apartment after they'd searched it for evidence Anchorage PD might've missed. Each and every single one of them shredded through her now. She'd given him everything, risked telling him her deepest, darkest secret for the glimpse of a normal life. With him. And he'd thrown it in her face.

"Thank you for saving my life. Three times." Somehow, even after all the tears she'd shed over the past few hours, her lower lash line burned. But she wouldn't let them fall this time. She was stronger than that. Her heart lurched in her chest. He might not be done with her, but she'd made her decision. She opened her eyes, pressed him away. She was done with him. "I warned you about the people you push away, Elliot. Not all of them come back. Have Sullivan send me the invoice for your services. Then you can be free of me."

Turning her back to him was one of the hardest things she'd ever done in her life. It'd be so easy to forgive him. So easy to bury herself in his muscled arms.

So easy to forget everything that'd happened the last five days. But what they'd had together had been a fantasy. Because no matter how close she'd come to death, she was the same person. And so was he.

She'd kept Officer Ramsey waiting long enough. Waylynn forced one foot in front of the other, heading toward the officer's cruiser.

"I don't care if you killed your father," he said.

Panic flared as she studied the crime scene techs and officers around them. "Why don't you say that louder? I don't think the entire police department heard you."

"I had Vincent run the prints on the gun, but I don't care what the report says. I don't care if you turn into a completely different person down the line because of your genetic makeup or if you don't want to leave Anchorage." Warmth slid down her spine as he closed the distance between them. She stepped back, but he only countered her move until her back hit the side of the ambulance. Elliot leveraged one arm above her head and leaned in, his mouth mere centimeters from hers. "I want to wake up to your face every morning and go to bed with you every night. I want to binge-eat peanut-butter Oreos until we're both sick to our stomachs and greet you with a beer after you come home from work. I want to see how much you know about country after the '90s. I want you, Doc. Since the moment I laid eyes on you that day I moved next door, I've wanted you. And I will do anything to make you mine."

His mouth crashed down on hers, his tongue sweeping past her lips to claim her. And she let him. Just like that first time he'd kissed her outside her apartment. One brush of his teeth against her bottom lip and she tumbled head over heels into intoxication. And she could almost forget the fact he'd called her a monster, or that he'd been collecting files on everyone he claimed he cared about.

The pain in her hand intensified as her fingers constricted around the fishing knife. Reality barged through her system and Waylynn ripped away. Escaping from the feel of him pressed against her, she gulped freezing oxygen to clear her head. "I can't do this."

"Here? Because I'm happy to do it somewhere else," he said. "My SUV's over—"

"No. This. Us." She motioned between them. "It's not that you called me a monster, Elliot. I've known what I am—what I might become—for years and have come to terms with it. It's that you said it right after we started talking about a future together. You needed a way out."

The sarcasm in his gaze disappeared. "A way out?"

"You keep blackmail files on the people you rely on to have your back. You're so determined to keep everyone at a distance with your jokes, you never let anyone in because you're afraid they might turn on you." And he had good reason. She shook her head, folding her arms across her midsection in an effort to keep the tremors at bay. "It couldn't have been easy growing up the way you did or easy behind bars after you were arrested in Iraq, but you're not in prison anymore. You're not supposed to look for a way out of the relationships you claim you care about, and I don't want to wake up one morning and find your side of the bed empty, Elliot. And until you realize some people—like the ones on your team—are worth hanging on to… I can't be part of your life anymore. So here it is. Here's your way out."

Elliot ran his palms down his face, the bloodstains on his clothing shifting in the newness of morning light. Tears welled in his eyes, but he refused to look at her. "Who's going to drink all my beer after work every night?"

"I don't know." Her insides shattered. She couldn't swallow around the lump in her throat. Couldn't breathe. Waylynn headed for Officer Ramsey's patrol car, determined more than ever not to look back. Tossing the fisherman's knife across the marina parking lot, she curled her hand around the thin cut across her palm as she walked. "But it can't be me."

Chapter Fifteen

Three days later...

An ear-piercing scream had Elliot reaching for the gun stashed under his pillow. He threw back the sheets and shoved out of bed, not bothering to check the time as the apartment blurred in his vision. He'd made it halfway to the front door before he slowed.

Damn it. Third night in the last three days.

Setting his forehead against the nearest wall, he forced his pulse rate to slow. He dropped the gun to his side. No matter how much he wanted to bust down her front door and chase back the nightmares she suffered from since Blake Henson had tried to drown her in the ocean, Waylynn had made herself perfectly clear. They weren't friends anymore.

He slammed the butt of the gun into the wall. Once. Twice. A growl ripped from his throat, but he forced himself to hide the gun back under his pillow. He might as well start the investigation for his new client. There was no way he'd be getting back to sleep. Not when he knew she was on the other side of the wall, scared, suffering. Alone.

"Hell." What he wouldn't give to drag her back to the cabin, make her forget everything that'd happened. Take back what he'd said, prove he didn't have a backup plan when it came to her. Swiping his hand down his face, he hauled his stupid ass to the kitchen and started the coffeemaker. He opened his laptop and took a seat at the bar, the glow from the screen lighting the rest of the kitchen and living room.

His attention immediately went to the only file folder on the desktop, the one Waylynn had broken into somehow. He entered in his password, the title of her favorite '90s country song, and hit Enter. The file exploded into separate documents, photos and research. Jane Reise, Sullivan's army prosecutor. Anthony Harris. Elizabeth Dawson. Kate Monroe and the intel he'd gathered from the attack on her and her husband last year. The rest of the Blackhawk Security team and then some. Every secret, every lie, every trace of his targets' existence was in these files. He scrubbed his hands down his face. "I hate it when she's right."

Which was often.

Every piece of intel he'd gathered over the last year and stored in this file had been leverage. A reason to distance himself from the people he claimed to care about, just as she'd said. His fingers brushed the small black-and-red thumb drive Kate had recovered from the side of the road. As far as he knew, Waylynn's father's police report was still stored on the device. Along with the research she'd tried to recover before her Genism access had been cut off.

He plugged the drive into the side of his laptop and waited as it loaded. There. At the bottom of the search window. He positioned the mouse over the Nathan Hargraves police report and dragged it into the virtual trash bin. Then he did the same with every single file he'd collected on his team, on his neighbors, on anyone whom he hadn't been assigned to investigate. Except one.

No, he'd keep that one. Because Kate Monroe deserved to know the truth about what happened to her husband. Printing off the pages from that particular file, he dressed quickly, then ejected the storage drive and grabbed the overnight bag he'd hung on to since the night he'd pulled Waylynn from the bottom of the ocean.

The sudden glow of his phone from the couch where he'd tossed it ripped him back. The team had been trying to reach him for three days. Amazing the thing still had a charge after so many damn calls. Scooping the device from the cushion, he answered. "Make it fast."

"Answer the door, Dunham," Vincent demanded.

Three knocks twisted him toward the front door. He disconnected and discarded the phone, rolling back his injured shoulder as he unlocked the dead bolt. Vincent Kalani stood on the other side. Falling back against the door, Elliot ushered the forensics expert inside, but the rigidity and tension in the man's body language announced his intentions before Vincent opened his mouth.

"I didn't steal your lunch if that's why you're here." Elliot closed the door, then set Waylynn's overnight bag onto the couch. He'd been about to break her door down if she didn't answer. This wasn't over. Not by a long shot.

"Ugh. You sound so depressed it makes me cringe.

I wish you would've answered your phone so I didn't have to see your face." The massive former cop handed him a manila file folder. "Thought you might want to see this."

Elliot took the folder with the single sheet of paper inside. Black smudges and a hell of a lot of technical terms stared up at him, but it wasn't hard to understand what was inside. "The fingerprints on the gun aren't Waylynn's."

"Your girl didn't kill her father after all. Fingerprints came back as Nora Hargraves. Her mother." Vincent Kalani studied the small apartment. "You know, some color would really brighten up this dark, sad cave of an existence you've decided to live."

He couldn't focus on the forensic expert's usual insults. He stared at the report. Read it again. And again. Waylynn had been protecting her mother all these years. "Where's the gun?"

"The blood on the woman's shirt belonged to the father. Wife must've been wearing it when she pulled the trigger." Vincent dived into his leather jacket pocket and pulled an evidence bag free, handing the gun that'd killed Nathan Hargraves over. "Case is officially closed."

The weight of the gun kept him grounded. Wouldn't have mattered what the report said either way but knowing Waylynn had been protecting her ill mother all this time only made him love her more. "Will Waylynn be charged with tampering with the evidence?"

"Not unless someone turns her in." Vincent circled around him toward the door. The former NYPD officer reached for the door but turned back. "Back at the docks, you said something about using files against us if something happened to her. You got one on me?"

"Not anymore," he said.

"Good." Vincent swung the door open. "I was afraid I'd have to kill you."

A short scoff escaped his mouth as his teammate closed the door behind him. Elliot had no doubt the forensics expert would follow through, too. As a former cop, Vincent Kalani had embedded himself with some of the evilest kinds of people in New York City. People who could destroy lives if they discovered Vincent had been a cop the whole time. But, the man's secrets were safe with Elliot. Always would be.

And so would Waylynn's.

Because he cared, damn it. About her. She was the person worth risking his own happiness for, the one he couldn't spend the rest of his life without. He grabbed her overnight bag and shoved the flash drive she'd stored her research on and the gun inside. Cool morning air slammed into him as he nearly ripped the front door off its hinges and pivoted in front of her door. Her apartment had been cleared as a crime scene, but pieces of police tape fluttered in the small breeze. He knocked, ready to face his future.

With her.

The door opened, the sight on the other side more than his lungs could bear.

She answered the door and all the reasons he'd thought of to keep his distance from her disappeared. A wavy waterfall of blond hair framed the healing bruises along one side of her jaw and skimmed across her collarbones. Those ocean-blue eyes narrowed on him, the same color as the sling wrapping her left arm. She was everything he'd dreamed of and more. Intelligent, sexy, defiant and strong. And, hell, he wasn't good enough for her.

"Elliot? What are you doing here?" Waylynn tried folding her uninjured arm across her chest, gaze locking on the bag in his hand as she shifted her weight onto one foot. Surprise smoothed the edges of her full mouth, but she didn't move to take her stuff from him. "If you came here to apologize—"

"I wanted to bring back your stuff. The flash drive's in there, along with my MIT shirt you like so much. Kate collected all your things from the side of the highway after…" He offered her the bag to distract himself from the rage burning through him at the thought of that night. "After you'd disappeared. The gun, too."

"Oh." Her mouth parted, hand relaxing down to her side right before she reached out to take the bag from him. "I thought Vincent was running prints on it."

"He did." But the results didn't matter. He knew the truth. The woman standing in front of him wasn't a killer, wasn't a monster.

"So you know who killed my father, then." Dropping the bag beside the door, she rested her weight against it but didn't move to slam the door in his face. Progress. "Are you going to turn me in for keeping the evidence all these years?"

"No." The statute of limitations was still in effect, but he wouldn't have said a damn word even if it wasn't. "I know you were protecting your mom so she didn't have to spend her last days behind bars. I don't blame you. If you can believe it, it only made me fall harder for you.

What I don't understand is why you couldn't tell me the truth. Why keep protecting her after she's gone?"

Her shoulders rose on a strong inhale.

"My mother was a good woman. I wanted her to be remembered that way. Not as a killer. And… I was afraid you'd have me arrested for tampering with the murder weapon." A weak smile played across her mouth, homing his focus to her lips. "Thank you for bringing back my things. But if the police do find out, I don't expect you to lie for me—"

"I deleted all the files I had on my team and your father's police report." He pushed his hands into his jeans. Silence stretched between them for a moment. "You were right. I've been looking for a way out of a lot of situations in my life. My debt to Sullivan, the relationships I have with my team. What I had with you." Rolling an invisible rock on the cement with his boot, he lowered his attention to her perfectly painted red toenails and smiled. "I thought my twisted sense of freedom was the most important contributor to my happiness, but I was wrong." He raised his gaze to hers. "You make me happy, Doc, and if nothing else, I want things to go back the way they were. The thought of losing you completely guts me from the inside, but I'll be happy just to be your friend again. If you'll let me."

Her hand slipped down the edge of the door. "It's not like you to give up."

"I'm not giving up." It was the truth. He'd fight to stay in her life, even if he couldn't have her for himself, and he'd spend the rest of his life trying to make her happy in return. "You're selfless, you're kind, you put others first and will go out of your way to protect the ones you care about, even if you're the one to take the fall. You deserve someone worthy of all those things, Doc. You deserve someone as good as you. You deserve someone better than me and I'm sorry."

"Yeah." She fisted her fingers in his T-shirt and pulled him over the threshold of her apartment. Notching her head higher, she leveled her mouth with his. Her geranium scent filled his lungs with every breath as his heart threatened to beat out of his chest. "You're probably right, but where's the fun in that?"

EVERYBODY HAD AN ADDICTION. Hers just happened to be him.

Need bubbled beneath her skin, moving and flowing as thick as molten lava. And if she wasn't careful, she'd erupt all over the damn place. Hot. Destructive. Unforgiving.

Waylynn kissed him—hard, fast, trying to quench the desire for him she'd ignored for the last three days. Every second without him had been agony. Every night waking up alone from her nightmares had torn her apart a little bit more. She dragged him inside and used her foot to close the door behind them, all the while never taking her mouth off his. Happiness throttled through her unlike anything she'd experienced before. Her hand shook as she framed his jawline and pulled back to catch her breath.

Her skin tingled where he touched her, her nerve endings on fire. For him. He'd risked his life for her, given up his most valuable possession for the chance to be with her. His willingness to try to make this work between them deepened the ache behind her sternum. "What's it like not having a backup plan for once?"

"Not sure yet. I literally deleted the files ten minutes ago. Still hasn't sunk in, but I can tell you the time I took to put them together is now free." His eyebrows bounced on his forehead and she couldn't stop the laugh forcing its way up her throat. "I should tell you I kept one file."

Vulnerability claimed her, and she sank flat on her feet from her toes as she stared up at him. Her hand slipped to his shoulder, careful to avoid the bullet wound on one side. "What file?"

"Kate's," he said.

"Are you going to tell her the truth?"

"I have to. She could still be in danger." Elliot ran a hand through his hair, clearly affected by the event. "She thinks it's over."

Kate had helped save her from Blake Henson's clear coffin at the bottom of the ocean. All this time, the team's psychologist had kept it together after losing the most important person in her life. How? "She deserves to know."

"Nobody knows outside of the team." He held her a bit tighter, reflecting the growing need inside her to keep him as close as possible. Because if she lost him again… No. She couldn't think like that. Couldn't imagine a life without him in it. Didn't want to. "I didn't tell you I was the one who looked into it after the ambush happened and found the shooter a few days later. He'd been off his meds for a while and I got him the help he needed in a hospital."

"Then why keep the file?" she asked.

"Kate needs to know what really went down that

night." Elliot threaded his fingers into her hair at the base of her neck. "If something like that had ever happened to you, I'd want to know the truth."

"Then you should tell her." She nodded. "Just, however you do it, remind her you're the messenger and don't get yourself killed in the process, okay? I almost lost you once. I'm not about to let it happen again."

He buried his nose in her neck and inhaled deep. Elliot squeezed her tight until air pressurized in her lungs, but she didn't dare push away. Lifting his head, he brushed a strand of hair out of her face and tucked it behind her ear. Electric jolts speared through her, her insides, down to her bones as he locked those mesmerizing gray eyes on her. No one had ever looked at her as he did. Like she was important. Like he needed her to breathe. "Careful, Doc, you're starting to make me think you care about me."

"Maybe a little." Her lips spread thin in a wide smile. "I mean you're the only one who knows my secrets. Kind of freeing in a way. I'd like to hang on to that feeling for a while."

"Oh, is that all I'm good for?" Elliot slipped his hands to her waist, swaying them back and forth in a slow rhythm. Taking her uninjured hand, he extended it out away from them and swung her to one side. He set his mouth against her ear as they danced in the middle of her living room, one hand pressed against the small of her back, the other tightening in hers. Thoughts of their first dance outside this very apartment pulled her deeper. "I'll take it. I'll take anything I can get from you for the rest of our lives, but you're going to have to tell me why you have moving boxes all over your apartment sooner or later."

"Aren't you a private investigator?" She studied her living room and the dozens of open boxes, rolls of packing tape and labels. This apartment had once been a safe haven, somewhere she could get away from the demands of her job and binge on peanut butter Oreos and her favorite TV shows as long as she wanted. All the while knowing her best friend lived next door. "Or was kissing me too much of a distraction?"

A deep laugh rumbled through him and she reveled in the vibration running through her body. "You think highly of yourself, don't you?"

"I'm going to be honest. I haven't showered in two days because I can't stand the thought of going back in that bathroom. I've been brushing my teeth over the kitchen sink. It doesn't feel the same as it did before." The images ingrained in her head when she'd found Alexis would stay with her for the rest of her life. And she couldn't stay here anymore. Nerves fired through her as she turned back to him and she licked the dryness from her lips. "So… I bought a place. I'm moving in two days, but it'd be nice to have a bodyguard living with me in case someone else at my company decides to kill me."

"Why, Dr. Hargraves, are you asking me to move in with you?" He stopped swaying, pulled her closer. A brightness in his eyes speared straight through her, filling her with hope, chasing back the darkness that made up her DNA. "Are you sure that's a good idea considering your Dr. Jekyll, Ms. Hyde situation?"

"You've already taken down one monster." She refused to let the events of the last week encroach on this moment and slipped her fingers over the gauze taped to his shoulder. "I think you're up for the challenge."

"You're not a monster, Waylynn." He notched her chin higher and forced her to look at him, all sarcasm, all joking leaving his voice. "You're the kindest, sexiest woman I've ever met and nothing in this world will ever convince me otherwise. Besides, if it turns out you are, I could chain you to the bed, right?"

A wide grin deepened the lines at the edges of his mouth.

"You could try." A soft laugh escaped her throat as she closed her eyes and set her ear over his chest. The strong beat of his pulse kept rhythm with hers, as though they were the same body, the same soul, and she never wanted to move. Except the movers would force her to when they came to load her boxes onto the truck.

"No matter what happens, we're in this together," he said. "I was stupid to push you away. I love you, Doc, and I will prove it to you every day of our lives to make it up to you if I have to."

"Yes, you were, but I still love you. Always have. Always will." The nightmare was over. Officer Ramsey had informed her Blake Henson would serve life behind bars for the murder of her assistant and for his stunt trying to drown her in the ocean. The board had overturned Dr. Stover's decision to let her go and she was free to return to work as soon as she was ready. With a promotion and a raise, considering the events of the past couple of weeks. But maybe taking her work to a different lab wouldn't be the worst thing in the world. As long as Elliot came with her.

Waylynn pulled his mouth to hers and lost herself in him all over again. Would she ever get used to the way he affected her? His clean, masculine scent dived deep into her lungs and sealed the deal. No. Never. He was hers. No matter what happened from here on out, they were in it together. Forever. "Now help me with these boxes. They're not going to pack themselves."

Most important, she had Elliot.

Her best friend. Her bodyguard. Her everything.

Epilogue

Kate Monroe pulled two photo frames from the box and arranged them on her desk in her office, skimming her thumb over the glass. The team had left everything the same since she'd taken her leave, but couldn't they have at least watered the plants?

Three knocks on her door snapped her head up.

Elliot Dunham stood in the doorway, a manila file folder in his hand. The cocky private investigator always had a smile on his face these days. One of the upsides to being in love, and her heart panged. Not out of jealousy. Out of admiration. "Looking good, Monroe."

"Thanks. Glad to see you back, too." She shuffled the paperwork from her last case for Blackhawk Security to a corner on her desk as a distraction. The case had been assigned to her a year ago. Before... She stopped that thought in its track. She'd have to look into that one and see what became of the profile she'd written for Vincent. "How's your life? Does Waylynn need—"

"No, thank you. She's great. Other than she still has nightmares a couple times a week." Hesitation deepened the lines in his forehead as he moved fully into the office. "But she's not why I'm here."

Confusion slithered through her. Elliot hadn't been assigned any new cases as far as she knew. He wasn't supposed to be back in the office until next week. "Do you need a profile?"

"Actually, I'm here because of you." He tossed the folder onto her desk, the sharp corner hitting the back of her hand. The label spelled out her name and she narrowed her attention on him. What was this? "I'm here because your husband is alive, Kate."

* * * * *

COLTON'S RESCUE
MISSION

KAREN WHIDDON

To my dog rescue family, Legacy Boxer Rescue.
Because of you, so many dogs have found
new beginnings. You truly are the heart of the
organization and I love you all!

Chapter One

Snowfall—check. Festive music playing on speakers in all the outdoor common areas—check. Ornate and glittery Christmas decorations both inside and out—final check.

Remy Colton stood on the sidewalk of downtown Roaring Springs, Colorado, and surveyed the merry atmosphere. As director of public relations for The Chateau, the premier luxury destination also known as a little piece of France, Remy couldn't have asked for more perfect holiday weather. With both his family's ski resorts—The Lodge up on Pine Peak and The Chateau, here in the Roaring Springs valley—booked to capacity for the two weeks leading up to Christmas, any snow was always welcome. And they were definitely getting a lot of the beautiful white stuff.

Remy liked to keep busy during the holidays, especially since he'd never really gotten into the holiday spirit. That was never a problem, even though the PR department pretty much shut down until after the New Year. The Chateau attracted a wealthy clientele—sometimes celebrities—and those patrons could be quite demanding. He never minded pitching in, especially on Christmas Eve or Christmas Day, so his employees could spend the holiday with their families.

As for himself, out of necessity, he always made sure to spend a few hours with his own extended family at the elaborate holiday dinner his uncle Russ and aunt Mara hosted at Colton Manor, the 35-million-dollar showpiece of a home they'd constructed up on a hill. While he enjoyed visiting with his cousins and their significant others, he usually hightailed it back to The Chateau as quickly as he could. As far as he could tell, no one ever noticed or minded. If there was one thing his father, Whit, understood, it was the concept that work came before anything else. Clearly, it had never occurred to Whit that Remy might be lonely.

Pushing away the unsettling thought, he forced himself to focus once again on the positives. Nothing like a great snowfall to make the guests happy.

"Excuse me?" A feminine voice, both sultry and with a faintly northeastern accent. Before he could react, she tapped him on the shoulder.

He turned and eyed a tall, blue-eyed woman wearing top-of-the-line ski gear. Not only was she athletic, but she was also strikingly beautiful. He felt a jolt the instant he met her gaze. Probably one of the guests, though he had no idea how he could have possibly missed noticing her. "Yes, can I help you?"

"I asked at the front desk and they sent me out to talk to you. I'm looking for Seth Harris. I believe he's the hotel manager. I've already been up to The Lodge, but they said he wasn't working today."

Seth. His gut clenched. What had his brother done now?

Normally he would have directed her to the gondola

that ran between The Lodge and The Chateau. But she was correct. Seth was off today. Remy caught himself staring and rapidly checked himself. Something about her eyes...

Whoever she might be, she wasn't his brother's usual type. Seth's taste usually ran to leggy, busty blondes.

Since Remy knew better than to let this woman— whoever she was—drop in on Seth unannounced, he simply shrugged. "I believe he'll be working tomorrow, so I'd suggest you check back at The Lodge then."

Instead of nodding and thanking him, she didn't budge. "I've been told you're his brother. I really need to talk to him."

Remy made a mental note to find out which employee had seen fit to give out such personal information. "Are you a friend of his, Ms. ...?"

"Fisher," she stated. "Vanessa Fisher. And I'm not sure if Seth still considers me a friend or not. We were recently engaged, though we're not any longer."

Engaged? This was the woman Seth had wanted to marry? She looked nothing like the shy woman the rest of his family had described. This woman was tall, true. And she did have dark, silky hair. What everyone else must have forgotten to mention was that she was beautiful. Stunning, punch-in-the-gut gorgeous. Her dark blue eyes studied him.

Years of practice had taught Remy how to hide his shock. Nothing Seth did should have surprised him, but when he'd learned his baby brother had gotten engaged, shock hadn't even begun to describe how he'd felt. Sure, Seth had mentioned dating someone named Vanessa. He'd made several trips down to Boulder to visit her. But first he'd gotten engaged and then, in typical Seth fashion, the engagement had been broken off.

Which meant now Remy was actually meeting his brother's former fiancée for the first time.

"Remy Colton," he said automatically, removing his glove and holding out his hand.

She tilted her head before doing the same and slipped her fingers into his. Touching her sent a pleasurable jolt through him, though she appeared completely unaffected. "Remy," she mused. "Interesting name."

Entranced by her smile, he froze. But then the rest of what Vanessa Fisher had said dawned on him. It sounded like Seth had dumped her. Which meant what?

He started to ask, but his befuddled thoughts must have shown on his face because she shook her head before he even got the words out.

"It's not like that." She touched him again, this time on his jacket arm. Remy normally wasn't a touchy-feely kind of person, but for whatever reason he didn't mind *her* touch. "I'm the one that broke things off," she continued. "Seth and I haven't spoken since."

Cocking his head, he considered her. He'd never once in his life envied his younger brother, but for the first time, he did. Something about this woman knocked him off his feet. While he knew none of this was his damn business, he asked, anyway. "And you're now here because…?"

She met his gaze directly. "That's personal. Now can you tell me where to find Seth or not?"

Since he was meeting Seth a few doors down in the trendy faux-Western bar called The Saloon, he shrugged. Hopefully, his brother wouldn't kill him when he walked in with this woman. "Come with me."

They walked along the snowy sidewalks, mingling in with the happy tourists. This time of year, everyone in Roaring Springs seemed to be in a celebratory mood. They came, they skied, they shopped and ate and drank. Since the townspeople earned seventy-five percent of their income in the winter, the locals were grateful for the crowds.

When they reached The Saloon, the line that had formed spilled out onto the sidewalk. Despite this, those waiting laughed and chatted without the typical impatience that moneyed people often exhibited.

"Excuse me," he said, taking Vanessa's arm as he soldiered through the crowd. "I'm meeting someone inside."

The harried hostess working the front desk recognized him and smiled. "Hey, Remy. Your brother's got a booth in the bar," she murmured. "Go ahead back and join him."

"Thanks." Remy glanced at Vanessa, again feeling a strong sense of attraction. She unzipped her parka, then removed her gloves and shoved them into her pocket. As they walked, he leaned in close, taking in her scent, which, unbelievably, seemed to be a holiday mix of peppermint and chocolate—two of his favorite things this time of the year. "Promise me you're not here to make a scene," he said, taking hold of her elbow.

One corner of her lush mouth quirked up in the beginning of a smile as she glanced back at him. "I promise. I'm not the scene-making type."

He spotted Seth in the corner booth, intent on scrolling through his phone. He barely looked up when Remy slid into the seat across from him. "Um, Seth?"

His brother raised his head, his gaze skittering right past Remy to Vanessa. His mouth fell open. Seth had never been good at hiding his emotions, Remy thought. Surprise first, and then anger crossed his face, which finally changed to a sort of sullen resignation. "Vanessa. What are you doing in town? I thought you always skied Winter Park."

"Do you mind if I sit?" she asked instead of answering the question.

"Go ahead." Seth waved his hand, finally eying his brother. "I'm guessing you and Remy have already met."

"We did." Sliding in next to Remy, Vanessa placed her elegant, long-fingered hand on his arm. "Thank you so much for escorting me here."

When she pulled her fingers away from him, he exhaled, wondering why he felt like leaning into her touch. Predictably, the skin-to-shirt contact, however brief, made him ache for more. Damn. His brother's former fiancée.

Remy let out a breath, suddenly feeling like a third wheel. "I'm guessing I should go," he offered, half-hoping Seth would refuse. "It seems you two have a lot to talk about."

"We do," Vanessa replied softly, barely glancing at him. "Thanks for understanding."

Avoiding looking at anyone, Seth simply nodded, then took a long drink from his beer.

Though Remy hadn't eaten dinner yet—that being the reason he'd been meeting Seth here—he started to slide back out of the booth. Vanessa stood and stepped aside to let him pass, her cool, direct gaze revealing nothing.

Again, envy shot through him, along with shame at feeling this way. Remy loved his troubled half brother and would never do anything to hurt him. He'd spent the last several years trying to forge a family relationship with a sibling he hadn't even known he had and wouldn't jeopardize it for anything, especially not for a woman. He might not be able to explain the strength of his attraction to Vanessa Fisher, but he definitely could refuse to act on it. Staying as far away as possible from her would be a great way to start. Assuming she was even here for long. Knowing Seth, he'd send her packing as quickly as possible.

As he made his way through the crowded pub away from the booth, a stool opened up at the bar just as he reached it. Moving instinctively, Remy took it. After all, he needed to eat. He ordered a draft beer, glad he had his back to his brother's booth. Watching Seth and Vanessa would be a form of slow torture. Which made zero sense. He barely knew her, after all.

When Gary, the bartender on duty, tried to hand him a menu, Remy waved it away. He knew what he wanted. "I'll just have the buffalo burger and sweet-potato fries," he said. "Medium well on the cook."

Gary grinned. "I almost went ahead and put in the order the second I saw you sit down, but there's always a chance you might want something different."

"Not today." Remy smiled back, then took a long swig of his beer.

"Who's the babe with Seth?" Gary asked. "I've seen her up on the slopes over at Sunlight Mountain a few times, though I haven't seen her ski here. She's a real pro."

"She is?" Unable to keep from glancing back over his shoulder, he observed his brother and Vanessa engaged in what appeared to be an intense conversation. "Maybe that's how the two of them met. Skiing."

"You don't know her?" Gary raised his brow, eying the two in the booth. "She's not Seth's usual type."

Since he'd had the exact same thought himself, Remy simply nodded.

"Be right back," the bartender said. "Looks like Seth wants another beer. And I need to see if his lady friend needs anything to drink."

Remy couldn't help but turn and watch as Gary headed over to his brother's booth. Seth had his back to him but Vanessa looked up and met his gaze. Again, he felt that undeniable sizzle of awareness and wondered if she did, too. If so, she did nothing to reveal it. Instead, she dipped her chin in a quick nod, before returning her attention to Gary and Seth.

And just like before, he felt that unfamiliar twinge of jealousy, combined with a longing so fierce it stunned him. What the hell? He forced himself to turn around and focus on his beer.

VANESSA HADN'T EXPECTED the butterflies in her stomach upon meeting Seth's charismatic and sexy-as-hell brother. Which made absolutely no sense. She hadn't come to Roaring Springs looking for a new relationship. Especially not with the half sibling of the man with whom she'd broken things off.

Pushing the thought of Remy from her mind, she focused on Seth. While initially he'd appeared shocked to see her, he'd visibly relaxed the instant his brother had walked away. Still, something seemed off about him, though she couldn't quite put her finger on what it was. Of course, part of her would now always feel uneasy around him, due to the way he'd handled their breakup.

"So, tell me, Vanessa, how long have you been in town? And more importantly, why are you here?" With his sandy blond hair and hazel-green eyes, when he turned on the charm, Seth could make women melt. Once, when she'd been particularly vulnerable after losing her parents, he'd affected her this way, though they'd been friends first.

"I just got in this morning," she replied, resisting the urge to tell him her trip had been made impulsively. "I'd hoped to stay a night or two and do some skiing while I was here, but it seems every place is completely booked."

"They are." He sat back, the slightly smug tone in his voice at odds with his sympathetic smile. "This time of the year is our busiest. A lot of wealthy, important people spend their holidays with us. They book their rooms months in advance."

"With us?" she echoed, before remembering he was employed as hotel manager at The Lodge.

"But no worries," he continued as if she hadn't spoken. "If you want to ski Pine Peak, you should. You're welcome to stay with me for as long as you want."

She squirmed, once again remembering his out-of-control anger when she'd broken things off. He'd punched a hole in the wall, and the violence of his re-action had terrified her. She'd cringed away from him, startled and afraid, at which point he'd stormed out. Nope. She didn't think she'd be staying with him now. "That's very kind of you, Seth," she replied, choosing her words carefully. "But I didn't come here to see about the possibility of us getting back together. I felt bad about the way I broke things off and realized I owed you an explanation."

"I didn't think you wanted to get back together." His expression darkened. "And, no, you don't owe me an explanation. I get it. I'm over it, Vanessa."

"Maybe so, but please let me talk." Swallowing, she hesitated. "I'd feel much better."

"Fine." He took another long pull of his beer, then set the empty mug on the table with a thunk and gestured at the bartender for another. "Go ahead and unburden yourself. Even though I basically figured it out when you wouldn't sleep with me. Not once, the entire time we were together."

Wincing, Vanessa glanced around, hoping no one had overheard. She told herself she shouldn't blame Seth for being deliberately cruel. She might have been the same way had their situation been reversed. After all, she'd done him a great disservice. Not only had she ruined their friendship, but she'd also let him think she might be able to love him. "Please don't be like that," she began. "You and I were always friends before we were anything else. I hate that we've lost that."

The bartender brought over another beer for Seth and asked what she'd like. She ordered a glass of chardonnay and waited until the man had walked away before continuing. "One of the things I'll always be grateful for is how you were my rock when I fell apart after my parents were killed. Seth, you saved me. I'll never be able to repay that. But…"

"But I fell in love with you," he said, finishing for her. "And you didn't feel the same way."

Was it wrong to feel relieved that she didn't have to spell it out? Sighing softly, she murmured, "Exactly."

"Then why did you accept my proposal?" He searched her face. "I can understand everything else but that. Why would you agree to marry me if you didn't love me?"

Her gut twisted. Not so easy after all. "I didn't want to hurt you," she explained, aware she might be making a mess of this. "And to be honest, I found myself clinging to…" Aghast at what she'd almost said, she stopped, searching for another way to explain she'd chosen what had seemed safe and familiar, and that she'd been briefly afraid of being on her own.

"I get it," Seth interjected, once again inadvertently rescuing her. "To tell the truth, I think I knew all along that you didn't feel the same way I did. I just wanted…" He took a deep breath. "More."

She nodded, aware that acknowledging the pain in his voice might be worse than pretending not to hear it. "I'm sorry, Seth. That's what I came up here to say. I don't think I can love anyone right now with my life in such an uproar. You deserved more. We both do. When you wouldn't take my calls, I felt like I needed to explain in person. Maybe understanding why will help you move on."

"I've already moved on," he informed her.

Her wine arrived. Grateful, she smiled at the bartender before taking a sip. "Perfect," she said. "Thank you."

"No problem." The man moved away. When she looked across the booth, she saw that Seth watched her intently, his eyes narrowed into slits. Again, she felt a shiver of unease, which was ridiculous. Emotions had been high that day. Enough time had passed and she knew Seth would be calmer now.

After all, he'd never raised a hand to her.

Still, she suddenly realized she wanted out of there, away from him. She'd done what she'd come to do and now maybe they both could have closure. Digging in her purse, she extracted a ten-dollar bill and laid it on the table next to her still-full glass of wine before rising to her feet. "Thanks for listening," she said, hoping her smile looked more genuine than it felt. "I'm going to head out now. It was great seeing you."

"Wait." He stood as well. "Please don't run off, Vanessa. I accept your apology." He pushed out a breath from both cheeks. "I'm really hoping we can still be friends." He pinned her with his gaze, his hazel-green eyes earnest. "Can we? We have a long history of friendship. I'd hate to lose that."

How could she resist? After all, that's what she'd wanted. She'd missed their friendship. Slowly she lowered herself back into her seat. "I'd like that," she said, wondering if it was really relief she felt, or more gratitude that he truly seemed to be over her.

"Great." He pushed her wineglass toward her. "Enjoy your wine. It's been a while since we talked. I'm sure we have a lot to catch up on."

Instead, they ended up discussing only generalities, like a couple of strangers on a first date. The closing of her favorite Irish bar in Boulder, the skiing up at Sunlight Mountain near Glenwood Springs...

"Have you skied Pine Peak yet?" Seth asked. "I like it a lot better than Sunlight. It's got some great black-diamond runs. Of course, I'm prejudiced since I live and work here."

She thought of her skis, still strapped to the roof of her car. "Not yet. I was hoping to do that while I was up here." Taking a sip of her wine, she shrugged. "Maybe another time."

"How about tomorrow?" He grinned at her over the rim of his beer mug. "It's best first thing in the morning, right when the lift opens. I like to go before work. Come with me?"

"I'm tempted," she admitted. "But like I said, there's not an available room in this town. Believe me, I've checked."

"I told you, you can stay with me." He held up a hand as she started to protest. "I have a guest room. You can stay there. Completely platonic. Please, I insist. There's nothing I'd like better than skiing with you again."

Maybe because she really, really wanted to ski Pine Peak, or perhaps because she felt like she owed him at least that much, she found herself acquiescing. "Just for one night."

"Sure." He raised his nearly empty mug. "I'll have another to celebrate."

Her stomach growled, reminding her that she hadn't eaten since breakfast. "How about some dinner instead?"

REMY HAD JUST climbed into bed and shut off the lights when his cell phone rang, startling him. Sitting up, he glanced at the digital clock on his nightstand—eleven thirty. Damn it. A call at this time of night was never a good thing.

"Hello?"

"Remy, this is Liam Kastor. Did I wake you?"

Instantly alert, Remy explained he'd been awake. Since Liam was a detective with the Roaring Springs Police Department, he suspected this call involved something his younger brother had done. It certainly wouldn't be the first time.

"It's Seth," Liam continued, confirming Remy's suspicions. "We got a call earlier from The Saloon. The bartender, Gary, said Seth had been there drinking all evening and got belligerent when they cut him off. I headed down there to check it out, but by the time I arrived, he was gone."

"Driving?" Remy asked, horrified.

"No, thank goodness. His car is still parked in the lot. Either someone gave him a ride or he left on foot. Since it's snowing pretty heavily outside, I sent out a couple of patrols looking for him. Being drunk out in freezing temperatures is never a good combination. There's no sign of him, at least downtown."

Remy swore. "I'll go look for him. Thank you for calling me."

After ending the call, he immediately dialed his brother's cell. After several rings, it went to voicemail. Remy left a quick, terse message asking Seth to call him.

Now he had no other option than to go out and search.

He threw on warm clothes, then snagged his coat

and gloves and headed out into the frigid cold. In the time since he'd been home, several inches of perfect powder had accumulated. The plow would be by in the morning, but this kind of snow was easy to drive on.

He retraced the route Seth might have walked if he'd decided to head home to his condo from The Saloon. Since it was only a few blocks, it was definitely doable, at least when sober.

When Remy reached the trendy apartment building without seeing any trace of his brother, he parked and considered what to do next. First, he punched redial, hoping against hope that Seth would pick up. When he got voicemail again, he sighed and shut off his engine.

Inside, he rode the elevator up to the third floor and trudged down the hall until he reached Seth's condo. Glancing at his watch and seeing that it was nearly midnight, he winced but rang the doorbell, anyway. While dealing with a drunk Seth was never pleasant, he had to make sure his brother had made it home safely.

When nothing happened, he pressed the doorbell again and again and again. Sooner or later that kind of noise would get through to even a passed-out drunk.

Sure enough, a moment later the door opened a crack. But, instead of Seth, a tousle-haired Vanessa peeked out at him. The sight of her sleepy, sexy blue eyes hit him like a punch in the stomach.

When the implications of her presence registered, he felt like a fool. Swallowing hard, he nodded at her. "Is Seth home?"

Covering her mouth while she yawned, she opened the door a bit wider and stepped aside so he could enter. She wore flannel pajamas in a plaid holiday pattern with some sort of fuzzy slippers. Somehow, she managed to look both cute and alluring at the same time.

"Is Seth here?" he asked again, reminding himself to focus.

"I'm not sure." Brushing her hair back from her face, she lifted one shoulder in a delicate shrug. "He was earlier. We had dinner and then came back here so I could get settled. He wanted to go back out but I was tired, so I went to bed. In the guest bedroom," she said pointedly. "Anyway, I've been asleep. At least until you started ringing the doorbell over and over."

"My apologies." He thought about explaining and decided against it. Surely, she knew what kind of trouble her former fiancé could get himself into. "I'm just going to check on him," he said. "Make sure he's okay."

"Knock yourself out." She wandered into the kitchen, still yawning.

Seth's bedroom door was closed. Remy knocked—three sharp raps of his knuckles on the wood. No answer. Reluctantly, he turned the knob and squinted into the dark room, hoping he could make out whether or not Seth occupied the bed.

No such luck. Bracing himself, he flicked on the light switch.

An annoyed groan came from Seth, sprawled out, fully dressed, on the bed. "Turn that the hell off."

Instead of complying, Remy eyed his baby brother, trying to judge how drunk Seth might be. Deciding it didn't matter—he'd learned long ago how pointless it was trying to talk to someone while they were inebriated—he turned out the light and backed out of the room.

"Is he all right?" Vanessa asked, her fingers curled around a tall glass of ice water.

Remy grimaced. "I think so. I'm sorry to have disturbed you. I'll come back and talk to Seth in the morning."

She regarded him, her gaze steady. "He and I are supposed to go ski Pine Peak in the morning before he goes to work. You might want to call him instead."

Again, the stab of envy. Though Remy wasn't a skier of Seth's caliber, he enjoyed a few runs up on the slopes as often as he could, time permitting. Though knowing his brother, he doubted Seth would feel much like skiing tomorrow. He'd be way too hungover.

Saying none of this, he nodded. "Thanks. I'll keep that in mind. Again, I apologize for waking you."

She waved him away with a sleepy smile. "No worries. I guess I'll be seeing you around."

Damn, he hoped so. And once more, that odd combination of guilt and longing assailed him. Swallowing hard, he gave her a quick nod and left.

All the way home, he called himself every kind of fool. He'd just met the woman, for Pete's sake. And while he could definitely understand the lure of physical attraction, he wasn't the kind of man who'd even consider making a move on his brother's lady, no matter how irresistible he found her.

His brother's lady. The notion made him shake his head. Seth never stuck with anyone very long, never mind proposed marriage. Despite the fact that Remy helped his brother any way he could, Seth constantly seemed to be barely treading water. Maybe resuming his relationship with Vanessa would be the thing Seth needed to completely turn his life around.

Remy definitely hoped so. But he couldn't help but think there was something...off in all of this. For one thing, the reconciliation between Seth and Vanessa sure had happened quickly. Especially since she claimed she'd broken off the engagement. Yet they'd had one dinner and Seth had immediately installed her in his condo. Strange. But none of his business.

Except for the insane pull of attraction he felt toward the woman who was once his almost-sister-in-law.

Chapter Two

Back home, Remy shed his clothes and once again climbed in between his sheets, then pulled his comforter up to his chin. He couldn't shake the image of Vanessa in the soft flannel pajamas, wondering what it would be like to slip his hand under them and caress her warm skin. Guilt immediately followed that thought, because he knew he didn't have the right.

Despite thinking he wouldn't, he managed to drift off to sleep. When he opened his eyes again, he saw his alarm was due to go off in five minutes. He shut it off and pushed himself up.

Thirty minutes later, showered and dressed, he drank his black coffee and nuked instant oatmeal for breakfast. When he'd finished eating, he checked his watch. He had a morning meeting with a new advertising firm from Denver, so he wouldn't have time to stop by Seth's.

As he drove to work, he couldn't help but wonder if his brother had felt well enough to ski. He found himself wondering if Vanessa would go by herself, anyway, and wished he had time to head up to Pine Peak.

Wishful thinking. And foolishness, completely unlike him. Remy considered responsibility his middle name and rarely took time off from work.

Though right now, he sorely wanted to. He hadn't been skiing at all this season. Of course, his sudden desire to go now had way too much to do with the intriguing beauty ensconced in Seth's condo. Trouble, any way he looked at it.

Shaking his head at his stray thoughts, he parked and reminded himself to concentrate on his job. When he walked into the elegant lobby of The Chateau, he greeted Mary, the redheaded concierge who was married to Johnnie Web, a firefighter and local hero. She smiled and greeted him back, her cheerful words making him smile the entire elevator ride up to his floor.

As he stepped off and entered the bustling office, the uncharacteristic quiet made him pause. Usually, phones were ringing, people were talking and the hum of various printers or copiers made a pleasant cacophony.

Today, more than half of the cubicles were empty—people taking off for the approaching holiday. He ought to know because he'd personally approved everyone's requested vacation time.

He'd actually been a bit surprised the Denver ad agency had requested a meeting today to pitch their ideas for a new campaign. While Remy had let it be known that he was actively searching for a new company, all the other major players had scheduled meetings for after the New Year.

Since he actually admired this firm for wanting to get a jump on their competition, he'd agreed to the meeting, despite being short several members of his decision-making staff.

Walking into his office, he looked around for his assistant, Heather. She came out of the break room carrying a donut and a cup of coffee, her long, brown hair up in her usual jaunty ponytail. "Well, good morning," she chirped. "Someone brought donuts, if you're interested."

Before he could reply, her phone rang. Heather rushed past him toward her desk, managing to get there without spilling any coffee. "Remy Colton's desk," she answered. Listening for a moment, her eyes went wide. "Please hold." She eyed Remy, her expression carefully blank. "It's The Lodge. You'd better take it."

"Okay, thanks." He strolled into his office and closed the door. He couldn't imagine why anyone up there would be calling, but picked up his phone and answered.

"I'm sorry to bother you," Denise, one of the shift managers, said. "But Seth didn't show up this morning."

Remy glanced at his watch. "What time was he scheduled to be in?"

Denise hesitated. "Nine. However, when he pulls a time slot that early, he's always a little late."

Remy hadn't known this. "How late?" The question came out a bit sharper than he'd intended.

"He's usually in by ten," she said quietly. "But it's after that and he isn't answering his phone."

Remy cursed silently. If he hurried, he could make it to Seth's condo and back before his meeting, which seemed to be running late. "I'll run over and check on him," he promised.

"Thank you." Again, he sensed her hesitation. "If he's…sick, just let us know so we don't expect him."

"Will do." He hung up, gritting his teeth. Almost immediately, his assistant buzzed him.

"Your ten o'clock canceled," she said. "They were driving up from Denver this morning. Since the pass is closed, they have no way to get here."

He thanked her, actually glad. Now he wouldn't have to worry about rushing things with Seth. It sounded like his baby brother needed a good talking-to.

VANESSA WONDERED FOR the umpteenth time if she'd made a mistake agreeing to stay in Seth's condo, even if only for one night. When his handsome brother, Remy, had shown up after midnight, worried, she felt a jolt of attraction low in her belly. Again. And she hated drama of any kind. Getting in between two brothers could create chaos of epic proportions.

Still, after Remy left and she'd wandered back to her bedroom, she couldn't stop thinking about him.

When she woke shortly after seven, she hurriedly showered and dressed before heading to the kitchen, where she hoped to get a cup of strong coffee. Seth's bedroom door remained closed, making her wonder if he'd forgotten their plans to ski. Loath to knock, she texted him instead.

What time are we leaving?

No answer, which might mean he was in the shower. She went ahead and made her coffee, glad Seth stocked milk and sweetener. After a couple of sips, warmth flooding her throat, she felt her original optimism again. There was nothing she loved better than skiing and she could hardly wait to try out the slopes at Pine Peak. She glanced at her gear piled over in a corner near the door. Rather than leaving it in the car and taking a chance on it being stolen, she'd brought it inside Seth's condo.

Speaking of Seth… She checked her watch. They'd agreed on early morning, before he had to go in to work. While she wasn't sure what his schedule looked like today, she figured he'd have to start by nine at the latest. Which meant they were running out of time to ski.

She walked over to the window and peered outside. Snow still fell in a steady curtain and judging from the amount piled up on cars, they'd gotten over a foot of fresh white powder overnight. But there didn't seem to be any wind, which was a good thing.

Perfect for skiing. As long as conditions weren't whiteout, the slope would be rocking and rolling. She could hardly wait.

Gathering up her nerve, she went ahead and tapped quietly on his door.

Nothing.

With her heart racing, she turned the knob and peeked her head in. Judging by the man-size lump under the covers, Seth was still asleep.

Sleeping it off?

"Seth?" she ventured, staying in the doorway. "Seth, are you going to get up?"

A loud groan was his only answer.

Damned if she would go any farther into the room. She wasn't sure what Seth thought this was, but she could clearly see what might happen if she stepped over and attempted to shake him awake. He'd pull her down and start kissing her, likely ignoring her protests that they weren't intimate anymore.

Nope. Not happening. Suppressing a shudder, she called him again. "Seth. We're supposed to go skiing before you go to work. I'm not sure what time you have to be in, but if we're going to hit the slopes, I'm thinking we need to head out now."

"We'll go later," he mumbled. "I'm taking the day off from work."

"Okay," she replied, backing out and closing the door. Drinking the rest of her coffee, she debated whether or not to head out alone. While she could certainly ski an unfamiliar mountain by herself, it was always much more fun with a friend like Seth, who was a damned skilled skier. And whatever else he might be, she hoped the two of them could remain friends.

She decided to give it a few hours. After all, she had no place she had to be.

Since Seth had told her to make herself at home and to help herself to anything she wanted, she rummaged in the fridge in search of something she could make herself for breakfast.

Surprised to find a wide variety of foods, she settled on scrambled eggs and toast, along with a second cup of coffee.

After she ate, she checked the weather app on her phone. While she personally felt there was no such thing as too much snow, she knew ski resorts didn't always agree. If visibility got too poor, they'd shut down the slope and send the ski patrol out to bring in any stragglers. Her heart sank as she realized the snowstorm had caused exactly that situation. Though they hoped for perfect conditions tomorrow once the storm had passed, those in charge had decided it was too dangerous at the moment.

Which meant Seth's refusal to get out of bed had actually been a good thing. With the passion of a thousand purple suns, she hated getting suited up in anticipation of a couple of good runs and being stopped at the base of the mountain as she was about to get on the lift.

Should she go home then, and leave skiing Pine Peak for another time? After all, she'd done what she came to do and hopefully Seth would now have some closure.

Another quick internet search revealed they'd closed Loveland Pass. She could still take the I-70 tunnel, though she wasn't sure of the road conditions right now.

Her motto when it came to snowstorms had always been Better Safe Than Sorry. Which meant she'd be sticking around Roaring Springs at least one more night, maybe longer.

Glancing once more at the still-closed bedroom door, she knew Seth wouldn't mind her staying with him an extra day or two. If she could just get past this uneasiness. Since she'd been here, Seth had been nothing but a perfect gentleman. Sure, he'd gone out and had a little too much to drink last night, but he hadn't come pounding on her door or anything.

A sharp series of knocks on the front door made her jump. Hurrying over, she checked the peephole. Her stomach did a somersault when she saw Remy standing there, all bundled up in a down parka, a light dusting of snow on his broad shoulders.

Hurriedly, she opened the door. "Come inside," she said. "It's freezing out there."

"I know." As he stepped inside, his solemn expression gave her pause. "They closed down the slopes."

"Yes, I saw. Ditto on Loveland Pass, which shouldn't be such a surprise." She took a deep breath. "Would you like some coffee?"

One side of his mouth quirked up, but he shook his head. "No thanks. This isn't really a social visit. Is Seth around?"

"In there." She inclined her head toward the closed door. "Is everything all right?"

"He didn't show up for work." Remy removed his parka and hung it on the back of a chair. "He didn't even call, so they didn't know if they needed to bring someone else in to cover his shift."

Seth had said he was taking the day off. Clearly, he'd managed to forget to inform his employer of that.

Again, their gazes met and held for a second too long. Remy looked away first. "Is he still asleep?"

Feeling slightly dazed, she nodded. "I think so. I tried to wake him earlier but he was having none of it. We were supposed to hit the slopes first thing this morning. Though I guess since they closed them down, it was lucky we didn't."

"True." Remy grimaced. "Please excuse me while I go talk to my brother."

She nodded, trying to decide if she should retreat to her room or not. As he disappeared inside Seth's room, she elected to remain in the kitchen. She couldn't help but find how seriously Remy appeared to take his role of elder brother fascinating. Obviously, Seth could use the help.

"Get the hell out of my bedroom," Seth shouted. "Who let you in here, anyway?"

"Your houseguest," Remy replied, his tone measured and controlled. "I was here last night, too, after Gary called me all worried about you."

A string of curse words followed. "I don't work for you, Remy." Seth stormed out of the bedroom, briefly stopping short when he saw Vanessa. He'd put on a sweatshirt and a pair of wrinkled jeans and shoved his feet into snow boots. "Sorry about this, Van," he muttered, before snagging his down parka out of the front closet. He turned to glare at Remy. "I'm just living my life and trying to have some fun, bro. I don't need you coming in here and giving me a hard time."

Remy started to speak, but Seth cut him off with a furious command. "Don't." He held up his hand. "I'm out of here. Don't follow me, either of you. I need to be alone." With that, he bolted out and slammed the front door, knocking down a picture that had been hanging on the wall and shattering the glass.

Not sure what else to do or what to say, Vanessa went in search of a broom and a dustpan. She located them in the laundry room and went to clean up the glass.

"Here, let me." Remy took them from her and immediately got busy. Surprised, she hung back, wishing she had something to do with her hands. Maybe then she could better resist this unexpected urge to touch him.

Once he'd dumped all the glass shards in the trash, Remy retrieved the vacuum and went back over the area. Vanessa watched him, amazed how he could manage to look so sexy while performing the most mundane task.

Finally, he shut off the vacuum, wound up the cord and put it back in the hall closet. "There," he said, dusting his hands off on the front of his jeans. "All done."

She nodded. "Thanks." Then, because she felt awkward, she checked her watch. Since she'd had such a late breakfast, it seemed a bit too early for lunch. But since cooking was one of the things she loved and did well, she asked Remy if he'd eaten.

"Not for hours." The grim set of his mouth told her food had been the last thing on his mind.

"How about you let me make you something? I can rustle up breakfast or lunch or brunch, if you want to call it that. Seth told me to help myself to anything I wanted in the kitchen."

Though his gaze narrowed, he finally nodded. "I'd like that, thank you. But something simple. I don't want to put you out."

Relieved, she grinned. "Actually, I love to cook. And right now, I'd feel a lot better if I could keep busy."

He followed her to the kitchen. "Again, I apologize about all that. You just got here. I'm sure you didn't sign up for all this family drama."

Did she hear the hint of a question in his voice? Deciding to ignore that possibility, she began rummaging in the fridge. "So...what are you in the mood for?" she asked.

"Have you had breakfast?"

Slowly, she nodded. "I made myself scrambled eggs earlier. But that doesn't matter. I can whip you up some breakfast if that's what you want."

Watching her, he considered. "It's still early enough

for breakfast to be a respectable option. The Chateau restaurant serves it until ten thirty."

"Breakfast it is, then. Bacon, eggs and toast? Or…" She took a peek inside the refrigerator again. "There are enough ingredients for eggs Benedict with ham. Would you like that instead?"

"If it's not too much trouble." He grimaced and glanced at the front door. "I wonder if Seth will be back to eat."

Though she privately doubted that, she nodded. "I'll make extra just in case. As long as I keep the eggs and the English muffins separate, it won't get too soggy."

Humming happily, she got busy. Next to skiing, cooking was her favorite pastime. And privately, she considered herself pretty darn talented at it. Her friends back in Boston had always raved about the meals she'd made. And since moving to Boulder, she'd hosted a couple of dinner parties with the same results.

And now she'd be cooking for Remy. Why that felt different, she wasn't sure.

"Is there anything I can do to help?" he murmured from behind her, his voice so close she knew if she spun around, she could reach out and touch him.

Forcing herself to continuing stirring the hollandaise sauce, she simply glanced over her shoulder. "Not really. Why don't you make yourself a cup of coffee and sit down and relax? This won't take too much longer."

"Would you like a cup, too?" he asked. "You look like you're about empty."

Though she rarely had more than two coffees per day, she liked the idea of sharing a cup with this man. Maybe they could talk and get to know each other a little bit better. As long as that's all they did, that should be safe.

"Sure," she answered.

"Cream and sugar?"

"Yes, please." She smiled as he did a double take. "I know, black coffee is better. According to Seth, you can best taste the coffee that way."

"I agree with my brother on that." Remy made them both a cup, then carried hers over to her before taking a seat at the table. "You seem to know what you're doing," he commented. "Do you cook professionally?"

"No." She risked another glance over her shoulder. "I've thought about it. Though I'm afraid if I started doing it for a living, that would take some of the joy out of it."

Just then the front door blew open and Seth burst inside. He shook off snow before removing his coat and barreling through to the kitchen. At the doorway, he stopped short, staring at the two of them.

"What are you doing?" he asked as he came up behind Vanessa and gave her a huge kiss on the side of her neck. "That smells interesting. Why are you cooking for my brother?"

At his touch, she froze. Again, she had the sense of barely leashed violence, though she managed to shrug lightly. "He was hungry, so I thought I'd make him something to eat while he waited for you to get back. There's plenty, if you'd like some, too."

Instead of immediately answering, he leaned around her and peered into the pan. "What is that?"

"Hollandaise sauce. I'm poaching some eggs and

serving them on English muffins with cheese, topped by this sauce."

"You know, eggs Benedict," Remy chimed in, his tone dry. "I'm pretty sure you've had it before."

Though Seth didn't respond, judging by the hard set of his mouth, he wasn't pleased.

Why Remy was pushing his brother's buttons, she wasn't sure. But she sure as heck planned to stay out of it. She kept busy, putting the English muffins under the broiler now that the poached eggs were in the water. "Seth, why don't you get some coffee and sit?" she suggested. "Breakfast will be ready in a few minutes."

Seth narrowed his eyes and glared at her, then stalked over to the coffee maker. Relieved, she relaxed her spine slightly, though she couldn't help but wonder if coming here for closure might have been a huge mistake.

The eggs were done just as the English muffins turned the perfect shade of brown. She tossed a few thick slices of ham in a frying pan and when they'd begun to crisp, she put everything together and ladled the hollandaise on top. Perfect, she thought, suppressing the urge to snap a quick pic with her phone. Instead, she smiled and carried the plates over to the table.

"Here you go," she said, placing the meals in front of each man. "Enjoy."

"Aren't you going to eat?" Seth asked, eyeing his food. "Seems like you went through an awful lot of trouble for my brother."

Still smiling, she ignored the snide tone. "I had scrambled eggs and toast earlier, while you were asleep. And you know how much I like to cook. This wasn't any trouble at all."

"Thank you," Remy said, and he dug in.

Seth eyed his brother, using his fork to move things around on his plate. When he finally cut a piece, he got only the egg and ham, leaving the English muffin and most of the sauce on his plate. He chewed and then set down his fork. "You know," he mused, "I think it's time I hired a professional chef."

When he glanced at Vanessa, she wondered if he was actually going to offer her the job.

"One who can really cook." He pushed his plate away. "Nice try, Van."

Stunned, she could only stare. To her horror, she felt tears prick the back of her eyes. She turned away, ostensibly to clean up the pans. The casual cruelty coming from a man she'd always regarded as a friend hurt. Clearly, Seth hadn't gotten over the breakup, and they couldn't go back to being friends. In fact, as soon as the roads were clear, she needed to pack up and go. Maybe a room at either The Chateau or The Lodge would have become available just for one or two nights, so she could ski Pine Peak. Heck, she'd even take a room in one of the chain motels on the edge of town.

She ran the water, then scrubbed out the pans and placed them in the dishwasher. Seth had gone silent, making her wonder if he might apologize. She glanced back at the table, only to find him glaring at her, his expression furious.

"What were you two doing here alone while I was gone?" he demanded, including Remy in his stare. "And come on, Vanessa, why were you trying to impress my brother with a fancy breakfast? We have oatmeal. Scrambled eggs and toast is what you said you had.

But no, that wasn't good enough for him. I'm thinking you—"

"Enough!" Remy pushed to his feet. "I don't know what's gotten into you, Seth. Leave her alone. She was simply being kind. She doesn't deserve this treatment from you."

"Really, Remy?" Standing so quickly he knocked back his chair, Seth faced his older brother. His hands were clenched into fists. "You come in my place, hit on my girlfriend and have the nerve to try and tell me how to act?"

Remy appeared as stunned as she felt. "Seth—"

Again, Seth cut him off. "Mind your own business. Vanessa belongs to me. Our relationship has nothing to do with you." He pointed toward the door. "Leave."

Remy took care not to glance her way. Part of her didn't want him to leave. But when she didn't correct Seth, what else could he do?

"Thanks for breakfast," he finally said, meeting her gaze. "It was delicious." He grabbed his parka and left.

Seth dropped back into his seat, muttering under his breath. Vanessa cleared her throat. "Seth, we need to talk."

"Do we?" He shook his head. "Don't be mad because I didn't like your cooking. I've never been fond of eggs Benedict, that's all."

"It's not that," she said. "Actually, that's only part of it. You were unnecessarily rude, both to me and your brother. Not just that, but I don't belong to you. And we don't have a relationship."

His harsh expression softened. "Then why'd you come here? Come on, Van, I know you missed me as much as I missed you. You didn't drive up all the way from Boulder just to ski."

Even though the lure of skiing Pine Peak had factored into her decision to come to Roaring Springs, she knew better than to bring that up. "Seth, I came here to explain why I broke things off so abruptly. I wanted to give us both closure."

"Closure?" He spat the word as if it left a bitter taste in his mouth. "What is it with women and closure? Who the hell cares? Either you want to get back together or you don't. Which is it?"

Heart aching, she took a deep breath. "Actually, I was hoping we could go back to being friends. But clearly, that was a foolish idea. I'll pack my things and get out of your hair. I'm sorry to have put you out."

She kept her chin up and her back straight as she walked to the guest bedroom. Luckily, she hadn't done much unpacking, so all she had to do was grab her toiletries and put them in her suitcase.

When she emerged, Seth was nowhere to be found. She had no intention of going in search of him to say goodbye. Essentially, she'd already said that.

It took two trips to get her small suitcase and her ski gear loaded back in her car. Seth didn't bother to make an appearance, something that both saddened her and filled her with relief.

At least the plow had been by. She'd put snow tires on her car right before the first snow and she had chains in the trunk in case she needed them. Either way, she wasn't sure she could make it back home in this weather. With snow still falling heavily, she drove a slow and cautious couple of blocks until she reached The Chateau. If worse came to worst, she'd sleep sitting up in a chair in the lobby.

There were no parking spots open in the small lot, but she finally located one on a side street. This time, she left her skis on top of her car, though she grabbed her suitcase and trudged toward the hotel entrance.

Stepping through the ornate glass doors, she felt as if she'd entered a different world. Though she doubted anyone would have checked out since yesterday, she approached the front desk, anyway.

Just as the polite, well-coiffed young woman asked her if she could help her, Vanessa had an idea. "Yes, I'm looking for Remy Colton. I was told he works here." After all, she'd met him out in front of the hotel yesterday.

"I'm sorry, but Mr. Colton isn't taking visitors today," the woman, whose badge announced her name was Tena, said.

"Could you contact him and ask him to call me?"

Slowly, Tena nodded. "I could take your number, yes."

Vanessa rattled off the digits, then asked that Remy call her as soon as possible. "I'll be waiting in the lobby," she said. "Unless you happen to have any vacancies?"

"I'm sorry, we don't. We're fully booked through Christmas."

Which was the same answer she'd gotten when she'd inquired yesterday and clearly nothing had changed on that front.

Choosing an unoccupied, overstuffed chair facing the front door, Vanessa took a seat. She began scrolling through her phone, checking social media and catching up on the news. Barely five minutes had passed when her phone rang.

Chapter Three

After getting a message to call Vanessa, Remy dialed her number immediately. When he heard her soft hello, he exhaled. "Are you all right? I was worried about you," he said.

"I'm fine," she replied, her voice shaking. "But I've left Seth's condo. I'm not sure what to think about his behavior."

Remy wasn't sure, either. In all honesty, his brother's mood swings, heavy drinking and barely leashed rage worried the hell out of him. The breakup with Vanessa must have affected him strongly, though if his end goal was to get her back, he was going about it the wrong way. He couldn't blame Vanessa for being scared off.

"Is there somewhere we can meet and talk?" Remy asked, pushing away the sharp thrill of anticipation that went through him at the thought of seeing her again. He only wanted to make sure she was safe, he told himself. Nothing more. "Where are you now?"

Her answer surprised him. "Well, actually I'm in the lobby of The Chateau. I was hoping a room would miraculously open up, but no such luck. I'm still not sure the tunnel is open yet. I seriously doubt I could get back home to Boulder in this storm." She laughed self-consciously. "And I really was hoping to ski Pine Peak once it opens. As long as I'm up here…"

"I'll be there in five," he replied. He could tell she wasn't the kind of person who enjoyed asking for help from anyone. "We'll go grab a cup of coffee or something to drink and I'll see what I can do to find you a place to stay."

Sounding relieved, she agreed to wait for him.

"Save my number in your phone," he told her. "This is my cell. You can call or text me anytime."

She promised she would.

Hanging up, Remy walked out into the still-too-quiet office and told everyone they could take the rest of the day off. Despite The Chateau being booked to capacity, the PR department took it easy over the holidays. With so many already on vacation or personal days, they weren't getting any work done anyway, and if the snow continued to fall at the same rate, the plows would have trouble keeping up. They might as well go home and stay warm.

His good-natured order was met with cheers. He stood near the door and watched everyone gather up their coats and head out. A few people high-fived him and one of the older women gave him a hug. Hiding his impatience, he wished they would hurry up so he could lock up the office and go spend the rest of the day with Vanessa.

The rest of the… The realization should have shocked him, but he could barely get past his eagerness to see her.

Finally, everyone had gone. He busted out the door

with an unusual spring in his step before he reminded himself to slow down. Vanessa needed a friend, not a suitor. Plus, with Seth so volatile, he didn't want to take a chance of doing something to set him off.

Before heading out into the lobby, he decided to get a breath of fresh air. Mostly so he could get a handle on the conflicting emotions that filled him when he thought of spending time with Vanessa.

Stepping outside, he stood for a moment, letting the snow swirl around him, barely feeling the cold. He took several deep breaths, letting the icy air fill his lungs. He'd always found winter exhilarating, which made living high up in the Rockies perfect.

Glancing at the street and the tire tracks left by his employees, he decided he'd go ahead and walk around to the front entrance of The Chateau and go in that way.

As usual, when he strolled around to the front of The Chateau, a sense of pride and contentment filled him. He loved the structure, inside and out, and loved the people who worked there and made it one of the top vacation destinations in the United States even more.

Stepping into the lobby, he stuffed his gloves into his pocket and caught sight of Vanessa seated on one of the ornate chairs under the skylight, sunlight illuminating her dark hair. Scrolling through her phone, she didn't see him until he'd gotten a few feet away. When she looked up, their gazes met and locked. Once more, something intense flared between them. One-sided? he wondered. Or did she feel it, too?

"Hey." Vanessa stood, greeting him with a smile and an outstretched hand. "Thanks so much for meeting with me."

When his fingers connected with her slender ones, he fought the completely ridiculous urge to pull her up against him. Instead, he managed a civilized handshake and reluctantly released her.

"Let's go get something to drink and see what we can figure out," he offered.

"Here?"

He debated with himself, weighing the chances of Seth walking in, since the last thing he wanted to do was provoke some kind of scene. Deciding that possibility highly unlikely, he nodded. "There's a wonderful little coffee shop right off the lobby," he said.

"I saw it. It was very crowded, though. I don't think there was any place to sit."

Which wouldn't be surprising. "Let's go check it out." But even before they were close, he could tell they'd need to make another choice. "I tell you what," he told her. "Since the slopes are closed right now, everywhere downtown is going to be packed."

She nodded, eying him. "How about we take a walk? Or are you averse to a little snow?"

Unable to help himself, he laughed. "I love to be out in the snow and cold. People are always acting like I'm crazy when I say I want to go out for a stroll in the winter."

Eyes sparkling, she nodded. "I have snow boots in my car. How about you?"

"Of course," he replied. "In my back seat."

Impulsively, she took his arm. "Then let's go."

Side by side they hurried out of the hotel. He felt giddy, as if he was seventeen again and a love-struck teenager. While rationally, he knew he had to get a grip, for now he decided to go with the flow and simply enjoy the day.

She led him to her vehicle first, a practical and sturdy Subaru. "Four-wheel drive," she said, grinning as she unlocked the doors. "She also gets great gas mileage." Grabbing her boots, Vanessa sat down on the front passenger seat to put them on.

"She?" he asked. "Don't tell me you named your car."

"Of course I did." Boots in place, she hopped out and tugged on her gloves. "Your turn."

Her infectious enthusiasm made his heart pound. Slipping and sliding, he took off for his Jeep, hoping he had an extra pair of socks, too, since his were already soaked.

Luckily, he'd had the foresight to tuck a pair into his snow boots. He motioned her to hop inside, front or back—her choice. She chose the front passenger side, which probably was a good thing. He got in the back seat and closed the door to keep the blowing snow out while he peeled off his wet socks and slipped his feet into a pair of dry ones. Once he'd laced up his Sorel Caribou waterproof boots, he gave her a thumbs-up. "Ready."

She hopped out, pulling on a jaunty ski cap with a pom-pom on top. "I'm hoping the storm has driven most of the people inside," she said. "But with this being a ski resort, you never know."

Debating, he gave in to impulse and took her arm. "I'm sure there'll be a few other hearty souls, but I guarantee it won't be anywhere near as crowded as inside."

"Good." Her teeth flashed as white as the snowflakes. For someone with nowhere to stay, she seemed awfully chipper. Maybe she was one of those people who never worried, and simply figured things would always work out. He'd often wished he could be like that. Instead, he planned and scheduled, feeling as if he had to have control over every aspect of his life.

Walking side by side with Vanessa, he realized it felt amazing to be able to let that überpreparedness slide, if only for a little while.

After a few steps, she pulled her arm free, turning this way and that, surveying the picturesque downtown area with wonder. Bright lights shone from inside the shops and cafés, and in most of the eating and drinking establishments, it appeared to be standing room only. Quite a bit different than the normally bustling sidewalks.

The heavy snow and blowing wind had discouraged most of the tourists from venturing out. Those few people they encountered were bundled up so much that they were unrecognizable. Glancing at Vanessa, he saw she'd pulled out a scarf and wrapped it around her lower face. He reached into his pocket and did the same. They needed to talk, but for now he wanted to simply enjoy being with her like this.

When they reached the end of the commercial part of Main Street, she turned. "I guess we can go back down the other side," she said. "Though I wouldn't mind going in somewhere and warming up a bit."

Since the chill had begun to seep into his bones, too, he nodded. "There's another coffee shop one block back on the opposite side of the road. Maybe since everyone seems to be frequenting the bars, it won't be as bad."

She nodded, her long lashes white with snow. "I've reached my limit on coffee, but I can get hot cider or tea." She missed a step and nearly fell. Without thinking, he reached for her hand and took it, helping to steady her. If this surprised her, he couldn't tell.

Gloved hand in gloved hand, they crossed the street. Traffic was almost nonexistent and even the streetlights had taken on a magical glow. The deep, powdery snow had begun to make walking difficult, even though a few intrepid shop owners appeared to have attempted to shovel the sidewalk.

By the time they reached the No Doze Café, they were both out of breath. Luckily, the inside appeared to be only moderately crowded, rather than packed.

The instant they stepped through the door, Vanessa pulled her hand out of his and removed her gloves. "Oh, it smells wonderful in here," she said, inhaling deeply. "And look—a table just opened up over there in the corner!" She made a beeline for it, grabbing a chair and taking a seat before anyone else could. Grinning triumphantly, she beckoned Remy over.

Entranced by her, he went. "Do you mind ordering while I guard our spot?" she asked. Rummaging in her pocket, she pulled out a crumpled five-dollar bill and slid it across the table. "Here. This will take care of mine. I'd like a large hot apple cider with whipped cream."

"I've got this," he said, ignoring her money. "I'll be right back."

At the counter, he waited in line. Finally, he placed their order—the cider for her and a black coffee for him—and paid. The drinks were ready quickly and he carried them back to the table, noticing how a group of twentysomething guys were eying Vanessa. He had to love the fact that she appeared to be oblivious as she scrolled on her phone.

As soon as he approached her, she put it down and reached for her drink. "Thank you so much." She took a deep sip and made a throaty sound of pleasure that had him aching with desire.

Damn. He reminded himself to focus. He sat, wrapping both hands around his coffee cup. "Are you ready to tell me what's going on with Seth?"

Her eyes widened. "Wow, you clearly believe in getting right to the point."

"I do," he admitted, aware he couldn't tell her he'd simply needed a distraction from the way he couldn't stop wanting her.

She sighed. "I came here because I felt I owed Seth an explanation for the way I broke things off with him. I was abrupt and…" Expression rueful, she shrugged. "I was wrong. Not for ending it, but the way I handled it. I wanted closure. I forgot guys don't seem to get that word."

Her comment made him smile. "Truth. We—or at least I—tend to see things a bit more cut-and-dried. Either something is or it isn't."

Considering him, she shook her head. "Despite my best efforts, Seth seems to believe I'm here for another reason—to get back together. He's hurt and angry…understandably so." She took a deep breath. "He's your brother, but I'll be honest with you. Seth's taking it to another level." Leaning forward, she met his gaze. "He's frightening me."

"Me, too," he admitted gruffly. Then, because he was curious, he asked her how long she'd known his brother.

"A couple of years. We met on the slopes. We were friends, just that, nothing more. Then I went through something..." She bit her lip, her dark blue eyes huge. "Both my parents were killed in a car crash. Seth was there for me. He became my port in the storm."

Surprised, Remy simply nodded, hoping she'd continue. Maybe his brother *had* matured in ways he didn't always reveal. For Seth to stand by Vanessa while she endured her own private hell, expecting nothing in return... That showed the sort of personal growth, the kind Remy had long wished Seth to have.

She fell silent. He didn't press her, and instead drank his coffee in silence.

"I'll be right back," she said, getting up quickly and heading toward the restroom. Right before she reached the short hallway that led to the ladies' room, she turned and looked at him. "Please wait for me." And then she disappeared behind the door.

For reasons he didn't entirely understand, that broke his heart.

HAD SHE SAID too much? Or not enough? Standing in front of the washroom mirror, Vanessa put her hands to her flaming cheeks. She needed to remember that Remy and Seth were related by blood, while she was merely a stranger who'd come to town for what now seemed to be entirely selfish reasons. Clearly, Seth would have been better off without her attempt at obtaining a respite from her guilt at the knowledge that she hadn't handled their breakup well.

Turned out maybe that had been all in her head. She should have left well enough alone. And she couldn't believe she'd almost revealed the fact that she and Seth had never even been intimate. If she had, then Remy would know what a cold fish she was.

During her brief engagement to Seth, she'd managed to deflect every attempt he made to get her in his bed. At first, she'd chalked it up to her sheltered upbringing, but she'd come to the realization she didn't want him at all that way. She'd seen the way other women looked at him—he was a handsome man, after all. So it had to be her. With that bit of awareness, she'd understood they both deserved better.

But she'd lacked the courage to say that to Seth. Of course, the fact that when she'd called off the engagement, he'd been so furious that he'd punched a hole in the wall might have had something to do with it. He'd scared her so badly, and after he'd stormed out she'd had all her locks changed so he couldn't come back.

He hadn't. He'd hightailed it back to Roaring Springs, which had given her both relief and peace. Until she'd gotten the foolish idea that she needed to make things right with Seth so they could both move on.

All she'd managed to do was make everything worse.

Though she had learned one thing about herself. Apparently, she wasn't as much of an ice princess as she believed. One look from Remy Colton's hazel-green eyes set her on fire. She craved his touch, wondered about how his lips would feel on hers and imagined carnal scenarios she'd only previously read about.

Had she lost her mind? Seriously, she needed to get a grip on this ridiculous attraction she felt toward Remy. Talk about creating a huge mess! That's what it would be if she even considered acting on these forbidden desires.

So nope, nope, nope. Luckily, Remy seemed oblivious to her feelings. Thank goodness. She needed to remember she simply needed his help to find a place to stay for one or two nights and then she'd be out of this town for good. Hopefully before she managed to make an even worse mess out of things.

Once she managed to regain her composure, she left the sanctuary of the restroom and went back to her table. Remy looked up from his phone and smiled. The warmth of it went straight to her heart.

Shaking her head at herself, she sat back down and took a sip of her hot cider. Though it had cooled down significantly, the drink still tasted delicious.

"I've done some checking," he said. "We keep a family suite at The Chateau and since no one is using it at the moment, it's yours."

She stared. "A suite? That's amazing."

"And in case you're worrying about the cost, we're not going to charge you anything. You can have it for as long as you need it, within reason."

Within reason. His caveat made her smile. "Don't worry. I won't be moving in or anything. I'd just like to ski the mountain once it reopens. And then I'll be out of your hair."

Gaze steady, he shrugged. "How long is up to you. No one will be using the suite until after the holidays."

"Wow. Okay, thanks. I confess I'm a bit surprised you don't have family coming in for Christmas, though."

"We do. But they'll be staying at Colton Manor," he replied.

"Colton Manor?" She couldn't help herself. "That sounds like something out of a movie about royalty or something."

He laughed. "That's closer to the truth than you realize. My family has this huge and utterly pretentious mansion where my uncle Russ and my aunt Mara like to entertain. My grandfather, Earl, has a separate suite of rooms all to himself."

"Your father doesn't live there?"

"No. He tends to do his own thing."

"What about your mother?" Utterly intrigued, she leaned forward.

"Cordelia?" His mouth twisted. "She dropped me off on Whit's doorstep when I was five. She has... substance-abuse issues. My grandparents basically raised me. And Cordelia has been out of the picture ever since I got legal custody of Seth."

"That's a lot to take in," she mused. "You must have been so young yourself and yet still took on trying to raise your little brother."

He shook his head, his expression distant. "I didn't have a choice. I simply couldn't leave him in that environment."

She wanted to tell him how much she admired him for that, but kept it to herself. Remy clearly was a good, honorable man, and men like him weren't comfortable with compliments on actions they considered to be second nature.

They finished their drinks in companionable silence while the snow continued to fall outside. She liked the way Remy put her at ease without even trying.

"Would you like another cider?" he finally asked.

"I think I'm done," she said and stretched, even though she was reluctant to move. "Thank you so much for helping me."

Wearing a pleased expression, he nodded. "We've solved your immediate problem. But I'm still worried about Seth."

"I'm sure he'll be fine," she began.

"Oh, he will, once he thinks about things rationally and calms down. But that's not what I meant. I love him—he's family I didn't even know I had until fifteen years ago. But he's had his share of troubles since we reconnected. He's not always successful in conquering his demons."

Intrigued, she grabbed her empty cup and stood. "You know what? Let's both get another drink. On me this time. That's a story I'd really like to hear, if you don't mind sharing."

"I don't mind at all." His steady gaze touched on her and she felt it like a caress. "Though I have to say, I'm surprised Seth never told you."

She was, too, though she didn't voice that thought. "I'll be right back."

Instead of a line, only one other person waited at the counter. She placed the order and paid, waiting just a minute until the drinks were ready.

"Here you go," she said, placing Remy's coffee on the table in front of him. She waited until she'd gotten settled back in her seat before she took a sip of her own hot cider drink. "Seth didn't really talk much about his past. He always said he liked being an enigma."

Though Remy raised one eyebrow at that statement, he didn't comment. He drank his coffee, appearing contemplative, as if trying to figure out the best way to tell his story.

She waited patiently, enjoying the warmth of the room, the scent of fresh-roasted coffee, the delicious drink and the intriguing man seated across from her.

"When I was five years old, my birth mother dropped me off on my dad's doorstep," he began. "Whit Colton has always been a playboy. Still is, even though he's well past fifty. He had no time for a son, but he made sure to take care of me financially, for which I'm grateful. His parents were delighted to have a grandchild to coddle, so they took care of me and loved me."

He looked down, wrapping his hands around his coffee cup.

Unable to help herself, she made a sound of sympathy and reached across the table to put her hand on his. "That must have been hard on you. You were so young to go through such a thing."

Remy grimaced. "It wasn't easy. For years, I was convinced I must have done something wrong for my mother to send me away like that. And when my father didn't seem to want to have much to do with me, well, that reinforced my belief that it was all my fault." He released a ragged breath then went on. "As a consequence, I became very, very well behaved. Straight-A student, outstanding athlete, all of that. My grandparents cheered me on, encouraged me and treated me as if I mattered. Despite their belief in me, I always felt something was missing. So when I was twenty, I set out to find my birth mother."

Vanessa gasped. "Did you have any luck?" Then, as she realized what that meant, she shook her head. "Of course you did. I'm guessing that's also how you found Seth."

"Exactly. My mother, Cordelia, was an ex-model, which is how she met Whit Colton. She became a drug addict, probably before she dumped me off on Whit." He took a deep breath, his gaze faraway, as though he was lost in his memories. "Though she'd gotten married to Seth's father, he also had drug problems and, worse, anger issues. She'd neglected Seth the way she'd neglected me, except he spent his entire life in that environment. Seth's dad was abusive, verbally and physically, which in turn caused Seth to take out his anger on others, even animals. Though he was only fifteen, he started to have problems with drugs and alcohol too."

Stunned, she covered her mouth with her hand. "That's horrible. I had no idea. Seth never mentioned any of this to me."

Remy shrugged. "He says he prefers not to look back at the past. I'm sure he didn't want your pity."

Pity. She considered Remy's choice of word. Maybe he was right. But then again… "Knowing about this might have helped me understand him better. The anger issues. The times he got falling-down drunk."

"Well, now you know." Remy's matter-of-fact tone didn't fool her one bit. Raw emotion shone from his eyes. "I couldn't leave my half brother there. He wouldn't have stood a chance. I took over legal custody of him, even though I was only five years older."

"His parents let you? Just like that?"

"No." Remy drank his coffee. "I got a loan from my father and paid them to relinquish custody. Not surprisingly, they were eager to waive parental rights for some cold, hard cash."

"Yikes." She winced. "But this was a good thing, right? I'm assuming you must have brought him to your grandparents."

"No. I enrolled him in rehab and sent him to counseling. Once he was off the drugs and had learned to deal with his rage, then I brought him home. I loved him the best I could, as much as he would let me. Things were rough between us for a while, but then seemed to settle down." He sighed. "But you've seen him. Something is…off. He's back to binge drinking. And that anger still lurks right under Seth's skin, ready to erupt at the slightest provocation. I worry about him constantly."

Vanessa wasn't sure what to say. She settled on going with the truth. "Well, that explains a lot. The night I broke up with him, he punched a hole through my wall. He told me to consider myself lucky it wasn't me."

Remy's jaw tightened. Fists clenched, he turned away, his breathing harsh. She watched as he clearly struggled to get himself under control. "I'm sorry," he muttered, slowly moving to face her. "I wish I could have been there to protect you."

She took a deep breath. "He scared me to death. And then the way he's acted since I came here… While knowing about his past helps me understand why he behaves the way he does, I still think it's best if I don't see him again. At this point, I don't think we can even be friends."

To her surprise, Remy smiled. "Maybe it's time you make some new friends."

Chapter Four

Though he knew he shouldn't, Remy couldn't help but hope Vanessa took full advantage of the free luxury suite in The Chateau and stayed for a few days longer. Despite her clear worries over Seth, he really didn't feel his brother was a danger to anyone but himself.

Just in case, Remy would personally keep an eye on Vanessa to make sure she was safe. At least that's the reason he told himself, as he gazed at the beautiful woman sitting across from him. Anything else would make things way too complicated.

"What about you?" he asked, aching to both change the subject and hear her story so he could get to know her better. "Tell me about your childhood. Where did you grow up?"

A brief shadow crossed her face, so swift he might have imagined it. "In Boston. I've worked hard to lose the accent. And my childhood was nothing extraordinary," she said. Her tone was matter-of-fact, but he sensed she'd had her own trials and tribulations to deal with. Most everyone did, it seemed. Individuals who'd had a picture-perfect youth were few and far between.

"Tell me, anyway," he prodded. "I'm genuinely interested."

She gave him a sideways glance, as if she found that difficult to believe. "My parents were older and I was their only child. I always felt like an afterthought and I probably was. They sent me away as soon as they could, to an all-girls school in Switzerland."

"I can relate to that," he told her. "I wasted a lot of my younger years hoping if I was good enough, my dad might notice me." The rawness of his own admission left him stunned. He hadn't meant to tell her that. He considered it private, one of his deepest, darkest secrets. Yet on some level, he truly believed Vanessa would understand.

She nodded. "Me, too. I spent all my time trying to please my folks, because I believed if I did well enough at something, at *anything*, maybe they'd love me enough to let me return home to Boston." She laughed, a painful sound. "Pretty silly, wasn't I? Because they never did. Instead, they viewed each success as validation they were doing the right thing, that I belonged in Switzerland. By the time I realized I'd been knocking myself out for nothing, I was about to graduate. I felt like such a fool."

"No." This time he reached out and covered her hand with his. "You weren't. And I felt the same way as a kid." He took a deep breath and then forced himself to remove his hand. "What did you do after graduation?"

She shrugged. "Though I toyed with the idea of taking a year off, I didn't. In keeping with their plan to have me as far away from them as possible, my parents wanted me to go to university in London. This time,

rather than falling in with what they wanted, I refused."
Her chin came up and she smiled, though a touch of
sadness remained in her pretty blue eyes. "I had my
own plans, you see."

Intrigued, he waited.

"In Switzerland, I learned to ski. And it turned out
I was pretty darn good at it." Her smile widened, inviting him to take part in her joy. "While all the other
kids were partying and living it up, I was on the slopes.
I spent all my spare time perfecting my skill."

"You must have truly enjoyed it," he commented.

Just like that, her expression turned serious. "Yes. I
did. Skiing was the only thing that gave me pleasure."

More than anything, he wanted her to look happy
again. "Does that mean you became a ski bum?" he
teased. "Can't say I blame you. We get more than a few
of those here in Roaring Springs."

"I wanted to, but I'm too ambitious to just drift along,
spending all my time in pursuit of pleasure."

Her self-conscious half smile made his chest ache.
"Me, too," he said. "That's why I work so much."

Gaze faraway, she nodded. Remy let his own eyes
roam her features while she sat lost in thought. He was
amazed once more at how beautiful he found her, even
though her features weren't classically perfect.

When she didn't speak again, he prodded her, just a
little. "If you didn't become a professional skier, then
what did you do?"

"I decided to go to the University of Colorado in
Boulder, mostly due to the proximity to the slopes. I
had vague dreams of competing."

"Did you?" Intrigued again, he watched her.

"No. My parents would have been appalled. I think they were relieved I hadn't chosen a school closer to home. Once I graduated, I decided to stay in Boulder. End of story."

Except he sensed there might be more. "Now that you're an adult, why haven't you pursued your dream of competing? If you're that good, it seems like a waste of talent not to."

Sorrow darkened her eyes. "Thank you for saying that. Actually, I'd reached the same realization myself. I started skiing a lot—that's how I met Seth, you know. He seemed to understand my drive. Oh, I was fiercely intent on getting ready for my first competition. I'd entered and had my number and everything."

"Did you win?"

She shook her head. "I never even made it to the competition. Instead of spending every waking moment on the slopes, I truly wish I'd have made a trip home to Boston. The day before the big competition, both my parents were killed in a car wreck. I got the news in a phone call."

Aching to comfort her, he tightened his hand around hers. "I'm sorry."

"Thanks." She lifted her face and met his gaze. The pain and grief in her eyes made him long to take her into his arms. Luckily, the table separated them so he settled for holding on to her hand. She didn't pull away.

"Everything was a blur after that," she admitted. "Since my parents and I never managed to have a close relationship, I felt cheated. And was beyond devastated. I went back east to plan their funeral and begin settling their estate. I'm still dealing with all that. Through it all,

Seth was there for me, without question. That's partly why I felt like I owed it to him to explain."

Seth. She'd managed to effectively remind him of his brother. Yet he still couldn't bring himself to let go of her hand. A second later, she did it for him, as she gently pulled her fingers free and wrapped them around her cup.

Lump in his throat, he took out his phone and made a show of checking his emails. Nothing work-related or even slightly important.

Once he'd placed his phone back in his pocket, he looked up to find her watching him. "I'm glad you came here," he said gruffly. "It takes a big heart to try and make things right after a breakup."

Taking another sip of her cider, she sighed. "I don't know. Clearly, I messed that up, too. It would have been better if I'd never contacted him. I should have just stayed away."

He wanted to tell her again he was glad she hadn't. Because then, he never would have met her. Instead, he kept his mouth shut and said nothing. Flirtation, even if heartfelt, was the last thing either of them needed right now. Plus, as long as his brother still had feelings for her, Vanessa would be strictly off-limits as far as Remy was concerned.

Maybe forever.

Damn, how that possibility burned.

"Seth will be fine," he assured her. "It's likely he just needs a little more time."

"I hope so." She drank more of her cider. "I really hope he's able to move past this and everything else. Conquering demons is never easy. Believe me, I know."

"I do, too," he admitted, enjoying this feeling of camaraderie that was developing between them. This woman made him feel a lot of things, and he barely knew her. He could only imagine how it would be if they had the luxury of time to get acquainted without complications.

"I'd like to go skiing with you once they reopen the slopes," he blurted, inwardly wincing as soon as he said it.

Her eyes widened, letting him know he'd been right to question his timing. "I'd like that," she finally replied. "As long as it doesn't cause problems between you and your brother."

Before he could reply, her phone rang. Pulling it out of her jacket pocket, she stared. "It's Seth. I'm not sure I should answer it."

Leaving that choice up to her, he simply drank his coffee and said nothing.

She ended up letting the call go to voicemail. A moment later, her phone chirped.

"He's texting now," she commented, glancing at her screen. "He wants to know if we can talk. I just don't know. Part of me feels I've said all I had to say. I don't want to stir things up again."

Once more, Remy held his tongue. That would be her decision. He couldn't let himself get involved in whatever was between her and his brother. Even if it really was over, he wouldn't interfere.

Shaking her head, she shoved the phone back into her pocket. "I'll deal with him later. And sure, I'd love to ski with you. If you can keep up with me, that is." A quick flash of a smile. "I'm going to guess that you're pretty skilled, since you live up here."

"I'm not too bad," he admitted. "I've skied the black diamonds."

Black diamonds were for advanced skiers.

"Double or triple?" Which should only be skied by experts.

That made him laugh. "I've done a few double diamonds but I'm more of an advanced skier rather than expert. I'm good, but not great, if you know what I mean. I don't go often enough to have spent a lot of time perfecting my skills."

Clearly aghast, she stared. "You live in a ski resort but you don't go often? Why not? Do you have an injury or an illness that you haven't mentioned?"

"No." Still chuckling, he shook his head. "I work a lot."

Even he knew how lame that sounded. "Honestly, though, while I enjoy skiing, I don't have a passion for it."

"Then you've been doing it wrong," she instantly replied. "Or going with the wrong people. I'll show you. Skiing is the closest I've ever been to anything resembling heaven."

He couldn't help where his mind went at that. Not anywhere he could actually say out loud.

Staring at him, she blushed, as if she knew his thoughts. She opened her mouth and then closed it, looking down at her cider.

"Maybe you can teach me a few tricks," he said, deciding to let her off the hook. "Skiing, to clarify."

If anything, her blush deepened. But then, with the

dogged determination he was coming to know, she lifted her chin. "Maybe I can," she replied. "As soon as the slopes reopen, let's go. For now, can you help me get checked into my room? I'd like to get settled before this snowstorm becomes a blizzard and the roads become impassable."

Remy nodded. "That's always a possibility." Even though the weather forecast had only predicted heavy snow, this area of the Rockies had become known for its mercurial winter weather. "Are you ready?"

She pushed to her feet and carried her cup to the trash can, then returned to put on her jacket, hat and gloves. "Now I am," she said.

REMY WALKED WITH her to her car, then helped her unload and carry some of her belongings, though she insisted on taking her skis. Foot traffic on Main Street had thinned out and the snowfall showed no signs of slowing.

"You might be right about that blizzard," Remy commented.

She squinted at him through the snow and grinned. "I usually am. I have a thing about weather."

"You dabble in meteorology?"

"No." She laughed, joyous again now that they were outside. Snow stuck to her lashes and she blinked it away. "For whatever reason, I can tell when it's going to rain or snow and for how long. It's a special talent of mine."

He stared at her, his expression incredulous.

"You look like you don't know whether to take me

serious or not," she commented. "It's okay. A lot of people have told me I'm a little bit weird."

"Weird?" He shook his head. "Not hardly. I'd say intriguing, more than anything."

At that her entire body went warm—not an easy feat with the wind gusting and snow swirling. She barely knew this man, but he made her feel things she'd never experienced before.

When they reached The Chateau, Remy asked her to wait in the lobby while he went to speak with the people behind the counter. It didn't take long. A few minutes later he returned with a key card. "You're on the top floor," he said. "We only have four, but the suite has a wonderful view. This way to the elevator."

Following him, she looked around, awed despite herself by the elegant luxury of the hotel. While in Switzerland, she'd traveled Europe extensively. This hotel reminded her of several places where she'd stayed in France and Germany.

They were alone in the elevator. The piped-in music played Christmas carols, which again made her feel sad.

Pushing away the melancholy threatening to engulf her, she stepped out eagerly when the elevator stopped on their floor. The hallway seemed to extend out forever. Each doorway was framed in ornately carved wood and her feet sank in the plush carpet.

"Here we are," he told her, using the key card to unlock the door and then holding it open for her.

She stepped into a room larger than her first apartment. A leather couch and recliner had been arranged near a stone fireplace, with a flat-screen television over the mantel. Beyond, she could see a bedroom.

"Check out the view," Remy said, drawing aside the curtains proudly.

Unzipping her jacket, she went over and stood beside him, gazing out at the snow-covered town spread below. "This is…amazing." Troubled, she turned to face him. "Are you sure it's okay that I stay here? It seems like you could get bookings for a room like this and make quite a bit of money."

He smiled warmly down at her. "We never book this room. It's reserved for friends and family only."

About to protest that she was neither, he forestalled her with a light touch on her shoulder. Even through the parka, she wanted to lean into him.

"I consider you a friend, Vanessa," he said. "This room wasn't going to be used at all. As I mentioned earlier, you're welcome to stay as long as you like."

She thanked him, half hoping he would stay a while, half hoping he'd go so she could take a nap and get some rest. He smiled at her for the space of a few heartbeats, and then cleared his throat and turned toward the door.

"Have a good rest of your day," he told her. "I'll be in touch tomorrow, okay?"

Nodding her acceptance, she followed him as he let himself out, turning the dead bolt and adding the chain for good measure. Then and only then did she allow herself to truly explore the suite. She'd never stayed in any place this nice. While her parents had always had money, they were frugal travelers, especially on the rare occasions they'd allowed her to accompany them.

Eying her suitcase, she debated whether or not to unpack. For now, she decided to simply leave her belongings inside. A nap might do wonders to restore her flagging energy.

To her surprise, she slept for two hours. After a hot shower, she changed into her flannel pajamas and perused the room-service menu, too exhausted to drag herself downstairs to eat.

Later, warm and fed, she watched television for a while and then crawled between the softest sheets she'd ever experienced. She immediately fell fast asleep.

The next morning, she woke and stretched before padding to the window and peering out.

The snow was still falling, though now instead of a heavy curtain, fat, big flakes fell relentlessly from sky to earth, swirling on the north wind that stirred up snowdrifts and turned them into icy weapons. After getting dressed, then going downstairs and having breakfast, she decided she'd venture outside briefly after stopping at the front desk to find out if Pine Peak had opened yet. When the desk clerk had informed her that conditions were still too bad, she wanted to check it out for herself.

A few seconds out in front of The Chateau and she had to concur. This hotel sat in the valley. She could only imagine what things would be like up on the mountain.

Disappointed, she went back inside and wandered the lobby area of the elegant hotel, allowing herself to appreciate the festive holiday decorations. Her parents had been big on Christmas, and they'd had their servants put up two tall trees loaded down with decorations. Since her boarding school closed for winter break, she'd always traveled to Boston and returned to a bedroom that felt more like a stranger's than her own.

She might have thought reflecting on the fact that this was her first Christmas without them would have sent her into a downward spiral, but to her surprise, being around so many others intent on celebrating raised her spirits.

Seth had never been able to reconcile how she could yearn after people who made no secret of the fact that they found her a nuisance. After learning his story from Remy, she could better understand his viewpoint. As for herself, she'd never stopped hoping for her parents' love. Now, with them both gone, she'd never receive it.

Though she still had misgivings about meeting Seth, she couldn't help but remember all the times he'd been there for her. His strong, silent presence had helped her get through emotional lows that might have decimated her otherwise.

Impulsively, she texted him and asked him if they could meet for lunch. He immediately agreed, inviting her over for a home-cooked meal. Still skittish, she declined to go to his condo and instead insisted they meet somewhere public. Which happened to be the extremely crowded bar and grill at The Chateau. He'd agreed and they'd set a time—two hours from now.

Which gave her a little time to explore the rest of the hotel. She did some shopping in the gift shop and when she finished, she carried her purchases back up to her room. Then she sat down and put on a little makeup. The simple act of wearing mascara and foundation always gave her confidence. While she wanted things to get back on good footing with Seth, she couldn't discount the possibility that things would go south. She'd need all the confidence she could get.

Finally, a few minutes before the agreed-upon time, she made her way downstairs to the bar and grill. Eying the line at the reception desk, she decided to go ahead and wait for a table for two. Luckily, the line moved quickly and she soon found herself sitting at a cozy spot near the window with a great view of the snowy landscape.

She went ahead and ordered a drink, deciding on a hot rum toddy for warmth. When the waiter brought her drink and offered her a menu, she perused it, trying to decide what she was in the mood to eat. Though she'd have to wait to order until Seth arrived, it never hurt to have an idea of what she wanted.

Checking her watch, she took another tiny sip of her drink. Seth was late. Since he often ran behind, she'd expected this, but she'd been nursing her rum toddy for close to thirty minutes now.

If he didn't show up in the next five, she planned to go up to her room. Since Seth didn't know she was staying at The Chateau, he wouldn't disturb her. Remy had registered her under an assumed name, making a joke out of it, winking and smiling and generally making her feel better.

Her phone chimed, indicating a text. From Seth. Reading it, she wasn't sure what to think. I fell and hurt my ankle. Not broken, but swollen. I'm not up to meeting you. I can barely walk. Is there any way you'd consider stopping by here?

Dubious, she felt slightly ashamed that her first reaction was skepticism. She wouldn't put it past Seth to do whatever he felt necessary to get her alone.

But why? What would be the purpose? She'd already done what she'd come to do. She'd offered him her explanation. He'd reacted badly. What else was there to say?

Another text came through before she'd even answered the first. Please, Van. As your friend. I just need to make things right.

That one word made her waver. Friend. Because Seth had been that, first and foremost. She still owed him for always being there for her.

I'll stop by, she finally texted back. If I can even get there in this storm.

The city is plowing the roads several times a day, he texted. You should be fine.

Assuming he was correct, he had a point. She'd check out front and see if there were any cabs. If so, she'd use one of them for transport. Deciding, she texted him. Okay. But I can't stay long.

That's fine, he replied. See you in a few.

She tossed back the rest of her drink, then asked for the check. Once she'd paid, she put on her parka. After walking through the crowded lobby that hummed with activity, she stepped outside and stopped for a moment in wonder at the fierceness of the storm and the purity of the white landscape. All her life, for as long as she could remember, she'd felt this way about snow. As if each time it covered the earth, the pristine, silent landscape signified a new beginning.

Evidently, Roaring Springs taxi service had either been overwhelmed by demand or, more likely, people were staying put until the storm passed. Disappointed, she turned back toward the entrance, debating whether or not to text Seth and reschedule.

The plow went by just then, breaking the silence and sending arcs of snow onto both sides of the street. Since this completely obliterated the sidewalk, at least until it could be shoveled, that meant going to Seth's on foot was out, even if she had considered the possibility. Still, she'd probably have to shovel snow off her car.

Walking up and down the lot, she could no longer feel her feet. By the time she finally located her buried vehicle, she'd begun to seriously rethink the idea of leaving The Chateau. While the plow had just been by, with this rate of snowfall, it wouldn't be long until the street got buried again. And she didn't want to get stuck at Seth's.

It struck her that he hadn't even asked her where she was staying or been the slightest bit concerned about her safety out in this blizzard. When conditions were considered so dangerous that a ski resort closed the mountain, she thought he at least should have asked.

No point in worrying about that now. Since she'd gotten a little stir-crazy cooped up in the hotel, she decided to risk it. After all, Seth lived only a couple of blocks away.

It took her a good ten minutes, but she finally cleared enough of the snow from her car to be able to drive. She got in and started the engine, sitting in the cold seat for a few minutes until the vehicle warmed up.

By the time she got to Seth's condo, nearly an hour had passed since his first text. Her hands ached from gripping the wheel, but the short drive had been uneventful despite greatly reduced visibility. She'd had to take it slow, watching for icy patches on the streets. Luckily, very few other vehicles were out. It seemed her earlier guess had been correct. Most people must have decided to hunker down by the fire.

She reached Seth's condo without incident. Though she'd only been there once, luckily she remembered the location. He lived in a trendy part of town right off Main Street. His building was one-of-a-kind, with fully restored, modern styling.

After she parked, she walked across the lot, headed inside and rode the antique elevator to his floor. His door had a red welcome mat in front.

Taking a deep breath, she raised her hand and knocked three times, instinctively using the old coded cadence they'd agreed on during her rough times. She hadn't been taking visitors then and Seth had been the one exception.

The door swung open. "Hey there!" Wearing a big, goofy smile, Seth waved her inside.

She could tell he had been drinking the instant he closed the door behind her and awkwardly tried to take her into his arms. More than just the nearly overwhelming odor of whiskey, his red-rimmed, bleary eyes and delayed coordination told her that he'd had quite a few before her arrival.

Chapter Five

Making a snap decision, Vanessa spun around to leave. "I don't need this. Not today." Not ever.

"Wait." He grabbed her arm. "It's okay. I promise. I just needed to take the edge off. I'm not drunk."

While she wasn't sure she believed him, since he seemed to be in a good mood, she relented. "Just for a little bit. I don't want to be gone too long with this storm still going strong."

"Is it?" He seemed disinterested. "I've been holed up here and haven't checked outside at all. Would you like a beer, or a glass of wine? I also have some whiskey I can mix with cola or pour over ice. I'm drinking it on the rocks. Your call."

"I'm good with water," she said. "Or coffee, tea or cocoa, if you have any of those."

He laughed. "I'm sure I do. Come on into the kitchen and you can choose."

Turning to lead the way, he stumbled into the wall. At the last moment, he caught himself and kept going. Not sure how to react, Vanessa eyed the door. Should she leave or simply pretend not to notice?

"Don't go," he pleaded, glancing back at her over

his shoulder. Apparently, he was at least sober enough to notice her hesitation. "I promise, I've got this under control."

Despite her instincts, she trailed along behind him into the kitchen. She wished she'd thought to let Remy know that she'd come here.

"What about your ankle?" she asked.

"It's better now," he said, with a lopsided smile.

After getting her a bottle of mineral water, Seth picked up his own drink—something with ice in a tall, plastic glass—and gestured toward his living room. "Want to sit and talk? I want to apologize for the way I acted when you were here last. Plus, since you were generous enough to explain everything to me, I think I owe you an explanation, as well."

Doing a quick mental evaluation—he wasn't slurring his words and seemed relatively focused—she nodded and followed him into the living room. He'd built a fire in the stone fireplace and had the TV on, though the sound had been turned down so low she couldn't hear it. The curtains were open, revealing the wintry wonderland outside.

He still hadn't asked her where she might be staying. She needed to decide how she would answer if he did, since she'd actually prefer him not to know.

Taking a seat in the overstuffed chair on one side of the fireplace, he motioned her to the other one. Relieved he wasn't going to try to get her to snuggle up next to him on the couch, she did.

"Relax, Van," he chided. "I know I was an ass last time. I'm sorry for that. The breakup just hit me hard. Part of me really wanted to believe you'd come here to get back together, even though I knew somewhere deep inside that you hadn't."

Releasing a breath, she watched him closely. Seth's vibe seemed mellow and not the least bit threatening. Maybe now that he'd had a chance to reconcile himself with the truth, she could finally get that closure she'd come for.

Sipping his drink, he eyed her over the rim of his glass. "Sorry we weren't able to hit Pine Peak before they had to close it."

"Me, too," she admitted. "I'm hoping they reopen before I have to head back to Boulder."

He nodded. "It's a good slope. I get up there as often as I can. Have you been keeping up your normal skiing-every-week thing?"

"When I can, yes. I've had to go back east twice since November, which of course meant I couldn't ski. I did manage to get up to New Hampshire once, but most times I was too busy to spend any time on the slopes."

"Speaking of which, when are you going back to Boston next?" he asked. "Or did you just get back?" Seth knew all about her frequent and necessary trips to try to settle her parents' estate.

"I'm due for a trip," she replied. "Though I decided to go after the holidays. I'd rather wait until ski season is over, but since we still can get snow into March, that might be stretching it a bit too much."

"Skiing still comes number one with you, I see." Seth made the statement without judgment. After all, he was one of the few people outside of the competition set who knew just how skilled she was.

"You know it." Access to difficult mountains had

been one of her primary considerations when she'd decided to live in Colorado. That, and she liked the natural beauty of the state and the way the air always felt clean due to the lack of humidity.

"Can't say I blame you." Continuing to sip from his drink, Seth appeared unusually relaxed. She remembered what Remy had said about drugs and wondered if he'd taken something and combined that with alcohol.

While she tried to come up with a way to ask, he nodded off, still sitting up, drink in hand.

Afraid he might spill it, she cleared her throat. When he opened his eyes, she smiled at him. "Maybe you should put the drink down if you're going to nap?"

His bleary gaze drifted from her to his glass. He cursed softly, but placed his drink on the coaster on the coffee table. "Sorry," he muttered. "Probably my cold meds interacting with the whiskey."

"I figured," she replied. Though she hadn't even been there an hour, the time had come for her to leave.

"Don't go yet," Seth begged, as though he'd somehow read her mind. "I'm sorry I'm such a poor host, but I really don't want to be alone right now. I need you to be here for me, Van. Just for a little bit longer."

He needed her. And since she'd said virtually those exact words to him in the dark times right after her parents' deaths, she'd be a jerk if she left now.

But what did he expect her to do? Watch him sleep? Grab the remote and watch some television? Or scroll social media on her phone?

Then she caught sight of Seth's laptop, open on the kitchen table. While she could always wait to check flights until she got back home to Boulder, it wouldn't hurt to check rates now. Especially since she had need of a way to occupy her time.

"Do you mind if I use your laptop to see about flights to Boston next month?" she asked. "It's kind of a pain to do on my phone and I'd like to get a jump on things."

Eyes half-lidded, he heaved himself up and padded to the kitchen without answering, where she could hear him making himself another drink. "Are you sure you don't want something besides water?" he called. "I have some really good whiskey. Or rum, vodka or tequila, if that's your preference."

"No, thank you." She eyed the laptop, wondering if he'd even heard her. Either way, it really wasn't a good idea for him to keep drinking. Gathering up her courage, she spoke up. "Hey, Seth. From one friend to another, don't you think maybe you've had enough?"

At first, he didn't respond. She could hear the sound of him stirring his drink. Finally, he came back into the living room and dropped himself into his chair. The sudden movement caused his drink to slosh over onto his jeans. He didn't appear to notice. "Why are you giving me such a hard time?" he asked, his voice as mournful as his expression. "I'm just relaxing inside my own home. I'm not planning on driving anywhere."

"I'm worried about you," she said, relieved the anger hadn't returned. "That's the truth. It kind of seems like your drinking might have gotten out of control."

He took a long sip from his glass before answering. "I don't have a problem, if that's what you're inferring."

Since she wasn't going to argue, Vanessa simply focused her attention on the leaping flames of the fire. They sat in silence for the next several minutes while she tried to work up what to say so she could leave. More than anything, she wished she could help him, but she understood she couldn't assist someone who didn't want to help himself. Whatever path Seth had now taken, he had to make his own choices.

She just didn't want to be around to watch him crash and burn. It would be far too painful. Whatever else he might have become, he'd been a good man once. He'd been the actual definition of a true friend. And maybe, just maybe, he needed her to be one to him now.

"Is there anything I can do to help you?" she asked quietly. "Anything at all."

He looked at her then, really looked at her. "What do you mean?"

Waving her hand vaguely, she shrugged. "I don't know, Seth. I can tell something is wrong, but you act like you're fine."

"I *am* fine," he protested, then tossed back half of his drink. "Please stop worrying about me. I get enough of that with my brother, Remy."

Remy. Just the mention of his name made her heart skip a beat. Luckily, Seth had never been the most observant of men. Especially now, while more than halfway to intoxicated.

"I'll try not to worry," she promised, leaning forward. "Seth, you were there helping me in one of the darkest times in my life. I want you to know that I will do the same for you. We won't ever be a couple, at least not in a romantic way. But if you'd like to be friends again, I'm open to that."

"We'll see." He drained his glass and awkwardly pushed up out of his chair, clearly on his way to make another. If he kept drinking like this, he'd be three sheets to the wind in no time.

"Wait," she said, desperate to find a way to distract him. "Would you mind letting me use your laptop to look up ticket prices on flights from DIA to Logan?"

Maybe if she could get him using the computer with her, he'd forget about getting another drink, at least for a little while. Seth had always been really into computers. So much so that she'd always wondered why he hadn't looked for a career in that field.

Swerving unsteadily toward the table, he grabbed the laptop and brought it to her. Dumping it unceremoniously on her lap, he shrugged. "Knock yourself out. My password is 'beginagain2020.'"

She blinked. "Okay. Thanks."

"No problem." Seth waved his hand and resumed his journey into the kitchen.

She powered up the laptop, and when the prompt came up, she typed in Seth's password. The usual assortment of desktop file folders came up. One marked "Loves" caught her eye.

She glanced at the kitchen. No sign of Seth. Feeling daring, she clicked on the folder.

Inside were two subfolders. One marked "Vanessa Fisher," the other marked "Sabrina Gilford." More than curious now, she clicked on the latter and found dozens of photographs. Several were of Seth with his arm around a pretty woman. Others were clearly screenshots of typed notes. Apparently, he and Sabrina had been dating while he and Vanessa were also seeing each other.

She glanced around. Still no sign of Seth. Finger

poised above the built-in mouse, she took a deep breath. "Are you all right?" she called.

"Yeah." He poked his head around the corner. "I'm going to the bathroom, okay? Don't run out on me while I'm gone."

"I won't," she promised. The instant he disappeared, she returned her attention to the laptop and quickly clicked on the folder marked with her name. Just like the Sabrina one, there were numerous photos of her and Seth together, as well as several of just her. And like the other folder, there were also notes, detailing his thoughts and emotions.

Not sure she wanted to see this, she closed that file and returned to the other one.

A screenshot of an obituary caught her eye. Enlarging it, she realized Sabrina had died. Hurriedly, she read the obituary, and then went back and clicked on some of the notes.

Then, considering the possibility that Seth might return and ask her about airline fares, she opened up a popular travel site and typed in a ticket-price search for a random date in mid-January. Once those selections were displayed, she minimized the file and went back to reading Seth's notes and screenshots of text messages between him and Sabrina.

From what she could piece together, Sabrina had broken up with him in a similarly vague way as Vanessa had. Judging by his text messages to her, he'd been both furious and threatening.

And then Sabrina had been murdered. Vanessa felt sick. If she remembered correctly, there had been some serial killer in Roaring Springs. Sabrina must have been one of the victims.

Since Seth had still not returned, she took a couple of pictures with her phone.

She closed the file and returned to the travel website and took a snapshot of that. Then she powered down the laptop and closed it.

Still no sign of Seth. She wondered if he'd fallen asleep or passed out in the bathroom. Though she in no way wanted to check on him, she'd never be able to live with herself if she left and found out later that something bad had happened to him.

About to get up and go knock on the door, relief flooded her when Seth emerged, once again heading into the kitchen.

"Did you find your flight info?" he asked, using the ice maker to fill a glass. Which meant he was making another drink.

She'd had enough. About to tell him she needed to go, she stood. This might be better to do once she had stepped into the hallway, she thought. Halfway to the front door, the sounds of an awful crash came from the kitchen. Immediately followed by Seth cursing.

"Are you all right?" she asked urgently.

"No. I cut myself. There's blood. A lot of blood. And it hurts."

Hurrying into the kitchen, she found Seth standing in the middle of the room, surrounded by shards of glass and holding his bleeding hand. Blood dripped from between his fingers, pooling on the floor.

"That looks like a bad cut." She grabbed a dish towel. "Here. Let me wrap this around it so we can stop the bleeding. Then I'll take a look at it. It might be a good idea for you to go to the hospital if it's really deep. You could need stitches."

He swayed, appearing as if he might pass out and tumble face-first into the dangerous pieces of glass. Going to him, and wincing at the crunching under her feet, she steered him toward the kitchen table and helped him settle into a chair. "What happened?"

"I'm not sure." Expression bewildered, he looked at the glass and blood as if he had no idea how he'd gotten there. "I was about to pour another drink. The bottle must have slipped, or my glass did, because the next thing I knew, they were both broken. And I was bleeding."

REMY MUST HAVE checked his phone ten times that morning, hoping against hope that Vanessa would call or text. When the cell finally rang shortly after lunch, relief flooded him. He realized he'd waited all day simply to hear her voice. Except not like this. Breathless, she stumbled over her words, clearly panicked. "I need your help."

All senses instantly on alert, he asked her what was going on.

"It's Seth," she said. "He's been drinking and he fell and cut himself pretty badly. I think he might have mixed something else with his alcohol, though I don't know what. He claimed it was cold medicine, but I doubt that. He's refusing to go to the ER."

Briefly, Remy closed his eyes. "Where are you?"

"Seth's place," she replied, her voice still shaky.

He inhaled sharply. Why the hell that answer surprised him, he didn't know. He shouldn't have expected otherwise. "I'll be there as quickly as I can." He glanced at the window and the blinding swirl of snow. "How are the roads?"

"They're keeping the streets plowed," she said. "I drove here. It was manageable."

"How long ago?" he asked, pinning his phone between his shoulder and his ear as he shrugged into his coat.

"Not long. A little more than an hour."

More relieved than he should have been, he told her he'd see her soon and ended the call.

His Jeep had gotten buried by snow, but after a few minutes, he'd cleared enough off to head out.

The roads weren't awful, though clearly the snowplow couldn't keep up with the swiftly falling precipitation. When he reached Seth's condo, he couldn't find a parking spot and ended up double parking behind another car buried in snow.

As soon as he stepped off the elevator, he saw Vanessa, standing in Seth's doorway, watching for him. Relief lit up her face the instant she spotted him. "I've bandaged him up as best I could," she said, leading the way into the kitchen. "And I cleaned up the broken glass. But he's lost a lot of blood and the combination of whatever he took and the whiskey isn't helping."

In the kitchen, a haggard-looking Seth sat slouched on the floor, back braced up against one of the cabinets. When he saw Remy, he grimaced and glared at Vanessa. "What's he doing here? Did you call him?"

"I did," she replied softly. "You need help, Seth. More than I'm able to give you."

He cursed, stringing together several swear words that would have made a sailor blush. Vanessa didn't react to them. Instead, she kept her gaze trained on Remy. The hope and trust he saw in her eyes made him feel both humble and proud.

He could fall for this woman. Where that thought had come from, he didn't know. What he did understand was that such thoughts had no place in this scenario.

Crouching down near his brother, Remy reached for Seth's shoulder. With a violent move, his brother knocked away his hand. "Don't touch me."

"Fine." Remy stood and pulled out his phone. "I'm going to give you a choice. Either you let me take you to the emergency room, or I call 911 and you can ride in the ambulance. Your choice."

"I'm fine," Seth insisted. "I'm not even drunk. My cold medicine didn't mix well with my whiskey. I just need to sleep it off."

Ignoring the fact that his brother *always* needed to sleep it off, Remy pointed to the rough tourniquet Vanessa had placed on Seth's arm. "I'm talking about your cut. Looks like you may need stitches."

"And antibiotics," she interjected, earning another irate look from Seth. Vanessa took a step back before glancing at Remy. "You got this?"

Remy nodded. "Yep."

"Then I'm going to head out." Snatching up her coat, she marched toward the front door. "Take care. I hope you feel better soon, Seth."

And then she was gone. Remy felt her absence with the same sort of chill one feels when the sun disappears behind a cloud.

He returned his attention to his brother. "What'll it be, Seth? Ambulance or riding in my Jeep?"

"Jeep," Seth replied, his voice as sullen as his expression. Remy helped him up, noting the strong stench of whiskey. Somehow, he got a coat around his brother's shoulders and a ski cap on his head. "Be careful on the snow," he warned, keeping a grip on Seth's uninjured arm.

Once at the ER, the triage nurse greeted them by name. Once Remy explained the reason they were there, she asked them to take a seat and promised they'd be seen shortly.

Luckily, since the slopes were closed down, the ER was mostly empty. Dr. Reynolds stitched up Seth's arm, and they did some blood work despite his protests. When the doctor came back to discharge them, he asked Seth if he was aware of the dangers of mixing benzodiazepine with alcohol.

At least Seth appeared sheepish. He concurred that he did know, but claimed to have forgotten he'd taken the pills before he started drinking. His words mollified the doctor, though Remy had his doubts. His brother would say whatever felt convenient to get him out of trouble. It had become Seth's pattern recently and Remy had no idea how to break the cycle.

Pen poised to sign the discharge paperwork, Seth asked if he could have some pain medication.

Incredulous, Remy met Dr. Reynolds's gaze and gave a half shake of his head. "I think ibuprofen will take care of any pain," the doctor said. "Take two before you go to sleep tonight."

Seth frowned, then opened his mouth as if he meant to argue.

"He'll be fine," Remy said, forestalling him. "Come on, Seth. Sign the paperwork so we can get you home before the storm gets any worse."

A surly Seth did as Remy asked. Bundling him up, Remy hustled his brother out into the snowstorm.

They didn't speak for the entire drive home, which was fine by Remy. He'd actually expected his brother to issue a litany of complaints.

Only when they reached the front of Seth's condo building did Remy address his brother. "I'm just going to drop you off here. Please do as the doctor said and try to stay out of trouble."

Seth turned to look at him. The flatness of his gaze matched his voice. "Why did Vanessa call you? How'd she even get your number?"

"She called The Chateau and left a message for me to call her. When I returned the call, I used my cell and told her to save it to her contacts."

"I knew it!" Seth exploded. "You have the hots for my girl."

Remy shook his head. There were several possible responses to that statement, each of which would only add fuel to the fire. He decided to go with a simple version of the truth. "Look, Seth, I like Vanessa. She seems like good people. However, leave me out of whatever is going on between the two of you. I'm only trying to do what's right."

"Of course you are." Seth rolled his eyes. "Mr. Goody Two-shoes, walk-the-straight-and-narrow, black-and-white Remy Colton. I'm thinking it would never occur to you to hit on Vanessa Fisher, especially considering who she is."

Refusing to allow himself to be insulted, Remy focused on the last part of Seth's statement. "What do you mean, 'who she is'?"

"You really don't know? Google her. She's the only daughter of Clive and Celeste Fisher."

The names sounded familiar, but Remy still couldn't place them. Not wanting to prolong this discussion with his brother, he simply nodded. "Take care of yourself."

"I will." After exiting the Jeep, Seth slammed the door. Remy watched until he'd disappeared inside the building, then drove back home in the snow.

Once inside, he did a quick internet search. As Vanessa had mentioned, her parents had been killed in a car accident six months ago. What she hadn't said was that her father, Clive Fisher, was the well-known, wealthy investment banker and author of several self-help books. Vanessa truly was an heiress, with a fortune that rivaled the Coltons'.

As if thinking of Vanessa had somehow summoned her, his phone rang, caller ID displaying her name. Despite everything, his heart skipped a beat.

"I've been meaning to call you," he answered. "I just dropped Seth off at his condo."

"How is he?" Vanessa asked.

"He'll survive." He sounded grim, revealing his frustration. "The doc said his blood pressure was dangerously low, and the tox screen revealed he'd taken a high dose of a benzodiazepine. He finally admitted it, though he claimed it was an accident."

"Did they keep him overnight?"

"No." He dragged his hand through his hair. "They stitched him up, gave him a prescription for antibiotics, told him to take ibuprofen, and sent him on home. I debated whether or not to stay with him, but he didn't want me to. And he's an adult, so I left."

"I can't blame you." Her soft voice felt like a balm to his soul. Suddenly, he ached to see her.

"What are you doing for dinner?" he asked before he could stop himself.

"I'm not sure. I've been debating whether to use room service or go eat by myself in the restaurant."

Taking a deep breath, he decided to go for it. "Do you like steak?" he murmured, deliberately keeping his tone light.

She laughed. "Who doesn't?"

"The Lodge has a great steak house called Del Aggio," he continued. "How about I take you there?"

She went silent for a moment, making him wonder if he'd made a mistake. "That sounds wonderful," she finally said. "But won't you need reservations?"

"They'll fit us in," he told her. "I'll just need to make a quick call. Would seven work for you? If the tram was running, we could ride that up to the resort. But since I believe they shut it down due to the storm, we'll have to take my Jeep. As long as the roads are passable, we'll be good to go."

"Seven is perfect." Though a tinge of hesitation still colored her voice, she also sounded happy. That sent an answering warmth through him. "I'll see you around what…six forty-five?"

He agreed and ended the call. Filled with anticipation, he called up to The Lodge and let them know his plans.

Chapter Six

Del Aggio, in keeping with the general decorating scheme of The Lodge, sported a combination of Western and down-home, country decor. A huge two-sided fireplace sat right in the middle of the restaurant and the crackling blaze they had going did much to keep the diners warm and cozy.

Vanessa and Remy waited in the bar until their table was ready. Though she'd been inside The Lodge lobby a few times, she hadn't taken the time to really check out the interior of the restaurant. Now she realized she much preferred The Lodge's rustic comfort to The Chateau's old-world-style elegance.

"This place makes me feel right at home," she mused, sipping from her glass of Shiraz.

"That's because you're a skier," Remy replied, smiling. "My family did a ton of research and decorated this place accordingly. The Chateau is more for those who like the idea of a ski vacation, but prefer to spend more time shopping and getting pampered."

His comment made her laugh. "You hotel moguls think of everything, don't you?"

"We have to." He gave a modest shrug. "Research matters if you want to be a success."

And The Colton Empire definitely was a success. Seth had gone on and on about his brother's family. Being her father's daughter, she'd checked into them. Seth had been right. The Colton businesses were definitely fiscally solvent and growing.

Remy's name was called. He took her elbow as they walked toward the hostess. At his touch, her entire body warmed. Honestly, she felt as if they were on a date instead of two acquaintances working toward a possible friendship.

Due to Remy's status, they were given a secluded table near the fireplace but with a floor-to-ceiling window on the other side. Outside, the snowflakes danced in the decorative lanterns that circled a large, snow-covered patio with a seating area that must be popular in the summer and fall.

Vanessa perused the elaborate menu that featured every cut of steak, as well as a few token chicken and fish entrées. There was nothing she loved better than good prime rib, cooked medium rare. A well-cooked T-bone would be a close second.

Closing her menu, she saw Remy had already done the same. "You decided quickly," he commented.

"It was an easy choice." Smiling, she sipped her wine. She truly enjoyed being with this man, despite the push-pull of attraction that constantly simmered between them.

The waitress arrived, blushing when she saw Remy. She asked if they wanted another drink. Vanessa asked for a second glass of wine, plus water. Remy did the same.

Once the waitress walked off, Remy leaned forward. "Service is a bit slow here, on purpose. It's a deliberately unhurried dining experience."

Vanessa had to grin. "I'm not in a rush to go anywhere. Are you?"

This made him throw his head back and laugh. "I like you, Vanessa Fisher."

She blushed as deeply as the waitress had. "Thanks. I like you, too."

They placed their orders—Remy got the T-bone, and if she'd known him better, she would have definitely asked for a taste.

He told her about his job in public relations, which had always interested her. In return, she told him about Boston and how her passion for the New England Patriots had now been relegated to second place, behind the Denver Broncos, which her old Boston friends would consider sacrilegious if they knew.

"But I'm still a Red Sox fan," she said breathlessly, as if that made all the difference in the world. "Though the Broncos come first in my heart, I also watch the Pats."

"You like football?" Remy asked, sounding as surprised as if she'd just admitted to belonging to a secret society or something.

"Love it. I try not to miss any games. I actually DVR them so I can watch them later if I have to miss them."

He laughed again. "This is going to sound so weird, but I do that, too."

"Wow." She eyed him, not sure if he might be pulling her leg. "I've never met anyone else who did that."

"Well, now you have." He turned the conversation to

other topics, ranging from the snowfall forecast to what Roaring Springs was like in the summer.

"Is it empty?" she asked.

"It's less crowded than during ski season, but we get different kinds of tourists. Hikers and bikers, people who want to train for endurance bike rides and such. And people who like to shop. For the first two weeks in July, Roaring Springs hosts a film festival similar to Sundance. It's been a tradition for the last ten years."

Intrigued, she made a mental note to check that out. "I'd be interested in attending something like that," she said.

"Great. I'll keep you posted on the details." His easy reply sounded as if he took it for granted that they'd stay in touch.

She realized she liked that idea a lot. But she knew he might change his mind once she revealed what she'd discovered on Seth's computer.

Since they hadn't ordered appetizers, their steaks came just then, perfectly cooked. She cut into hers, anticipation making her mouth water. Remy did the same.

She waited until they'd both eaten most of their meal before bringing up what she'd found on Seth's computer. She wasn't even sure she should. After all, she'd been snooping on Seth's computer. No matter how she tried to spin it, what she'd found had been none of her business. So what if Seth kept computer files on his previous girlfriends? Despite being creepy and a little weird, doing that wasn't illegal.

Still, it bothered her. A lot. Maybe because Seth had never mentioned Sabrina at all, even when she'd been murdered. She really wanted to see what Remy thought about all of it, even if telling him changed his opinion of her. Which shouldn't have mattered, but it did.

A lull had occurred in the conversation. Now or never. She took a deep breath.

"What do you know about Sabrina Gilford?" Vanessa asked, aware her casual tone might be at odds with her intent expression.

In the act of eating a piece of his steak, Remy stilled. "She is—was—my cousin, on my father's side. She was murdered, strangled just like the other victims. We all believed she'd been killed by the same serial killer—the Avalanche Killer—but when Curtis Shruggs was brought into police custody, he said he didn't kill her."

"Maybe he lied?" she suggested, her heart beginning to pound.

"I thought that, too. The only problem is he confessed to all the other murders. Why not claim that one? He said he only wanted credit for his own work. As far as the police are concerned, Sabrina's killer is still out there."

She took a deep breath, unsurprised to realize her hand was shaking. "Remy, please don't think I'm crazy. But do you think Seth might know anything about her murder?"

Inwardly cringing, she waited for Remy's reaction. She wouldn't blame him if he stormed out, after accusing her of being crazy.

Instead, he eyed her and chewed, seriously considering her question. "As far as I know, he didn't even know her. So I doubt it. Why?"

Debating whether or not to simply drop it, Vanessa pulled up her photo albums on her phone. She clicked on the first shot she'd taken of the pics on Seth's laptop and slid her cell across the table to Remy.

"I was looking at airfare to Boston on Seth's laptop—with his permission. I saw a folder marked 'Loves' and it intrigued me, so I clicked on it. Inside, there were two subfolders, one with my name and one with Sabrina's. Both had lots of pictures. Take a look and see for yourself."

Picking up her phone, Remy studied the images, scrolling from one to the other. His frown deepened as he read Seth's typed notes, and when he came to the newspaper clippings, his mouth twisted in pain.

When he finished, he wordlessly slid her phone back to her. "I wonder why Seth never mentioned he dated Sabrina," he mused. "That doesn't seem like something he would want to hide."

She shrugged. "Did you know about his engagement to me? Or even that he was in a serious relationship?"

"I heard about it." Eying the last bite of steak on his plate, he finally popped it into his mouth and chewed slowly. Once he'd swallowed, he took a drink of his wine. "I wasn't able to make the party when Seth announced his engagement."

"I know," she replied in a soft voice. "I would definitely remember meeting you."

Looking dazed, he started to apologize for not making more of an effort to meet her. "Work had been crazy and I took off for a bit of a mini-vacation. By the time I got back in town, you'd already gone. And then Seth said you'd broken up. I have to say, I wasn't surprised."

"It was all very sudden. Both the engagement and the breakup. I realized it wasn't going to work out, Seth and

I getting married." Slightly embarrassed, she sighed. "Seth is—or was—my friend. While I don't recognize the man he's apparently become since we separated, I have to believe he still has a good heart."

Expression relieved, Remy sipped his wine. "Thank you for that."

Not sure how to respond, she stirred her food around on her plate and simply nodded. "I'm sorry I brought it up. Heck, I'm sorry I snooped. I just saw the folder and my curiosity got the best of me. I know it was wrong."

"It's okay." Unbelievably, he seemed to be attempting to comfort her. "You're only human. I think most of us would have done the same thing."

Would he? She wanted to ask, but decided not to. Remy Colton seemed like a pretty black-and-white kind of guy. She doubted he'd ever intrude on anyone's privacy like that.

"Look," he continued, "my brother has been having issues recently. I'll be the first to admit it. And lately, with the drinking and whatever else, I think his addictive tendencies might have gotten the best of him once again. If I can convince him to get help—"

"I think that would be awesome…"

Tilting his head, he studied her. "But? I can tell there's something you're not telling me."

"He's your brother. And my friend. But the Seth I've seen since I've been here scares me. I'm more than a little afraid."

Gaze locking with hers, he finally nodded. "I'll look into this, I promise you. For now, maybe it's best that you make sure you're not alone with him again."

"I don't plan to be."

The waitress returned, bringing with her an elaborate dessert tray. Though Vanessa's first impulse had been to decline, a bowl of berries in cream caught her eye. "I'll have that," she said.

Remy ordered a cheese plate, along with coffee for them both. They spent the rest of the time chatting about inconsequential things, the kind of superficial small talk between two people who had no idea what else to actually say.

She hated it. And wondered if she'd managed to ruin things between them before they'd ever begun.

REMY WATCHED THE beautiful woman across from him struggle. More than anything he wished he could reach over, take her hands in his and promise to protect her. From his own brother. That's where things had begun to feel as if he'd stepped into an alternate universe.

Deep inside, Remy had always longed for family, the one thing his self-involved father had no desire to give him. When he'd discovered the existence of a half brother, he'd known he'd move Heaven and earth to make sure the kid was safe.

And so he had. Seth had been his number one priority since the day he'd first seen that skinny, sullen, scared teenager slouching in a rickety chair in their mother's filthy apartment. He'd known right then like a punch in the gut that no matter what he had to do, he'd be getting Seth out of there. Remy never would have guessed that by having his mother dump him off on Whit Colton's doorstep, she'd been doing him a huge favor. He'd wanted to do the same for Seth, and so he had.

And now this. Vanessa's discovery made him question it all again.

Had Seth done something to hurt Sabrina? He wanted to believe that wasn't the case with everything within him. But that one little niggling piece of doubt hung in there, making him question just about everything.

Meanwhile, Vanessa had gone quiet, contemplative. Her long-lashed blue eyes stirred a complicated swirl of emotions inside him. She intrigued him, worried him and made him happy all at once. A combination both dangerous and full of potential.

"I'll do some checking," he reassured her.

Though Vanessa nodded, she seemed distracted, eating her berries one at a time. After she'd finished them, she gazed at the bowl as if she'd like to lick it clean. "I'm sorry if I ruined the evening," she finally said, clearly unaware of her effect on him.

He blinked. "You didn't." Now he did allow himself a light touch on the back of her hand. "I don't blame you for freaking out. To be honest, I'm a little concerned myself. I'm worried about my brother."

"I am, too." She sighed, her pretty eyes going soft. "Maybe I shouldn't have come here."

"I'm glad you did," he told her, meaning every word. He didn't know how a woman he'd just met could manage to make him feel so alive, just by her presence. Every time her gaze met his, his heart turned over and his body stirred.

Remy signaled the waitress for the check. "Well, we aren't going to solve anything tonight. Let me get you back to The Chateau and tomorrow I'll make some phone calls and see what I can find out."

After dropping off Vanessa at The Chateau, Remy continued on to his home, driving slowly in the thick curtain of snow. Once he'd gotten inside, he started up his gas fireplace, poured himself a drink and began flipping through old movies available on Netflix.

When his cell rang, he answered it without looking at the screen, assuming it was Vanessa. Instead, his father's voice boomed at him with his standard greeting. "I'm glad I caught you," Whit Colton said.

"Where else would I be at ten in the evening during a blizzard," Remy pointed out, his tone mild as he sipped on his Scotch.

Apparently feeling as if he'd made enough small talk, Whit cut directly to the chase. "Who is the woman you've put in the family suite at The Chateau?" he demanded. "Are you up there now?"

"No—" Remy replied.

Whit cut him off. "Imagine my surprise when I learn my son has decided to make use of the suite without even checking with me."

The anger in Whit's voice was no surprise. Remy frequently managed to make his father mad, most often without even trying.

"I made sure we weren't going to be using it," Remy said, refusing to allow Whit to make him defensive. "She came up here from Boulder and the storm hit and she had nowhere else to stay. They've closed the tunnel and the pass, so she's stuck here in Roaring Springs until this storm blows over. I let her stay there since she's a friend."

"A *friend*?" Whit drawled the word as if he found it offensive. "Well, I need the suite so you need to get her out of there immediately. Let her stay with you, if she's such a good *friend*."

Remy refused to allow his father to goad him. "No. I'm not going to be waking her up in the middle of a blizzard and kicking her out. That's ridiculous. This can wait until morning."

"It can't." Whit cleared his throat. "You know I use that suite. It's my own personal, private, uh, nest."

"Nest?" Remy repeated, not understanding.

Whit swore. "Are you really going to make me spell it out?"

It took an effort for Remy to keep from groaning out loud. "Let me guess. You're wanting to bring someone up to the room tonight."

"Bingo," Whit growled. "Now get your gal pal out of there so I can have the room cleaned. Pronto."

"Now?" Still disbelieving, Remy scratched his head. "It's snowing like crazy out there and the plows have stopped for the night." He decided not to mention that he'd just gotten home not too long ago.

"Not my problem. You should have thought of that before you used the room without my permission. Just get it done." Whit hung up.

Remy swore. And swore again. Though he hated to call Vanessa this late and possibly wake her, he knew if he didn't, his father would simply go barging into the suite and order her out. That would be infinitely worse.

She answered on the second ring. At least she didn't sound asleep. Remy abandoned all attempts at delicacy and flat out told her what had just transpired.

After a moment of stunned silence, she laughed. "I guess I'd better get packed."

Her laughter puzzled him, but since it seemed infinitely preferable to panic or anger, he'd take it. "I'll be there in a few minutes to pick you up."

"Remy, you don't have to do that," she protested. "I'll figure something out."

"You're staying with me," he said. "I have a guest room, too. And since I got you into this spot…"

"You don't owe me." Her gentle reply made his chest ache.

"Of course I don't. But there's nowhere you can stay in town and it's too damn cold to sleep in your car. Plus—" he softened his tone "—I'd really enjoy your company."

She laughed again, the easy sound spreading warmth through him. "Sold," she said. "I need a few minutes to get packed. I'll wait in the lobby. Just let me know when you get here and I'll run out. There's no reason you should have to park or anything."

Glad he had snow tires on his Jeep, he made it to The Chateau without any problems. Pulling into the circular drive, even now he had to admire the way the warm light spilling out from the windows seemed like a welcoming beacon through the swirling snow.

Under the covered valet-parking area, he texted Vanessa, letting her know he'd arrived. One of the valets hurried over, hunched against the cold, and looked relieved when Remy waved him away.

A moment later, she came out, bundled up and beautiful, struggling as she tried to balance her suitcase with her ski gear. Remy jumped out to help her, then stowed her gear in the back. Once she'd settled into the passenger seat, she looked at him and grinned.

That grin settled into his heart like a shot of fine whiskey, momentarily knocking the breath from him.

"What an adventure!" she exclaimed, peering out past the light as if trying to see through the swirling snow. "Did you have any trouble getting here?"

"Not really. The plows have stopped for the night, but this Jeep has four-wheel drive."

To his amused disbelief, she appeared excited. "I love four-wheeling," she said.

He drove slowly, his grip tight on the wheel, ready for the slightest skid. Though the snow had filled in any previous tire tracks, as long as it was just powder, the roads would be fine.

"No one else is out," she commented.

"Because everyone has better sense. I imagine they're either in bed under multiple blankets or sitting by roaring fireplaces."

"I hear that. I love a good fireplace."

Suddenly he wanted nothing more than to be cuddling on his couch with her in front of a fire. Blinking, he pushed the tantalizing images from his mind.

Finally, they pulled onto his street. On one side, all of the homes sat on small hills—on the other, the land was flat. He'd always considered himself fortunate to have his little hill with a view.

"Is this where you live?" she asked.

He answered in the affirmative.

Vanessa gave him a sideways glance. "Okay, I'm going to ask you something weird." She took a deep breath, while his imagination went wild. "Could you do a few donuts before we pull into your driveway?

I've always loved doing them in fresh powder, as long as there's nothing around to hit."

This made him chuckle. "Are you serious?"

"Yep." She nudged his shoulder with her own. "It's already been a strange night. Indulge me."

Eying her, he shrugged. "I don't know. The streets seem clear of other vehicles, but there are still mailboxes and evergreens I could hit."

She snorted. "Fine. Never mind then." The amused scorn in her tone made him blink.

The seventeen-year-old boy buried deep inside him responded. Easing up on the gas, he pressed the brake and turned the wheel, sending his Jeep fishtailing. Though he hadn't even thought to try doing donuts since his youth, he hadn't forgotten how.

And the joyous purity of Vanessa's laughter was all the reward he needed.

Back at his house, he pulled into the garage and killed the engine. "You can leave your ski gear in the car for now," he told her. She followed him inside, her expression curious.

"Nice decorating," she said, turning in a slow circle. "Did you hire a designer?"

"No. I'm not much for that kind of stuff. All the artwork came from the last time my aunt and uncle had their house redone. They were going to toss the discards, so I picked everything up. Luckily, all this happened to be in a Western theme, which I can live with. What I didn't use, I donated to Goodwill."

"Interesting."

He crossed the room and relit the gas logs in the fireplace, instantly sending flames dancing. "Make yourself comfortable," he told her. "Would you like something to drink?"

Shaking her head, she covered her mouth with her hand to mask a yawn. "I'm good, thank you."

"I need to go make up the guest bed. It should only take me a few minutes."

She turned to face him. "No need to go through the trouble. If you'll just give me the bed linens, I can do it. I'm kind of tired and would really like to just get some sleep."

Remy felt his expression soften as he looked at her. Considering she'd been rushed out of the hotel suite he'd promised her she could use as long as she wanted, she seemed to be in pretty good spirits. Most women he knew would have been complaining bitterly. Not Vanessa. She seemed resilient as hell.

This only made him like her more.

"Come this way," he said. "Two work faster than one, so we can make the bed up together."

After making a stop at the linen closet to grab a set of sheets and a blanket, he led the way into the guest bedroom. With Vanessa on one side of the bed and him on the other, they made quick work of getting it ready. He hadn't realized how intimate such a mundane task could be, or how her presence would make the room seem to shrink.

"There you are." He managed to speak normally, despite his supercharged awareness of her.

Her answering smile nearly undid him. "Thank you," she murmured. "I really appreciate you doing this for me."

He nodded and turned to head for the door, intending to tell her to sleep well as soon as he'd reached the relative safety of the hall. But she moved at the same moment and they nearly collided.

Remy froze. Vanessa gazed up at him, her huge blue eyes guileless and shining. What else could he do then but give in to the impulse to kiss her?

The first brush of his lips on hers, meant to be casual, slow and tender, instantly became anything but. As she met him halfway, his hunger flared and his senses reeled. The taste of her was heady, demanding more. When she returned his kiss with reckless abandon, he forced himself to rein in his desire to devour her.

Except she was having none of that. Pulling him down to her, she had them both tumbling onto the freshly made bed.

In that instant, he was lost.

Chapter Seven

They locked lips, tongues as tangled as their bodies, the kisses deep and wet and sensual as hell. The two of them touched and caressed and made love with their mouths until Vanessa thought she might combust. Damn. She wanted more. *So much more.* This man—his taste, his touch—drove her wild, made her feel wanton and hungry. Aching, burning, melting, she knew she'd never been so close to losing control.

And she couldn't let herself. Not now. Not yet. Maybe not ever.

"Wait," she said breathlessly, shuddering, barely able to find the strength to pull out of his arms. "We can't. I'm sorry. But—"

Remy looked as shaken as she felt. "You're right," he said, his voice whiskey-rough and sexy as hell. He pushed to his feet, but not before she'd seen the very visible proof of his desire. Her knees went weak. "I don't know what got into me. I apologize."

She wanted to tell him no need, that they'd both been responsible for the kiss. But she didn't, thinking maybe it might be better this way.

"I hope you don't think that this is the reason I invited you here," he continued. "Because I promise you, it isn't."

He looked so miserable, she knew she should say something to ease the tension and make him feel better. But how could she, when every second she spent with this man had her wanting more?

Though she'd never been a risk taker except on the slopes, she decided to take one now. "Remy, I like you. A lot. I think maybe we should just take things slow, but I definitely want to give this a shot. If it goes somewhere, great. If not, that's fine, too."

"This?" He raised an eyebrow. "Do you mean...?"

His hopeful expression made her laugh out loud. "Maybe eventually." She waved her hand vaguely toward the bed. "I mean getting to know each other. I don't know, but I have a feeling that this could be—"

"Something special." His intent gaze told her she'd made the right decision. "I agree. I want you to stay here as long as you like. We can take our time. I'd like to court you, date you and learn everything I can about you."

She laughed. "Sounds like fun. But let's not get ahead of ourselves. We'll just take it a day at a time. Either way, I think we'll have lots of fun."

Slowly, he nodded. "I got ahead of myself there."

"I think we both did." She smiled gently to let him know the encounter had been more than mutual.

He exhaled. "But what about Seth?"

Seth. For a moment, her heart fell. Then she raised her head. "All my life, I've had other people make decisions about what I should and shouldn't be doing. Seth knows exactly how I feel about him. I'd love to remain friends with him, nothing more. Besides that, I owe him." She cleared her throat. "But while I want to be there for him, if he doesn't want assistance, there's little I can do. I've been nothing but honest and up-front with him."

Pausing, she took a deep breath. "All that said, I think we should be careful. Whatever comes of this, I don't want to hurt him. And I never want to cause prob-lems between two brothers."

The smoldering flame in his eyes warmed her.

"Thank you for that. Keeping any sort of relation-ship with Seth is already difficult enough," Remy said. "And I definitely don't want to do anything that might push him to do anything crazy. Or," he amended, "cra-zier than he's already done."

Sobering, she nodded. "Agreed. I'm hopeful you can talk him into going to rehab again. I really think he needs the help."

"I'll do my damnedest." Reaching for her again, he pulled her close for a hug, letting her feel the full force of his arousal. She melted, but managed to keep her-self still.

After a moment, he released her—reluctantly, she thought.

"Get some sleep," he said. "The weather forecast said this snow should let up by tomorrow afternoon. Hope-fully, Pine Peak will be able to reopen. If not, feel free to hang out here. I'm planning to go into the office for a little bit, though not too long. With most of my staff on vacation, I'm not going to make anyone struggle through the storm to make it in."

He stepped back, moving through the door until he

stood in the hall. "I'll see you in the morning, Vanessa. The bathroom is right across the hall and I'll put fresh towels in there for you." Then he closed the door, leaving her alone in the small room.

To her surprise, she felt his absence like a cold draft. She shivered, already missing the warmth of his arms.

What had she gotten herself into? She wasn't sure, but the thought of going back to Boulder without giving Remy a chance made her ache with the kind of loss she'd felt when she'd learned her parents were gone. It was damn near unbearable.

Before she could lose her nerve, she opened her suitcase and unpacked it, hanging some things up in the closet, putting others away in the empty dresser drawers. Weird, maybe. But this decision to stay with Remy felt right.

The next morning when she woke, at first she had no idea where she was. Bright whiteness, the kind that only came from a good snowfall outside, came through the window despite the blinds. Stretching, she sat up in bed, and remembered. Warmth and joy slammed into her, along with a healthy dose of trepidation.

The kiss and all the heat behind it had invaded her dreams. She finger combed her hair, thinking that she hadn't felt like this since she'd been a teenager infatuated with the neighbor, a boy two years older than her named Taylor Hopkins. Of course, nothing had come of that. She'd been way too shy and her crush had been complicated by the fact that she'd only seen him on the few occasions when she'd been allowed to go home to Boston. Somehow she'd made it through four years of university in Boulder without getting involved in a serious relationship.

She'd dated, certainly. And a couple of the boys had wanted to take things to the next level, but since she hadn't been feeling it, she never had. Even with Seth, she'd always felt detached, as though she was viewing the relationship from a distance.

This thing with Remy was different. Or could be. Since being with him she felt more alive, more *present*, than she'd ever felt. For the first time in her life, she had high hopes, which might be ridiculous. Who knew?

After taking a hot shower, she blow-dried her hair and applied a little makeup, secretly amused at how badly she wanted to look good for Remy.

Finally, dressed and ready to face the day, she went out into the hallway, following the scent of coffee to the kitchen. She stopped short in the doorway, taking it all in. This room surprised her, too. Instead of being a utilitarian kitchen, Remy's could have been featured in a magazine spread on gourmet kitchens. It featured white cabinets, a beautiful quartz countertop, top-of-the-line stainless-steel appliances and a huge vent hood. She stood for a moment with her mouth open, staring around her in awe.

Remy sat at the kitchen bar, scrolling through his phone while nursing a cup of coffee. He looked up when she entered, his intent gaze locking on hers.

Again she felt that fierce pull of attraction.

"Coffee?" he asked, pointing to his single-cup coffee maker. "I've got several varieties of pods stored in the caddy underneath it. Pick whichever one you want."

Tongue-tied, she chose a bold coffee she'd had often

while in the Pacific Northwest. Once it finished brewing, she fixed her cup to her liking, then took a seat on the bar stool next to him. "Any word on Pine Peak?" she asked.

"Not yet. They sent out the ski patrol at first light to check on conditions. They said they'd update the web page as soon as they knew."

Grimacing, she sipped her cup. "After that much snow, I bet they'll have some cleanup to do."

"Most likely," he agreed. "I'm going to go in to the office for a little while. There's plenty of food in the fridge—eggs, bread, whatever you might want. I have oatmeal in the pantry. Feel free to help yourself to anything. I want you to make yourself at home."

Suddenly feeling shy, she nodded. "Thank you. At some point, I'll need a ride back to The Chateau so I can get my car."

"We can do that." He hesitated, and then leaned over and kissed her cheek. "I'll see you later. Call or text me if you need anything."

She promised she would.

After Remy left, she wandered his house, feeling aimless. The snow had finally stopped falling, but the wind gusts remained in the dangerous category, so Pine Peak remained closed. She'd read on their Facebook page that controlled avalanches were being set off to minimize the risk of a real one occurring and injuring or killing skiers later.

Since she loved snow, she put on her parka and went out into his backyard. Just a few minutes of watching the wind blow the snow into drifts was enough, and she went back inside.

While she was out there, she saw she'd missed two calls and two messages. Before she could even listen to them, her phone rang again. When she saw Seth's number on the caller ID, she let it go to voicemail. A moment later, she heard the chime that signified she'd received a third voicemail. Since she needed to warm herself up, she'd check it along with the others after making a cup of hot tea.

Five minutes later, feeling slightly warmer, she sat down with her hot drink to listen to her messages. They were all from Seth, and with her heart in her throat, she played the first one.

"Hey, Van. Just checking to see where you are and if you're okay. I realized you never told me where you ended up staying. Maybe you made it back to Boulder? If you're still in town, please give me a call back. I need to talk to you about something important."

The second and third messages were repeats of the first, though the tone became angrier and more insistent.

She sighed. Right now, she wasn't in the mood for drama, and the instant she told Seth she was now staying at Remy's, she knew he'd get upset. And that would be putting it mildly.

Barely ten more minutes passed before her phone rang again. Seth. He left a fourth message. She decided not to listen to it just yet. She'd begun to realize he had every intention of blowing up her phone until she gave in and answered. This made her even more determined that she wouldn't. She hated manipulation and games.

During the course of the morning, Seth called eight times more, for a total of twelve. He left messages with every call. Staring at the steadily rising number showing on the message display, she shook her head. Seth had gone off the rails for no reason. She could only imagine what he'd do if he knew where to find her. The thought made her shudder.

Finally, she put her phone on silent mode. She wasn't sure how to deal with all this, and briefly considered calling Remy. But she didn't want to start their first day together by bothering him at work.

Since there seemed no point in going into town, she puttered around the house. Remy had said to make herself at home, so she did. When he called around lunchtime to check on her, she missed the call, but knowing he'd be home soon, she decided she'd wait to talk to him then instead of phoning him back. Seth's constant barrage had given her a major headache. Trying to focus on the positive, she thought she'd see about cooking them both a nice dinner.

Checking in Remy's freezer, she located a package of meat. In the fridge, he had fresh carrots, celery, onions and potatoes—in short, everything she needed to make beef stew. Remy even had a nice bottle of Shiraz they could have with dinner. The only thing missing would be a nice loaf of crusty French bread, but she didn't need the carbs, anyway.

Glad she had something to do to occupy her time and help her ignore her phone, she happily got to work chopping up vegetables, humming as she worked. She felt very domestic all of a sudden, something she rarely ever experienced. Her first home-cooked dinner for a member of the opposite sex. And not just any guy, but Remy. The sexiest, kindest, most generous man she'd ever met.

As SOON AS he got to the mostly deserted office, Remy called his cousin Molly, Sabrina's sister. "Did you know anything about Sabrina and Seth dating?" he asked, keeping his tone casual.

"I knew she was seeing someone, but she never mentioned anyone specifically," Molly answered after considering his question for a moment. "Sabrina and I pretty much lived separate lives and we hardly ever even talked, except to comment on each other's Facebook or Instagram accounts. She'd been posting some random things just before her death."

As someone who'd always yearned for a family, Remy truly didn't understand when those who were lucky enough to have one didn't appreciate it. But that was just him.

"Okay." Remy cleared his throat. "Anyway, send me what you've got, please." Ending the call, he waited while the texts came in. Molly sent ten photos, three of them from Facebook, three from Instagram and four from Snapchat.

She was right, he thought. They were intense ramblings about the dark side of life and love, not the sort of factual, day-to-day life things Sabrina usually posted. Unless, he thought, she had been high on drugs. Since she'd been a big party girl, that would always be a possibility, but he'd never seen her post anything that weird, ever.

Which meant what? That someone else had been posting to her social media? Maybe even the killer? But why? The only thing Remy could come up with was the possibility the posts had been meant to throw police off the killer's tracks.

He called Molly back. "I got them."

"Weird, aren't they?" Molly said.

"Yes, they are. I agree with you. None of those seem like something Sabrina would have posted. Did you show the police what you sent me?"

"I never mentioned it to them," she admitted. "I've been so overwhelmed by my grief that it slipped my mind, and I honestly never thought it was very relevant to the case."

"I think it's relevant now," he said, feeling certain. "Especially since the authorities have learned she wasn't murdered by the Avalanche Killer. I suggest you get ahold of Daria Bloom, the deputy sheriff in charge of the case, and show her what you've got. I'm pretty sure she'll want to see them."

"Do you think so?" Molly sounded uncertain. "I guess I can try. Do you really think they mean anything?"

"I'm not sure. But the police will know. It couldn't hurt."

After ending the call, Remy sat in silence for a moment trying to gather his thoughts. Why Sabrina? Why had she been singled out? Of course, he and everyone else had wondered the same things about each and every one of the women the Avalanche Killer had murdered. And as far as he knew, the entire town had believed Sabrina had been another one of his victims.

Sabrina had been strangled, just like the others. But the Avalanche Killer, aka Curtis Shruggs, had been eager to confess to his kills after he'd been apprehended last month. Curtis had been proud of his work, defiant in his belief that his actions had been not only necessary, but also justified. He could name each and every one of his victims, in chronological order.

He'd been emphatic that Sabrina Gilford hadn't been one of them.

At first, the police hadn't wanted to believe it. They'd thought they had their killer caught, the case solved and it had all been wrapped up in a neat little bow.

And then they didn't. If Curtis hadn't killed Sabrina, then who had?

Remy shook his head, reluctant to face up to the truth. While in college, Sabrina had been a party animal. She'd gotten worse once she'd graduated. He couldn't help but wonder if her getting together with Seth might have had something to do with that. Seth and his predilection for drugs, combined with Sabrina's never-ending quest for fun, would have been a nightmare waiting to happen. Alcohol, drugs and two people who didn't know when to stop.

But would Seth really have killed her? Was his baby brother even the type of person who could kill? And why would he? Sabrina had been strangled in a deliberate attempt to mimic the Avalanche Killer. Remy thought if Seth had managed to do something stupid while under the influence, it wouldn't be murder by strangulation.

Relieved and a little bit ashamed that he'd even been considering the possibility that his brother could be a cold-blooded murderer, he shook his head. Seth might be a mess, but he wasn't a killer.

He couldn't help but wonder how someone like Vanessa, who didn't seem to be big on partying, had gotten along with his brother. It almost was like Seth might have had two different personalities, showing one side to Vanessa and a completely different side to Sabrina. Especially since it appeared he'd dated both women at the same time.

Had Sabrina been aware of this? Vanessa clearly hadn't.

Now Sabrina was gone. Dead too soon. And the police didn't seem to have any idea who might have killed her. Did Seth?

Uneasy, Remy shifted his weight in his chair. Now that Vanessa had told him about the files she'd found on Seth's computer, he had no choice but to consider the possibility that Seth might have been involved. Even if he hadn't actually taken Sabrina's life, he might know something that could be of use to the police in helping them find the killer.

Remy didn't think the police had even questioned him. Why would they? No one had even known he and Sabrina had been dating. How had that been possible? Had the two of them snuck around, relishing their shared secret?

Seth had even kept this from his own brother. What else had he kept secret? Remy wouldn't have known about any of this if Vanessa hadn't looked at Seth's personal computer.

What a mess. While he didn't want to give away Vanessa, he had to figure out how to best bring up the subject with Seth. It was time he found out exactly what was going on in his baby brother's head.

Checking his watch, Remy saw it was nearly lunchtime. Since the snow had stopped falling and the plow had been through, Remy decided to see if Seth wanted to get together for a bite to eat. He dialed his brother's number. Seth answered on the second ring, sounding both out of breath and furious.

"What?" he snarled.

"Are you okay?" Remy asked. "I'm calling to see if we can get together for lunch. We need to talk."

No response, only by the harsh rasp of Seth's agitated breathing. "I don't know," he finally said, still sounding as if his teeth were clenched. "I'm trying to get ahold of Vanessa. I have no idea where she is. She just up and disappeared when you took me to the hospital."

Not sure how to respond to that, unless Seth asked, Remy knew it would be best not to mention Vanessa at all. "I'm sure she's fine. How about lunch? Getting a good burger in your stomach might make you feel a little better. I can pick you up in ten minutes."

Another moment of quiet, during which Remy prayed Seth wouldn't ask him if he'd seen her.

"Fine," he finally responded. "I could eat. Are you buying? Because I don't have any cash and my credit cards are maxed out."

Though this comment made Remy wince, he kept that to himself. "Of course I'm buying." He always did. Not once in all the time Seth had been working here in Roaring Springs had he offered to pick up the check. Remy figured he never would. After all, that's what big brothers were for.

Before he left, he decided to call and check on Vanessa. She didn't answer, so he left a voicemail, letting her know he was just checking on her and he'd see her when he got home later.

Vanessa. Seth still seemed obsessed with her, and Remy could understand why. She was special, the real deal. And while he didn't want to skulk around with her behind his brother's back, he also had no intention of setting off Seth.

Swinging by Seth's condo, Remy tried not to think of the last time he'd been here. He pulled up out front, texted his brother to let him know he'd arrived and waited. Seth came out the door a few minutes later, wearing a beat-up down puffer jacket that had seen better days. With his five o'clock shadow and bloodshot eyes, he looked as if he'd just gotten off of a three-day bender.

When he let himself into Remy's Jeep, a foul odor of alcohol mixed with sweat and cigarettes came with him, so strong Remy had to force himself not to react.

"You look like hell," he said, frowning. "What is going on with you?"

"I don't want to talk about it." Seth slouched down in the seat. "You promised to feed me. Let's do that."

While Remy drove, his brother messed with his phone, sending text after text and then waiting for a reply. When nothing came, he texted again. "Why won't she answer me?" Seth finally asked out loud. "What kind of friend avoids me after I was just in the hospital?"

Swearing softly under his breath, Remy glanced sideways at his brother. "Are you talking about Vanessa?"

Seth shot him an aggravated look. "Who else would I be talking about? I already told you I've been trying to reach her all day. I know she's not skiing since they haven't opened up Pine Peak yet. So why is she avoiding me?"

"I don't know," Remy drawled. "Maybe because you scared the hell out of her?"

"How?" Seth scoffed at the idea. "I was a perfect gentleman."

"Are you serious?" Remy chided. "You got drunk off your ass and cut yourself badly on broken glass, and then blatantly refused to go to the hospital." He tightened his grip on the steering wheel, trying to keep his temper in check, and a stony silence fell between the two of them for the remainder of the ride to the Honest Slims' Barbeque joint. Despite the weather, or maybe because of it, the small parking lot was almost full.

The instant they stepped out of the Jeep, the delicious aroma of barbeque smoke made Remy's mouth water. Even Seth appeared to perk up. "I thought you said burgers," he protested half-heartedly.

"I changed my mind." For Remy, the decision to eat at Slims' had been spur-of-the-moment. He'd been about to drive past and head to one of the burger joints at the south end of town. Instead, he'd realized he craved brisket and potato salad. Since Seth had always loved Slims', he'd figured it would be a win-win situation.

"You know what? I'm glad. This sounds better." Grinning widely, Seth glanced around and rubbed his stomach. "And I'm starving."

"When was the last time you ate?" Remy held the door open, allowing his brother to precede him into the restaurant.

"Not sure." Seth wouldn't look at him. "It's probably been a while."

Remy held his tongue as they went through the order line. Both men placed identical orders—brisket, potato salad and fried okra. Seth got sweet tea while Remy chose unsweet.

They carried their trays to a table near the front window. Not Remy's first choice—he'd hoped for a quieter booth but they were all full.

As soon as they sat down, Seth began chowing down, his head bent and completely focused. After a moment's hesitation, Remy did the same, giving himself time to figure out the best way to bring up Sabrina.

Before he could, Seth brought her up himself. "I think I must be bad luck. I dated Sabrina Gilford and she ended up dead. I hope the same thing hasn't happened to Vanessa."

Remy almost choked on his brisket. He fought the urge to bring out his phone and call Vanessa instantly, just so he could hear her voice. Luckily, he got himself under control, aware Seth had no idea where she was staying and would never think to look at Remy's place.

"What do you mean?" he finally asked, in as calm a voice as possible.

"Just commented on bad luck." Seth shrugged. "It just about killed me to learn what had happened to Sabrina." He made a face. "Right after Sabrina and I broke up, she was murdered. And they haven't found the killer. I hope the same thing doesn't happen to Vanessa. Especially since she's hanging around Roaring Springs."

Remy could hardly believe what he'd just heard. "Is that a threat?" he asked quietly, his stomach twisting.

"Of course not." Seth shook his head. "You know me, bro. I'd never hurt a woman I loved like that."

He sounded sincere. Remy relaxed slightly. Seth was his brother, after all. Damaged, true, but not a killer.

Chapter Eight

At least Seth had finally stopped calling, though when
Vanessa picked up her phone again, now that the stew
was simmering, she saw he'd sent thirty-eight text messages to go along with the twelve voicemails.

This scared the hell out of her. Excessive much? The
Seth she'd known before would never have done something like this. This Seth seemed to be skirting on the
edge of violence.

And the other woman he'd been dating had ended
up dead.

Shivering, she shook her head. Seth had been a friend
to her when she needed one. She couldn't wrap her
mind around the possibility that he might have killed a
woman in cold blood and tried to make it look as if she
was just another of a serial killer's victims.

Maybe she was looking at this the wrong way. Al-
coholism and drug issues did not make Seth a murderer. Neither did dating two women at the same time.
She knew Seth, had known him for a long time, and
she couldn't imagine him intentionally hurting another
human being. *Intentionally* being the key word. What

kind of things he might be capable of when under the influence, she didn't know. But surely not murder.

Then why was she so afraid of him?

Tired of questions she couldn't answer and having awful speculations without proof, she stirred the stew and got busy tidying the kitchen. When she'd finished that, she decided to do a load of laundry. Since she'd packed limited clothing for what had been supposed to be a short trip, she needed to wash what she had or she would have to go out and buy herself some more things to wear. Exploring the house, she discovered Remy had built a really nice home gym in the basement. She spent a good hour down there lifting weights and running on his treadmill.

Finally, after taking a quick shower, she returned to the kitchen, double-checked the stew and waited for Remy to get home. Funny, this domestic feeling. She'd never felt like this, not even when she'd purchased her first home in Boulder. She wasn't entirely sure why she did now.

Finally, she heard Remy's Jeep pulling into the driveway and her heart began to race. Smoothing her palms down the front of her leggings, she wondered if she should try to appear busy, as if she hadn't been breathlessly anticipating his return all day.

In the end, she decided the heck with it and raced to meet him at the door.

"Hi!" she greeted him, feeling heat turn her cheeks pink. He stopped short, his lean frame both casual and serious.

"Hi yourself."

Uncertain how to act, she stepped back so he could

come inside. "Did you have a good day?" she asked, aware she might be babbling, but unable to stop it.

"I did. Things are kind of slow at the office, but I talked to Seth today at lunch," Remy said, finally pulling her in for a hug and kissing her cheek. "At first, judging by the way he was talking, I thought he was about to confess to killing Sabrina Gilford." He gave a short, uncomfortable laugh before releasing her. "Instead, to my relief, he shared a few insights with me. They were actually valid. He thinks he might know who killed her."

Feeling both cautiously optimistic and skeptical, Vanessa crossed her arms. "Did he talk to the police?"

"Not yet. He's promised to, later today. I'll follow up with them tomorrow morning." He laughed, a painful sound that matched the haunted look lingering in his eyes. "I can't tell you how much better I felt after hearing that. I'd seriously begun to worry Seth might have been involved."

Lifting his head, Remy glanced into the kitchen at the stove. "Whatever you've got simmering there smells delicious."

"Thanks. It's beef stew. It'll be done in a few hours, just in time for dinner." She refused to be distracted, even if she wanted to kiss him until she couldn't think straight. "Did Seth actually pass along his information to you? Or did he just vaguely mention he had some?"

Remy chuckled. "That's exactly what he tried to do at first, but I pressed him. No way was I letting him off the hook that easily. It turned out Sabrina was cheating on him."

"Like he was cheating on her?" Vanessa interjected. "And me?"

"Yes. He showed me text messages and a few snapshots on his phone of Sabrina and her other boyfriend. Apparently, he accidentally ran into them."

Or he stalked them. Vanessa didn't voice that thought out loud. Though she hated to burst Remy's bubble, she had to point out the obvious. "But doesn't that make him even more of a suspect?" she asked. "Now he would have a motive."

Remy froze. "I can't believe that didn't occur to me. I guess I'm just having difficulty thinking of my baby brother as a killer."

Now or never. Without saying anything else, she handed him her phone.

At first, he stared at the screen, not comprehending. "You have thirty-eight text messages?"

Slowly, she nodded. "And twelve voicemails. All from Seth."

Remy had already opened the text messages and started reading. His frown deepened. "This is crazy."

She kept silent, letting him make his way through them. When he finished, he raised his head and met her gaze, his own tortured. "I can't believe this."

Taking a deep breath, she nodded. "I know. Me neither. The voice messages are worse."

"Worse?" Remy's voice rose. "I just had lunch with him. He mentioned he was trying to get ahold of you, but nothing about blowing up your phone with incessant texts." Clearly stricken, he tried to hand her back her phone.

"Did you want to listen to the voicemails?" she

asked, refusing to take it. She hated the way she felt—
like she'd just crushed his heart. But none of this was
her fault, and if Seth was as dangerous as he had begun
to seem, someone needed to stop him before he hurt
someone else.

"No. Not right now." Remy dragged his hand through
his hair. "I'm not sure I can take it. To be frank, I'm not
sure what to think."

"You need to play them," she gently pointed out.
"Please. I'm scared and worried."

Still holding her phone, he took a deep breath and
then nodded. Gaze locked on hers, he pressed Play on
the first voice message.

She stood, silent and still, while Remy doggedly
made it through all of the increasingly awful voicemails Seth had left. While he had never come right out
and actually threatened her, some of the creepy things
he'd said could definitely be construed that way. Hearing them replayed hurt her heart.

Once he'd finished listening, Remy shook his head.
His complexion had gone ashen. "I'm so, so sorry," he
said quietly. "You shouldn't have to go through this. No
one should. This has got to stop now." Then he pressed
the icon to call Seth back.

Eyes wide, she took a step back. Though doing so
might be ridiculous, she didn't want to be anywhere
near Remy when he and his brother spoke. As if Seth's
bad energy could somehow reach through the phone
and hurt her.

Gaze locked on hers, Remy put the call on speaker.

"It's about time you called me back," Seth answered,

his voice flat and eerily calm. "Where the hell are you? And why haven't you been picking up your phone?"

"It's me, Seth," Remy said, the sharp edge to his tone letting his brother know he meant business. "Vanessa just let me see her phone with all the texts you sent, and I've listened to the voicemails, too. I've got you on speakerphone. What the hell is wrong with you?"

"Vanessa is with *you*?" Seth roared. "What the—"

"Stop." The single barked order had immediate results. Seth went silent, and Vanessa nervously twisted her hands, wondering for the hundredth time what had happened to the kind, caring man she'd once known.

"You've been frightening the hell out of Vanessa," Remy continued, his voice like steel. "And quite honestly, after reading those text messages, me, too."

For a moment, Seth didn't respond. When he finally spoke, he'd clearly dialed back his anger and resentment. "You're right," he said, surprising her. "I acted like an ass. Vanessa, will you ever forgive me?"

Remy started to reply, but she held up her hand to let him know that she wanted to handle this herself.

"Seth, I'm not sure an apology is going to do it this time," she said, her voice resolute. "I really feel you need to get some help, whether it's for addiction or anger issues or both. Either way, for the first time since I met you, I felt as if I was in danger from you."

"I would never hurt you, Van."

"Maybe not," she concurred. "But the way you've been acting since I arrived in Roaring Springs is nothing like the guy I know. Nothing."

"I know." Subdued, Seth suddenly appeared to be on the verge of tears. "I need help. Remy, I promise I'll go back to rehab after the holidays. In the meantime, I can start going back to the AA and NA meetings. Will that be enough for you, Vanessa?"

"Seth, this shouldn't be about me. You have to want to get help for *you*. I shouldn't factor into this at all."

Remy cleared his throat. "She's right," he finally said. "Unless you want to do this for you, it's not going to stick."

"I know, I know." Conciliatory now, Seth sighed. "I'm messed up. I love you both and I appreciate you sticking with me through all of this. Van, I'll try harder to improve on being your friend and, Remy, I know I need to be a better brother. I should have told you that at lunch today. I'm sorry. I'll leave you alone now."

"You're not going to start drinking, are you?" Vanessa asked worriedly. "I know you're upset and that's your default coping mechanism."

A thread of bitterness ran through Seth's self-deprecating laugh. "While I will admit that is tempting, I plan to pour out every bit of any alcohol I have left. Then I'm going to call the guy that was acting as my sponsor before I went off the wagon and talk to him. I won't bother you again tonight. Take care, both of you." And he ended the call.

Placing her phone on the table, Vanessa sat down on one of the bar stools before her legs gave out. Putting her head into her hands, she took several deep, shuddering breaths. When she finally raised her head, she found Remy watching her. His hands were clenched into fists, as if to keep himself from touching her. That's when she realized he struggled with this attraction as much as she did.

"Seth sounds very sincere," she breathed.

"He does." Remy swallowed, still holding her gaze. "I worry so damn much about him. He's really messed up, but there's a good person somewhere inside him, I know it."

"There is." She hastened to reassure him. "He just got a little lost."

Remy lowered himself onto the bar stool next to her, sitting so close their knees touched. "Are you all right?"

The concern in his deep voice warmed her. Slowly, she nodded. "How about you?"

He smiled. "I'm about to be a lot better," he said, right before he leaned over and kissed her.

She melted into him, matching the heat of his lips on hers with a passion of her own. He didn't touch her—not yet—and she didn't touch him either. The only place their bodies fused was their mouths. She wanted to devour him, her tongue dancing with his, every movement searing her. He slanted his mouth over hers, caressing her lips again and again, until she couldn't restrain herself any longer. She pulled back and, quivering, she reached for him. Then, ever so slowly, she slid her hand down his muscular chest. Heart hammering against her ribs, she reveled in the feel of him, enjoying the heat blazing from his eyes as he watched her. Emboldened, she let her fingers explore every inch of his upper torso, stopping just short of his belt.

"Go ahead," he rasped, still watching her with those hot, hungry eyes. She liked that he kept his hands locked on the counter, loved that he let her do this in her own time, her own way.

Body tingling, she continued her lazy exploration.

His harsh intake of breath when she reached for his belt buckle caused a shivery ache inside of her.

When the buckle came free, she undid his jeans, letting his magnificent arousal spring free. Eying him, she licked her lips. She ached to take him into her mouth, but as she bent to do exactly that, he stopped her. "Not yet," he groaned, his voice raw. "I want to be inside you first."

Immediately, blood surged to her lady parts. He kissed her again, his lips scorching her skin as he moved from her mouth to her neck. With one deft movement, he unhooked her bra, helping her remove it and her shirt. Grinning at each other, they both divested themselves of the rest of their clothing, standing naked and unashamed in front of each other.

Now she let her gaze feast on him, loving his lean, athletic frame with broad shoulders and narrow hips. Muscular, too, the kind that came from regular workouts in the gym.

Heat blazed from his eyes as he caressed her, cupping her breasts before lowering his head to taste. His tongue lathed her sensitive nipples and she groaned. Pleasure radiated to her core, and she felt liquid heat flowing through her. She was ready. More than ready.

"Now," she ordered, tugging him to her. Tangled together, they moved into his bedroom and, kissing ravenously, fell backward onto his bed.

Finally, Remy lowered his body over hers. She pulled him close, welcoming him. With one swift movement, he buried himself deep inside her, filling her. Savage, such primal, raw possession. He groaned, she sighed, and again, they paused and grinned at each other.

Though he was already hard, she felt him swell even more inside. As he began to move, the pure, explosive pleasure made her arch her back and cry out.

She met him thrust for thrust, as hungry for him as he appeared to be for her.

This, she thought. This was what she'd been missing all along. And then she felt herself ride the crest all the way to the top, before shattering into a thousand stars.

LYING WITH VANESSA snuggled in his arms, in the aftermath of what had been the most powerful, earth-shattering lovemaking he'd ever experienced, Remy marveled at the miracle that had brought her to him. He breathed in the clean, strawberry scent of her silky hair, with his eyes half-closed, wondering if he'd actually drift off to sleep. Just the feel of her soft skin and lush curves pressed against him had him half-aroused again.

Realizing he'd forgotten to set the alarm, he considered the plausibility of easing out from her arms and walking naked over to the keypad so he could do that. Especially since they had a killer on the loose in Roaring Springs, he would feel safer with the alarm set. He guessed that came from growing up in Whit's mansion. His father had always been an overly paranoid sort, and Remy had come to feel having to set and disarm multiple alarms anytime he arrived or left was normal. Now, in his own home, he had only one, very high-tech system for which he paid dearly.

Best to get up and set it.

No sooner had he reached a decision than he heard the sound of someone unlocking the front door. Or *trying* to. Heart pounding, he leaned over Vanessa to get his pistol from his nightstand. She woke and sat up, her elbow banging him hard in the nose. Head reeling from that, he moved her aside, pushing past the sudden pain to focus on the danger.

The bedroom light came on. Cursing, Remy grabbed his pistol and flicked off the safety. He spun, pushing her behind him as he brought up his weapon, ready to defend Vanessa at all costs.

Seth stood in the doorway, staring at both of them with an expression of shocked disbelief.

Vanessa gasped, yanking the sheet up to cover her breasts.

"I knew it." Seth didn't bother to conceal the bitter hurt in his voice. "The two of you have been getting it on behind my back."

"It's not like that," Remy began. "How did you get in here?"

"You gave me a key," his brother reminded him, his expression dark. "Not once in my wildest dreams did I imagine I'd walk in and find the two of you doing the nasty."

"It's not like that," Remy repeated.

"Oh, really? Because it sure looked like that to me."

Looking from one man to the other, Vanessa shook her head. "We are so not having this discussion right now, right here. Seth, please wait for us in the kitchen. We'll be right out after we get dressed. Then we can all talk like reasonable adults."

For a second or two, Remy actually thought Seth was going to do as she asked. Still framed in the doorway, he actually hesitated. Then his expression crumpled. "You don't want me to see you without your clothes on."

"That's right." Vanessa spoke with a calmness Remy

knew for certain she didn't feel. He knew because her heart pounded under his arm.

"Please close the door behind you and wait for us in the kitchen," she commanded softly. "As soon as we're dressed, we'll meet you there and we can all talk."

Seth slammed out of the room without another word.

Remy let out a breath he hadn't even been aware he'd been holding.

"Oh, wow," Vanessa said, her blue eyes huge. "This isn't going to go over well."

"I agree." Grimly, Remy put the safety back on his gun and returned it to the nightstand drawer. Still wide-eyed, she watched him, but made no comment. He began gathering up their clothes, handing Vanessa hers, and they both got dressed in silence.

"This—us—meant more than what it must have looked like to Seth," he commented, swallowing hard.

"Yes," she agreed. "It was." She tugged her shirt over her head.

When they were done, Remy took her hand. "Are you ready?"

She gave a slow nod. "At least we don't have to hide anything now."

"True." He opened the bedroom door and, still hand in hand, they went out to face the music.

Seth was in the kitchen, slurping up a bowl of Vanessa's beef stew. "Is this your specialty?" he asked her. "Or did Remy make this?"

"I did."

Seth nodded. "This is really great."

Clearly uneasy, she shrugged. "Thanks."

"Get some. Join me," Seth prompted. "Let's all have a meal together like we're one big, happy family."

Remy sighed, his gut twisting. Even though his brother's voice hadn't contained even one ounce of sarcasm, what else could it be? "We'll eat later," he said. "Right now, we just want to talk."

"I'm sure you do." Still cordial and pleasant, Seth grabbed his now-empty bowl and returned to the stove to get a generous helping of seconds. He whistled as he filled his bowl.

Vanessa exchanged a worried glance with Remy. He dipped his chin, trying to let her know he felt he could keep the situation under control. Especially since Seth now appeared determined to kill them with kindness. Though it worried him that his brother now acted as if he had multiple personalities.

Inwardly wincing, Remy waited until Seth sat back down. "I'm really sorry that you had to walk in on us like that. Once we knew what direction we were heading, we'd planned to tell you about it."

"It?" Seth asked sharply. "Just because you two couldn't keep your hands off each other doesn't mean anything serious, does it?"

"We don't know," Remy clarified, willing to overlook his brother's overly simple analogy. "This has been very sudden."

"Yes," Vanessa interjected. "After I left your place, I didn't have a place to stay. Remy let me stay in the family suite at The Chateau. I'd still be there now, but…"

"But *what*?" Narrowing his eyes, Seth glanced from one to the other. "Remy's house seemed a bit more welcoming?"

"My father showed up with one of his lady friends,"

Remy said. "When he found out Vanessa was using the suite, he called me and demanded that I kick her out. There's not a single vacancy anywhere in town. Would you rather she'd stayed in her car and froze to death?"

Seth looked hurt. "She could have stayed at my condo."

"No, I couldn't," Vanessa replied. "You scared the hell out of me the last time I was there. When Remy called to tell me I had to vacate the suite, he very kindly invited me to use his guest bedroom. I accepted."

Now Seth rounded on his brother. "You invited her here with the intention of getting her into your bed, didn't you? None of this is Vanessa's fault."

"Fault?" Vanessa pushed her hair back from her face. "You're acting like I didn't have a choice here." She took a deep breath. "I'm sorry if this caused you pain, Seth."

Remy swallowed. "We had no intention of hurting you." He dragged his hand through his hair, feeling as if his insides were shredded. "But we—"

"We?" Seth roared. "There is no *we*, not with you two. Vanessa and I, we're the *we*."

Vanessa winced. "Seth, you and I are over. You know this. You even agreed that we could try to become friends again."

"Friends?" he scoffed, looking from her to Remy and back again. "Come on, Van. I know you didn't drive three hours up here just because you wanted to be *friends*. You regretted breaking up with me and you came to see if there was a chance we could get back together. And then you met my brother and decided to go for him instead. After all, he's got much better prospects than I do."

"Prospects?" Remy asked, puzzled by Seth's choice of word.

Instead of elaborating, Seth shrugged.

"It's not a competition," Vanessa said softly. "It never was. We aren't together, Seth. We're never going to be, whether or not I see Remy. You need to understand that."

Remy admired her courage. She spoke in an even tone, clearly refusing to allow Seth to ruffle her.

"I know," Seth finally responded. "But geez, Van. My *brother*?"

Again, the knife to the gut, twisting. Remy knew Seth probably wanted him to say something along the lines of "if it bothers you so much, we'll stop." And he knew, deep down inside, he should. Even if he knew that Vanessa and his brother would never be together again.

Remy considered himself a good man, an honorable man. He knew the best thing to do would be to keep his distance, to back away.

But he wasn't sure he could let Vanessa go. Whatever they'd started between the two of them felt too powerful.

"Seth, Remy knows I'm not staying in Roaring Springs long. This wasn't planned, not at all. We simply got swept away." Vanessa took a deep breath, her expression tormented. "Maybe it will go somewhere, maybe it won't."

Remy somehow managed to keep his face expressionless. While she was absolutely right, he'd managed to get ahead of himself, too. Even though he and Vanessa had talked about it, he could sympathize with Seth there. Something about Vanessa was damn near irresistible. If he wasn't careful, he knew he might just end up getting hurt.

Expression bored, Seth nodded. "Look, you guys, I know I've been messed up lately. Vanessa, I get it now." He lifted one shoulder, clearly trying for indifference. When he met her gaze, he appeared earnest. "I just figured it was worth a shot." Jerking his head toward Remy, he smiled a tight smile. "I'm sure my brother thinks the same."

Seth pushed to his feet and ambled toward the front door. Hand on the knob, he turned to face them. "No more alcohol. No more drugs. I'm going to walk the straight and narrow, but I'll need your help to do it. Both of your help, okay?" He looked from Remy to Vanessa and back again.

"Of course," Remy said. Vanessa seconded that.

Seth nodded. "Thanks. I'll talk to you tomorrow. And, Remy, remember this—you owe me."

With that, he let himself out the door.

"Oh, my goodness." Vanessa exhaled loudly. "That was..."

"Intense." Remy dropped into a chair. "I feel awful."

"I do, too." Her mouth trembled.

When he met her gaze, her shiny eyes told him she was blinking back tears. His gut wrenched. "Are you okay?"

Instead of answering, she covered her face with her hands. He gave her a moment, then, unable to keep from touching her, he squeezed her shoulder. "It's going to be all right," he promised gruffly. Even though he had no idea if that was the truth.

Chapter Nine

Having Seth walk in on her and Remy right after they'd made love had been one of the most surreal experiences of Vanessa's life. She wasn't sure how she felt about it, or how she *should* feel about it.

On the one hand, she refused to be ashamed of the relationship developing with Remy. And it wasn't technically like she'd cheated on Seth. True, clearly she'd made a mistake coming back and trying to get closure with him, but under no circumstances had she left him with the wrong impression of her actions. She'd been clear and up-front and Seth had even agreed that they'd try to regain their earlier friendship.

But to come between two brothers? That was the last thing she wanted to do.

"I'm a grown man," Remy reminded her, when she voiced her concerns. "As is Seth." Despite his definitive statement, he still frowned. "Though I never meant for him to find out this way."

She knew what she ought to do, though the thought of actually following through with it tore at her heart. "Maybe I should go home as soon as the roads are cleared," she offered.

"Why would you do that?" Remy demanded.

"Because I'm thinking maybe you two need to work things out without me being around and getting in the way."

"Vanessa." Remy kissed her cheek. "Ever since I found Seth living in that dump with our mother, I've dedicated my life to helping him." He took a deep breath. "Maybe by making sure life was easy for him, I did more harm than good. Seth hasn't had to stand on his own two feet because he always knew I'd be there to pick him up."

Not sure how to respond to that statement, she stuck to her guns. "Regardless, I don't want to come between you two."

Remy kissed her cheek again, this time lingering a moment. "Vanessa, if you want to run off, there's nothing I can do to stop you. But don't use Seth as an excuse. If he hadn't walked in on us, he would have found another reason to find fault with me."

Bemused, she eyed him. "I don't know what to think."

"Then don't." This time, his mouth found hers for a slow, deep kiss. "Stay and ski Pine Peak. Once, twice, or as many times as you want. Stay until we figure out if this thing between us is going anywhere."

"Persuasive devil, aren't you?" she murmured as his lips moved over hers.

"I try." When they finally came up for air, they were both breathing fast. "Let's go back to bed and try and get some sleep. Maybe we can hit the slopes tomorrow."

The next morning, Remy's alarm woke them. Blinking back her dreams, Vanessa shouldn't have been surprised to find herself in Remy's arms, his aroused body pressing hard into her backside. She stretched, arching herself into him, not even minding the delay when he reached into the bedside table and pulled on a condom.

They made love fast and furious, the kind of rough and primal sex that she'd only read about. Thrilling to each thrust, she climaxed quickly, and then again just as Remy found his own release.

After, he padded to the shower. When he emerged, his dark hair still damp, he checked his phone. "If I can clear up my schedule, I'll go ski with you."

This made her happier than she could have believed possible. She rushed through a shower, emerging to find he'd made them both egg-and-bagel sandwiches. She wolfed hers down as she drank her coffee and checked the resort's website on her phone.

"Nothing yet," she mused. "When will they post whether or not Pine Peak is open?"

"It'll be open." He spoke with great confidence. "I checked the weather and even walked outside. The wind is gone and the skies are clear. I know they were setting off some small avalanches as a precaution, but skiing conditions are perfect."

"Yay!" She wanted to jump up and down but settled for clapping her hands. "I'd already bought my passes and lift tickets. Since they were for the days the resort was closed, I'm pretty sure they'll honor them today."

"They will." Remy checked his phone. "I need to make a call and make sure there's nothing pressing going on this morning at the office, and then we can suit up and get on our way."

After Remy cleared his schedule, he and Vanessa

loaded all their equipment in his Jeep and headed up to the mountain.

"We should get there right when the lifts start running," he told her.

Feeling like a gleeful little kid, she nodded.

As soon as they'd parked, she bounded out of the car. She could scarcely contain her excitement. This—the cold air, the perfect powder, waiting in line to get on the lift—was when she felt the most alive. Each mountain had its own personality, and she'd skied many. Some were unforgiving, tempting those daring enough to brave the slope to make it to the bottom unscathed. Others were flirty, at first seeming deceptively simple, before one skied around the corner to find themselves on a treacherous and challenging run.

The first time she skied a mountain, she always waited a moment before pushing off, savoring the anticipation.

"You look so happy," Remy commented, his voice warm.

She grinned and turned to face him. "I am. I've been waiting for this a long time. I've heard such great things about Pine Peak. I can't wait to see if they're true."

His hazel-green eyes sparkled, rivaling the sight of the sunshine glittering off the snow. "I dare to say they are. It's been far too long for me, so I'm excited, too. This is going to be fun."

Fun. While his innocuous choice of word might seem banal, she found a celebratory joy in the contrast of control and freedom while racing down a mountain. In skiing, she'd found both her escape and her salvation.

One of the reasons she'd become so skilled had been her eagerness to do it over and over again.

She and Remy took the first run together, choosing a challenging slope labeled as a black diamond. She whooped out loud as she sped down, around turns marked by trees, avoiding large boulders and other skiers.

When she finally reached the bottom, she swirled to a stop and beamed at Remy, who came in right behind her. "Fun was right! I want to go again. Now am I imagining things, or did I hear there's a double black on this mountain, too?

Grimacing, he waved her away. "There is. You'll have to do that one alone, though. I haven't quite got the skill to tackle it."

Though she wanted to make a comment informing him he'd never get better if he didn't practice, she also understood how annoying a comment like that could be. Not everyone was as in love with the sport as she.

"I can do it another time," she said, struggling not to reveal her disappointment. "Let's ski this same one again. Or another, your choice."

"Vanessa." He studied her, his expression patient. "How about you take a pass at the double and I'll wait for you in the coffee shop. I haven't skied in at least a year and I'm already sore."

Again, she bit her tongue. For the life of her, she'd never understand how anyone could live in a ski resort and rarely take advantage of it. "I don't know…"

"I'm serious," he persisted. "Enjoy yourself. I plan to. Come find me when you're done and we'll grab something to eat or we can pick something up on the way home."

Maybe she should have hesitated, but she'd waited way too long to give up after one run. "Okay," she said. "I'll come look for you when I'm done. Are you sure you don't want to have at least one more go?"

"I'm sure. Maybe after I rest up a minute, I'll hit it one more time. Meanwhile, I need to return a few calls."

Work again. While she admired his work ethic, she also wanted to remind him he'd taken the morning off to ski. One turn down the mountain wasn't much of anything. But she didn't want to nag, so she held her silence.

Something must have shown in her face. "All right," he relented. "Let's do this one again. Then I'll take a break and you can go test your skills on the black diamond. How's that sound?"

Instead of answering, she flung her arms around his neck and kissed him. Though their lips were both cold, heat still sparked between them. She grabbed his gloved hand with hers and beamed. "Let's do it."

This time, she asked Remy to go first, mainly because she wanted to be able to see him ski. Honestly, she'd been so caught up in the experience that she had no idea of his skill level.

Remy appeared to be a capable, though cautious skier. He took no chances, stayed right in the middle of the run and appeared focused on simply getting from the top to the bottom.

She caught up with him a few seconds after he'd skied to a stop. "Thank you!"

His gaze went to her mouth and for one breathless moment, she thought he might lean in and kiss her. Instead, he shook himself, as if brushing off snow. "I'm going for coffee now," he said. "Enjoy yourself and I'll see you when you're done."

She liked that he didn't ask her how long she'd be or how many times she intended to ski the mountain. For that, she wouldn't have had any kind of definitive answer since she tended to keep going until she either got too cold or too tired.

"I will." Hesitating, she decided to go ahead and give him an out. "If you have other things you need to do, I don't mind if you leave. I can hang out at The Lodge until you're finished or I can ride the gondola back to The Chateau."

Meeting her gaze, he shook his head. "Nope. I'll wait. Who knows, I might decide to take another run down the mountain later." This time, he gave her a chaste peck on the cheek and turned to walk away.

Heaven help her, she wanted to run after him, grab him by the collar and kiss him senseless. Instead, she knew they'd have all the time in the world that evening, so she simply smiled. "See you later," she said, her voice full of promise.

Back in line at the lift, she waited, shifting her weight from one ski to the other as she inhaled the sharp, clean air. The higher altitudes energized her, made her feel invincible. These days, when she went back to Boston, the combination of being at sea level and the humidity weighed her down and made her feel sluggish.

Finally her turn to get on the chair came, along with an older man with silver hair and a charming smile. He made small talk the entire ride up, not flirting, simply one stranger sharing his love of the sport with another.

When they reached the top, he saluted her before turning away and skiing off. She turned the other way, searching for the sign that marked the double-black slope.

There. Heart pounding with anticipation, she breathed deeply, finding her center. When she felt steady, she pushed off.

The double turned out to be everything she'd hoped for. Challenging, even to a skier as skilled as she, with twists and turns and downhill runs so steep she'd clenched her jaw so hard it hurt.

Three quarters of the way down, a man stepped out of the trees, right in her path. Seth. At her rate of speed, if they collided, bones would be broken. Or worse, one or both of them could die.

She leaned hard to the left, throwing all of her weight into the turn, praying she could maintain enough control to stay on the path and out of the trees.

Luckily, her skilled reflexes enabled her to avoid crashing into him. As she flew past, he yelled something at her. While she didn't catch the exact word, she knew he'd screamed an insult.

It didn't matter. Not now. She battled her furious anger, aware if she gave in to emotion, she'd run the risk of losing control. And that wasn't going to happen. Not on her first double on Pine Peak.

As soon as she reached the bottom, she quickly skied out of the way and bent over to catch her breath. What the hell was wrong with Seth? Why would he try a stunt like that? He was also a skilled skier and knew all too well how dangerous stepping into her path would be.

And then a second thought occurred to her. How had

he known where to find her? While she hadn't taken great pains to hide from him, she'd figured he'd be at work at The Lodge.

Instead of meeting Remy at the coffee bar, she called him and asked him if they could go home immediately. He met her at his Jeep, his expression laced with concern. "Done already?" he asked. "You sounded upset. Is everything all right?"

"I'll tell you about it later," she replied, feeling jumpy. Unable to keep from looking behind her, as if Seth might appear at any moment, she hopped into the passenger seat the instant Remy unlocked the door.

Picking up on her cue, he started the engine and drove away without any more questions. She liked how he didn't badger her and could wait until she felt ready to talk.

As soon as they pulled into his garage, she got out and stormed into the house. Remy followed close behind.

"Are you all right?" he asked again, catching hold of her arm.

Surprised to realize she was both shaking and on the verge of tears, she let him pull her into his arms and hold her.

"What's wrong, Vanessa?" He kissed her temple. "Did you fall or something? Are you hurt?"

Grim, she pulled away and faced him, bracing herself as she told him what Seth had done. As she spoke, arms crossed, she couldn't stop rubbing herself on her upper arms.

Remy's expression turned from concerned to furious. "You're sure it was him?"

"Yes. What the hell is wrong with him? He used to be my friend. I could have been killed. We *both* could have. Luckily, I was able to make a hard turn and avoid him without hitting a tree. It's like he wants me dead."

As much as it pained her to say those words, she could tell it hurt Remy more. He swore and reached for her again. "I should have been there to protect you," he gritted out. "I'll have a word with my brother. And maybe you should go to the police."

"I can't," she said, her voice muffled up against his chest. "He's already messed up. If I got him arrested, wouldn't that make things worse?"

"I don't see how they could be worse." Remy swallowed hard. "Seth is spiraling out of control. He needs to be stopped before he hurts you or anyone else."

For whatever reason, his words allowed her to let go and cry. She sobbed, while he kept her close, her entire body shaking with the force of her sorrow. She cried for a jumbled mix of reasons—the fallacy of her good intentions of coming here, her lost friendship with Seth and his clear deterioration. She wept because her feelings for Remy were so new and she didn't want to give him up, not just yet.

And when he put a gentle finger under her chin and raised her tearstained face to his, she knew she wanted him to kiss her before he lowered his mouth to hers.

WATCHING VANESSA SLEEP, Remy forced himself to breathe slowly and deeply. Making passionate love had released some of the pent-up fury he'd buried deep inside himself, but he still had to figure out what to do.

Seth had tried to hurt Vanessa. She could have been seriously injured or even killed.

Finally, his brother had crossed a line from which there could be no returning. Remy didn't understand why Seth directed his anger at her rather than at him. He'd been so determined to believe that deep down Seth was a good guy that he'd failed to protect Vanessa.

This had to stop. First thing in the morning, he'd be visiting Seth and setting him straight. If he had to have Vanessa take out a restraining order against his brother, so be it. Somehow, Remy must have managed to fall asleep, because when he opened his eyes again, it was 4:00 a.m.

And someone stood at the end of his bed, watching them.

Vanessa stirred, perhaps sensing something. Remy held himself perfectly still, willing her to go back to sleep. Instead, she opened her eyes. Catching sight of Seth, she gasped.

Seth stood for one second longer, then turned without speaking a word and left.

"I'm going after him." Remy pushed back the sheets and swung his legs out of the bed.

"Wait!" Vanessa caught at his arm. "Don't follow him. We need to call the police. That wasn't heartbreak I saw in Seth's eyes. It was malice. He wants revenge."

This time, he couldn't even argue. Because as much as he hated to admit it, she was right.

With Vanessa wavering between leaving or staying, he instructed her to keep all the doors locked. Since he hadn't had time to get his key back from Seth, he asked her to put chairs under both the front and back doorknobs.

"Why?" she'd asked, her eyes going wide.

"Just in case. I don't think Seth will actually try anything—but we can't take the risk."

She sighed, but finally agreed to do as he asked. He kissed her cheek, aching for more, and headed into the office early. As soon as he was there, he began calling all his cousins for help. Family stuck together and no matter how embarrassing the situation felt, he knew they wouldn't judge.

If Seth turned out to be the one who'd murdered Sabrina, he wanted everyone on full alert. There was no telling who his brother might decide to hurt next.

The first person he called was his cousin Trey, the Bradford County sheriff. Since it went straight to voicemail, he had to settle for leaving a message. He didn't worry, since he knew Trey would return his call. The sheriff took his job seriously and he was the most by-the-book man Remy had ever met.

Next he called Wyatt, asking him to put them on a conference call with Decker, Fox and Blaine. Wyatt ran the Crooked C Ranch, Fox bred quarter horses, while the other two worked at The Lodge. Blaine managed The Lodge's extreme-sports division, something he excelled at since he was ex–Special Forces, and Decker was The Lodge's director of operations. Both were sensible men, and although he felt slightly disloyal talking about his brother, Remy knew he needed all the reinforcements he could get.

Once all four were on the line, Remy outlined the events of the past few days. He held nothing back, including what Vanessa had found on Seth's laptop. Once he'd finished, Fox swore. "I wasn't going to mention this to you, but Sloane's husband, Liam, swears it was Seth's car that followed them back from Denver the night Sloane was almost killed."

"Did you tell Trey?" Remy asked, his stomach twisting in knots. It was one thing to have all these suspicions about his brother and quite another to have other people come up with more.

"I did," Fox said. "Trey's been looking into it. He's also learned that the person who threw a brick through Bree's gallery was not the same man who took a shot at her. It's possible it could have been Seth, but without proof, Trey's hands are tied."

Wyatt spoke next. "Phoebe found out that Seth was at the same premiere where someone threw water on her. She thinks it was him, but again since she has no concrete evidence, she didn't want to make it an issue."

"I have more bad news," Decker interjected. "I've recently learned that some of The Lodge payroll accounts have come up short. The books were doctored. I've been keeping this quiet until I get a full report from my CPA, but Seth had access to them as the hotel manager."

Remy swore.

"Now, I have no proof it's him," Decker cautioned. "And until I do, I won't be pursuing criminal charges. But since you've brought all this other stuff up, I thought you should know."

"I don't usually pay attention to gossip," Blaine chimed in. "But there's been a lot of talk among some of the other employees about Seth and money. Again, like Decker said, there's no proof. But I agree you should know."

"I've got a call in to Trey," Remy said. "Is he aware of this?"

"I've alerted him to my suspicions," Decker replied cautiously. "That's all they are at this point—suspicions. However, if I obtain evidence, I will be pressing charges."

"I don't blame you." It was almost too much for Remy to process. His phone chimed, indicating another call.

"Trey's calling me," he told the others. "I'm going to have to let you go."

Instantly, they all agreed and he clicked over. It took him a few minutes to fill in the sheriff, and some of what he mentioned Trey already knew, but he had to get it all out.

Some of his panic must have shown in his voice. Trey listened and when Remy finally wound down, he told him to take a deep breath. "How about we just go over and have a talk with Seth?" his cousin offered. "I can swing by your office and pick you up in about fifteen minutes."

Remy agreed and ended the call. He deliberated whether or not to phone Vanessa, but in the end, decided he'd rather tell her in person. No sense in getting her all freaked out while home alone.

He went down to the lobby to watch for Trey. When the sheriff's cruiser pulled up five minutes early, Remy hurried outside. As usual, Trey appeared competent and unruffled—Remy felt grateful since he felt like such a mess inside.

"It's not your fault," Trey said, once Remy had buckled himself in. "You did the best you could with that kid. No matter how this turns out, you need to know that."

Tight-lipped, Remy didn't even try for a fake smile, knowing the other man would see right through it.

When they got to Seth's condo, he wasn't home. Though Remy didn't see his pickup truck in the parking lot, he and Trey went inside the hall and knocked, anyway.

No one answered. Just in case, Remy tried the doorknob. To his surprise, it turned easily. "It's unlocked."

Trey raised an eyebrow, but didn't comment.

"I'm going inside," Remy said. "Are you with me?"

"Do you honestly feel as if your brother's life might be in danger?"

Hesitating, Remy nodded. "I do. He's not himself. Who knows what we might find if we open the door."

Jaw tight, Trey considered. "I don't have a warrant," he told him. "I'd need probable cause."

Remy pushed open the door. What he saw just inside made him stop short, his heart in his throat. On the table just inside the door were several firearms—pistols and shotguns and AR-15s. What the actual hell?

Turning to look at Trey, Remy opened the door wide enough so his cousin could see, too. "I don't know about the laws, but is finding a cache of weapons enough of a probable cause?"

"I'd say yes. Exigent circumstances," Trey explained. "That means I have a reasonable belief that evidence may be destroyed in the time it would take to get a warrant."

Once inside the condo, the sheriff called in for

backup. While they waited, he meticulously photographed each weapon. "These will be bagged for evidence. Even though there hasn't been a crime yet that we know of, we'll need to see proof that your brother legally purchased these guns."

Still in shock, Remy grimaced. "I'm going out on a limb and saying I'm guessing he probably did not."

Two deputies arrived and Trey stepped aside to let them take over. "Bring them back to headquarters and we'll store them in evidence," he said. "Seth will have to come in and claim them if he wants them back."

Remy could imagine how little Seth would like that. He dreaded telling Vanessa. Like him, she'd jump to the inevitable conclusion that Seth had been planning something deadly.

"We've got to find him quickly," Trey said, no doubt sharing Remy's silent speculation. "We don't know what other firepower he might have on him or what he's planning. It's imperative we stop him before someone gets hurt."

Worried, Remy dialed Vanessa. After three rings, the call went to voicemail. He left a detailed message, hoping she was all right.

Chapter Ten

At the sound of the front door opening and then closing, Vanessa froze, the flow of her graceful movement interrupted. On the YouTube video she was streaming, the yoga instructor continued giving instructions in her soothing, serene voice, though Vanessa's calmness had instantly gone right into panic mode.

She'd forgotten to wedge the chair under the doorknob as Remy had instructed. Heart pounding, she wondered if her carelessness would result in yet another unwanted, angry confrontation with Seth.

Maybe not. *Hopefully* not. Remy could have simply decided to surprise her at lunchtime.

"Remy?" she called out, willing him to respond. Instead, nothing but silence answered her. Tense, her stomach twisting, she looked around for something she could use as a weapon in case she needed to defend herself.

Coming up short, she wondered if she should hurry into the kitchen and grab a knife, just in case. But she'd read that more people are hurt by the weapon being used against them by their attacker, so she stayed where she was. Frozen, heart hammering in her ears, she waited for whoever, whatever, to make their move.

When nothing happened—no noise, no movement, no furious Seth jumping out to confront her—she wondered if she'd imagined the sound of the door. She'd been in a half-meditative trance, but still…

Finally realizing she needed to pause the video stream, she did that. Definitely not Remy, since he hadn't responded to her when she'd called out his name.

Moving slowly, she went to check the door. Still locked. Which meant either she'd imagined everything, or the intruder had locked the door after gaining entrance.

What to do, what to do? Part of her shouted "run," ordering her to head for the door as fast as she could, and get out, right *now*. The other, more skeptical part chastised her for letting her imagination get away with her and for overreacting.

Had she? Eying the paused yoga stream longingly, she wished she could simply return to her session, where she'd been stretching and posing and pushing herself to the max. Truth be told, all along she'd been hoping Remy would come home and surprise her. She'd actually allowed herself to daydream, in love with the idea of him walking in and watching her move her body in ways that felt both sensual and empowering.

She wavered too long, stuck between gut instinct and feeling foolish.

There. Another sound, this one barely discernible, as if someone was trying to move quietly but a misplaced foot and a random squeak of the floor betrayed them.

Damn it. The back of her neck tingled. She hadn't

been wrong—someone *was* in the house, and she needed to get out immediately.

She spun, nearly tripping over her own feet as she raced for the door. But before she could, Seth stepped into the foyer, between her and the door, his expression impassive.

"Seth," she gasped, putting her hand to her throat in fright. "You startled me. What—"

His arm came up. He held a pistol pointed right at her. "Hello, Vanessa."

Think fast. Maybe she could talk her way out of this.

"Seth." Despite her best efforts, her voice quavered. She slid her phone into her yoga pants pocket and tried to compose her expression into something she hoped appeared neutral.

"In the flesh," he mocked, his expression as cold as his gaze.

She swallowed hard. "Why are you here, Seth? And what are you doing with that gun?"

"What I should have done a long time ago," he drawled, his eyes narrow as he glared at her. "Driving the karma bus straight for you."

Part of her wanted to ask if he had taken something—some drug judging by the way his pupils looked—but she knew a less antagonistic approach would be best. For the first time she understood that the Seth she'd known and loved like a brother had vanished completely. This Seth, with the flat stare and mean twist to his mouth, was not only lost to her, but also deadly. She and Remy had known he was spiraling out of control, but they hadn't grasped how far gone he already was.

He wanted to kill her. She shivered, trying to hide the stark terror that realization brought.

"Seth, let's sit down and talk," she offered, schooling her expression into one of concerned politeness. "Please. Put the gun down. There's no reason for you to act like this."

Sneering, he let loose a string of profanities, calling her every name in the book and some she hadn't ever heard of. She felt each word rain on her like a blow and it took an effort not to hunch over from the pain of hearing a man she'd once considered her best friend talk to her this way.

Fear turned her blood to ice as she waited, silently, for him to finish. He hated her—the contempt and disgust in his voice was testament to that.

"I'm going to kill you," he declared once he'd run out of expletives. "You understand that, don't you?"

Somehow, she found her voice. "I really wish you wouldn't."

He laughed at her and came closer, his gun still aimed directly at her.

"Would you please put that down," she asked, her legs going weak from fear. She couldn't help but wonder how quickly she'd die. Would it hurt? If he shot her in the head, she hoped she'd be killed instantly.

"You want me to put the gun down?" he asked, smiling a shark's smile. "I guess you want to die in a more personal way. Maybe I should strangle you with my bare hands."

Though she wanted to tell him she didn't want to die at all, she couldn't seem to push the words out of her frozen mouth.

He came closer, still smiling. Because the sight of that patently evil smile chilled her to the bone, she closed her eyes.

"Look at me," Seth demanded. "I want you to look at me while I kill you."

A shudder snaked up her spine. Slowly, she opened her eyes and did as he asked. He stared at her, that same malicious smile turning smug. "You deserve this," he declared. "You know that, don't you?"

She gave up the idea of even trying to formulate a response. There was no reasoning with him, anyway. Eying the gun and Seth's dead, cold eyes, she decided she'd take a chance, anyway, and make a run for it. At the worst, he'd shoot her. Maybe she'd make it out. She had to try.

Taking a deep breath, she braced herself. And then Seth launched himself at her, slamming her up against the wall so hard she saw stars. With his hands around her throat—what had he done with the pistol?—he choked her, his grip tight. Painful. Deadly.

Wheezing, she fought back, primal instinct taking over. But she refused to die, craving air, needing to breathe. She brought up her knee and got a lucky shot right between his legs, and he gasped and released her, cursing, and doubled over. She squirmed away, ready to go for his eyes if need be, too panicked to try to find the gun. Sprinting for the front door, she nearly made it, but Seth caught hold of her shirt and spun her toward him. Luckily, the fabric tore.

Free again, she ran outside onto the front porch, screaming at the top of her lungs. She jumped over the stairs, intent on getting away, praying Seth wouldn't shoot her in the back.

An elderly man came out three houses down and called to her so she ran there, letting him usher her inside and ordering him to bolt the door.

Once he'd done so, she asked him to call 911 before she broke down into a blubbering mess. Where was Seth? Would he shoot out the windows, bash down the door, come after her and kill her, anyway? She couldn't stop shaking, couldn't talk to the police dispatcher, and finally had to hand the phone to her rescuer so he could tell them to come help her.

Still no sign of Seth. Did he know where she'd gone? At any moment, she expected him to crash through the window or the door and finish what he'd started.

She wanted Remy... She wanted her parents. She wished she'd never come to Roaring Springs. All she could do was cry while the elderly Good Samaritan awkwardly patted her shoulder and waited for the police to arrive.

Finally, she asked for a tissue and blotted her face and blew her nose. She took a deep breath, dug her phone from her pocket and dialed Remy, but the call went straight to voicemail. That's when she saw she'd missed a call from him. When? She hadn't even heard the phone ring.

He'd left a message. She played it back, trying to draw comfort from the steady sound of his voice, but he sounded worried. Though he didn't say why, he'd asked her to call as soon as she could.

Had he somehow known what Seth was going to do? Surely not, or he would have called the police. Right?

Two deputies arrived and the elderly man—his name was Chris, she remembered him saying—let them in. When she haltingly told them what had happened, they immediately called for backup. The second set of deputies went to search Remy's house while the first two took her statement.

"You need medical attention, ma'am."

"No." She shook her head. "I want to go to the station and make a report. I'm pressing charges. And I need you to make sure he can't get to me again."

"We will," the young deputy assured her. "But I really think you should at least get checked out. Those bruises on your neck look bad."

"I'll live." Then, at his incredulous expression, she relented. "I'll go after I make my report. I want to make sure Seth is arrested and charged. He's off the rails and dangerous."

"Let's take you down to the sheriff's office," the older of the two said. "I'll have Dispatch put in a call to Trey. We'll get this thing straightened out."

Though she wanted to snap back that there was nothing to straighten out—that Seth needed to be arrested—she held her tongue. She'd save everything for the sheriff, including her wrath if they tried to sweep this under the rug.

TREY'S POLICE RADIO crackled as he and Remy got back into the cruiser. "Sheriff, you'd better get back to the station pronto. We've got a young lady here who says Seth Harris attacked her. She's pressing charges. We've got men out looking for Seth to bring him in, but so far no one has been able to locate him."

A young woman? Remy swallowed hard. Vanessa? Who else could it be? "What's the woman's name?" he croaked.

"A Miss Vanessa Fisher," the dispatcher replied. "She's refusing medical attention."

Which meant she wasn't seriously injured, didn't it? Remy opened his mouth to ask, but the dispatcher spoke again, this time to Trey. "What do you want me to do, Sheriff?"

"Put out an APB immediately," Trey barked. He turned to Remy. "What kind of vehicle does Seth drive?"

"Ford F-150 pickup," Remy answered, his heart racing. "Black with oversize tires."

"Did you get that?" Trey asked the dispatcher.

"Yes, sir. I'll get the APB out immediately."

As soon as Trey replaced the radio, he turned to Remy. "You okay? You're looking a bit pale."

As soon as Remy managed a nod, Trey grimaced. "Then buckle up and hang on."

After flipping a switch that turned on his police lights and siren, Trey sped away from Seth's building.

"She was at my house," Remy said. "The woman Seth attacked. Her name is Vanessa Fisher."

"The one you've been telling me about?" Trey asked. "She used to be engaged to Seth?"

"Right."

Trey eyed him. "And what? Since she was at your place, I'm guessing she's seeing you now?"

Remy nodded. "Sort of. Seth's been threatening her, but neither of us realized she might be in any real danger from him."

"But tell me you took precautions, anyway. You said he had a key to your place. Did you at least change the lock?"

Feeling like a fool, Remy shook his head. "I planned to, but I haven't had time yet. I told Vanessa to wedge a chair under both the front and back doors."

"Well, either she forgot or Seth managed to get inside, anyway." Grim-faced, Trey drove with a single-minded intensity.

Though it was usually a ten-minute drive to the sheriff's office, they made it in five. Trey had no sooner pulled up into his designated parking spot than Remy opened his door and bolted from the car. His cousin followed, his pace a bit slower, but not by much.

Inside, Remy started trying to articulate where he wanted to go. Trey shook his head and took Remy's arm, then told the front-desk officer, "He's with me." He led Remy to the back, toward his office. "I'm going to give you some time alone with her," he said. "I'll read over her statement and she and I can talk once you've gotten her settled."

Grateful, Remy thanked him.

The instant he saw Vanessa, head in her hands, her long hair a curtain hiding her face, Remy's legs almost buckled. He went to her, dropped to his knees in front of her chair and gathered her into his arms. "It's okay," he murmured. "You're okay."

Immediately, she burst into tears. His strong, capable Vanessa. The ache that had begun in his throat spread to his chest.

Holding her close, he murmured soothing, nonsensical words. Trey took his place behind his desk, steepled his hands in front of him and waited.

Grateful for this kindness, Remy held on tight, wishing he could take her pain from her and into himself. Part of him wanted to find his brother and beat the tar out of him. But he knew right here, right now, this was where he belonged. With her. Time for reckoning would come later.

Finally, Vanessa's weeping slowed. Taking deep, shuddering breaths, she tried to gather her composure. Trey slid a box of tissues across the desk and Remy handed them to her, waiting patiently until she'd grown calm enough to try to tell them what had happened. What Seth had done.

When she lifted her head, he caught sight of the horrible, purpling bruises around her neck. Damn. He bit back the curse word, his jaw clenching. For a moment, he saw red. "Seth did that?" he asked, letting his shocked disbelief and helpless rage show in his voice.

Tears welling in her eyes, she nodded. "He wanted to kill me," she rasped. "I think he meant to shoot me first, but then he decided to make it more personal."

The thought of what might have transpired sent a chill through him. "Tell me what happened," he said, still holding on to her with both hands. "I'm guessing you didn't block the doors with chairs."

She shook her head. "I meant to, but I forgot. I wish I had." Blinking back tears, she told him everything. By the time she finished, he struggled to contain himself.

Seth had tried to kill Vanessa. Horror and blinding, all-consuming fury filled him, though he struggled to keep it from showing.

"You're okay now," he whispered, smoothing back her hair from her bruised face, the sight of the purple and yellow marks on her neck making him feel sick.

"I'm guessing this means he probably killed Sabrina," he added, handing her another tissue and waiting while she blotted at her eyes.

"Do you feel well enough to let me take your statement?" Trey asked, his voice gentle. "I heard everything you told Remy, so I just need to ask you a few questions and then we're done. Okay?"

Slowly, Vanessa nodded. With Remy's arms still around her, she answered the sheriff's questions, which were mostly clarifying the circumstances around Seth's attack.

Finally, Trey thanked her and said he had everything. "You can take her home now, Remy. I'll drive you both since I brought you, if that's all right."

Outside, in the crisp, cold air, they all hurried to Trey's cruiser. He offered the front seat to Vanessa, but she wanted to sit in the back with Remy. Gratified, Remy pulled her as close as the seat belt would allow and held her, breathing in her clean, fresh scent and aching down to his marrow. "Are you sure you don't want to get checked out by medics?" he asked. Vanessa simply shook her head no.

On the drive home, she stared straight ahead, subdued. Trey made several attempts at light conversation before finally giving up. When they reached Remy's house, the sheriff suggested Remy get a locksmith there as soon as possible.

"I'm calling as soon as we're inside," he promised.

"Good. Because another blizzard warning has been

issued for tonight. I've got as many men as I can spare out there searching for Seth, but if we don't find him before the storm hits, he's going to be looking for someplace warm to hide. Make sure he can't get in."

"I will."

"Let me go in with you and make sure no one's there," Trey suggested.

The thought hadn't even occurred to Remy, but his cousin was right. "I appreciate that," he said. Helping Vanessa out of the cruiser, Remy kept his arm around her as they hurried up to the house after the sheriff.

"The front door is unlocked," Trey commented, drawing his service pistol. "Maybe you two should wait in the car."

Vanessa started to tremble. "I ran out of here screaming. Seth was still inside." She turned to Remy, her expression worried. "I'm sorry. One of the deputies came back to look for Seth and I didn't even think about asking him to make sure to lock up."

"I wouldn't have expected you to." Trey squeezed her shoulder. "You did what you had to in order to stay alive. Let's check this place out. Once we know it's clear, I'll leave. But I intend to have deputies do drive-bys constantly."

"Thank you," Remy responded.

"Maybe we should stay somewhere else." Vanessa's voice trembled. "I wonder if your father is done with that suite at The Chateau."

One look at the stark fear in her eyes and Remy knew he'd do whatever it took to make her feel safe. "I'll call him and find out," he promised. "Don't worry. I'll figure out something."

Trey stepped inside, followed by Remy, who didn't want to wait while Trey cleared his home. Expression panicked, Vanessa joined them. "I can't stay here alone. I'm going in with you."

Remy put his arm around her and kept her close.

Inside, the three of them stuck together as Trey swept every room. Finally, they returned to the living room after he'd declared the place clear. About to leave, the sheriff hesitated at the front door. "Remy, are you armed?" he finally asked.

"Yes," Remy answered grimly. "I have a Ruger I keep in my nightstand, plus a twelve-gauge."

"Good. Hopefully, it won't come to that, but better safe than sorry."

Though the idea of having to shoot his own brother sickened him, Remy agreed. He knew he'd do whatever he had to do in order to protect Vanessa.

As soon as Trey left, Remy wedged chairs under the doors and closed all the blinds. He called a locksmith that he'd used before and they agreed to send someone out that evening. Remy asked for a call when they were on their way. After instructing Vanessa to wedge the chair after him, he ran next door and left a spare key with his neighbor, a trucking company owner named Charlie, and asked if he wouldn't mind letting the locksmith in once he arrived. Since the weather had all but shut down his fleet, Charlie readily agreed, even after Remy offered a halting warning about Seth.

"I'm not surprised," Charlie drawled. "That boy's been a loose cannon for a while now."

Not sure how to respond to that, Remy simply nodded. "I'll pick up the new keys from you sometime to-morrow, weather permitting."

With this accomplished, he returned home, knocking and announcing himself to a clearly spooked Vanessa, who let him in. He told her that his neighbor would be meeting the locksmith for them. Though she nodded, her distant expression made him realize she'd retreated somewhere deep inside herself. As he watched her, she shivered, seemingly unaware that she did so.

"Would you like to get out of here?" he asked. "We can go into town or just for a drive. Whatever you want?"

Blinking, she finally seemed to focus on him. "I had a panic attack when you went next door," she admitted. "I never have panic attacks." She took a deep, shaky breath. "Now that you've gotten the locksmith taken care of, will you call your father and see if we can stay at The Chateau?"

"Of course." Glad of the reminder, he dialed Whit's private cell phone. His dad answered on the second ring.

"I need to use the suite," Remy said, making his request a statement rather than a question. "Today. Right now, actually."

"For how long?" Whit asked, sounding distracted.

"I'm not sure. At least a few days."

"Fine," Whit answered. "I won't be needing it until after the holidays, anyway. Knock yourself out." And he ended the call.

Since Remy had been prepared to argue and insist, his father's easy capitulation surprised him. When he relayed the news to Vanessa, her relief made her entire face light up.

"Let me get packed and change out of my yoga clothes," she said. "Will you come with me? I don't want to be alone, not even if you're in the next room."

"Of course." He followed her and stood in the doorway while she threw her things into her suitcase, keeping out a bulky sweater, jeans and boots. When she'd finished, she peeled off her yoga outfit and put on the much warmer clothes, her back to him. Then she zipped the bag closed and looked at him.

"Your turn," she said. "I'll come watch you pack now."

He made quick work of this chore. At the last moment, he took his pistol out of the nightstand and slipped it into a shoulder holster he could wear under his coat.

"All done." Grabbing his suitcase, he reached for hers but she shook her head.

"I'll carry it. I can swing it like a weapon if someone comes after me."

Since he knew she'd seen him put on the holster, he didn't comment. Whatever it took to make her feel safe was fine with him.

They hurried to his Jeep. Outside, the sky had turned an ominous shade of gray, warning of the approaching storm. "Back-to-back blizzards are unusual," he commented.

Vanessa nodded but didn't reply. Instead, she kept up a constant scan of the landscape, as if she expected Seth to appear at any moment.

They made it to The Chateau and Remy headed around back, using the employee parking lot. The leaden sky hadn't yet opened up, though an icy wind blew down off the mountains, carrying a warning of the storm yet to come.

Once inside, Vanessa stuck to Remy's side, glancing around them constantly. His heart ached for her—and with the knowledge that his own brother had caused this fear.

He got their room key and ushered her into the elevator.

She kept her head down, not speaking, clearly still grappling with everything that had happened.

If she wanted space, he'd make sure she got it. Ditto, if she needed comfort. Whatever Vanessa required, she'd have.

The suite sat at the very end of a long hallway, the dark mahogany double doors tucked in a small alcove. Remy used his key card to unlock the doors, holding one open with his body so Vanessa could slip past him.

Moving like a wraith, she did. Chest heavy, he nudged the door closed, wishing he knew what to do to help her.

"Make love to me," she said, as if answering a question he knew he hadn't spoken out loud.

Slowly, he turned, and she came to him, her soft curves molding to him as he wrapped her in his arms. On fire, she kissed him with an intensity that drove everything but red-hot desire from his mind.

"Are you sure?" he asked, when he came up for air. Though already hard, he had to make sure she knew what she really wanted. "You've just been through—"

"I want to feel alive." With that, she touched him, the insistent intimacy of her caress leaving no doubt. He struggled to regain self-control as she stroked and caressed him, then helped him shed his clothes at the same time as she got rid of hers.

There was an intense urgency in her movements. "This," she demanded, guiding his hand to her core, letting him feel her heat, her wetness. She arched her back as he stroked her there and then, with one fluid motion, she pushed him back onto the bed and straddled him.

More aroused than he'd ever been in his life, he groaned as she settled herself over the top of him, sheathing him tightly. He slid his hand down her taut stomach to the curve of her hips, his gaze locked on hers, his body bucking helplessly as she rode him.

"Too soon," he rasped, trying to make her hold still. "Please. Give me a moment to—"

But she only shook her head, the wildness in her eyes matched only by the way she moved. She took him, claimed him, propelled him to ride the crest of fulfillment in one shattering explosion. As he emptied himself into her, he realized too late that he hadn't used protection.

Then Vanessa shuddered, her body clenching around his as she reached her own peak. The tremors, an aftershock of pleasure, continued through her as she held him fiercely, as if she'd never let him go.

That's when he knew. *He loved her.* This woman, proud and passionate, prickly and stubborn, was meant to be his. He could only hope she felt the same way.

Chapter Eleven

The snowstorm came with a vengeance, waking up Vanessa from a sound sleep. Her first reaction—instant, wide-eyed terror—subsided as she realized she was at The Chateau and that Remy held her securely in his arms.

Remy. After that first mad, passionate round of love-making, they'd gone at it again a couple of hours later. She couldn't get enough of him. And while she knew some of it was due to the adrenaline rush and the need to reconfirm life, that didn't even scratch the surface of how much she'd begun to care for him.

Outside, the wind howled around the building corner. She slipped from the bed without waking Remy and went to the window. Peering out, she could barely make out the light poles below through the swirling maelstrom of snow.

Trapped. Her first thought made her feel slightly ashamed. She shouldn't think that way. Even though she once again couldn't leave town due to a snowstorm, she had Remy. He alone made all of this worth it. If she'd never come to Roaring Springs, she'd never have met this amazing, wonderful man. She only wished he wasn't Seth's half brother.

Thinking of Seth sent a shudder through her. He'd been her friend, then briefly her fiancé, and now clearly her enemy. How had she missed his addiction issues and anger problem? How could the man who'd been a rock and supported her through her parents' deaths have tried to kill her?

While she might never have the answers to those questions, she could only hope he was found and brought in without any bloodshed. Gazing out into the swirling whiteout, she wondered where Seth was. The last she'd heard, the sheriff's department had organized a massive manhunt in Roaring Springs and the surrounding area. They'd hoped to apprehend him before the blizzard hit. She wondered if they had. Doubtful, since they most likely would have let Remy know.

Despite everything, she wanted Seth to get help, not to die alone in the freezing snow. She thought back to the times they'd been together, tried to remember if there'd been something she'd missed, some hint or clue of the darkness hidden inside him.

She'd thought him a bit self-centered, she mused. And he'd always seemed to have a deep-seated mistrust, maybe even envy, of people who were better off than him. For the first time she wondered how much of that stemmed from his involvement with the clearly wealthy Coltons.

She'd always treated Seth more like a brother than a mate, she realized. She'd refused to allow the physical part of their relationship to progress beyond kissing and some heavy petting. This had never appeared to bother Seth. If it made him angry, he'd managed to keep his feelings hidden from her.

Of course, he'd been dating Sabrina Gilford on the side. What he hadn't gotten from Vanessa, he no doubt received from her. She thought of the photos she'd seen on Seth's computer. The dark-haired woman had laughed up at him, her fondness for him evident on her pretty face. She hadn't seemed abused or worried in any way. And Seth, with his arm around Sabrina's slender shoulders, had gazed down at her with the same adoration with which he'd once looked at Vanessa.

How much of that had been feigned? Was Seth really that good of an actor? Why bother to pretend to be in love with two different women? Her eyes widened as she found herself wondering if he'd actually proposed to both of them. Had Sabrina broken off things just as Vanessa had? Was that the reason she'd ended up dead?

Seeing where her thoughts had gone, she wrapped her arms around herself and forced herself to face the truth. The man she'd once considered her best friend most likely was a murderer. If he'd succeeded when he'd grabbed her, would that have made him a serial killer?

Vanessa sighed. She supposed she should consider herself lucky that he hadn't killed her that day at her place in Boulder when she'd given him back his ring.

Some of the chill from outside mixed with her dark thoughts made her shiver. She turned, went back to the bed and slipped between the soft flannel sheets, squirming just enough to put herself back into Remy's arms without stirring him. This was where she belonged, she knew. But how could she and Remy forge a future with his brother between them?

Morning brought that particular brightness of sun on fresh snowfall. Which meant the storm had ended as quickly as it had appeared. Sitting up in the bed, loath to leave the warmth of the covers, she debated whether or not to go back to sleep.

"Hey there." Smiling, Remy stretched, drawing her gaze to his muscular chest. "Come here."

Unable to resist, she slid down next to him. His morning arousal delighted her and she reached for him.

"Wait." He grabbed her hand before she could touch him. "We didn't use a condom last night."

"Should I worry?" she asked, half teasing. "I'm clean and I'm on birth control. What about you?"

Expression relieved, he kissed the hand he'd captured before guiding it back. "I'm clean, too." He looked around for his jeans, his body already pushing into her expert strokes. "Do you want me to grab one now?"

"No." Her unequivocal answer came straight from the heart. "I don't want anything between us."

After making love again, she dozed, secure in Remy's strong arms. "Do you want the first shower?" he asked. "I've ordered breakfast from room service. It should be here in about thirty minutes."

"Yes, thank you." Happier than she had a right to be, she dashed for the ornate bathroom and took a hot shower.

Blow-drying her hair while Remy showered felt cozy and domestic. If not for her niggling worry about Seth, she might have allowed herself to relax and enjoy the feeling.

They enjoyed a leisurely breakfast. Though he had to be worried, Remy appeared more concerned with making sure she was comfortable. She caught him glancing at his watch a few times and finally asked him if he was due in at the office.

"No," he answered, clearly distracted. "This time of the year things are super slow, so I texted my assistant and had her let everyone know to stay home due to the storm." He took another long sip of coffee before pulling out his cell. "I'm going to check in with the sheriff."

She nodded. "Okay." And then she held her breath while she waited to hear what he found out. Judging by his sober expression, the news wasn't good.

After ending the call, he met her gaze. "They shut down Pine Peak due to the storm, but got word of multiple avalanches." He swallowed hard. "And one of the ski patrol got a call about a man stranded up there. They're not sure if he was caught in one of the avalanches or not. Either way, Trey thinks it might be Seth."

Her stomach twisted. "Are they sending the ski-rescue team out?"

"Yes, but they're severely undermanned. I'm going to go offer to help."

She stared at him, trying to find the best way to divulge her thoughts. "Remy, you're not a strong enough skier. I don't want to lose you."

"Maybe not." Grimacing, he shrugged. "But I don't have a choice. Seth's my brother. I can't let him freeze up there alone."

"I'll go," she said, surprising herself. "You know I can handle it. I even volunteered on a ski patrol when I was in Switzerland."

Remy started shaking his head before she'd even finished. "Please stay here, Vanessa. If it is Seth, with him being so unstable, there's no telling what he might do if he sees you."

He had a point. Wavering, she let him pull her into his arms. "Can we at least go to The Lodge and sit in with whoever is coordinating the rescue?"

"Yes." He kissed her cheek. "That we can do. It might be a bit of a struggle getting up there—the plow will be busy digging downtown out first, but we'll figure something out."

"How about we ski there?" she asked, itching to get going.

"It's all uphill," he reminded her. "Snowshoes might work better."

She saw his point. "Do you have any?"

"Not personally, but we always keep several pairs in the extreme-sport area. I'll call my cousin Blaine— he runs that program. They should be able to deliver them to our room."

Vanessa nodded, still trying to figure out a way to go along with the rescue team. She had confidence in her skiing skills and knew she would be an asset, no matter what Remy thought. Though he wasn't wrong about a possible bad reaction from Seth if he saw her or caught her alone. After all, he'd tried to kill her once. No doubt if he saw a second chance, he'd take it, regardless of the circumstances.

Reluctantly, she knew she had to stay behind.

Remy finished his call and told her the snowshoes would be delivered in a few minutes. "Go ahead and suit up," he said. "No idea how long getting up to The Lodge might take. We have a tram, but they shut it down until they can get the snow cleared off the rails."

The trek up to The Lodge might have been arduous, but the bright blue sky and sunshine made it actually pleasurable. Though her legs were well conditioned to skiing and snowboarding, using the snowshoes for such an uphill distance made her muscles burn. Beside her, Remy appeared to be feeling it, too, though he made no complaints. Instead, he appeared fixated on reaching their destination.

When they reached the large sign at the entrance to the resort, Remy stopped, his labored breath producing puffs of steam in the frigid air. "They haven't even cleared the driveway," he said, clearly disappointed. "That's usually one of the first things the grounds crew does."

She understood. If the drive had been plowed, they could have taken off the snowshoes and simply walked it. Now they were facing another steep grade they'd have to climb.

"I'm guessing they were busy with more important things," she murmured, glad for the opportunity to catch her own breath. "Just think of this as conditioning for the next time you strap on skis."

Her comment made him laugh. She smiled back, basking in the warmth of his grin. A second later, it faded. "If the snow is this deep at this lower elevation, just imagine what it's like up there on the mountain."

Though he hadn't said his brother's name, she knew exactly what he meant. Focused once more, they began trudging up toward The Lodge.

When they reached the parking lot, Vanessa stared at the private luxury cabins dotting the mountainside before eying the main building itself. The modern construction managed to look both historic and decadent—

the place to be if one wanted to stay at the best ski resort in the state. Each time she saw The Lodge, she fell in love with it a little bit more.

Though she'd never booked a room here, she could honestly say that nowhere else could possibly hold a candle to this one.

"This way," Remy said, snapping her out of her thoughts. "We're not going inside the main building. There's a ski-patrol cabin right before the road that leads to the lift."

"Lead the way."

The one-story frame building looked deserted on the outside, though she knew had the lift been open, the place would have been buzzing with activity. But the instant they stepped inside, the small but focused group of people gave off an intense vibe that showed they meant business.

She should have been surprised, but this ski patrol was high-tech. A large computer screen monitored each member's GPS location. Impressed, she slipped in the middle of a group of three men and a woman. "Any luck so far?"

If they were surprised to see her, no one showed it. "Nothing yet," the woman said grimly. "Though our people are just now reaching the area where the stranded man was last seen."

Remy came up behind her and placed his hands on her shoulders. When the others registered his presence, their eyes widened.

"Hey, guys," Remy said quietly. "I know you'll do your best to locate our stranded guest and bring him back safely."

"Yes, we will, Mr. Colton." A petite young woman, her blond hair in a long braid, regarded him solemnly. "We're all hoping it's not Seth. He's a skilled enough skier that it seems unlikely he'd be in this position."

Vanessa couldn't believe she hadn't thought of that. "If it's not Seth, then who...?"

The young blonde lifted one slender shoulder. "It could be any one of our guests. We have a group of guys from Longmont up here celebrating a bachelor party. They'd been warned several times about taking unnecessary risks. My bet is that it's one of them."

Vanessa exchanged a long look with Remy. If the stranded skier wasn't Seth, then where was he? He couldn't have left town, not with all the roads closed. Unless...

"Does Seth have a snowmobile?" she asked Remy, keeping her voice pitched low.

"No," he replied. "At least not that I know of."

"Maybe he borrowed one, so he could get out of town."

Remy shook his head, taking her arm and leading her away from the others. "He has nowhere to go. No matter how desperate he got, I don't think he'd go back to our mother and that hellhole apartment. Not when he's invested so much time and money creating a nice life for himself here in Roaring Springs."

"They found him!" One of the rescue team shouted. "Alive. They're bringing him in now."

REMY AND VANESSA joined the small group of people waiting to meet the injured man and his rescuers as they came down from the slope. Vanessa gripped Remy's hand so tightly her nails dug into his palm, but he didn't mind. So far, no one had mentioned the guy's identity, so they had no idea if it was Seth or one of the young men from the bachelor party. Though odds were high it was the latter, Trey had joined them just in case. If they brought Seth down on a stretcher, he'd promptly be arrested and charged.

"There they are!" someone shouted, pointing at a speck way up on the mountain. Everyone grew quiet. As the group drew nearer, Remy strained to make out the features of the man on the stretcher.

"It's not him," Vanessa breathed, at the same moment he realized the exact same thing. On Remy's other side, Trey grunted and walked over to the man's group of friends, who'd celebrated with a few unrestrained cheers. They fell quiet the instant the sheriff approached.

"Well." Still holding Vanessa's hand, though her grip had loosened somewhat, Remy tugged her close. "What do you want to do now?"

"I'm not sure," she answered. As she glanced over her shoulder, her eyes widened. "The crowd size has doubled."

Turning, he saw she was correct. Alerted by the ski patrol, most of The Lodge management staff had come out to watch them bring the injured skier down from the mountain.

Catching sight of Remy, one of Seth's counterparts hurried over. "The plow is on the way, with an ambulance right behind it. We've got people working on a press release, too."

"Good. Make sure they run it by me before releasing it."

"Will do." The man moved away.

"Listen." Vanessa tugged on his hand. "That sounds like the plow."

Everyone around them murmured, some craning their necks to see if they could catch a glimpse of it. A moment later, the plow made its way up the driveway, shoving aside snow into great piles on either side.

Another cheer went up as everyone caught sight of the ambulance, lights flashing, following right behind. As the plow made a slow circle to go back down, the ambulance parked and three EMTs jumped out. As they surrounded the young man, whose name apparently was Eric, the ski patrol relinquished custody and vanished into the crowd.

Eric's group of bachelor-party attendees remained at his side, unusually quiet while they watched the paramedics set up. Remy suspected one or two had bad hangovers, but they all seemed genuinely concerned.

"Looks like he's going to be okay," Vanessa said. "Let's go inside and maybe get something to eat or a cup of coffee."

He squeezed her hand. "Great idea."

Hand in hand, they walked toward the side entrance.

As usual, the interior lobby of The Lodge was packed full of skiers. Today, with nowhere to go, they seemed hell-bent on spending money and having fun. The gift shop had a sign up noting they'd sold out of souvenir T-shirts, scarves and knit caps. The bars were packed and it was standing room only.

Remy sensed an impatient vibe. The vast majority

of the guests were here for the snow sports. Since the storm had stopped, they were all biding their time until Pine Peak reopened.

If no one seemed concerned about the man who had been rescued from the mountain, Remy knew there was good reason. They didn't know. Per policy, Lodge employees kept the worrisome news under wraps and would continue to do so until a successful rescue had been announced by Decker. He'd be releasing a statement very soon. Luckily, they'd been successful.

If they hadn't been successful, they'd figure out a way to do a press release that wouldn't scare off any of the guests. They had procedures in place for handling fatalities. Even if someone died in a skiing accident, once the slopes were determined safe, the skiing would continue.

Luckily, Eric hadn't died. Remy figured he'd find out later what exactly had led to the young man becoming stranded.

"Each time I see this place, I'm more and more in awe. I notice more and more details, like these absolutely beautiful Christmas decorations," Vanessa breathed, turning her head and trying to take them all in. "It's impossible to take them all in on one visit. I love that they're totally different than the ones at The Chateau."

"They are." He grinned. "The decorator there is instructed to go for an elegant, old-world, European vibe. Here, they strive for a more artsy, outdoorsy feel." Gazing at her, blue eyes sparkling, creamy skin pink from the cold, he wanted to kiss her senseless. Of course, that would have to wait for later. "Which do you prefer?"

he asked, gesturing at a huge tree decked out with deer and moose among all the other ornaments.

She took his question seriously, studying the tree. "I like them both," she finally said. "Although, if and when I ever put up my own Christmas tree, I think I'd lean toward a more casual approach, like the rustic look here."

"If and when? Are you saying you've never put up your own tree?"

With a slightly embarrassed grimace, she shrugged. "I always visited my family and my parents had a tree there. Until six months ago, I never had my own place and nowhere to go." She swallowed. "This will not only be my first Christmas alone, but the first in my Boulder house."

"Makes sense." Giving in to temptation, he bent down and lightly kissed her mouth. "There's the café. Let's go get in line."

Relaxing into him, she nodded. "Sounds good, though I can think of something else I'd rather be doing..."

Sorely tempted, he hugged her. "Coffee first. We can always go to the room later."

They joined the line, which seemed ridiculously long, waiting with her in front and him pressing himself into her. Cozy and tempting at the same time. He felt a moment of happiness so pure, so bright, it hit him like a lightning bolt. This woman made everything better. They completed each other. As soon as possible, he would tell her, though he really wanted to wait until Seth was captured and safely locked away.

Just thinking his brother's name felt sobering. Pushing away the entire train of thought, he decided to focus on only what was good and bright about this day. Vanessa was unharmed, and they'd found each other. He had to believe Seth would get caught or turn himself in and finally get the help he so badly needed.

The line moved slowly. There were still five or six people in front of them when a shot rang out. Where? Spinning around, trying to keep himself between the shooter and Vanessa, Remy tried to locate the threat.

Another shot. There were screams, though Remy wasn't sure if they were because someone had been hit or just from general panic.

All hell broke loose. People bolted, running in every direction. Over the roar of the crowd, someone else shouted, *"Run!"* In full panic mode, everyone took off, a confused, terrified, thundering herd of people all scattering in different directions, no one sure which way to go.

Remy eyed the nearest decorative pillar and shoved Vanessa behind it. "Stay down," he ordered. "Don't move, not for anything, you understand?"

"Wait." She grabbed at him, her expression frantic. "Where are you going? Get down here with me."

"I can't." He shook off her grip. "This is my family's hotel. I've got to find the shooter."

Another shot, then two more in rapid succession. More screams, the smell of gunpowder, desperate perspiration and maybe even the coppery scent of blood. The lobby emptied out, despite the melee and crush of guests all running in opposite directions.

Trey appeared at Remy's side, his pistol out. "They're saying the shooter is near the lobby fountain," he growled, glancing sideways at Remy. "I'm guessing you're not armed?"

"No. I didn't see a reason to carry it when Vanessa and I snowshoed up here from my house."

Another shot. And another scream, a long one, trailing off into sobs. Trey cursed. "Stay behind me." Crouching low, he took off and pushed through the crowd going in the opposite direction. "Come on." Remy followed his lead, dodging between pillars and at the same time urging the terrified guests toward the emergency exit.

And then, amid the chaos of the fleeing people, Remy saw him. Seth, standing at the top of the small maintenance staircase that ran up behind and looked over the huge lobby fountain.

Seth surveyed the stampede below him with a smug smile, clearly taking pleasure in the panic below. Even worse, he had his arm around the neck of a terrified young girl, who appeared to be around thirteen or fourteen years old. He must have dragged her up there with him, Remy realized. The teen wept unabashedly, clearly out of her mind with fear.

Trey appeared at Remy's side, dragging him back behind one of the pillars. "Stay out of sight," he warned. "For all we know, Seth could have come here with the intention of taking you and Vanessa out."

"Maybe. Either way, he's shooting innocent people." Remy heard the shocked disbelief in his voice. "Do you know how many people he's injured or killed?"

"I don't know." Grim-faced, Trey clasped Remy's shoulder. "I'm sorry, I know he's your brother, but I'm going to have to take him out."

"What about the girl? He's using her as a shield."

"Daria's on the way. She's the deputy sheriff and my best sharpshooter." Since Roaring Springs was so small, they didn't have a dedicated SWAT team.

Remy shuddered. "Let me try and reason with him."

"I think he's beyond reasoning."

"No! I refuse to believe it. Come on, Trey. You have to at least try to talk him down. If it doesn't work, then by all means have Daria put a bullet through his head."

"We don't have a skilled negotiator," Trey admitted. "I can try, but…"

"Let me do it." Remy swallowed hard. "I think if anyone can get through to him, I can."

"I don't know about that. I can't let you put yourself in danger."

"Look." Remy pointed. Seth had raised his pistol again, eying the dwindling crowd of people as if searching for his next victim.

Trey swore. "Daria needs to get here now. She's having a bit of trouble because some of the roads are still not plowed."

"I can't let this happen." Jerking away from Trey, Remy stepped out into the open. Just about everyone had fled the lobby, except for two clearly terrified people who were huddled together behind another pillar. Judging by the way the woman wept and the man held her, they were Seth's hostage's parents.

"Let her go, Seth," Remy shouted. "You need to stop this right now."

For maybe two seconds, Seth froze. And then he laughed. The awful mocking sound seemed to echo in the nearly empty lobby.

"Let the kid go," Remy repeated. "Take me instead."

"I don't want you. But I will take Vanessa. Send her out here and this girl can go free. She's shaking, can you see that?"

"You son of a bitch. I'm not sending Vanessa. She's not here. You're angry with me, not her. Take me."

Narrow-eyed, Seth appeared to be considering. "Let me get this straight. You want to die for Vanessa Fisher. Do I have that right?"

Though he wouldn't have put it that way, now wasn't the time to be splitting hairs. "If I have to, yes. Just let the girl go."

"No. Get. Vanessa." Seth screamed so violently, spittle flew. His young captive closed her eyes and swayed, looking as if she might pass out from terror.

"I'm here." Vanessa's voice, coming from the other side of the fountain. Too far away for Remy to protect her.

"Vanessa, no!" He stepped forward, determined to get to her any way he could.

Ignoring him, Vanessa continued to move toward the staircase. "If I come up there with you, will you let her go?"

"Yes." Glowering at her, Seth kept the pistol pressed up against the teen's head. "But get up here fast, before I change my mind."

Remy made it about halfway across the room before Seth shouted at him to stop. "Take another step and she dies."

Remy froze. He wondered how much longer until Daria showed up with her high-powered rifle. It didn't seem like he had a chance in hell of talking

Seth down, not now. Especially not since Vanessa had revealed herself.

"Do as he says, Remy." Taking deliberate steps, Vanessa never took her gaze off Seth as she moved closer. "Seth, I know you're not a monster. Give me your word that you'll let this girl go once I reach you."

Instead of promising, Seth laughed maniacally, never moving his gaze from Vanessa. The sound echoed—the cackling of a madman. Remy's gut twisted as he realized he'd severely underestimated just how unstable his brother had become. "Don't hurt her," he called, hoping against hope that Seth still had a small shred of decency.

Both Seth and Vanessa ignored him. "I'm here," she said, speaking in the soothing kind of tone one used with irritable small children.

Heart in his throat, Remy watched her as she reached the bottom of the massive fountain. Even now, she'd made herself a perfect target. If Seth wanted her dead, he had a clear shot.

While Seth focused on Vanessa, Remy took the opportunity to move a few feet closer, praying Seth wouldn't notice.

So far, so good.

Vanessa had now climbed up, not on the bottom step of the small staircase which she probably hadn't noticed since it was blocked off with a chain and hidden mostly behind the massive fountain, but on one side of the fountain itself. The same thick concrete edge that kids like to balance on while they tossed their pennies into the water. Seth stood several feet above her, glowering at her while still holding the young girl in a tight grip. Remy noticed he didn't seem sure where to aim his pistol, as he switched from the teenager's temple to Vanessa and then back again.

While Seth was preoccupied, Remy took advantage and moved another couple of steps closer.

"Come up here, Van," Seth ordered. "It's just a few more feet."

"No." Vanessa's voice, clear and certain, rang out. "Bring the girl to me. Once she's here safe, then I'll go up there with you. Or someplace else—whatever you want."

Remy held his breath, praying that her gambit worked. If they could get Seth down from his vantage point, he'd be much less of a danger to any other innocent bystanders.

"Why?" Seth finally asked, squeezing the teenager so hard that she cried out. "Why would I want to go anywhere with you?"

"Don't you have plans for me?" she asked, sweetly reasonable. "That girl hasn't done anything to hurt you. She doesn't deserve to get caught up in any of this. Bring her down and let her go."

To Remy's shocked disbelief, Seth began hustling down his captive...one step, then another.

Head held high, Vanessa waited for him, looking for all the world like a queen awaiting her subject.

Meanwhile, Remy inched a little bit closer. Seth never even glanced his way.

Two more steps, and Remy could see the wide-eyed girl visibly trembling. Now Seth had come halfway down. Still a clean target, should Daria have arrived and gotten set up. But as long as Seth kept that pistol pressed up against the teenager's temple, Remy knew the deputy sheriff wouldn't risk it. Since he didn't want his brother to die, Remy hoped like hell Vanessa could talk Seth into giving himself up.

Movement caught his eye. Trey, moving briefly from behind his pillar, gave Remy a quick thumbs-up before ducking back into the shadows.

Thumbs-up. Did that mean Daria had taken up her position and had a high-powered rifle aimed at Seth?

Chapter Twelve

Heart pounding, Vanessa struggled to keep her voice steady. Instinctively, she knew she couldn't let Seth see her fear.

As if this was a perfectly normal circumstance, she checked her watch. "Come on, Seth. Bring the girl down and let her go. You and I have unfinished business."

She caught her breath as Seth manhandled the teenager another couple of steps. The girl's eyes locked on hers, the terror in them clear, amplified by her tears. Silently, she pleaded with Vanessa to help her, save her, not to let her die.

One more step. Two. Seth's captive held herself rigid, moving like a robot, clearly afraid to make the wrong move.

Vanessa couldn't blame her. She was pretty damn petrified herself.

Only three steps remained until they reached the bottom. Vanessa took a deep breath. She could do this. She *would* do this.

On the other side of the fountain, she saw Remy, carefully and slowly moving closer. She wanted to shake her head at him and warn him to stop. They didn't need to risk Seth noticing and flying into a rage.

She crossed her arms, tapping her toe in feigned impatience. She wasn't sure why or how she knew this, but somehow she realized the best way to deal with this crazy, out-of-control situation was to pretend everything was fine.

Frowning at Vanessa, Seth hustled his captive down the remaining steps. "Come over here," he ordered, his arm still around the teen's neck.

Heart thundering in her ears, Vanessa complied. She walked until only a few feet separated them. Wondering if she dared, she decided to reach for the girl, hoping to pull her from Seth's grip.

Before she could, Seth shoved the teenager away. She stumbled, too shocked to realize she was free. "Go," Vanessa urged her, watching as the girl half ran, half crawled to a small group of people who must have been her family.

Once she knew the teen was safe, Vanessa returned her attention to Seth. "What now?" she asked, her voice quiet and, amazingly, calm. "Are you going to shoot me in the head, right here, in the lobby of this hotel?"

"No," he answered, the bleakness in his gaze both startling and frightening. "I've messed up, Vanessa. I didn't mean to hurt anyone, except maybe you. So now, I'm going to use this gun to put an end to my misery— to *everyone's* misery."

Shocked, she stared. Unbelievably, Seth was smiling, though his eyes remained pools of darkness and despair. "And if I know you," Seth continued, "you'll blame yourself. My death will haunt you for years to come."

Then he lifted the gun to his head, pressing it against his own temple. Horrified, Vanessa wasn't sure what to do. Several scenarios flashed through her mind. Should she try to jump him, maybe knock away the pistol? Undecided and uncertain, she hesitated a moment too long.

Remy did not. He ran and leaped across the space separating them, landing on top of Seth and sending the gun flying.

Miraculously, it did not go off.

"Stay down," Remy ordered, struggling to restrain his brother. Seth fought him, crying and laughing at the same time, his expression a study in confusion.

"You should have just let me die," Seth cried out.

"Never," Remy responded, his voice heartbroken. "You're still mine to protect."

At that, Seth stopped struggling, his gaze meeting Remy's.

"Why?" Remy asked. "Why hurt innocent people? What brought you to this point?"

"You're a Colton," Seth replied, the anger in his voice matching the emotion in his eyes. "You couldn't possibly understand."

The sheriff appeared, seemingly out of nowhere, and joined Remy. Working together, they got Seth's hands behind his back and then Trey put him in cuffs. Once he'd been restrained, Trey motioned to two of his deputies to take him away.

"Take him out the back," Trey ordered. "The news vans have started showing up out front. I've got people warding them off, but the last thing we need is them showing video of Seth on the evening news tonight."

For a second, Vanessa thought Remy might go with

the two men escorting Seth. But he visibly checked himself and remained in place.

"That was a close one." An athletic woman with short brown hair wearing a Bradford County Sheriff's Department uniform sauntered up, carrying a deadly-looking rifle. Her golden-brown eyes briefly touched on Vanessa. "There were a few times when I had a perfect shot. Luckily, Trey refused to give me permission to take it."

Vanessa realized this woman must be the sharp-shooter from the police department. If Seth had made one more wrong move, she would have taken him out. Despite all he'd done, the thought of him dying that way made her stomach hurt.

"I'm glad it all worked out," Vanessa finally said, hoping she sounded calmer than she felt.

"Me, too." The other woman studied her. "You were really brave out there. Good job talking him down." She stuck out her hand. "I'm Daria. Daria Bloom."

"Vanessa Fisher." They shook. Vanessa appreciated Daria's cool, firm grip.

Daria glanced past her, her gaze landing on Remy. "Are you okay?" she asked, her smooth brow wrinkling in concern. "You look a little pale."

"I'm fine." Remy attempted a smile, which clearly said he was not. "What about the guests? Were there any serious injuries?"

"A couple of minor gunshot wounds, but nothing too bad." The sheriff smiled reassuringly. "No fatalities. I've got paramedics treating everyone now."

Another uniformed deputy walked up and joined them. "We got Seth loaded up out back and he's on his way to the station for processing and booking. The mayor has been trying to reach you. Mayor Dylan would like to get with you to formulate a statement he can give to the press. He's stressed his highest priority is reassuring the people of Roaring Springs that they are now safe."

For a moment Remy raised his head and opened his mouth, making Vanessa think he planned to take issue with that statement. She saw the second it sunk in that his own brother had made the entire town feel threatened. The flash of pain in his gaze made her ache to go to him and offer comfort, but she knew this wasn't the place or time.

"I assume you're going to keep him locked up until the judge sets bail?"

"I think it's safe to say the DA is going to deem him a flight risk. There probably won't be bail," Trey answered, his expression solemn.

"Will you at least try to keep an eye on him? After this stunt, I'm afraid he might try to hurt himself."

"Of course." Trey clapped Remy on the shoulder. "We've already placed him on suicide watch."

"Thank you," Remy said, his expression both defeated and sad. Vanessa knew that he still felt responsible for the acts of his brother. She resolved to talk to him later about that.

A tall, well-built man with wavy brown hair walked up. "Is everything under control?" he asked.

Trey nodded. "Yes, Decker. We've already taken Seth off premises and the wounded have either been tended to on-site or transported to the hospital."

Decker dipped his chin before turning his attention to Remy. "Have you dealt with the press?"

Remy looked stunned. "I...no."

"I've got men keeping them back," Trey interjected. "I know Decker's head honcho at The Lodge, but I'm going to need to take his statement. Is there someone else you could send?"

Remy straightened, smoothing out his miserable expression. "I don't work at The Lodge, but I'll handle this."

"Thank you." Decker turned away, calling out to someone else, his attention already elsewhere.

As Remy visibly composed himself, Vanessa joined him. "I'll go with you, if you don't mind."

Remy took her arm and put a bit of distance between them and the others. "This is not my job, Vanessa, but I'm helping out." His voice shook.

"It's okay, Remy," she insisted. "This involved your brother, for goodness' sake. I don't know who that Decker guy is, but he either doesn't realize what you just went through or he's an idiot."

After a startled glance, Remy laughed. Some of the tension left her hearing that sound.

"Decker is another one of my cousins. Not only that, but he's the director of operations here at The Lodge. He's in damage-control mode right now. I get it."

Abashed, she swallowed. "I'm sorry. I didn't mean to disparage your cousin."

"Oh, honey." He kissed her cheek. "I appreciate you wanting to defend me. Thank you."

Stunned at both his insight and the endearment, she froze. *Honey.* She kind of liked that.

Trey came up. "Hey, Remy. I know you're about to go do your thing with the press, but remember Mayor Dylan wants to do a joint statement. He's on his way here. Can you hold off on helping Decker with the press for a bit longer?"

Though his expression seemed pained, Remy nodded. "Trey, I'll be honest with you. I'm still trying to process what Seth has done. There's no way I can handle a press conference right now. I'll send someone out to let them know. That way they won't get too restless. But I'll probably be delegating the actual conference to someone else."

Trey immediately nodded. "Of course," he said. "I completely understand. Do what you have to do."

"Thanks." Remy turned to her. "I don't know about you, but I need to go somewhere quiet, where I can think."

From the corner of her eye, she saw Trey grab Decker, who appeared to be making a second pass of the room. The two men conferred, heads close together. Finally, Decker glanced at Trey and nodded before someone else claimed his attention.

Trey returned. "It's all set. Decker is going to take care of everything. And he said you could use his office if you need some privacy."

Vanessa watched Remy closely. His guarded expression almost crumbled, but he appeared to wrest control of himself at the last minute.

"Thank you," Vanessa told Trey, taking Remy's arm. As long as she kept her focus on him, she didn't have to deal with the fact that her legs were trembling so much that she could barely walk.

"Outside," she told Remy. "I need to get away from the people, the sounds, all of it. Let's go for a walk."

"Okay." He nodded. "I'm with you on that."

Once outside, they walked to the outdoor seating area for one of the restaurants. Now closed, she chose a long bench and carefully brushed off the snow. "Sit."

Remy sat. She took a spot next to him.

They sat in silence for a few minutes, the cold seeping through her jeans and into her bones. Still she didn't move.

Finally, she turned to Remy. He sat as still as a statue, gazing off into the distance. "Where do you think Seth is now?"

He blinked and checked his watch. "By now I think he'll have arrived at the police station. They'll book him and put him in a holding cell until they decide whether to send him to the county jail. It depends whether the feds pick him up or not."

"It's so sad." She shivered, the cold finally getting to her. "Do you mind if we go back inside? My feet are numb."

Immediately he jumped to his feet. "Of course I don't mind. Let's go. We can always take Decker up on his offer to use his office, if you still need more quiet time."

"I think we both do," she said.

After they walked inside, the lobby still a chaotic mess of people and police and reporters, Remy led her through a door marked "Employees Only" and then down a long, carpeted hallway.

Her cell rang. Glancing at the screen, she didn't recognize the number, or the caller ID. Stepping away from Remy and Trey, she answered.

"Van, don't hang up." Seth's voice, sounding desperate. "I insisted on my one phone call and since right now they're keeping me locked up in the Roaring Springs jail, they let me. I called you."

Her chest hurt. Closing her eyes, she took a deep breath. "Why?"

"I wanted to let you know I'm sorry." He sounded so young and afraid that, despite everything, her heart went out to him. "I didn't mean to hurt anyone. I just wanted to get your attention."

She steeled herself. "What about Sabrina? Did you kill her?"

"It was an accident," he said. "I swear to you. We'd both been partying pretty hard and we started arguing. She pushed me and I fell and hit my head."

"And then what?" she asked. "You strangled her?"

"She'd gotten too clingy and threatened to tell you about us. I lost it and I strangled her. Just like that Avalanche Killer. I'd just watched a news story on him, so that might have been in the back of my mind."

She realized Seth always had an excuse for everything. Nothing was ever his fault. "What about Remy?" She couldn't help but bring him up. "He's devastated by what you've done."

"The hell with Remy. It's bad enough that he's got everything." The viciousness of his tone revealed his rage.

"That rich, snooty family of his thinks he can do no wrong. He never got tired of rubbing my face in his good luck."

Speechless, she didn't know how to respond. Was Seth actually putting the blame on Remy for his own bad behavior?

"Are you listening?" Seth had dialed down his tone. "Because I've got more to say. Remy always had more than me. Always. The final straw was when he got you, Van. I just couldn't take that. It broke me. That's why I went crazy there at The Lodge."

Now Seth was blaming *her*? "Seriously?" Unwilling to hear any more, she ended the call.

When she looked up, both Remy and Trey were watching her. "Everything all right?" Remy asked, putting his arm around her shoulders.

She gave a tight nod. "That was Seth."

"What?" Both men appeared shocked.

"He's in custody," Trey said. "How did he gain access to a phone?"

"He said he demanded his one call and they let him have it."

Trey cursed under his breath. "I need to have a talk with my men. Did he threaten you?"

"No." She inhaled deeply, still trying to digest the awfulness of Seth's claims. "He wanted to let me know that his behavior was all my fault. Not his."

Remy shook his head. Trey laughed. "If you believe that, I've got oceanfront property in the mountains to sell you."

"You know that's not true, right?" Remy growled, pulling her closer.

"Of course I do. It just hurts that he apparently believes that."

"Seth believes whatever he thinks will paint him in a better picture," Trey volunteered. "Sorry, Remy. He's always been envious of our family. You just couldn't see it."

"That's true." Vanessa relayed the rest of what Seth had said. "Apparently he's been eaten up with envy."

Remy nodded. "I need to find Decker. I should participate in the press conference."

Trey's cell phone pinged. He checked it and jerked his thumb toward Remy. "Well then, you're up. The mayor just arrived and is waiting for you. You'll need to put your heads together for a minute to collaborate your statement."

THE ABSOLUTE LAST thing Remy felt like doing right now was dealing with the press, but since Seth had been responsible for all this mayhem, he felt obligated to do his part. Squaring his shoulders, he thanked Trey and asked him to keep an eye on Vanessa.

"What for?" Vanessa asked. "I'm going with you. Don't worry, I promise to stay in the background."

Sensing she needed a distraction, he agreed.

Mayor Dylan waited near the yellow tape that marked the crime-scene area where Trey's men were still working. He grunted when he saw Remy. "Helluva mess, isn't it?"

"It is." Briefly, he outlined the facts, sparse as they were. Decker walked up, pivoting when Remy waved him away.

"You know they're going to ask if he confessed to killing Sabrina Gilford," the mayor said.

"We're not going to let them dwell on that." Remy kept his voice firm. "All we're going to talk about is what happened here today."

"I'll let you take the lead then," Mayor Dylan said.

"I'll wrap things up with a brief speech about keeping Roaring Springs safe."

"Perfect. And we're not taking any questions."

Though the mayor raised his eyebrows at that, he agreed.

When they stepped outside, the number of reporters present surprised even Remy. There was Ben, from the Roaring Springs paper, of course. But Remy didn't even recognize the seven others, some of whom had brought camera crews with them. In retrospect, he figured the Denver and Colorado Springs stations would want to send a few of their people, but considering the massive amount of snowfall and the road closures, he had no idea how they'd managed to make it up here.

As soon as Remy and the mayor stepped up to the group, video cameras started recording. Remy outlined the events, beginning with the fact that there had been only minor injuries and no fatalities. "We have the suspect in custody," he continued, bracing himself. "His name is Seth Harris."

Ben jerked up his head at that revelation and he began writing furiously in his notebook. Ben believed in reporting the old-fashioned way. He didn't carry a tablet or even a smartphone. Remy supposed he must use a computer somewhere, but if so, he didn't know where. He'd never seen Ben with even a laptop.

Remy stepped back, gesturing to the mayor. Mayor Dylan stepped forward and launched into a practiced speech lauding the safety of their town and ski resorts.

As soon as he'd finished, both he and Remy turned around and hurried back inside, ignoring the reporters' shouted questions.

The rest of the day passed in a blur. Remy knew at some point he needed to go talk to his brother, but right now his own emotions were too high. Instead, he and Vanessa packed up their bags and moved back to his house. The snowplows had done a great job clearing the roads and downtown Roaring Springs had sprung back to life.

That night, Remy and Vanessa sat together in front of the fireplace and held each other. Remy didn't feel much like talking and either Vanessa got that or she felt the same way. The crackling of the fire was the only sound and provided the only light. He felt cozy and warm and...loved. He'd finally found the one woman who completed him—his other half—and the circumstances surrounding his brother tarnished what otherwise would have been a joyous time.

Seth blamed Vanessa and Remy for everything. Remy would much rather Seth blame only him. The only thing Vanessa had done wrong was coming here and trying to gain closure on the end of what she'd regarded as a friendship. *Closure.* That term seemed to be something women valued more than men. Either way, he was glad she had. Otherwise, he might not have ever met her.

But he couldn't keep from worrying that he'd been the one who'd caused his little brother to finally snap. That guilt was something he knew he'd have to live with for the rest of his life.

As the evening wore on, they dozed. Vanessa finally roused them to go to bed, asking him if he needed to eat anything since they hadn't had dinner.

Remy wasn't hungry, though he told her to go ahead and eat if she was.

"I'm only hungry for you," she said, tugging him into the bedroom with her.

They made love and fell asleep holding each other. Maybe because they were both so exhausted, but the next thing Remy knew, it was morning and the insistent sound of his doorbell ringing over and over and over woke him.

"What the...?" He glanced over at Vanessa, with her tousled hair and drowsy eyes. She shook her head and pushed him toward the edge of the bed. "Whoever it is, either get rid of them or stall them until I get some clothes on."

Despite his gnawing despair, he couldn't help grinning as he hopped out of bed and pulled on his pants. Barefoot, he padded out of the room, trying not to think about what he'd like to do when he got back in bed with Vanessa. Which he would. As soon as possible.

Whoever stood on his doorstep wasn't giving up. They kept pressing the doorbell, again and again. Remy knew only one person that tenacious. When he yanked open his front door and saw Trey standing there, he knew he'd been right.

"Did I wake you?" his cousin asked innocently.

"What?" Remy growled. "Don't you think Vanessa and I deserve to sleep in after the day we had yesterday?"

Trey dipped his chin. "Sorry. I guess I could have called, but I thought I might as well check in and see how you both were doing."

"Are you going to make him stand out there in the

cold?" Vanessa chided, coming up behind Remy and nudging him with one hip. "Come on in, Sheriff. Would you like a cup of coffee?"

Trey pushed past Remy, grinning as his cousin reluctantly stepped aside. "Thanks," he said. "I never turn down coffee."

After closing and locking the front door, Remy followed everyone to the kitchen, unable to keep from admiring the sway of Vanessa's backside as she strolled along. He blinked, realizing she'd put on one of his sweatshirts over her leggings. She looked so sexy, for a moment he couldn't think.

Until he caught Trey looking at him, a knowing smile playing on his cousin's lips. Trey had recently gotten engaged to Aisha Allen, who'd been his best friend since grade school, and Remy had never seen him so happy. Until now, Remy had never understood the kind of blissful fog newly betrothed men seemed to walk around in. Now he completely got it, even though he wasn't engaged. *Yet.*

Reining in his thoughts, Remy took a seat at the kitchen table. He thanked Vanessa as she placed a steaming mug of black coffee in front of him, and waited for the sheriff to tell him what warranted a personal visit. He figured if it had something to do with his brother, Trey would have already spit it out. Since he didn't appear to be in a hurry to do that, Remy guessed it wasn't anything urgent. Still…waiting for Trey to speak felt like torture.

"Is Seth all right?" he asked, unable to take it any longer.

"Last report I got, he was fine," Trey answered, taking a drink of his own mug of joe. "But that's not why I'm here."

Smiling, Vanessa moved one of the chairs and sat down next to Remy, nudging him with her hip. "We just woke up," she explained, ducking her head shyly.

"I kind of got that." Trey grinned. "Both of you deserved it."

Remy cleared his throat. "And you're about to tell us why you're here?"

Vanessa groaned. "Remy…"

"It's okay." Trey's grin widened. "I'm used to it."

Unrepentant, Remy leaned back in his chair and crossed his arms.

"Fine." Trey sighed. "We're calling a family meeting. Bree's going to let us use her gallery since we don't want to meet anywhere public. She's closing it for the evening."

"Why not have it somewhere public?" Remy scratched the back of his head. "Wouldn't it be nicer if we could all sit down and talk over a meal and a beer?"

"Nicer, yes. But we can't take the chance of anyone else overhearing. I'm sorry, Remy, but we need to get together and talk about Seth."

Though he privately winced, he agreed. "Is this in the nature of a formal police investigation?" he asked. "I mean, he's already in custody, so I don't see the point."

"Of course not. I'd never discuss something like that with the family. It's just a lot of people have been contacting me, putting two and two together and figuring out that Seth might have been behind a lot more mischief before he attacked Vanessa and then shot up The Lodge lobby. If so, I'd have to say he had a definite bone to pick with the Colton family. We want to compare notes."

The idea that his brother would have acted so spitefully toward Remy's family should have come as more of a surprise. Instead, he found himself asking how he could have missed it.

"Seven o'clock tonight," Trey said, rousing Remy from his thoughts. "Family only. Will you be able to make it?"

"I wouldn't miss it."

Vanessa looked from one man to the other. "I'm sorry," she finally said.

Trey reached over and squeezed her hand. "Not your fault." He pushed to his feet. "See you later, Remy. You both take care." He slugged back the last of his coffee and ambled toward the door.

Remy hurried after him, so he could see him out.

"Remember," Trey said quietly, glancing back toward the kitchen. "Family only."

"I got it."

When he returned to the kitchen, Vanessa eyed him over her coffee cup. "Are you okay?"

"Yeah. I'm just dreading whatever else I'm going to find out about Seth tonight. Apparently my entire family has been adversely affected by him in some way."

"Ouch. I'm sorry. Is there anything I can do to help?"

The concern shining in her pretty blue eyes touched him. Without thinking, he went over to her and kissed her. "Just be you," he drawled. "Will you be all right here while I'm gone?"

"Of course." She gestured at the television. "I'm

sure I can find an old movie to watch. Don't worry about me."

At six thirty, Remy grabbed his keys and got ready to head over to Bree's art gallery, Wise Gal. He'd only been there once or twice, not including her grand opening. Both times had been when she'd had a huge exhibit and wanted her family there to support her. And support was one of the things the Coltons did best.

As he turned to go, he walked over to where Vanessa sat in the living room, comfortably ensconced in the recliner, remote in hand. He bent down to kiss her goodbye, meaning only to brush his mouth lightly against hers. Instead, he found himself kissing her as if he might never see her again.

Finally, he reluctantly broke away, half-aroused. Judging by the smoldering lust in her blue eyes, she felt the same.

"I'll be back before you know it," he promised. "Keep the doors locked—even though Seth is behind bars—and call me if you need anything."

She grinned. "Will do. Don't be surprised if I call you and tell you how badly I want your body."

This made him laugh out loud. Damn, he loved her.

On the drive over, he reflected on how much his life had changed in such a short time. Vanessa had made everything richer—each day seemed more vivid. If not for the apparently escalating situation with Seth, he'd have to believe he'd never been happier.

When he arrived at the Wise Gal Gallery, even though he was ten minutes early, he saw that several others had gotten there ahead of him. Since Bree had prominently displayed a Closed sign on the front door, he had no trouble finding a parking space.

"Here he is." Blaine clapped him on the back, managing, as usual, to appear both rough around the edges and amiable. "Trey has some news."

Remy glanced across the room and met the sheriff's eyes.

Trey nodded, one quick dip of his chin. "He confessed," he said, his voice carrying across the suddenly quiet room. "Sabrina Gilford's death has finally been solved, along with the other strange occurrences surrounding the Colton family. Seth hated what the Coltons had so much, he set out to sabotage them whenever he could, even starting rumors to disparage the family in town. He felt Vanessa was his ticket to something better—that when they married, he'd have her millions and be just as wealthy as his brother and wouldn't need some management level job at The Lodge."

Trey looked down before resuming. "Seth figured out that Shruggs was the killer and secretly followed him, taking Bianca's body and dumping it on Wyatt's property. It was Seth, not Davis, who set off the avalanche that uncovered the bodies to cause even more havoc for the family. And he framed the Avalanche Killer for Sabrina's murder—she'd gotten too clingy and threatened to tell Vanessa about them."

Remy inhaled, his throat burning. As if he suspected, Trey paused, giving Remy time to compose himself.

"The FBI is now involved, too," Trey continued. "Stefan Roberts is handling the case. Not only has Seth been charged with terroristic threats, but he's also been charged with murder. He's being held without bail.

They'll be transferring him to the Federal Correctional Institute, Englewood, once he's sentenced. For now, we'll be keeping him here."

Chapter Thirteen

The instant Remy walked through the door, Vanessa saw the defeat in his posture. The idea that this self-confident, vital man had been knocked so low made her hurt with a visceral ache.

"That bad?" she asked, trying for a lighter tone even as she braced herself.

Slowly, Remy nodded. He swallowed hard. "At least I now have a pretty good idea why my brother chose to keep his relationship with Sabrina secret. Apparently, Seth has been harboring resentment toward the Coltons for some time now. My family can be overwhelming sometimes. Seth didn't really like to be around them much. If they'd gone public, my family would have wanted Sabrina to bring him around to family events. She would have insisted on it, too. She might have been a party girl, but Sabrina was proud to be a Colton." He looked down and swallowed again. "We all are."

"I'm sorry." She didn't know what else to say, so she squeezed his shoulder in commiseration. If she could, she would have done anything to take away his pain.

"Though no one has actual proof—like video or witnesses—all of a sudden, my family now realizes he was behind what they previously thought were random acts of violence or vandalism. He recapped a list of Seth's dirty deeds, from trying to run family off the road, to throwing a brick through the window at Bree's art gallery. When he ended with Seth doctoring books and imitating the Avalanche Killer, she shook her head. "I have no words," she finally said. She'd seen how badly Seth had deteriorated, but this...

"It's a lot to take in," Remy admitted.

Still trying to process all this, Vanessa tried to make sense of Seth's actions.

Murder, attempted murder, stalking and embezzling. So hard to believe the man who'd held her hand through her parents' funeral had done all that. Heartsick, she shook her head. "It's like I didn't really know Seth at all."

"You and me both." Remy sighed. "I keep asking myself how it was possible that I hadn't known. I talked to Seth at least once a week, sometimes more." He met her gaze briefly before his own skittered away. "I feel responsible."

"You're not." She understood Remy's internal struggle. She needed to help keep him from going someplace really dark. She got up and went to him, wrapping her arms around him and holding on tightly. "You can't blame yourself. I understand the raw guilt you feel, but stop it. No one suspects their brother is a killer. No one."

"I should have seen something. Some clue." Clearly not hearing her or believing her words, Remy moved away, rejecting her attempt to comfort him. "He murdered Sabrina. She was part of my family, even though she wasn't related by blood to Seth." Gaze tortured, he glanced at her. "And finally, he tried to kill you."

True. She managed to suppress a shudder. "Remy, Seth and I were friends for a long time. Not once would I have even remotely suspected he was capable of any of this. Never mind murder, but even the petty things like throwing water on someone or a brick through their window. You've got to stop torturing yourself."

"I'm trying." Still, he shook his head. "I'm still attempting to come to grips with the notion that my little brother is a psychopath."

So much anguish, so much pain in those words.

She had no words, hurting for him, with him. "Clearly, he needs professional help."

"I'm not sure anyone could help him," Remy finally said. "Though I'll leave that to the professionals to diagnose."

Again, she tried to comfort him and again, he shook her off. "I need to be alone." Then, clearly seeing the hurt flash across her face, he reached up and caressed her cheek. "Don't take it personally, Vanessa. I'm going to change and then go down to the basement gym and work out. Exercise is the best way for me to relieve tension."

Since she could understand this, she nodded, managed a smile and waved him away.

After he'd left, she thought about going for a run. But the sidewalks weren't all cleared and she wouldn't feel safe running in the street in the dark.

Instead, she decided to watch a Hallmark movie— exactly the kind of sweet, romantic escape she'd need to try to get in a better mood.

But thoughts of Seth kept running through her head. The *old* Seth, not the man he'd become now. The Seth who had gone skiing in Vermont with her, the Seth with whom she'd picked apples and done a 5K. That Seth—the man who'd been her friend—seemed like a completely different person.

She could only imagine what memories Remy had. He'd done his best to take care of his brother since Seth had been a teenager. Nothing but pain, all the way around.

The movie helped, somewhat. She tried earnestly to get into the emotional love story playing out on the screen.

An hour later, Remy walked into the room. She sat up, slightly groggy, hoping he'd been able to purge himself of some of the demons that haunted him.

When he crossed over to her, hair damp with perspiration, her breath caught. He looked at peace, relaxed and more at ease than he'd been since Seth had gone off the rails. When she met his gaze, he smiled. Love and heat blazed from his hazel-green eyes.

He crossed the room and dropped down next to her, pulling her into his arms. "I'm sorry," he rasped, lips against her cheek. "I needed to pound the punching bag for a bit. It helped me come to terms with everything."

If she turned her head just slightly, his mouth would capture hers. But she had something she wanted to say first. "Remy, I want you to always remember that we're on the same team."

He nodded. "I know. I'm not alone. Neither are you. We'll work through this together."

Relieved, she turned her face toward his. Happiness bubbled up inside her as she met his lips.

They moved from the couch to his bed, shedding clothes as they went. They made love, Vanessa losing herself in him. When she finally drifted off to sleep, he held her tight in his arms.

The next morning, Remy opening the blinds woke her. She blinked against the sudden onslaught of sunlight and at the naked, gorgeous man smiling down at her.

"You're finally awake!" he commented, as if that somehow surprised him.

"I am," she murmured. "Now that you let the sunlight in." Squinting at him, she sighed. "You look extremely...energetic."

Maybe he could expend some of that energy with her. Her entire body tingled at the thought.

He shook his head, even though she hadn't voiced the thought out loud. "We can't. Not right now. We have plans."

"We do?"

"Yes. Dress warmly," Remy ordered. "We're going out."

Eying him lazily from the warmth of his bed, Vanessa considered. "Going out where?"

"To buy a tree."

For a second, she wasn't entirely sure what he meant. "A tree? Like a Christmas tree?"

"Yep." His hot gaze caressed her, making her ache for his hands. "You said you'd never had one of your own. There's a big lot at the north end of town. And the hardware store downtown sells lights and decorations." He smiled at her. "We can stop for coffee and breakfast on the way."

The idea enticed her. Even better, Remy seemed almost himself again. "Okay." She pushed back the covers, immediately intrigued. "I'm in. I'll just need a few minutes to shower and get dressed."

"Take your time," he said, though his impatient glance at his watch said otherwise.

His excitement must have been contagious. She hurried through her shower, blow-dried her hair and applied minimal makeup. Proud that she'd gotten ready in twenty minutes, she rushed into the living room. "I'm ready!"

He smiled, the heat in his gaze making her reconsider her earlier plan to get tangled up in the sheets with him.

"That was quick," he commented. "You look beautiful, as always."

Tongue-tied, she nodded. "Thanks."

Once in his Jeep, she buckled up while he backed out of the garage.

The brilliant white of the landscape warranted sunglasses, so she dug in her purse until she found them. Briefly, as she gazed at Pine Peak in the distance, she thought longingly of taking a couple of runs down it, but she pushed away that idea. She could always ski tomorrow. Today, she'd make new memories with Remy.

They had a hearty breakfast at a small coffee shop off the beaten path, which meant only the locals went there. The place only had about ten tables and a long breakfast bar, so they had to wait twenty minutes. The heady scent of bacon and pancakes and coffee was intoxicating. "Best hidden gem in town," Remy said.

Her stomach rumbled. "Good. Because I'm starving."

"After we eat, we're headed to a hardware store that has a huge Christmas section. Think about what kind of colors and theme you want," he advised her. "Of course, if you want something eclectic, I'm down with that, too."

How she loved this man. The idea of them decorating their first Christmas tree together sounded amazing.

By the time they were seated, the line stretched outside and down the sidewalk. Despite the cold, no one seemed to mind. Instead, those waiting appeared at ease and chatted happily.

They were shown to a high-top table near the front window. From there, Vanessa could see the residential area to the east and the mountain to the west. "This reminds me a little of Boulder," she commented. "Though more down-to-earth."

This made Remy grin. The waitress brought them menus and coffee, promising to return in a few minutes.

He pounced on his coffee. Shaking her head, Vanessa doctored hers up and took a small sip. "Wow," she said. "That's a good cup of java."

"Just wait until you try the food."

Opening her menu, Vanessa decided on pancakes and eggs, with a side of bacon. She glanced up to find Remy watching her, his menu unopened in front of him.

"I already know what I'm having," he confessed. "I'm a creature of habit. Whenever I come here, I get the same thing. It's called the Old South breakfast. Eggs, bacon, hash browns, grits and biscuits and gravy."

"Yikes. That sounds like a lot of food."

"It is." He grinned again before taking a long drink of his coffee. "Yet somehow I manage to finish it all."

The waitress returned and took their orders and refilled their mugs. Once she'd left again, Remy reached across the table and took Vanessa's hand. "Which would you rather do first? Buy the ornaments or pick out the tree?"

Stirring another bit of creamer into her coffee, she shrugged. "I think the tree. Once we've chosen that, I'll know better how much decoration to buy."

"Sounds good."

When their food arrived, Vanessa ate until she couldn't manage another bite. Everything tasted delicious, especially the fluffy pancakes.

Finally, pushing her plate away, she sipped coffee and watched Remy devour his breakfast. Somehow, she found the way he single-mindedly ate with a determined purpose sexy as hell.

Bemused, she mentally shook her head at herself. The waitress winked at her as she took away Vanessa's plates. "Clearly, he's still working on his," she said, dropping the check in the middle of the table.

Vanessa smiled and agreed.

Finally, Remy had cleaned his plates—all three of them. With a self-satisfied sigh, he drank the last of his coffee. "Are you ready to go pick your tree?"

"Yes." And she was. Though she'd never had the experience of choosing a live Christmas tree before, she figured Remy had and would help guide her.

They drove to the end of Main Street, where it turned into a two-lane road. She recognized it as the one she'd taken on the way into town. Instead of turning right, they veered left, driving into a residential neighborhood with beautifully restored old homes.

"This is part of the original Roaring Springs," Remy told her. "These houses were here long before the town became a ski resort. The original owners got rich off the mines."

While she knew many Colorado mountain towns had mines, she hadn't heard anything about Roaring Springs. "Are any still open? I know I've been on a few mine tours in other places."

He shook his head. "No. They've long been boarded up."

They traveled a few more blocks down, then Remy slowed down. "There it is." He pointed to a huge parking lot with a few cars and one big, white tent. A large sign proclaimed Fern's Christmas Trees.

"They don't look too busy," she commented, not sure if she should be disappointed or not.

"Christmas is only a few days away," he reminded her. "Most people already have their trees."

She grimaced. "I hope they still have a few decent ones left."

For whatever reason, this comment made him laugh. "Oh, they will, I promise you."

Once he'd parked and gotten out, he took her arm. "You'll see," he said, leading her down a path and around a large boulder that shielded the place from the parking area and road. They went around the tent, which surprised her, but she followed his lead.

As soon as they scooted past the tent, she stopped and looked around her in awe.

A virtual forest stretched out in front of her. There

were more trees than she ever could have imagined. Tall trees, fat trees, pines and firs and trees that had been flocked to look white. Hand in hand, she and Remy roamed the lot, which felt more like getting lost in a forest than anything else. Now she was glad there weren't many other customers. She had the strangest urge to commune with the trees until she found the right one. They were all different and each beautiful. Any one of them would look perfect in Remy's living room.

"Let's take a look," he said. "Come on."

Hand in hand, they began strolling down the rows of trees.

"I can't decide," she murmured. "They're all so magnificent."

He glanced down at her, the tenderness in his gaze warming her. "Take your time. I'm a firm believer in finding the perfect tree. When you see the right one, you'll know it."

They'd reached the edge of the row and she turned to make her way down the next one. Three trees down and she saw it. A blue spruce, maybe six-feet tall, perfectly formed, not too wide and not too thin. "This one," she breathed, stopping in front of it. "I don't know how no one chose this tree, but I'm glad. Because it's coming home with us."

Her enthusiasm earned her an adoring look from Remy that turned her insides to mush. "Are you sure?" he asked.

"Yes." She nodded. "I've never been more certain of anything in my life."

"Perfect." He kissed her, long and deep. When the

salesperson found them, he stood back and eyed them as if he thought they were crazy.

"There." Still wrapped in Remy's arms, joy and love darkening her blue eyes, Vanessa pointed at the tree she'd chosen. "We'll take that one."

Later, with the tree all wrapped up and tied to the top of his Jeep, they drove to Race Hardware and chose the ornaments and lights and tinsel for their first tree together. Remy mostly stood back and watched as Vanessa loaded up her basket, his expression amazed as she laughed and sang holiday carols under her breath. She got it, because she would never have guessed that such a simple thing could make her so happy. *He* made her happy. Though she had a home in Boulder, a life there, she knew she planned to enjoy every second of her time with him.

Once they were back in his Jeep, all the holiday decorations stowed in the back, Vanessa glanced at him and smiled. "I can't wait to get back to the house and get all of this put out."

"Me, either," he said. "Though I helped my father choose a showpiece tree once or twice, this will be the first Christmas tree I've had at my house."

"What?" Eyes wide, she studied him, not quite certain if he might be teasing her. "Are you serious?"

"Yes." He shrugged. "I've been a single guy. Putting up a tree seemed like a lot of trouble just for me. There's a tree at the office and at Colton Manor, not to mention every single store, restaurant and bar in town. Including The Chateau and The Lodge. Anytime I got an urge to feel in the holiday spirt, I just had to venture out of my house."

"That means you and I aren't so different." She touched his arm, smiling big and wide. "That makes this even more special. It's not only our first tree together, but our first tree, period." Who knew? Maybe this would be the first in a long line of them. Dared she allow herself to hope for a future with this wonderful man? He kissed her once more before releasing her and opening his door. "Now let's get this tree unloaded and set up so we can get it decorated."

After she helped Remy get the tree off the top of his Jeep, she escaped to the bathroom to freshen up. Excited to share what hopefully would become a yearly ritual, she hurried back out to the Jeep and started carrying in the bags of lights and ornaments. Part of her wished she'd been able to do this in her new home in Boulder. One of the first things she'd decided when she'd purchased it had been where she'd planned to put her Christmas tree.

But no, she reminded herself. For now she'd live in the moment and enjoy this time with Remy. She inhaled deeply, breathing in the scents of fir and pine, and smiled.

Once Remy sawed a bit more off the bottom, he had her help him put the tree in the stand. Then they spent the next several hours turning the living room into Christmas Central. Remy streamed holiday music and made them hot cocoa, then helped her string lights and garlands on the beautiful tree. For the first time that year, she felt in the actual holiday spirit.

When "Rockin' Around the Christmas Tree" came on, Remy grabbed her hands and began dancing around

the living room in time with the music. She found herself laughing as he twirled her and hip-bumped her.

By the time the song ended, they were both out of
breath. He pulled her in for a long, deep kiss. "This is
fun," he murmured, resting his forehead against hers.
Smiling, she agreed, the tree twinkling merrily in the
background.

"It's beautiful and magical, too," she said.

Kissing her once more, he agreed and released her.
"Let's get it done."

"Okay. Next up, ornaments," she declared, handing
him a box of red glass balls. Grabbing a similar box
of gold ones, she put hooks on them and began placing them on the tree. This precious moment—decorating her very first Christmas tree with the man she now
knew in her heart she loved—would forever be etched
in her memory.

By the time they'd arranged every single ornament
on the tree, singing along to "Rudolph the Red-Nosed
Reindeer" and a few other classics, she felt happier than
she'd felt in years. This might be only temporary, but
she couldn't help but feel a bit optimistic.

Side by side, they stepped back to survey their handi-
work. Remy had placed the tree near the floor-to-ceiling
windows that looked out over the backyard. He walked
over and turned out the lights, so that the tree lit up the
room and reflected in the windows. Vanessa inhaled,
again blinking back tears. "It's beautiful," she breathed,
leaning her head on Remy's shoulder.

"So are you," he said, kissing her temple.

Remy cooked them dinner, a delicious lasagna with
salad and garlic bread. He opened a bottle of red wine

while he cooked. Watching him, she realized she needed to buy Remy a gift. This might be a bit challenging since he already seemed to have everything. She'd figure it out. They still had a few days before Christmas.

The next day, Remy went to work and Vanessa went skiing. When she'd finished her morning runs, she stopped by The Lodge intending to do a little Christmas shopping and have lunch.

"I know you!" a voice exclaimed. Vanessa turned. Daria Bloom, the woman who'd been carrying the rifle when Seth had gone crazy in The Lodge's lobby. She wore her Bradford County Sheriff Department uniform, though her demeanor was a lot more relaxed, understandably.

"Vanessa Fisher, right?" Daria asked, holding out her hand. She had long, elegant fingers with short, unvarnished nails. No-nonsense, capable hands. Liking her even more, Vanessa shook her hand.

"Yes. And you're Deputy Daria Bloom."

"I am." The other woman grinned at her. "Did you just get in from skiing?"

"I did. And now I'm thinking about having lunch. Would you care to join me?"

"I would love to," Daria answered promptly. "I've been dying to get to know the woman who—" She bit back the words.

"Who what?" Vanessa asked.

Daria shrugged. "Managed to get Remy Colton to focus on something other than work." Her easy smile put Vanessa at ease.

They walked to the café and were seated immediately. After ordering—they both wanted salads with grilled chicken—Vanessa discovered she and Daria had something else in common. They both were involved in brand-new relationships.

"Stefan—you'll meet him at the family Christmas party—just moved in with me." Daria's warm brown eyes glowed with affection. "He has the most adorable five-year-old son named Sam. I've never been happier." She took a drink from her water, eying Vanessa. "Are you and Remy living together?"

To her surprise, Vanessa felt herself blush. "Not officially," she said slowly. "At first, it was more of a thing where he was helping me out because I had no place to stay. But we realized pretty early on that we wanted more, so we'll make it official soon."

Daria laughed. "When you know, you know."

Their food arrived and while they ate, talk turned to the upcoming holiday. "I have no idea what to get Remy," Vanessa confessed. "He seems to have everything."

"Not everything." Daria's thoughtful tone matched her faraway expression. "Ever since Remy was small, he's always wanted a dog. Of course, Whit would never allow something as messy as a pet inside his pristine dwelling, so after a while, Remy gave up. He's only mentioned it in passing a few times since growing up." She took a deep breath. "Now normally, I don't advocate giving animals as Christmas gifts, but Remy has talked about this for so long. I think the only reason he held off was because he considered himself too busy."

A dog. Vanessa considered. The more she thought about it, the more she loved the idea. She, too, had longed for a dog of her own. In fact, she'd planned to get one once this year's ski season had ended. Now, with two people able to help take care of it, she realized there was no longer any reason to wait.

"I think you just helped me decide what to get Remy for Christmas," Vanessa said slowly. "I don't suppose you happen to know what kind of dog he would like?"

Daria never even missed a beat. Brown eyes sparkling, she leaned in. "I don't think he cares. He's talked about rescuing some poor shelter pup. And you wouldn't believe how full the shelter gets around the holidays."

"That's sad." Vanessa shook her head. "And rescuing a shelter dog has long been something I wanted to do, too. But before I take such a big step, I have to make sure he's on board with it. I'd also kind of like for the two of us to choose our dog together. That might ruin the surprise, but I think it's a fair trade."

"I have an idea." Daria's infectious grin invited Vanessa to smile back. "Let me know what you think of this plan…"

Listening, Vanessa grew more and more excited. "That just might work," she said. "Why don't you see if you can get that set up, and I'll take care of the rest."

After her lunch with Daria, Vanessa felt like she could skip all the way home. Of course, she drove, but she realized she'd just made her very first friend here in Roaring Springs. As an extra bonus, Daria was part of Remy's family.

Trey called later in the day. "How is Remy?" he asked. "I've phoned him a few times but he doesn't pick up. And even though I've left him a few messages, he isn't returning my calls."

"Seriously?" Surprised, Vanessa wondered what was

going on. "He's seemed pretty happy, considering. I mean, all the stuff with Seth hit him pretty hard, but he seems to be handling it okay."

"I don't think he is." The thread of worry in the sheriff's voice alarmed her. "I'm going to stop by his office before the end of the day, so he'll have no choice but to see me. But I thought I'd better check out his state of mind first."

She frowned. "As far as I know, Remy is fine." But now she wondered. He certainly seemed to have taken pains to stay away from even mentioning Seth. She'd actually thought avoidance might be helping him cope. But what if she was wrong? What if Remy still blamed himself, so much so that he couldn't face Trey, who had Seth locked up?

"He's avoiding everyone," Trey continued. "I've gotten a few calls from some of the others. They're all worried about how he's handling Seth's arrest."

He had a good point. She'd allowed Remy to keep her attention directed toward the bright and shiny new relationship they were forging together. *Was* he okay? Or was the situation with Seth tearing him up inside? She needed to find out.

"Keep me posted," she told Trey. "I'll talk to him tonight and make sure everything is all right with him."

"Will do," Trey promised. "And thank you."

When Remy got home, Vanessa watched him for any signs of internal distress. He acted completely normal. In fact, when she told him she'd had lunch with Daria, he grinned. "Due to some convoluted family shenanigans, she's technically my aunt," he said.

"You are fortunate to be part of such a large and

supportive family," she said warmly. "How's everyone else doing?"

He eyed her. "I'm sure they're all doing great. We'll see them in a few days at the Christmas party."

"Does all of your family attend?"

"Seth never went, so not all…" he began and then choked up. She understood. Because no matter what he'd done, Seth was still his brother. His *family.*

Though she watched him closely, Vanessa saw no signs he meant to reveal his inner thoughts or emotions. She took a deep breath. "I'm glad you brought that up. Speaking of your family…"

Slightly nervous, she twisted her thumb ring around on her finger. "I hate to be the one to bring this up, but Trey called me earlier. He's worried about you and he thinks you're avoiding him. He said he was planning to stop by your office this afternoon. Did you see him?"

"No." Remy frowned. "He must have gotten busy. As far as I know, he didn't come by."

"If he had, would you have seen him?"

"Maybe." He barely looked up, as if afraid of what she might see in his expression. "What does it matter?"

"You love your family," she pointed out. "And you and Trey seem close. Trey is worried about you. He says you've been avoiding everyone else, too, so I'm guessing others have reached out to you, too."

He got up, pretending to be occupied with putting another log on the fire. With his back to her, he spoke. "I've been to visit Seth twice. Both times, my brother refused to see me."

Shocked, she struggled to find the right words to

comfort him, but there were none. She settled on saying she was sorry.

"And that's why I've been avoiding Trey…and everyone else. Because of Seth. I failed him and I failed them. I need time." Though he attempted a casual shrug, the defensive tone in his voice made her ache.

"Remy." She kneeled down in front of him, lifting his chin and forcing him to look at her. "They care about you. No one blames you for Seth's behavior."

He sighed. "I know. I just can't get past my own guilt."

"Talking about guilt…" She took a deep breath. "I know. I have the same problem. I keep thinking of what I could have done differently. If I hadn't come to Roaring Springs, if I hadn't met you. Would that have changed anything?"

"This started long before we even met," he said, then gave a startled laugh. "You know what? Hearing the words spoken aloud actually makes me feel better. Still, finding out that he'd killed Sabrina blindsided me. If I'd known, could I have somehow saved her?"

"There was nothing you could have done to stop it. Don't you think Trey must ask himself the same question? Seth's a grown man."

"You're probably right," he admitted gruffly. "But I did everything I could to help my brother. Everything. I scrimped and saved so he could go to a better school, to rehab. I bought him clothes, his first car. I was always there for him, no matter what. He has to know how much I loved him."

"I'm sure he does." She hesitated. "Remy, you know Seth is troubled. Between that and his addictions, he's going to need a lot of help. All you can do is be there for him when he needs you."

"That will be kind of hard to do since he flat-out refuses to see me." Now, when he raised his face to hers, she saw the raw anguish in his eyes.

Her heart aching for the man she loved, she wrapped him in her arms and held him close. "Give him time," she said. "He's facing some serious charges."

"I know." He sighed. "He's made his choices and now has to suffer the consequences. And I've come to the realization that at this point, there's nothing I can do that could help him."

Since she'd come to a similar conclusion, she simply nodded. "He has his own journey he must make," she said. "All you can do is love him and be there if he ever asks for help."

THOUGH THE DAYS leading up to Christmas were typically the slowest of the year, at least as far as public relations were concerned, Remy found himself fielding a lot of questions from various media outlets about the Seth hostage situation. He'd even gone so far as to type up a statement, which he read verbatim on every phone call. He and the rest of the family managed to keep a lid on all the other things Seth had done.

Most of the staff had taken personal or vacation days, and the normally bustling office was quiet. After the New Year began, they'd begin taking meetings with various advertising agencies, but right now there was very little to do.

He'd thought going to work might help him come to terms with what happened with Seth, but to his surprise, Remy had reached a sort of peaceful place on his own. He'd come to understand how wonderful his life had become. Because of Vanessa, because of love.

And that made him realize he didn't want to hide out in the office any longer. Basically, the PR department was closed for the holiday season. He might as well take himself home and enjoy his first Christmas with Vanessa.

But first, he'd try to talk to Seth one more time. He just needed some sort of understanding as to what had made his brother do the awful things he'd done. Despite the long drive, he headed to the federal penitentiary where Seth was being held.

Third time's a charm, Remy thought, both relieved and apprehensive as the guard told him that Seth had finally agreed to see him. After divesting himself of all his personal belongings and being patted down, Remy was led into a small, colorless room with only a table separated by a glass partition, with a chair on either side. It appeared he couldn't be alone in the same room with his brother—instead, all communication would come through a phone with receivers placed on both sides of the glass.

Remy swallowed when Seth walked into the other half of the room. Gone was the urban, well-dressed sophisticate he'd gotten used to seeing around Roaring Springs. Instead, the savvy street rat Remy had found in that filthy, awful apartment had returned. Noticing him staring, Seth smirked. When Remy met his brother's gaze, he didn't bother to hide his disgust. "Seth." Then, remembering, he picked up the phone and motioned for his sibling to do the same.

"Why haven't you posted bail?" Seth demanded belligerently. "I want out of here."

"The judge denied bail," Remy replied, his chest aching. He felt anger, true, but also that same tangled mess of love and confusion and pain that seemed to swirl around Seth like a storm cloud.

"That's ridiculous." Swearing, Seth dragged his hand through his dirty blond hair. "Do something. I know you can. You Coltons have connections, influence. Use them."

"We don't—" Remy began, interrupted by a spate of virulent cursing.

"You won't, you mean," Seth snarled, his eyes slits in his once-handsome face. "Because I'm not one of you, not a Colton. That's why I've always hated you, all of you. Entitled, condescending pricks, each and every one. Acting like I'm not good enough to shine your shoes. Well, I guess I showed you, didn't I?"

Stunned, Remy needed every ounce of self-control he possessed not to recoil from his brother in horror. Not just to the virulent rancor, but his logic, which made no sense. "Seth," he pointed out, keeping his own voice flat and emotionless. "You killed someone. Hurt people. You did a lot of horrible things for no discernible reason. How is that in any way showing anyone anything?"

"I should have killed Vanessa, you know." Voice low, eyes crinkled with amusement, Seth leaned as close to the glass partition as possible. "It would have been fun to watch her die, slowly and painfully, just like Sabrina did."

Remy hung up the phone. Stomach roiling, he battled back nausea, aware that Seth wanted a reaction, would clearly take pleasure in getting one. So instead, he kept his face expressionless and merely shook his head. He'd wanted answers, hoped for an explanation, but instead this visit had only confirmed that his brother had become a monster. Seth would surely go on trial and be convicted; hopefully, hopefully the justice his crimes deserved would be meted out. And Roaring Springs would be a better, safer place without his brother.

Despite the certainty of that knowledge, as Remy turned to go, he felt sorrow settle like a stone inside his gut. Clearly, for far too long he'd seen Seth with blind eyes, chose to believe his brother could become someone he was not. It hurt. A lot. But finally he understood Seth was where he belonged, where he couldn't hurt anyone else.

The long drive home helped him reach a place of calm. He realized he had no more room for bitterness in his life. He could no longer look back, but keep going forward. After all, he had a future to plan, with a wonderful woman.

When he finally got home, he decided not to mention his visit to Seth. Not yet. He'd tell her later, once he'd had time to process everything.

Vanessa hugged him close when he walked in the door, almost as if she knew. While he didn't want to lie, he couldn't bring himself to talk of it yet. "I'm glad you're home," she said, her gaze quietly searching his face. "I didn't want to interfere with your work, so I'd been planning a couple of solo shopping trips and maybe a few more runs down Pine Peak."

"We can do all those things together," he said tenderly. "And more. There's a Christmas light-sleigh-ride tour that's really popular this week." He dug in his pockets and extracted a pair of tickets. "We go tomorrow night."

She kissed him then, thanks turning to heat. They made love there on the sofa in the afternoon, and afterward, simply held each other since neither was in any hurry to move.

This, he understood, was contentment. And the time had come to let her know about his brother.

Bracing himself, he casually mentioned that he'd been to see Seth. Vanessa nodded, watching his face. "He's unrepentant," he told her. "Still blames everyone else but himself."

"That's sad," she said, snuggling close. "Are you all right?"

"I am," he replied, meaning it. "I really am." The next few days passed quickly. For the first time that he could remember, Remy actually got the Christmas spirit.

"Me, too!" Vanessa exclaimed when he told her. "The last time I felt like this, I was too young to know better."

His heart squeezed. "Never again," he promised. "As long as I'm alive, you'll never spend Christmas alone."

"Right back atcha," she replied.

They went skiing—twice. The cold air and snow put a flush on her cheeks and a shine in her eyes. Once, he actually waited at the bottom of a run so he could watch her come down. When she skied, she was poetry in motion. Superbly confident and very skilled, she drew the eye. He wasn't the only one watching her.

"Hey!" She skied up to him. "What are you doing?"

"Watching you," he replied, kissing the tip of her cold nose. "Are you ready to go Christmas shopping?"

"Sure." They headed back to the ski lockers, where they'd stowed their shoes and her purse, grabbed their stuff and traipsed out to his Jeep.

Hand in hand, they wandered down Main Street, stopping for a cup of hot cocoa. He watched her as she shopped, taking pleasure in the tactile way she shopped, touching some things, almost caressing others.

She bought a few things, smiling at him as if shopping in downtown Roaring Springs might be the most fun ever. With her, he reckoned it was.

When they got back to the house, he put on Christmas music—amazingly, he hadn't gotten tired of it yet—and changed into sweats. Though lately they'd been going out every night, tonight they'd both agreed to stay in.

"I can't believe it's nearly Christmas." Smiling shyly, she put a brightly wrapped gift under the tree. There were a few others already there, one of them being a pair of sapphire earrings he'd bought her because they matched her eyes. "I know you said your family doesn't do gifts except for the children, but I got this for Daria. She's been really kind to me and I wanted to get her something."

"What did you get her?"

"A bracelet. I saw it in the shop and thought it would suit her."

He nodded. "She'll like that." This generosity of spirit was one of the many things he loved about her.

"I love the way Roaring Springs embraces the holiday season," she continued. "Not just the decorations, but the festivities. They seem to have something going on every night."

She should know. He'd accompanied her to just about every single event, often reluctantly. To his amazement, he'd enjoyed himself every time. He hadn't realized how much of a hermit he'd been until she'd come along.

"I love you," he told her, nuzzling her neck. "Thank you for being you."

Her grin made her eyes sparkle. "I love you, too. I can't believe we're finally saying that to one another, given everything that's happened."

"I know," he admitted, his voice husky. "Our love story is just beginning," he added, holding her closely.

"What are we doing on the actual holiday?" she asked. "I mean, shouldn't we discuss it, since it's only two days away?"

For a moment he stared at her, confused. Then he realized he must have forgotten to tell her. What he took for granted since it was a long-standing tradition, she had no way of knowing.

"Well, on Christmas Eve, I thought we'd have our own private celebration here." He gestured at his living room and the beautiful tree she'd decorated. "We can go out to eat or eat in, whichever you prefer."

"Hmm." Her grin widened. "That sounds heavenly. And on Christmas Day?"

"My family has a long-standing tradition. There's a big meal on Christmas Day at Colton Manor. Everyone comes and brings their significant others. The youngsters get gifts, and we eat. There's so much food it's ridiculous."

To his relief, she cocked her head and seemed interested. "Is it a potluck-type thing? Will we need to bring something?"

"No. Mara and Russ have their cooks prepare everything. Sometimes, one of the guys brings a cooler of beer. But there's a full wine cellar that's opened up to everyone, plus top-shelf liquor for those who prefer that."

"You seem to have a large family." She toyed with a lock of her dark hair. "Is it crowded?"

He couldn't tell if she was asking because she would find it overwhelming or if she had hopes of blending in with the crowd. "Yes." He kissed her again, this time on the lips. "But don't worry. They'll love you. I promise."

One corner of her mouth twitched before she kissed him back. "I guess I'll have to take you at your word for it. Tell me about their house."

He eyed her, wondering how to best explain the overstated opulence known as The Manor. "The Colton home is huge, but stark. I honestly don't see how anyone can love living there."

"Oh." She grimaced. "I've been to a few houses like that. Where everything seems designed to impress and awe rather than for comfort or real life."

"You nailed it." Then he remembered her parents had been wealthy, too.

"I take it that wasn't your childhood home?" she asked, watching him closely.

"No. My family had it built about ten years ago. Before that, they lived downtown near The Chateau. The house I was raised in was a much more normal place."

A shadow crossed her face. "I have no idea what normal is," she admitted. "My parents were well-off, but as I mentioned previously, I spent my childhood in boarding schools. Their main home was in Boston, in the Seaport area."

"I've never been," he replied.

"You can come with me next time I go, if you'd like," she offered. "I actually have to go sometime after Christmas. I'm still in the middle of settling my parents' estate."

"I'd love that," he said. "I've never been to Boston. We'll figure out dates so I can make sure to take off from work."

The excitement in her eyes made him smile. Just then, he realized he wanted to make their relationship permanent. But would she? Not only had she recently lost her parents, but she'd been engaged to Seth and broken that off. She'd just bought her first home in Boulder. Maybe she wasn't ready to chuck all that to build a life with him.

Remy had always been a confident man, certain he knew the right course of action. Around Vanessa, he couldn't see a clear path. He knew what he wanted, without a shadow of a doubt. But he also wanted to make sure to do what was right for her.

Even if that turned out to be letting her go.

Just the thought made his chest hurt.

Unaware of his thoughts, she smiled at him. "You know what? For the first time since my parents died, the prospect of flying back to New England doesn't seem daunting. I'm actually looking forward to showing you around. It's a beautiful city, even in the winter."

Grabbing his laptop, he powered up a travel website. "Let's check out tickets," he offered.

Chapter Fourteen

"It's Christmas Eve," Remy murmured in her ear, before kissing her awake with slow, languorous presses of his mouth to her neck and collarbone. Vanessa tried to burrow back under the covers, though she actually craved his attention as much as she craved sleep. When his touch became a caress and the press of his fully aroused body an invitation, she let herself get lost in the lovemaking.

Afterward, they lay together and held each other close. "That's what I'd call a perfect start to a holiday," he teased, kissing her once more before getting out of the bed and heading off to the bathroom.

She stayed in the bed, stretching, feeling as lazy as a sated cat. When she heard the sound of the shower starting up, she closed her eyes and reflected on how much her life had changed. If anyone had told her, even as recently as a couple of months ago, that she would have found her one true love, she would have rolled her eyes and refused to believe it. Even now, she fought the worry that their happy bubble could burst at any moment. Christmas Eve. Despite the awesome way the day had started, right now it didn't feel any different than any other day. No surprise there, since it never had. All her life, she'd heard of people who claimed to have had magical Christmas Eves. Whether spiritual or simply joyous, surrounded by family and friends, she didn't know. Either way, she'd always been slightly skeptical and maybe a bit envious.

In primary school, she always felt like the child standing outside the candy store, always separate, always looking in. Her classmates' excitement had been palpable—the tree shopping and decorating, the Christmas cookies baked, the pile of brightly wrapped gifts under the tree. They'd all fly home to be with their families the instant the holiday break dawned, but she didn't have many good childhood holiday memories that she could look back on, except for Christmas. The other holidays, she'd waited for those phone calls as if they were the most precious gift she could have been given, always wondering why they couldn't take her with them. She'd grown up unwanted and unloved, always feeling that if she could only somehow be better, do more, then maybe, just maybe, her parents might love her.

Now they were gone, taking with them any possible opportunity for a better relationship. This, she suspected, is what she mourned the most. The opportunities that would forever be lost.

She'd felt ashamed admitting this to Remy. But once she had, he'd said he understood, reminding her his childhood hadn't been a picnic, either, so he got it. He'd made her feel better, holding her close, and murmured endearments in her ear until she turned her head and kissed him. Those deep, drugging kisses drove everything else from her mind.

"Your turn." Emerging from the bathroom, toweling his hair dry, the brilliance of his smile filled her with love. "We've got a big day today, so we might as well get started."

"A big day?" She tried to remember. "I know we talked about starting our own tradition and having a special Christmas Eve meal, but what else do we have planned?"

His smile turned mysterious. "Wait and see. Now go get ready, before I'm tempted to join you in that bed one more time."

That made her laugh. And then, because she'd never been able to resist a surprise, she jumped up and ran for the shower.

When she emerged thirty minutes later, hair and makeup done, the smell of cinnamon rolls and bacon drew her to the kitchen. "Here you go." Remy handed her a cup of coffee, made exactly the way she liked it. "You're just in time for breakfast."

He brought over a plate of cinnamon rolls and another plate of bacon.

"Wow." She grinned. "I'm seriously impressed."

"New tradition," he said, his expression serious. "Cinnamon rolls and bacon on Christmas Eve morning, made by yours truly. Then I thought we'd head downtown and take in the parade."

"Parade?"

"Yep." Taking a seat, he helped himself to two rolls and four slices of bacon. "Every year Roaring Springs has one. It's a really big deal. There are floats and bands and horses and vintage cars—all the same stuff you'd see at any other parade anywhere else."

She thought for a moment. "I don't believe I've ever been to a parade."

"Seriously?" He eyed her skeptically, as if he wasn't sure if she might be joking.

"Seriously." Shrugging to show it wasn't a big deal, she took a huge bite of her cinnamon roll. "Mmm."

Shaking his head, Remy made short work of his food. Then he drank his coffee, watching her eat. "You really lived a sheltered life," he teased.

"I did." Blotting her mouth with her napkin, she eyed him. "Does that bother you?"

"Not at all. I think I'm going to look forward to being the one to introduce you to so many new things."

A lot of firsts, she thought, nodding. She couldn't think of a better person to share them with.

They got to the parade route early. Downtown Roaring Springs had already been blocked off and onlookers had begun to assemble. Remy led her to a café with outdoor seating and waved to another couple, who waved back.

The tall and muscular man stood as they approached. "About time you got here," he commented. With his dark brown hair in a crew cut plus the way he carried himself, Vanessa guessed he was either current military or former.

"Blaine Colton," he said, grabbing her hand with his large one and shaking it. "And this is my fiancée, Tilda."

"Hi there," Tilda greeted them softly. Her eyes were striking and she wore a knitted ski cap over her long, wavy, dark brown hair.

Remy introduced Vanessa, holding her left hand. "Blaine's in charge of the extreme-sports division at The Lodge," Remy reminded her as they took their seats.

"That's right," Vanessa murmured. "So…what kind of sports do you guys consider to be extreme?" She smiled. "I know which ones I do. I'm a competitive skier."

Blaine grinned. "We have quite a selection, depending on the season. Since it's winter now, we have ice climbing, snowboarding, skiing, of course, snowmobiling, monoskiing and snowblading."

Intrigued despite herself, Vanessa nodded. "And in the summer?"

"There are too many to list. But we do a lot of rock climbing, bouldering and free climbing, plus caving, slacklining, and the biggie, white-river rafting. The Lodge offers tours for just about anything."

"Vanessa's an amazing skier," Remy added proudly.

Blaine studied her. "Are you looking for a job? We can always use skilled snow athletes."

She laughed. "Thank you, but no. I've got more than enough to keep me busy between settling my parents' estate and practicing my skills on the slopes."

While they waited for the parade to start, she learned Tilda was a teacher, though she was off for winter break. She and Blaine had a thirteen-year-old son, who was there but had wanted to watch the parade with his friends instead of his parents.

"You'll meet him at the party tomorrow," Remy said, still holding her hand.

His offhand comment had Blaine regarding him with renewed interest. "Are you two serious?" he asked. "You must be, if he's dragging you to the family get-together on Christmas Day."

"Blaine." Tilda swatted his muscular arm. "Quit."

Instead of answering, Remy merely smiled a mysterious smile. Vanessa's insides twisted as she realized she'd allowed herself to believe they had something permanent, with a real future.

"Look." She pointed. "I think the parade is about to start."

"I'd better go get our drinks then," Blaine said. "Coffee okay for everyone?"

For the next hour, Vanessa watched high-school cheerleaders, braving the cold in their cute outfits and cowboy hats, band members toting instruments who looked as if they wished they'd had their jackets, floats made from fake flowers and glitter, and tractors pulling wagons full of people. There were restored hot-rod cars and an entire group of kids on horseback carrying a 4-H banner. Santa and his elves and even Mrs. Claus passed out candy, while a dancing Frosty the Snowman and a green Grinch rode on their own float.

It was all very festive and fun.

When the last group finally passed, all of the people lining the street began to move. The café instantly became packed.

"Time to go," Remy said, standing. He handed Blaine some cash and kissed Tilda's cheek. "See you two at the party tomorrow."

Vanessa slipped her hand into his. "Wow," she commented. "So far every single person I've met in your family is super nice."

"We try." Remy squeezed her hand. "I'm glad you got

to meet a few before the get-together tomorrow. There's so many people, it can be kind of overwhelming."

When they got back to the house, Remy went straight to the tree and retrieved something from underneath.

She had a moment of panic when he handed her a small, elegantly wrapped gift. "I'm giving you your present tomorrow," she said. "Maybe I should wait."

"It's okay." He kissed her, nuzzling her neck. "You really didn't have to get me anything. Having you in my life is gift enough."

Though she wanted to swoon at his words, she shook her head instead. "Same here. But still, I feel weird accepting a gift from you when I don't have one to give you in exchange. Yet."

"Don't." He kissed her again, his lazy tone matching the heat in his eyes. "It's not a competition. Plus, I want you to wear this tomorrow. Humor me, please."

Trying not to feel bad—what if the plan she and Daria had cooked up turned out to not go over well?—she slowly unwrapped the gift.

Inside, nestled in a black velvet box, was the most exquisite pair of sapphire earrings she'd ever seen. "My birthstone," she said, marveling. "How did you know?"

"I didn't. I got them because they match your eyes."

"They are beautiful," she breathed. "I love them. Thank you so much, Remy."

Keeping her gaze locked on his, she slowly put on the earrings. Then she stood and stripped off her clothes and helped him do the same. Once they were both naked, she made love to him wearing only his gift.

Afterward, wrapped in each other's arms, they dozed. When she opened her eyes again, Remy had pulled all the covers off her. Seeing her awake, he grinned. "Nap's over! We've still got a lot more Christmas Eve celebrating to do."

Though she couldn't imagine what else they could possibly do, she was game.

After they'd gotten cleaned up and dressed again, he checked his watch. "Are you hungry?"

She had to think about it for a moment. "You know what? I think I am."

"Good." He grinned. "We have reservations at a special Christmas Eve dinner in an hour."

Though that seemed kind of early, she didn't mind. They hadn't eaten since the cinnamon rolls and bacon earlier that morning. "Special?" she asked. "Does that mean I need to dress up?"

"Nope, not at all. This dinner is the most anticipated even of the holiday season. Luckily, I was able to snag a pair of tickets."

"Tickets?"

His smile turned enigmatic. "You'll see. Just wear comfortable—and warm—clothes."

Intrigued, she peppered him with questions, but all he would say was she'd have to wait and see. By the time they were ready to get into his Jeep, she felt like a little kid at Christmas, full of excitement and anticipation. Which, come to think of it, might have been the point.

VANESSA'S EXUBERANCE MADE Remy happier than he would ever have thought possible. He'd guessed he'd been living in Roaring Springs too long, because in years past attending the annual holiday feast and charity talent show had been more of a chore than a joyous event. Even though it certainly could be pleasurable, he'd been more focused on customer relations, making sure all of the well-heeled guests had a good time.

This year would be different. For one thing, he wouldn't be attending in an official capacity, but just as one of the guests. For another, he felt certain Vanessa had never seen anything like the frequently raucous fun. The decorations were over-the-top festive and the food extraordinarily delicious. Everyone who knew about it wanted to go, which was one of the reasons the tickets sold out weeks, if not months, in advance. He always was given two tickets, paid for by Colton Enterprises, due to his position as head of public relations of The Chateau. This year, he'd actually been grateful.

The organizers purposely held the event early, so that people could do midnight church services or family get-togethers after. Usually, a large group went caroling. Remy had never been part of that, but this year, if Vanessa was willing, he hoped to be.

He wanted to pull out all the stops and make this Christmas Eve one that they'd always remember.

Once they pulled into the very crowded parking lot, he told her what was taking place. "A talent show?" she asked. "Are you performing?"

Since the thought had never occurred to him, he laughed and shook his head. "No. But all the acts have to be Christmas-themed. It's really a lot of fun."

"As long as there's food," she replied, smiling. "I'm starving."

"Wait and see."

They got into the line, which snaked around the front of the building and down one side. Luckily, it moved quickly, as the sun had begun to set and the breeze turned chilly. Walking behind and close to Vanessa, Remy sheltered her from the wind.

After handing over their tickets, their hands were stamped and they stepped inside. People milled around, laughing, talking, holding drinks. There were bars at each end of the building, and rows of white-tablecloth-covered tables, each seating six.

"We have assigned seats," Remy said, checking the numbers on his ticket stubs. "Do you want to sit or walk around a bit?"

"Let's get a drink and then find our seats," Vanessa responded. "There's Daria!" She waved. From the other end of the room, the deputy sheriff waved back.

"Is there any chance we could trade seats and sit with Daria and Stefan?" Vanessa asked.

"I wish we could, but a lot of careful planning goes into the seating chart," he told her. "They try to put a Colton at every table. In the past, I've never been able to sit with my family."

Clearly disappointed, Vanessa nodded. "Maybe we can get together with them after the show. I really like Daria. I think with time, she and I will become good friends."

Once everyone was seated, the buffets that had been set up at each side near the bars were opened. The array of food choices—everything from seafood to steak to vegetarian fare—was astounding. The dessert tables were separate, but from past experience Remy told Vanessa to grab what she wanted before she sat down, because certain delicacies vanished quickly.

After everyone had gotten their meal, the lights

dimmed somewhat and the talent show started. Many of the acts were musical, from local bands rocking out to Christmas classics, to country crooners. There were a few magicians, one act with trained dogs and Mrs. Pauly's entire third-grade class playing bells.

As the talent show went on, Remy found himself watching Vanessa. Her rapt attention, her earthy laugh and the way the lights caught her cheekbones made her far more enjoyable then anything on stage.

When the show finally ended, everyone jumped to their feet and clapped. Eyes sparkling, Vanessa jumped up and down, applauding before turning to Remy and throwing her arms around him. "So. Much. Fun."

Though they looked around for Daria, she and Stefan must have left as soon as the show ended, because they didn't see them again. Vanessa said she was up for Christmas caroling, so, hand in hand, they joined the others and began trekking through the snow to all the downtown houses.

By the time they'd finished, they had wet feet, cold hands and warm hearts.

Vanessa hummed all the way back to his Jeep. "That was amazing," she said. "Thank you for a wonderful night." And then, right there, right in front of his Jeep, Remy slowly lowered himself to one knee in the snow.

Eyes wide, Vanessa tugged on his hand. "What are you doing?" she asked. "Get up. It's too cold to be playing in the snow."

"Wait." Remy shook his head. "I'm not getting up just yet. There's something I need to say, something I need to ask, and this is the right way to ask it. Vanessa, I love you. I don't have a ring—I thought if you'd like, we can pick one out together—but I want to make this permanent. Forever. Will you do me the honor of becoming my wife?"

Now he had her full attention. She lowered herself so that they were on the same level and gazed deeply into his eyes. "I love you, too," she whispered. "And yes. My answer is yes. And I'll relocate to Roaring Springs, to be here with you."

Full of joy and the certainty that he and Vanessa were meant to find each other, Remy kissed her right then and there, with the two of them both on their knees in the cold, wet snow.

Right then and there, he came to a decision. "We have one more stop to make on the way home," he said. "This might be the most fun of all."

"Really?" She shook her head. "I doubt you can top this. But I'm game. Where are we going?"

"You'll see." That's all he'd say, right up until he pulled up and parked in front of Mountain Luxe Jewelers. A sign on the window proclaimed them to be *the* ultimate fine jewelry destination. In fact, they were the only jewelry store in town, if one didn't count the sterling-silver-and-turquoise shop at the other end of Main.

Reading the sign on the marquee, she turned and eyed him. "Now?" she asked. "Today?"

"Why not?" Though he tried to sound casual, he saw the steady love in her gaze and leaned over and kissed her. "Every woman should have a ring on the day she receives a proposal."

Her husky laugh warmed him to his toes. "Well, when you put it that way..."

Sinclair Jones, owner and frequently the sole employee of the shop, looked up when Remy and Vanessa entered. He squinted at first, as if having trouble placing why they might be there. Then, he pushed up his round glasses on his nose and beamed. "Remy Colton. What brings you and your lady friend to MLJ today?"

Putting his arm around Vanessa's waist, Remy drew her forward. "Sinclair, this is my fiancée, Vanessa Fisher. Vanessa, Sinclair is the owner of this fine establishment."

"Fiancée?" Sinclair's entire face lit up. "Congratulations, you two. I'm guessing you'd like to see some engagement rings or bridal sets."

"Yes," Remy agreed. "Though I need to ask you to keep this between us until I get a chance to tell my entire family."

"Of course," Sinclair answered with great dignity. "Your confidence is safe with me."

Curious to see what Vanessa would choose, Remy took a seat next to her as Sinclair brought out trays of his finest diamond rings. He watched as Vanessa perused them, not touching anything. She searched as if she had a particular style in mind.

Apparently, Sinclair noticed this, too. "I have a large inventory," he said. "Not bragging, just stating a fact. If there's a particular style you're looking for, why don't you describe it to me and I'll see if I can locate it for you?"

She nodded, sitting back in her chair. "I'm not good with words, but I'll try. All of these—" she waved her hand at the trays of glittery rings "—are flashy. Showy. And while they're absolutely beautiful, I'd prefer something a little more…understated. And elegant. If you have a pen and paper, I can sketch out what I mean."

Immediately, Sinclair handed her a small pad of paper and a pen. Both men watched as Vanessa began to sketch a thick band, with elegant, scrolled Celtic knots and a total of three diamonds, a larger round one in the center and two smaller gems, one on each side.

"That's beautiful," Sinclair commented, his tone surprised. "Though that might be more of a custom-designed ring, I think I just might have something similar." He slid the trays they'd been viewing back into the display case, which he then locked. "Give me a moment," he said, disappearing into the back.

When he returned, he carried a single diamond ring in the middle of a black velvet box. The instant she saw it, Vanessa's face lit up. "That's it, exactly!" she said excitedly. "White gold, Celtic design and the perfect diamond."

"We'll take it," Remy informed Sinclair.

"Don't you want to know what it costs first?" Vanessa asked, still unable to tear her gaze away from the ring.

Smiling, Sinclair wrote something on a slip of paper and handed it to Remy. Reading the number, Remy nodded and got out his credit card.

"Thank you." Turning back to Vanessa, the jeweler removed the ring from the box. "Would you like to try it on? If it doesn't fit, we can have it resized."

When she nodded, Remy took the ring from Sinclair and slipped it on Vanessa's finger. The instant he did, he realized it fit as if it had been specifically designed for her. Maybe it had, Remy thought. Maybe the world still had a few miracles left for people who were in love.

ALTERNATING BETWEEN STARING at the stunning ring on her finger and the wonderful, sexy man driving them home, Vanessa battled an inexplicable urge to cry. Though her parents hadn't been the loving, caring types, they'd been hers and she suddenly missed them. She'd finally met The One and they were engaged to be married, and not only did she not have any family to tell, but she also wouldn't have her father walk her down the aisle. Until this moment, she hadn't even realized she wanted a traditional wedding.

Maybe she had once. Now, she just wanted to be married. A simple ceremony, no fuss. Just vows and love.

"We'll make our own family," Remy replied, once she'd vocalized her thoughts. "I'm with you on the simple ceremony, though I should tell you as a Colton, it's my duty to have an elaborate and ornate ceremony." The dry tone of his voice told her he wasn't serious. "Though they're going to want us to have a traditional wedding, with so many other engagements and weddings on the horizon, I'm thinking we might be able to pull it off. My family will just have to get over it."

Though she nodded, she still found herself blinking back tears. Noticing the look of concern on Remy's face, she shook her head and waved him away. "It's nothing," she began. "And it's everything. So much raw emotion today. I'm sorry, I'm not usually so weepy." She sniffed. "Tears of happiness, I promise you."

"I get it," he said softly. Glancing sideways at him, she could have sworn she saw an answering sheen of tears in his eyes. "I love you, Vanessa. That's what's most important."

"I love you, too," she said, before she found herself weeping in earnest.

He let her cry, tears running silently down her face. Though she felt slightly foolish, she couldn't help it, so she simply gave in and let her emotions have full rein. Beyond his declaration of love, he didn't comment or ask for reassurance, though she figured he had to be worried she was about to change her mind. "I'm not, you know," she sniffled.

"Not what?" Parking in front of the garage, he shut off the ignition and pulled her into his arms.

"Changing my mind."

"I never thought you were," he replied, holding her tight. "I have confidence in our love."

Yet one more thing she adored about him.

Once she'd gotten herself under control, he handed her a tissue and she wiped at her eyes. "I'm not the weepy type," she muttered. "I have no idea what just came over me. You must think I'm a mess."

"I don't. It's not every day that a woman gets a proposal of marriage. I get it. It's a lot to process." He kissed her, still holding her close. "But know this—I love every aspect of you."

He kissed her again. "Whether you're laughing or crying, I'll always be there for you."

How had she gotten so lucky? She kissed him back. "Thank you. And the same for me. Though maybe," she teased, "I should have you write that into your wedding vows."

That made him chuckle. "I have just one request.

Like I mentioned to Sinclair at the jewelry store, let's keep this engagement quiet until we can announce it to my entire family together, okay? People tend to get their noses bent out of shape if someone finds out before someone else."

"Of course."

"Perfect."

"The first Christmas Eve for the rest of our lives," he replied, making her so happy it hurt.

THE NEXT MORNING, Christmas Day, when Remy woke with Vanessa in his arms, he realized for the first time ever, he didn't dread the big get-together at Colton Manor. He still felt a deep twinge of sadness over Seth, but because he had this beautiful woman by his side, everything became better.

He made coffee and mimosas, along with Belgian waffles, strawberries and whipped cream. Accepting her mimosa, she shook her head and grinned. "You are spoiling me. I had no idea you were such a chef."

"You're not the only one who knows their way around a kitchen," he replied, kissing her on the neck.

They spent a lazy morning eating and drinking coffee and, later, snuggling in front of the fireplace. Finally, they knew they needed to shower and get ready for the family party.

"The main event," Remy called it, something he'd always done privately in the past.

When Vanessa put on her form-hugging, designer red dress, Remy thought he'd never seen her look more elegantly beautiful. She also wore her new sapphire earrings and several bracelets and a pair of sexy black stiletto boots. He wanted to devour her.

As for himself, he wore his usual black slacks, white shirt and red tie. Despite Whit's constant prodding, Remy never wore a jacket. It was, he argued, a holiday, after all.

"You look breathtaking," he told Vanessa.

"Right back at you," she replied, smiling. Dropping Daria's gift in her purse, she walked ahead of him to the garage, hips swaying. For a brief moment, he entertained a fantasy of skipping the party and taking her back to bed.

Of course, he did no such thing. They got in his Jeep and headed off, Christmas music playing on the radio.

Vanessa seemed unusually pensive as he drove.

"Are you nervous?" he asked.

"A little," she admitted. "I'm sure I'll get over it."

"I love you," he told her.

A slow smile lit up her face. "I love you, too."

"We're almost there." Deliberately taking the last curve in the road slowly, Remy watched for her reaction.

"Wow." She gazed up at the mansion perched high on the hill. All angles and glass, the modern-style mountain home had been designed to blend into the landscape. "You weren't kidding. That place is monstrously huge."

He grinned. "Just wait until you see the inside. It's so pretentious, it's almost tacky." He glanced sideways at her. "What was your parents' house like?"

"Old-school Boston. Elegant and restrained. The kind of place that almost felt like a church, where you were afraid to laugh or play or make noise." Her quick shrug didn't fool him. "I always told myself I was glad they didn't want me to live there with them."

Covering her hand with his, he squeezed. "I know it might not have seemed like it at the time, but you were probably lucky."

"Maybe. I'll never know now. But—" her expression brightened "—at least I had skiing."

"True. And now you have me." He placed a quick kiss on her neck, inhaling the light, feminine scent of her. "Here we are."

He pulled up the drive and stopped under the portico, where a line of other vehicles waited. Taking his place, he watched as one group of cousins exited the car, carrying bagged gifts and brightly wrapped parcels. As soon as they entered, their vehicle was driven away and another promptly took its place.

"They have valet parking?" Vanessa asked, her eyes wide. "For a family get-together?"

"Yep. Just wait until we get inside. There are servants tripping over each other. It's insane. But you'll get used to it."

Vanessa rolled her eyes, making him chuckle. "This is going to be interesting," she said. "Hopefully, even fun."

"It will be," he promised. "As long as you focus on the people rather than the pomp and circumstance. My family—your family soon—is really great. Oh, and I should warn you. I intend to announce our engagement this afternoon."

Waving her ring, she smiled. "I'm sure they'll figure it out once they see this."

"True." He pulled her close and kissed her. "But you deserve a formal announcement."

Finally, their turn came. When the young man opened the door for her, Vanessa swung out her shapely legs, tugging down her skirt at the same time. Her long legs and high-heeled black velvet boots drew the kid's gaze and Remy couldn't blame him.

She took his arm. "Let's do this," she said bravely.

"It's going to be all right, honey," he replied. "Relax. You've gone all tense."

Leaning into Remy, she exhaled and then shook her head. "I downplayed it earlier. To say I feel nervous would be an understatement. For whatever reason, I'm terrified."

"You have no reason to be, I promise. Look at it this way. At least you've already met a few members of my family."

"True," she mused, relaxing slightly. "Trey and Daria have both been nothing but kind. I have no reason to suspect the rest of the Coltons will be any different."

"Exactly."

At the front door, a uniformed servant took their coats. Smiling, Remy put his hand at the small of her back as they moved forward, her heels clicking on the marble floor.

The huge foyer led to a long hall, which opened out into the great room. This would be where the family gathered.

"Let's do this," he began. But before he could take another step, his cell phone rang. Caller ID showed the Bradford County jail. His heart skipped a beat. "It's Seth," he told Vanessa. "I have to take this."

She nodded. "Of course."

Taking a deep breath, he answered the call.

A robotic voice informed him that an inmate was placing a collect call and asked if he wanted to accept the charges. He replied yes without hesitation.

Click. "Seth?" Remy might have sounded too eager. Or maybe too cautious. He didn't care. "Seth, is that you?"

"Who else would be calling you from jail?" Seth said, the bitterness in his voice making Remy swallow. "I just wanted to call and see what you could do to get me out of here."

Stunned, Remy couldn't find any words. No "Merry Christmas" or "Happy Holidays." Just Seth, seeing what angle he would work.

"Hello?" Seth demanded. "Are you there? I hate it here."

"Seth, we've been over this already. You're in federal custody and bail has been denied. Not only are you a murderer, but you held a teenaged girl hostage with a gun against her temple. All of the horrible things you did hurt a lot of people." He took a deep breath. "You've got to pay for what you've done. There's nothing I can do to help you. It's time you learned how to help yourself."

"You're a sanctimonious jerk," Seth spat. "Where do you get off giving me advice? You've always had everything handed to you, just like all those other Coltons."

Not true, but damned if Remy would argue the point now. Suddenly tired, he rubbed his aching temple. "I hope you get some help, Seth. Maybe once you've had some time to reflect on what you've done, you can apologize to some of the people you hurt."

Silence. Then Seth laughed. "You always were such a sap, Remy. So desperate for love that you believed anything I told you, no matter how much evidence you had to the contrary."

"I'm going to hang up now," Remy warned, his chest tight, his heart aching. Anger mingled with sorrow, all twisting up his insides. "Merry Christmas," he said, before doing exactly that.

Dropping his phone back in his pocket, Remy eyed Vanessa and shook his head. She held out her arms and he walked into them, letting her hold him while he tried to sort out his chaotic emotions.

Chapter Fifteen

Entering the room packed full of strangers, the first thing Vanessa noticed was the children. There were several, some racing about, others sitting quietly, enthralled with a tablet or a phone. They ranged in age from infant to teen. This instantly made her feel better. She liked kids. For the most part, they were honest and down-to-earth. She knew if she started to feel out of place, she could always talk to one of the children.

Dragging away her gaze, she looked around the room.

Everyone had dressed up, most in festive colors. She spotted one woman whose style she instantly admired, loving the artsy, new-age flair to her flowy skirt and layered blouse. "Who's that?" she asked.

"My cousin Bree. She owns that Wise Gal Gallery I told you about." He looked around. "Her little dog should be here somewhere. She never goes anywhere without him."

Dog. Looking down, Vanessa hid a smile.

"How are you at remembering names?" Remy asked, his voice tender.

She raised her head to look at him and shrugged. "I

do okay." Scanning the room, she grimaced. "Though with this many people, I'm thinking I'll have some trouble. I'll try my best, though."

Some of her nervousness must have come through in her voice. "Don't be scared. Everyone is going to love you, because I do."

That made her smile. "Lead the way. I'm ready."

"Good. Let's do this."

After the first group of couples, Vanessa abandoned all hope of keeping up with the names. She met matriarch and patriarch Russ and Mara Colton, and Fox and Kelsey, along with their adorable adopted baby named John, who was eight months old. They met Fox's sister Sloane, her husband, Liam, and their brother Wyatt, a handsome cowboy, plus his wife, Bailey, and their infant son, Hudson.

Moving on from that group, Remy introduced her to Rylan and Bree, Skye and Leo, and Skye's identical twin, Phoebe, along with her fiancé, Prescott.

She already knew Blaine and Tilda and Daria and Stefan, though she had the pleasure of meeting Sam. Trey came over and greeted her, introducing her to Aisha, his fiancée.

After that, Vanessa simply smiled and nodded, especially when Remy introduced her to his father, Whit. The older man looked her up and down, his manner flirtatious, until his grandfather, Earl, rapped him sharply on his arm, which made Remy chuckle.

Vanessa slipped Daria her gift. Daria's eyes filled with surprise. "You didn't have to do that."

"I wanted to," Vanessa assured her.

"I'll open it later," Daria promised, dropping it into her purse. "Thank you so much."

Finally, they filed into a large dining room with a long, polished wood table, the size of which Vanessa had never seen. There had to be at least thirty chairs. Huge holiday centerpieces adorned the middle, one strategically placed about every four seats. Christmas plates and gold silverware, along with red wine and water glasses, completed the place settings. In two of the corners were smaller tables, most likely meant for the children. Even so, they were equally decorated, with slightly smaller flower arrangements.

"Assigned seating," Remy muttered. "Let's see if we can find our place cards."

Other couples roamed past them doing the exact same thing.

"Here." She pointed. "Remy Colton. Since the one right next to you says only 'Guest,' I'm assuming that's me."

This made him shake his head. "I'm sorry. I did give them your name. I'm not sure what happened."

His obvious concern touched her. "No biggie. Don't worry, I'm not taking it personally."

"Good." He kissed her cheek, which earned them several curious looks, though thankfully no one commented.

The room got noisy as everyone found their seats. Vanessa watched, grateful that so many of them had been kind and accepting. This would soon be her family, too. She suddenly realized the truth of what Remy had said. She'd never be alone again.

This in itself felt like another sort of miracle. She felt like the luckiest woman in the world.

"Are you ready?" Remy whispered, his warm breath tickling her ear and making her shiver. "I'm going to do this before we eat."

She nodded, her heart full of so much love it ached.

"May I have your attention?" Remy stood, tapping on his water glass with his fork. "Everyone?"

The room got quiet. Looking around, Vanessa caught Daria's eye. The deputy sheriff grinned and winked, as if she knew exactly what Remy was about to say.

"I wanted to let everyone know that Vanessa and I are going to be married," he said. "She has graciously consented to become my wife."

Everyone started talking at once, offering congratulations. Only Whit, Remy's father, said nothing. He sat stone-faced, eying his son with a narrow-eyed gaze. But he didn't seem angry, merely thoughtful. Finally, when the furor died down, the elder Colton stood and raised his glass.

"A toast," he said, finally smiling. "To my son and the beautiful Vanessa. May they have many years of happiness."

Everyone cheered.

"When's the wedding?" Kelsey asked. "If it's next summer, you'd better get with Blaine and Tilda. They're planning to get married in June."

Remy and Vanessa exchanged a look. "We haven't worked out the details about the ceremony yet, but as soon as we do, we'll make sure to let everyone know."

Several of the women came over and asked to see her ring. Vanessa showed them, glad when Mara ordered everyone back to their seats so the first course could be served.

The eight-course meal made the feast they'd enjoyed yesterday seem positively meager. There were actual servants, standing behind the chairs after they'd brought the food, which reminded her of a few occasions at her grandparents' Boston mansion. Because she'd been to a few of these types of shindigs as a child, she took small bites of each offering, aware that was the only way she'd make it through to the end.

Watching some of the others, she noticed many of the women did the same thing.

The men, on the other hand, appeared to be doing some serious chowing down. Watching Remy devour his entire prime rib, she wondered where he put it. Catching Daria's eye, she exchanged an amused smile as she noticed Stefan eating just as much as Remy.

As they slowly made their way through courses, Vanessa felt more and more jittery. Something big was coming after this was all over—Remy's gift. Assuming, of course, that what she and Daria had planned worked out and that Remy was on board if it did.

When the last dessert plate had been cleared away, Russ Colton stood, cleared his throat and made a toast. "To our Colton family," he began, his tone mellow after a few glasses of wine. "To our engaged couples—Rylan and Bree, Phoebe and Prescott, Trey and Aisha, Blaine and Tilda and, of course, now Remy and Vanessa."

Everyone politely clapped. Russ waited a moment for silence before he continued. "To our newlyweds Skye and Leo, as well as Fox and Kelsey, and to new arrivals like baby John and Hudson, and of course Stefan's young son, Sam. To Blaine and Tilda's Josh." He raised his glass, grinning. "To animal sanctuaries and art galleries, ranches and farms, The Lodge and The Chateau, and most of all, to our town Roaring Springs!"

He cleared his throat. "Mara and I are talking again and I've officially decided to retire after the New Year." Everyone went quiet at this. When they started to speak, Russ held up his hand. "Decker will be co-CEO with Blaine. Remy, I'm placing you on the board of directors along with Mara and Phoebe. We finally have a new little dynasty in the making. This year has been a tough one for our family but we've emerged stronger than ever before. Merry Christmas to all of you, with love!"

"Hear! Hear!" those assembled responded, raising their glasses high before taking a sip. "To the Coltons!"

Touched, Vanessa met Remy's gaze as she drank her champagne. So much emotion blazed in his eyes—love, contentment and joy—that she teared up.

When the time came to leave the holiday gathering, Vanessa caught Daria's eye. She'd managed to keep her excitement under wraps for the entire get-together, so much so that she felt confident that Remy didn't suspect anything. Daria dipped her chin in a casual nod and then tugged on Stefan's arm. He raised one eyebrow, then bent down and scooped up his son, Sam. The three of them would leave right after Remy and Vanessa and follow them to their destination.

Suddenly nervous, Vanessa asked Remy if he'd mind making a quick detour before going home.

"Sure," he replied, his gaze quizzical. "Where to?"

"It's a surprise," she promptly told him. "But I think you might like it." At least she hoped he would. Self-doubt momentarily plagued her. Their relationship was so new. What if she assumed too much?

Deciding Remy would surely let her know, she decided to make it clear that in the end, the choice would be up to him. "Remy, before we go…" Swallowing, she tried to find the right words.

Brow furrowed, he waited. "Should I be concerned?"

That made her laugh. "No. I just realized, though, that you might not feel you have a choice. I want you to understand that you don't have to worry about hurting my feelings. I can't say more without ruining things, but keep that in mind, okay?"

Slowly, he nodded. "That sounds ominous."

"It's not, I promise." She kissed his cheek. "Let's go."

As they drove, following the directions on Vanessa's phone's GPS, she wondered if Remy noticed Stefan and Daria following them.

"Here we are," she said, at the exact moment her GPS told them that they'd arrived at their destination.

"Bradford County Animal Shelter." Pulling up into the empty parking lot, Remy read the words aloud. He turned to face Vanessa, his expression puzzled. "You know they're closed, for Christmas, right?"

She nodded, unable to resist glancing in the mirror for Stefan and Daria's car. She didn't see it yet, but knew they'd be here soon.

"Then why are we here?" Remy asked, clearly still puzzled.

"I wanted to give you your Christmas gift," she said softly. "So if it's all right with you, I thought we could give one of the shelter dogs a true Christmas miracle." She took a deep breath, watching him closely. "Daria got special permission to let us in today. I've already filled out the paperwork and signed it, so all that's left is choosing a dog. *Our* dog."

Remy opened and closed his mouth. "Are you serious?" he finally said.

"Yes. Daria told me that you've always talked about rescuing a dog. I've wanted to as well, but my life was too unsettled. It's not now."

"No, it's not."

Determined to finish, she nodded. "But this is why I told you earlier that in the end, it had to be your choice. If you're not ready or want to wait, then we will. A dog is a big commitment."

Remy shook his head. He grinned from ear to ear. "So is marriage. I've wanted a dog for so long and I love that we'd be getting one together."

"Are you sure?"

"Yes!" He hugged her, still smiling. "I'm sure if you are. Let's do this!"

Just then, Daria and Stefan pulled up. They got out and as soon as they'd unbuckled Sam from his car seat, he started running circles in the snowy parking lot.

"Hey there." Stefan greeted Remy. "I hear you're about to get a new family member. Congratulations."

A slow grin blossomed over Remy's handsome face. "Thanks, man." He eyed little Sam, who'd stopped short and stared when he'd heard the word *dog*. "You know, I can think of someone else who might want their own pet," he said.

Stefan laughed at Daria's dumbfounded look. "I was just thinking the same thing," he said. "Sam's been wanting a dog for ages. Of course, if you're not on board, Daria, you'd better decide how you're going to dissuade him."

Daria stood on her tiptoes and kissed him. "We'll see," she said. "Now let's go get Remy and Vanessa their dog."

Unlocking the door, she flipped on the light. They stepped into a small reception area with a long counter. Daria pointed to another door leading to the back. "The animals are that way. The cat room is to the right and the dogs are past that. The shelter is full right now. Apparently, a lot of people dump their animals during the holidays."

As soon as she opened the door, the cacophony of barking began. High-pitched yaps and deep barks, some coming rapid-fire as if in desperation or alarm. Startled, Sam clutched his father's hand and drew back, unsure.

"It's okay," Stefan reassured his son. "I think we might have just woken all the doggies up."

"Go ahead, you two," Daria said, stepping back and motioning Remy and Vanessa to go past her. She wrinkled her nose. "It's a clean facility, but it still has that smell."

Gripping Remy's hand tightly, Vanessa swallowed. Together, they went through the doorway, walked down a short hallway and entered a room with concrete floors and tall, metal dog runs.

They both stopped, staring. "How are we going to choose?" Remy asked. "There are so many."

Though her heart had started pounding, she managed to shrug. "I have no idea. But I suspect when we meet the right one, we'll know."

Remy nodded. "I certainly hope so."

As they walked down the first row, dogs of every shape and size and breed greeted them. Long-haired and short. Broad noses and pointed. Ninety pounders and nine pounders. Many jumped at the bars. Most barked or pawed, seeming desperate for attention. One or two continued to lie on their cots, eying the humans with feigned indifference or disappointment, Vanessa couldn't tell which.

She stopped in front of a regal-looking golden retriever, considering, before moving along. Then she saw a beautiful, long-haired white dog and a cute hyper small terrier, and exhaled. "This is going to be more difficult than I thought," she said.

Remy had gone on ahead of her and stopped in front of the last cage in the row. "Vanessa, come here."

There, in the kennel, stood a medium-size, brown-and-white dog with huge brown eyes. He had a white flash around his neck and on his muzzle. He wasn't barking; instead, he twisted his entire body in apparent spasms of joy. "He's kidney beaning," Remy said. "Boxers are known for that."

Vanessa bent down and spoke to him through the bars, carefully holding out her hand for him to sniff. To her surprise—and joy—he licked her. And then he tilted his head as if to say "Come on, get me out of here, why don't you?"

"This one." The certainty in Remy's voice matched the feeling in her heart. "His name is Raider. He's a two-year-old boxer," he said, tapping the kennel card posted to the front of the pen. "Owner surrendered for constantly jumping out of his chain-link-fenced yard. Since we have a six-foot-tall wooden fence and don't intend to leave him out alone in the backyard, that shouldn't be a problem."

Vanessa dug in her pocket for the leash she'd purchased earlier. She hadn't gotten a collar, since she'd had no idea what size dog they'd end up getting. "I already paid and filled out the paperwork," she told him. "It's sitting on the front desk. All we need to do is let them know which dog we're adopting."

From the other row behind them, they heard Sam squeal. "Please, Dad? Look how much that puppy loves me. Can we take her home?"

Daria's voice joined Sam's. "What do you think, Stefan? I think she really needs us."

Stefan said something that sounded like agreement.

Vanessa and Remy exchanged a grin. "Looks like we're not the only ones giving a dog a home on Christmas."

Remy opened the kennel and slipped the leash around Raider's neck, using it as a collar until they could get a proper one. "Come on, boy. Let's get you out of here and take you home." He sniffed. "I foresee a bath in your very near future."

WATCHING VANESSA'S BEAUTIFUL face glow with love as she watched their new dog, Remy wanted to kiss her. But that would have to wait until later, since his hands were full right now with an excited flashy fawn boxer. Unlike most other women he knew, Vanessa didn't appear to mind the dog brushing up against her fancy dress with his nose.

The instant they stepped outside, Raider leaped into the air, jumping with joy. He did this over and over, like an end-zone happy dance. Amused, Remy watched him celebrate his freedom with gusto.

"Something tells me he's going to be a handful," Vanessa murmured, still smiling, clearly besotted. "In a good way."

"That's how boxers are," he answered. "I've read up on them because I've always wanted one. They do nothing half-heartedly, including love."

"That sounds perfect for us." Vanessa kneeled down. Immediately, Raider rushed her, licking her face and wagging his little nub of a tail so fast it looked like a helicopter prop.

She wrapped her arms around him and the dog leaned in, eyes half-closed, enjoying every second and absorbing the love.

"Our dog," she said. "I can hardly believe it. It's like a dream come true."

"*You're* a dream come true," he told her. "You and Raider both."

The shelter door opened. Daria, Stefan and Sam emerged. Daria held a tiny, fluffy dog in her arms while Sam ran circles around her, begging to be allowed to pet it.

Seeing Remy and Vanessa, Daria smiled sheepishly, letting them see her precious cargo. "Meet Xena, Warrior Princess. Her kennel card says she's a Cavapoo— half Cavalier King Charles spaniel and half poodle. She's eight months old."

"And I'm going to love her!" Sam announced.

"We're *all* going to love her," Stefan corrected. He eyed Raider, who'd caught sight of the puppy and was now wiggling his entire body in happy greeting.

"That one looks like a handful," Stefan said. His comment made Vanessa laugh.

"We were just saying that. But it's okay. He'll be *our* handful."

Daria handed Xena over to Stefan and went back to make sure everything was shut down for the night.

Overhead, a single bright star shone in the cloudless night sky. Remy caught Vanessa looking at it and pulled her close. "Christmas is full of miracles," he said.

"And love," she murmured back. "Always love."

He would have kissed her right then, a deep kiss that they both would have felt all the way to their toes, but Raider chose that moment to tug hard on the leash, sending Remy off balance.

He laughed and let the dog lead him over to the base of an evergreen. After Raider explored and marked his territory, he zoomed right back to Vanessa, who crooned baby talk to him and stroked his fur.

After Daria finished locking up the shelter, she joined them, once again taking little Xena from Stefan's arms. "I wish we could save them all," she mused. "There are so many dogs—and cats—who just need someone to love them."

Eying Raider and Xena, her expression softened. "The shelter is going to be running an adoption event right after the New Year. Drastically reduced adoption fees. Senior animals will be free. They're hoping to clear the shelter."

"Wouldn't that be perfect?" Still petting Raider, Vanessa smiled at her.

"For now, these two got their open happy ending," Remy interjected. "Let's go home."

"Merry Christmas to you both." Daria hugged Vanessa first, then Remy. Stefan followed suit.

Arms around each other, Remy and Vanessa watched the other couple climb into their car, Daria and little Sam now tenderly cradling their new puppy.

"I love my new family," Vanessa mused. "Thank you for that."

Trying to keep Raider from tangling his legs up in the leash, Remy laughed. "Thank you, too. Being with you has made me happier than I've ever been."

"Me, too." Smiling, Vanessa eyed him and their dog. "Come on, Raider," she said. "Time to go home."

They all loaded up in the Jeep.

Clearly Raider enjoyed car rides. He sat up in the back seat, tongue hanging out, alert and happy and at ease.

When they pulled up to Remy's house, he parked in front of the garage so it would be easier to get Raider out. Turning off the ignition, he met Vanessa's gaze.

"Merry Christmas," she murmured.

He leaned across the console and kissed her, putting all of the love he felt into the kiss.

Not wanting to be left out, Raider poked at them with his wet nose, effectively breaking them apart. Remy laughed, feeling a lightness of spirit he hadn't felt in a long time. "Merry Christmas," he replied. "Let's get this boy in and show him his new home."

They let Raider out in the backyard first and stood on the back deck with their arms around each other watching as their dog checked out his new surroundings. Once he'd taken care of his business, Remy called him, curious to see if he'd come.

Of course, Raider bounded over immediately, short nub of a tail wagging furiously.

"I bought a bag of dog food, some dog bowls and a bed for him a few days ago," Vanessa announced. "I hid them under the guest bed so you wouldn't see."

This made Remy laugh again. He couldn't recall the last Christmas he'd laughed so much. "Full of surprises," he murmured, nuzzling his fiancée's neck.

She turned her head, just so, and kissed him. "And many more just like this," she promised.

The next morning, Remy woke up early to let the dog out. After a bath to get the shelter funk off him, Raider had spent the night curled up at the foot of their bed, ignoring the huge dog bed that Vanessa had purchased. After exchanging quick looks, they allowed it, drifting off to sleep to the sound of contented boxer snores.

Raider fit right in, so quickly he might have always shared their lives. They went to the pet store located on the same street as the Wise Gal Gallery and bought their dog a collar, harness, matching leash and some toys. The clerk who rang them up commented on what a beautiful dog he was, and how he was obviously very spoiled. Her words made both Remy and Vanessa grin like fools.

"Proud dog parents, aren't you?" Bree said, greeting them when they walked down the street to her gallery. "I heard from Daria all about your Christmas-night adventure."

"You're one to talk," Remy said, pointing. Her little dog, Jekyll, sat up on a chair and surveyed them all with disinterested disdain.

Bree laughed. "Dogs rock. That's why I never go anywhere without mine."

Raider woofed quietly, wiggling his nub and straining to be allowed closer to the small dog. "Should I?" Remy asked.

"Not today. I wouldn't bring your big boy close to him," Bree answered. "He's having one of his off days. That's why I named him Jekyll. He has a split personality."

This made Vanessa chuckle. "It's a whole new world, isn't it?" she asked. "Being dog owners, that is."

Bree concurred, exchanging a quick look with Remy and giving him a thumbs-up in approval once Vanessa turned away to look around at some of the paintings.

"I'm really going to enjoy being part of your family," Vanessa commented on the way home. "Not only will I gain relatives, but I think I've made a couple of new friends. Soon, they'll be my in-laws."

Once they were married. A thought occurred to him. A radical, yet sensible thought.

"We should talk about the wedding," he ventured. "I don't want to wait."

A slow smile curved her mouth. "I don't, either. Are you saying what I think you are?"

"Yes. As long as you haven't been harboring a secret dream of a big, fancy, formal wedding, let's just keep it simple and quick."

She gave him a long look. "Won't your family be upset?"

"Yes," he admitted. "We'll have to allow them to throw us a big celebratory party to pacify them, but it'll all work out in the end. That is, if you're agreeable."

"I am." She kissed his cheek since he was driving, which made Raider bark and both of them chuckle. Their happiness must have been contagious, as their new dog spent the rest of the day amusing them with his antics.

They decided to put her Boulder house on the market as soon as possible, with her parents' Boston home to follow as soon as she finished cleaning it out. Remy offered to sell his custom home too, so that they could choose a new one together, but Vanessa vetoed that idea.

"We'll just make it ours," she said, warming his heart. "There's so much of you in it already, and since I love you, of course I love your house."

"Our house," he corrected, smiling. "Neither one of us will ever have to be alone again."

THE FRIDAY AFTER CHRISTMAS, Remy and Vanessa went down to city hall and got their marriage license. Since Colorado had no waiting period, blood test, or residency requirement, they walked over to the justice of the peace and quietly got married.

Then they went home and celebrated with Raider. Later, Remy would make phone calls and let his family know, but right now he wanted to enjoy the moment with his new bride.

"Vanessa Colton," he said, loving the sound of it. "My wife."

"My husband." Smiling, she kissed him, and this time their dog paid them no mind, too intent on romping in the snow.

* * * * *

COMING SOON!

We really hope you enjoyed reading this book. If you're looking for more romance, be sure to head to the shops when new books are available on

Thursday 12th December

To see which titles are coming soon, please visit

millsandboon.co.uk/nextmonth

MILLS & BOON

JOIN THE
MILLS & BOON
BOOKCLUB

* **FREE** delivery direct to your door

* **EXCLUSIVE** offers every month

* **EXCITING** rewards programme

50% OFF
YOUR FIRST
PARCEL

Join today at
Millsandboon.co.uk/Bookclub

MILLS & BOON
MEDICAL
Pulse-Racing Passion

Set your pulse racing with dedicated,
delectable doctors in the high-pressure
world of medicine, where emotions run
high and passion, comfort and love are the
best medicine.

Eight Medical stories published every month, find them all at:

millsandboon.co.uk

MILLS & BOON

THE HEART OF ROMANCE

A ROMANCE FOR EVERY KIND OF READER

MODERN

Prepare to be swept off your feet by sophisticated, sexy and seductive heroes, in some of the world's most glamourous and romantic locations, where power and passion collide.
8 stories per month.

HISTORICAL

Escape with historical heroes from time gone by. Whether your passion is for wicked Regency Rakes, muscled Vikings or rugged Highlanders, awaken the romance of the past.
6 stories per month.

MEDICAL

Set your pulse racing with dedicated, delectable doctors in the high-pressure world of medicine, where emotions run high and passion, comfort and love are the best medicine.
6 stories per month.

True Love

Celebrate true love with tender stories of heartfelt romance, from the rush of falling in love to the joy a new baby can bring, and a focus on the emotional heart of a relationship.
8 stories per month.

Desire

Indulge in secrets and scandal, intense drama and plenty of sizzl. hot action with powerful and passionate heroes who have it all: wealth, status, good looks…everything but the right woman.
6 stories per month.

HEROES

Experience all the excitement of a gripping thriller, with an inten romance at its heart. Resourceful, true-to-life women and strong, fearless men face danger and desire - a killer combination!
8 stories per month.

DARE

Sensual love stories featuring smart, sassy heroines you'd want as best friend, and compelling intense heroes who are worthy of the
4 stories per month.

To see which titles are coming soon, please visit

millsandboon.co.uk/nextmonth

GET YOUR ROMANCE FIX!

Get the latest romance news, exclusive author interviews, story extracts and much more!

blog.millsandboon.co.uk

JOIN US ON SOCIAL MEDIA!

Stay up to date with our latest releases, author news and gossip, special offers and discounts, and all the behind-the-scenes action from Mills & Boon...

 millsandboon

 millsandboonuk

millsandboon

It might just be true love...

LET'S TALK
Romance

For exclusive extracts, competitions
and special offers, find us online:

f facebook.com/millsandboon

@MillsandBoon

@MillsandBoonUK

Get in touch on 01413 063232

For all the latest titles coming soon, visit
millsandboon.co.uk/nextmonth

MILLS & BOON
A ROMANCE FOR
EVERY READER

- **FREE** delivery direct to your door

- **EXCLUSIVE** offers every month

- **SAVE** up to 25% on pre-paid subscriptions

SUBSCRIBE AND SAVE

millsandboon.co.uk/Subscribe

WANT EVEN MORE

ROMANCE?

SUBSCRIBE AND SAVE TODAY!

'Mills & Boon books, the perfect way to escape for an hour or so.'

MISS W. DYER

'Excellent service, promptly delivered and very good subscription choices.'

MISS A. PEARSON

'You get fantastic special offers and the chance to get books before they hit the shops.'

MRS V. HALL

Visit millsandboon.co.uk/Subscribe and save on brand new books.

MILLS & BOON
Desire

Indulge in secrets and scandal, intense drama and plenty of sizzling hot action with powerful and passionate heroes who have it all: wealth, status, good looks… everything but the right woman.

Six Desire stories published every month, find them all at:

millsandboon.co.uk/Desire